THE WARLORDS OF WOODMYST

The Warlords of Woodmyst

THE WOODMYST CHRONICLES BOOK IV

Robert E Kreig

WHITEKEEP BOOKS

For Noah, the warrior.

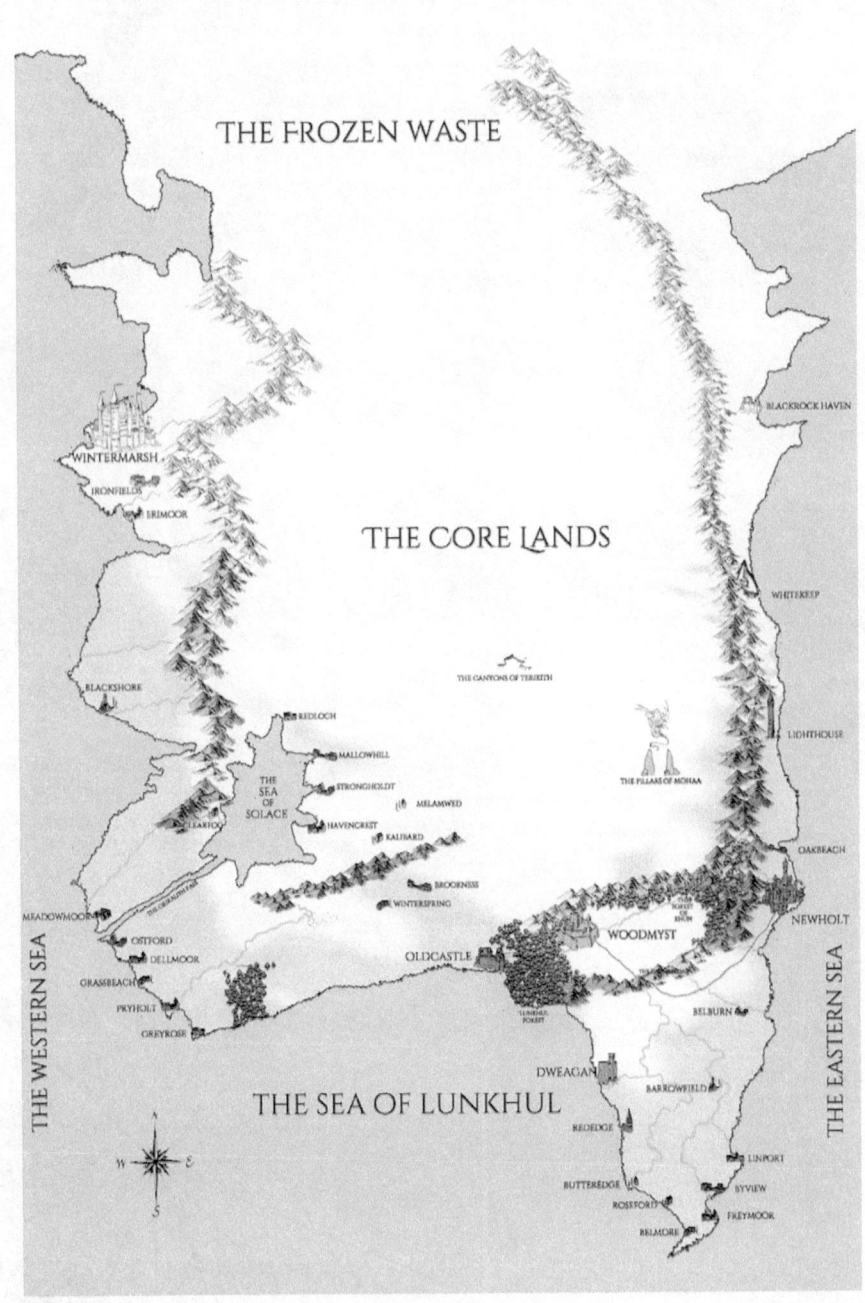

THE FROZEN WASTE

THE CORE LANDS

BLACKROCK HAVEN

WINTERMARSH

IRONFIELDS

BRIMOOR

WHITEKEEP

BLACKSHORE

THE CANYONS OF TERIRITH

REDLOCH

LIGHTHOUSE

MALLOWHILL

THE
SEA
OF
SOLACE

STRONGHOLDT

MELAMWED

THE PILLARS OF MOHAA

HAVENCREST

KALISARD

OAKBEACH

BROORNESS

FOREST
OF
BALM

WINTERSPRING

WOODMYST

NEWHOLT

MEADOWMOOR

OLDCASTLE

OSTFORD

DELLMOOR

LUNKHUL
FOREST

BELBURN

GRASSBEACH

PRYHOLT

GREYROSE

DWEAGAN

BARROWFIELD

THE WESTERN SEA

THE SEA OF LUNKHUL

REDEDGE

THE EASTERN SEA

LINPORT

BYVIEW

BUTTEREDGE

ROSSFORD

FREYMOOR

BELMORE

W   E

N

S

Prologue

White spray exploded over the bow as the *Adelandria* raced through the choppy waves of the Western Sea. The intended port was Strongholdt, a city on the shore of the Sea of Solace, a body of water set farther inland, accessible by a narrow gorge known as the Griralith Pass. Towering rock walls stood upon either side of the gorge, wide enough for two ships, three in places, to pass.

The Griralith Pass route twisted for over eighty miles and guarded by many forts that sat atop the cliffs along its course. The two largest garrisons, fortified with stone and armed with canons, sat upon each side of the mouth of the pass where vessels would enter and leave.

Captain Jeremy Schoenbach, standing in the wheelhouse behind a thick glass windshield, was always in awe whenever he saw the site. Even with the heavy weather and hard tacking that needed his attention, he took the time to peer through the teeming rain towards the tall cliff with its fortifications standing proudly on top.

"The wind is blowing strong from the west, Captain," Karlena, his first mate, called to him from the main deck. Several men and the other three Erilian women were busying themselves with their duties as they prepared to enter the passage. "Should we shelter until the storm has passed?"

"No," he shouted back. "We make for the pass. We only have three days to pick up our next freight and we still have this load to deliver. If we don't get those supplies for Byview, they'll go to someone else to deliver. We need that haul."

"So," Karlena yelled over the wind as she climbed to the quarterdeck, "we won't be harbouring for a day or two in the Sea of Solace?"

"We're running just within schedule," he told her as she entered the wheelhouse. He tossed her a towel that hung on the wall behind him. "If we get more weather like this, we could be late. I don't want to give our employers any excuse not to pay full charge."

"We leave early then?" She towelled her arms dry.

"Aye," he replied.

Without warning, the fortress atop the left cliff exploded into fire. Debris flew into the air, reminding Jeremy of a black flower spreading its petals. Giant fragments of rock and iron tumbled from on high, trailing smoke and dust in its wake before crashing into Griralith Pass.

"By the gods!" Karlena gasped. "What was that?"

The men on deck stopped their tasks to view the phenomenon as fire and stone tumbled to the sea.

"Perhaps their black powder for the canons erupted," Jeremy replied, staring with wide eyes at the tragedy.

Suddenly, the other fortress sitting on the cliff top opposite disintegrated into fire and smoke.

"Oh, no." Jeremy felt his knees weaken as Karlena wrapped her arms around him.

"It's happening," she said. "After all this time, it's happening."

He had to admit this was no mishap. Both fortresses were crashing into the tight passage, taking a good portion of the clifftops with them.

"Hard to port," he hollered, turning the wheel as fast as he could. Several men outside the wheelhouse repeated the order, snapping everyone on deck back to reality. "Man the sails. We're heading into the wind, lads."

"Aye," several chorused.

"I can feel it, Jeremy," she told him. "This is it."

"I think you're right," he replied.

Water burst into white spray at the base of the rock face to his right. The fallen rubble from both fortresses and boulders blocked Griralith Pass. No ships were going in or out.

"Where will we go now?" Karlena asked.

"We turn around and make for Oldcastle," he told her as he slipped an arm around her waist.

"Will we see them?"

He held the wheel in place, steering the *Adelandria* to the left. He kissed her forehead, tasting the salt on her skin.

"They need to know," he told her.

Moving the bow past the oncoming wind and directing the ship to the south, he manoeuvred the sails to tack through the breeze before bearing away.

Karlena ran back onto the deck to peer over the rails at the scene behind them.

Debris continued to fall into the pass. Plumes of white foam jetted into the air as heavy rubble hit the surface of the water after rolling from the pile of iron and rock building in the passage's mouth.

Sharek came to her side, placing a hand on her shoulder.

"Do you feel it?" she asked.

Karlena nodded. "One of them is near."

***

Standing high on top of the cliff, her scarlet robe trailing behind her like a waving banner as she watched the ship sail away on the rough seas, the witch sensed the warrior women far below. Her ruby eyes glared from beneath her hood as the vessel raced away to the south.

She knew of them.

She had been told.

She had been warned.

But it mattered not.

They were leaving on their vessel, fleeing for safety, away from her.

She turned her attention to the two pillars of smoke rising from the remains of the fortresses and into the stormy skies. Admiring the handiwork of her soldiers, she observed the scene for a short time before facing her waiting forces.

Five hundred men stood in formation, at attention, awaiting her orders.

"Ostford is ours," she hissed. Her voice carried on the wind as if pushed by some invisible force, reaching the ears of all who could see her. "The Griralith Pass is shut. We press south to Dellmoor and destroy all who oppose us."

The men cheered at the news.

"War," she told them, "has begun."

One

Tall, green grass swayed gently in the breeze as cattle and sheep grazed together on the meadow. Wildflowers dotted the pastureland, displaying many colours that attracted insects. Small birds fluttered from the grove, darting after the tiny bugs before returning to the trees to feed their young.

The river ran high; the winter snow from the mountains was still melting and making its long journey to the Sea of Lunkhul. Waterfowl had gathered to dive for fish and other tiny creatures that lived beneath the surface.

Sitting by the stream with her feet just beneath the surface of the water, Joanne Grenefeld sat with her eyes closed, soaking up the warm sun after another long winter.

Her house, built for her father, sat nestled at the bottom of the hill. She was sitting not more than a stone's throw away from it, relaxing by the water.

The sound of the river lapping by the edge, the gentle wind moving through the reeds and the tiny squeaks the ducklings and goslings made as they swam around their ever-watchful parents; all was soothing.

She opened her eyes and peered across the river to the vast expanse of land beyond. It had been nothing more than a marsh when she first arrived. Her first spring here sent winter's melting snow to that place where it remained, forming a boggy swamp.

The dragon fire and destruction brought on by the Night Demons nearly twenty years earlier destroyed the natural drainage for the excess build-up of water, so she had been told. The earth had been scorched and all life on the surface destroyed. Without plants and good soil to soak up the moisture, it simply collected.

When life did return, it was as reeds, moss, and algae. The water-fowl seemed to appreciate it more than the human inhabitants of the land. There were moments during summers, she remembered, when a southerly wind would blow through the valley, sending the stench of the bog into the village. It was almost unbearable.

Antony, her father, had helped the men of the village dig a trench that stretched across the southern fields from the river to almost half-way towards the southern mountain pass. She remembered it was an arduous task for the men and took three years to complete, not count-ing winters.

But it had paid off.

Grass had returned, the earth ploughed and crops grown.

They had built three hefty stone bridges, each just wide enough for one cart to cross. One stood near the edge of the woods, the Lunkhul Forest. They constructed a second one near the bulk of the village, near to where Richard Dering's cottage stood. The third sat just to her left.

"Joanne," a voice called from behind her. She turned to see a young blonde woman, not much older than herself, placing mugs on a table by the door of her cottage.

"Here," Joanne replied, lifting to her feet and waving.

The other waved back. "I've made lunch. Just toast and tea."

Joanne picked up her boots with one hand as she lifted her black dress away from her wet feet before starting across the grass.

"Coming, Lucy," she called, hurrying.

The table sat neatly on a wooden porch under a wide awning. When Joanne reached the platform, Lucy had placed a hot teapot in the centre of the table and two plates with burnt pieces of thin bread.

"Looks appetising," Joanne said as she sat down.

"Don't jest." Lucy smiled. "We know I can't cook. Dip your toast in honey and drink your tea."

"You didn't burn the water?"

"Not funny," Lucy said, and grinned.

"It's a little funny," Joanne replied as she lifted the teapot and poured a cup for the other, then for herself.

The girls took turns breaking bread and dipping it into a small bowl that sat on the side of the table. In the bowl was a thick, amber-coloured honey collected from hives they kept on top of the hill.

Joanne thought it was a peculiar pastime she and Lucy had taken upon themselves. They harvested honey while others harvested corn and wheat, fruit and vegetables, meat and wool. Theirs seemed the easiest of the tasks required in the community.

Joanne looked towards the houses in the small township, a discernible distance from her cottage. Her father had chosen to live away from them, perhaps for her sake more than his.

Upon arriving, ten years ago, the entire community took her in with open arms. After the word of what she had done at Blackrock Haven made its way to everyone's ears, they didn't look at her in the same way again.

Her father requested that his house be constructed by the hill. Both Richard and Tomas had allowed it without question.

He told her it was because he didn't feel as if he belonged. Yet they actively involved him in the construction of the lumber mill near the forest. He helped to build the new stable house that sat near the grove. The new meeting hall and many of the new cottages had his hand in their creation.

And then there was the trench.

The trench had taken three years, hard labour and a significant amount of blood and sweat. The men worked hard to establish the channel, often getting stuck up to their middles in mud and filth.

Even when he started to get ill, he would still venture out with the men, protesting that he was quite capable of working. It was Tomas who eventually ordered him off the site and to bed, seeing that the old man was much more afflicted with illness than he had let on.

She knew he had built the house here for her.

"What's the matter?" Lucy asked, perceiving her friend was in deep thought.

"I'm just remembering my father," she answered. "It will almost be a year since he..."

She felt a tear fall down her cheek.

"He was a kind man to me," Lucy told her. "There are few men I could feel safe with after Blackrock Haven. David and Tomas; perhaps Simon. But your father treated me like a daughter, and I hadn't felt like that in such a long time."

Joanne remembered seeing Lucy on board the black ship, usually at Martha Wyngrove's side, as if joined at the hip. Lucy Halloway was silent, always silent; traumatised by what many men had done to her in the warehouse near the docks, all because she had striking features that made her stand out from the others.

Ten years had passed, and Joanne still had trouble coping with her own memories of her time on board the black ship, of the scarred man with stinking breath and hungry eyes. She couldn't imagine what went on in Lucy's mind. The poor girl was fifteen when she was rescued. She had been there longer than Joanne and those who came with her.

"I am thankful to him for letting me stay here with you." Lucy sobbed. "I am thankful to you for letting me stay."

"You are a sister to me," Joanne told her. "This is *our* house now."

Lucy looked to the town. "What if one of them asks you to wed?"

"They won't," Joanne said. "They fear me. You, however..." she smiled, attempting to lighten the discourse. Their spirits should not be so low on such a fine day.

"I can't..." Lucy shook her head. "I don't think I could let another man touch me for as long as I live."

Joanne put her toast down. Suddenly, she didn't feel like eating anymore.

"I'm sorry," she said to Lucy.

"Why are you sorry?"

"I put us in such a dark mood," Joanne explained.

"It's a part of grieving." Lucy wiped her eyes. "We all go through it."

Joanne looked away from her friend and across the village. Something was still drawing her feelings downward, into the dark. It was more than the memory of her father.

"No." Joanne stood up and looked to the west. "There's something else. Something has happened. Something has made me feel this way. I mistook it for sadness and focused on my loss, but it's more. It's out there."

Lucy had seen moments when Joanne responded to some illusive attraction. Usually, it was heightened intuition about things that affected the community. She remembered the time when Emily was pregnant with her first, Catherine. Moments before the pain came, Joanne had ordered her sister to get to bed and lie down. The same thing had happened again with Alice, their second.

This time was different.

This time brought deep concern.

"What is it?" Lucy asked.

"I don't know," she replied. "It's like a storm is coming. But worse."

"We should call the rest of the Seven," Lucy told her. "Perhaps together, you can work this out."

"I'll speak to the others," Joanne told her. She stepped off the porch and onto the grass.

"Your boots!" Lucy pointed to her bare feet.

"Come along." Joanne beckoned with a wave of her hand, leaving her boots on the edge of the veranda. "We'll go and see Emily and Tomas first."

Leaving the tea and toast on the table, Lucy rose from her seat and crossed the grass to Joanne's side. The auburn girl reached out her hand and took the other's as they crossed the pastureland towards the township of Woodmyst.

***

"Tea?" Emily asked the two visitors as they sat together at the table, lifting her teapot, ready to pour the steaming beverage into cups she had placed before them. They both nodded as they watched two little girls playing with dolls on the edge of the veranda.

"I can't remember ever doing that," Lucy said, smiling as the girls made their dolls hug.

Emily felt the heavy presence resting upon both women, particularly Joanne. Knowing Lucy was susceptible to emotional breakdowns, she thought it would be best to find out why they had come.

"What can I do for you both?" she asked, moving her eyes over both of them.

"Something has happened," Joanne replied. "I don't know what it is, but I feel darkness and dread."

"She started mourning your father all over again," Lucy told the elder sister.

"It's more than that," Emily said, turning to Joanne, "isn't it?"

Joanne nodded.

"It made you feel depressed?"

"Yes," Joanne admitted.

"Then you thought of Papa?"

She nodded again. Her throat felt tight.

Emily lifted her cup and sipped. She glanced at her daughters playing nearby as she placed the cup into a saucer on the table.

"I thought of Mama," she said. "I thought of how she will never get to meet Tomas. How she'll never see her granddaughters, Catherine and Alice. How she'll never know how beautiful you turned out to be.

"I cried and thought that was really silly. We've been living here for years and I had finished my grieving for Mama long ago. Papa..." she paused for a moment. "Well, that's different. It wasn't that long ago since he left us."

Joanne thought that was an acceptable way to explain their father's demise, stating that he simply *left*.

"The girls felt it too, Joanne," Emily said. Joanne looked at her sister with wide eyes. "They don't understand what it is they have inside them. They just felt sad. I brought them out here to play, to get their minds off whatever this thing is. I intended to come to you later and talk with you, but you arrived shortly after."

"We should tell Tomas," Lucy said.

"He's working in the stables," Emily replied. "He'll be home shortly. I'll tell him about Catherine and Alice. But we need to tell him you and I both felt something dark. We will need to gather the rest of The Seven to see if they have experienced this as well."

***

Leaning against a support beam that held the awning over the veranda, Tomas sipped tea from a mug as he considered the words of the women sitting at the table.

He stood away from them to not offend them with the stench of straw, sweat, and horse clinging to his skin. He watched his two girls running around on the grass near the house, but from the corner of his eye, he could see Joanne watching him.

She was always watching him.

"We gather the Seven," he said after a long time of consideration. "Our concern is this dark sensation you both experienced. Let's see if they felt anything similar. If they did, you focus your abilities on that and see if you can locate it, or at least discover what it is."

He turned towards the women, and Joanne quickly moved her eyes to her cup of tea.

"I'll open the meeting hall for you," he told her. "Some men will keep watch so you are not interrupted."

"Thank you, but no," Joanne replied, meeting his eyes momentarily. "I would prefer to meet with the others on the ruins of the Great Hall. There is power there."

"A terrible evil took place there, Joanne," Tomas told her.

"I know," she said. "But the victims were all good and innocent people. Something of them remained in that place."

Tomas looked at her quizzically. "Their spirits are there?"

She shook her head, still not meeting his eyes. For ten years he had known her, and she had not looked him directly in the eyes for more than a mere fraction of time. He had always thought it was because of what had happened to her on the ship when she was a child. He guessed that, like Lucy sitting to her side, her trust in men had diminished and this included him.

She and Lucy had lived in the house farthest from the village, away from the men. Tomas understood that sometimes the deepest wounds take a long time to heal, and some wounds never do. Wanting both of the women to feel comfortable, he never pressed them about the issue.

But Joanne was family, and he thought she would feel some level of comfort around him, that she would allow herself to relax a little.

Her eyes remained on her cup.

"Not spirits," she replied. "More of a presence. An aura. There is sadness and loss there. But there is goodness and light that surrounds the ruins. It feels sacred."

Sacred.

Tomas liked that.

His mother had perished there, and he had never known a more wholesome or virtuous person until he fell in love with Emily.

He looked across to his elder daughter, who he named after his mother, Catherine. She was smiling at him with her nine-year-old grin; two teeth in the top front missing.

He couldn't help but to stifle a laugh.

Luckily, he thought, she had the features of her mother. Long auburn hair and hazel eyes.

Alice, the younger at seven, had similar features in her face. Again, he was thankful for that. But her hair was dark and her eyes were the same shade of brown as his.

She was more adventurous than her elder sister, often found high in a tree or swinging from the rafters of the bridges by her hands. Tomas believed she was life's form of revenge for what he had given upon his own parents as a child.

She was far more like him than he wished to admit.

He was a little saddened to learn they had both displayed a sensitivity to this sensation Emily and Joanne had felt. He'd hoped they would share none of the abilities that their mother and aunt possessed.

But he wasn't surprised.

Deep down, he knew this day would come.

"They will need to be taught," Tomas told the women sitting at the table. "They will need to be shown how to control it."

Emily moved to him and wrapped her arms around his neck.

"That time will come," she told him, before kissing his cheek.

Joanne looked away from the couple, forcing her eyes upon the children at play.

"You smell like horse," Emily told him.

"I'll bathe this evening," he told her before turning his attention to Joanne. "We should gather the others and head to the ruins. I'll see if David and Simon can attend to keep watch for you."

Two

_____

Four men stood on the eastern side of where the Great Hall once abided. The townsfolk removed the ruins of old Woodmyst some years before, and some of the stone used for the construction of the three bridges that crossed the river nearby.

Grass had reclaimed the village on both sides of the stream. Cattle moved into the area for grazing and some huts built a short distance from where they stood.

The only remnant of the old village was the Great Hall, or what remained of it.

The wooden beams and columns that were shaped like dragons, but which looked nothing like the monster that had burnt the building to the ground, were all gone. Only rubble and portions of the stone walls remained.

Inside the ruin, more grass covered the ground thickly, making Tomas think of a green carpet that neatly hemmed the toppled walls. In the centre of the wreckage, a lone tree grew.

It was still young and stood not much taller than David Gyfford, the tallest man in the township.

It was an oak. It would grow tall and wide, perhaps laying claim to the area on which the Great Hall once stood. What Tomas found perplexing about the sapling was just how it got itself so far from the forest.

The woods were still a good way to the west, and the grove was roughly the same distance to the north. Apart from a bird dropping an acorn right on that spot in the very centre of the ruin, he couldn't see any other way for the tree to have sprouted where it had.

He was tempted to pull it out when it first developed, but Emily asked him to leave it be. The council members agreed with her plea, seeing it as some good omen, and so it remained.

New life where death prevailed.

He was glad he had left it, not because he believed in omens, but because he thought it looked right. It belonged.

It was here, at the base of the oak tree, where the Seven gathered. Apart from Joanne, dressed in her black garments, the others had discarded their colours for regular attire.

They sat on the grass, talking for a long time.

Tomas, keeping his distance, could perceive they had all felt something today. He watched as they rose to their knees and formed a circle. Joining hands, they closed their eyes and lifted their faces to the sky.

He couldn't tell if they exchanged words as the Seven united, but he felt a change in the air. Something was transpiring between them.

"What are they doing?" David asked as he watched the women intently.

"I'm not sure," Tomas replied.

"It's the time," Oliver told them, shrugging his shoulders. "That's all it is."

"Time?" David scrunched his face. "What do you mean, *time?*"

"You know," the other replied. "When a woman has her *time.*"

Simon laughed.

"What?" he managed. "All seven of them at once."

"And my wife?" Tomas added.

"It doesn't happen like that," David said. "I've two wives and they don't share the *time.*"

Simon laughed again.

"Time," he chuckled before bursting into a laughing fit. Tomas grinned, responding more to Simon's reaction than Oliver's word of the day, so he turned to face the river so that the women couldn't see his face.

"Well, how am I to know?" the blond man asked defensively. "Unlike you, you giant ogre, I have only one wife."

"And two sons to his one," Simon mentioned, spurring the younger man on.

"And two sons to your one," Oliver repeated.

Tomas snickered, keeping his face turned away.

"Oh," David piped. "So, I'm inadequate in the sack? Is that what you're saying, Oliver?"

"Two sons to his one," Simon whispered.

"Oh quiet, you," Oliver told him. "You've none."

"Well, that was a little harsh." Simon frowned.

Something in Tomas' mind blinked to life. He had never considered Simon's lack of children an issue until this very moment.

"Have you ever wondered about that?" he said, turning back around to face the Seven. They were still engaged in their union, holding hands with their faces towards the sky.

"What?" Simon asked. "Why I haven't had children? It's not through lack of trying."

"Tomas?" David said to the other, taking on a serious demeanour. "I mean; a joke is a joke. But this..."

"I didn't mean it that way," Tomas replied. "And I'm not suggesting you're not capable, Simon. I'm wondering why none of the Seven has had children."

The three men followed Tomas' gaze to the women sitting by the tree in the middle of what once was the Great Hall. They hadn't considered it either.

"I just thought the gods didn't mean for us to have children," Simon said as he looked at Tricia, his wife.

She was to Joanne's right, her dark hair trailing over her back loosely. He remembered back to when they had brought her home from Blackrock Haven, wearing her scarlet garments. She was happy to be rid of them, burning the red clothing when she finally and gratefully received new vestments from the village's women.

At first, he had all but ignored her, seeing her advances towards him as nothing more than a simple infatuation from an adolescent girl. It wasn't until she was sixteen, and he twenty-five, that he had strong feelings towards her.

Still, not feeling comfortable within himself, he talked with Richard and Tomas extensively, seeking their guidance. Richard told him to look at his own relationship with Becka. She was young, around the same age as Tricia, when he fell in love with her, and he was much older than Simon at the time. Tomas simply told him to ask her how she felt. If she shared his feelings, then he should act.

So, he did.

For five years, they had been trying for children. For five years, he believed one of them could not do so.

Now that Tomas had pointed out the obvious, that none of the Seven had given birth, he realised there was more to the issue than he had first believed.

"Are they cursed?" he asked.

The men turned to him and sensed his concern.

"Do you love her?" Oliver asked him.

"Of course, I do," Simon replied. "I would die for her."

"Then, what does it matter if you don't have children?" The blond man clasped a hand on his friend's shoulder. "You have each other."

As Tomas observed the women rising to their feet and dropping their hands to their sides, he thought it was a strange phenomenon that not one of them had children. Apart from Joanne, they had all married men in the village and were still young; just out of their teenage years. Having children was not something Tomas placed on a schedule, but it was unusual for the wedded women of his village to not have at least one baby before the age of twenty.

Joanne came to Tomas's side and gave him a quick smile before turning her gaze to the other women of the Seven. Most of them started back across the grass towards the village as Tricia wrapped her arms around Simon's neck, planting a long kiss on his lips.

"Not through lack of trying," Oliver mumbled, shaking his head as he turned to follow the other five women towards the township.

"What's the time, Oliver?" David said with a cheeky smile as he started away from the ruins.

"It's about..." the other replied, looking to the sun, before he realised the giant was taking a shot at him for his earlier remark. "Bastard!"

Tomas snickered again.

They strolled across the field, side by side. Tomas felt her eyes upon him as he looked away, but she moved them to the ground, obscuring her face beneath her hood as he turned to look at her.

She walked with her arms folded inside the sleeves of her cloak. Apart from her mouth and chin, she concealed herself beneath her dark apparel.

"So," he began, "what did you discover?"

"We have all felt it," she reported. "Each of us took it as our own mood initially. But it is something more."

"Do you know what it is?"

"We know it is far away," she replied. "But all around. Like a wall closing in. There is something familiar about it. It reminds me of how I felt around the White Mistress. But more and darker. I don't know how else to explain it."

"Do you remember when we were in the throne room?" Tomas asked her.

"Yes," she answered. She pictured the Green Mistress being pushed through the air and into the wall behind her throne. She remembered the violent scene as blood and flesh slapped loudly onto the stone floor after she and the other young girls of the Seven had finished with Yasmeen Svoboda, the Sovereign. "How can I forget?"

"Do you remember when she said that war would come?"

"I do." Joanne looked at him. He was facing the village, not watching her. She traced his firm jaw to his lips with her eyes. He turned his head towards her. Quickly, she lowered her gaze to the grass and swallowed hard.

"There are others like her," he told her. "Maybe they are on the move?"

"I don't know for certain," she told him. "But it would seem there is a strategy at work."

He looked to the southern valley; the plateau filled with freshly ploughed ground. Some of it sown, the rest waiting for seeds.

Hoping his gut instincts were wrong, he considered how to defend his little community. If this was the birth pangs of war, and if it was the war that the green witch had warned them of, then the Mistresses would come for them.

The Seven had destroyed their leader, and the white witch had escaped. She knew where Tomas had come from, which would place Woodmyst amongst her chief targets.

Another would be the crew of the *Adelandria*. But they had canon, Tomas thought, and they could put up a good fight.

Woodmyst, however, had no defences except for natural obstructions that would force an enemy into the open. The only advantage the little village had was that they would see their demise coming.

She was watching him again. He could feel her eyes on him.

He wondered if it was a dislike towards him that made her avoid his eyes.

Was she angry, even after all this time, because he had wedded her sister?

Was it something else entirely?

Perhaps her resentment of men was silently being directed towards him.

Maybe she was having difficulty learning how to trust him after what that bastard did to her on the ship.

He felt angry, remembering she was only eleven at the time. How he wished he could have flayed the scarred man. He imagined himself chopping pieces from the man, saving a certain body part for last before administering the final blow.

Emily had the honour of taking the scarred one's life, and he envied her for it.

Still, after all this time, Joanne still wouldn't look at him directly face to face.

He wondered if she ever would.

***

"Goodnight," Tomas said as he leaned in to kiss Alice on the head. She pulled the covers up to her face.

"Ew," she whined. "Scratchy."

"Papa needs a shave?" he asked her.

"Yes," she replied with a wide grin.

"Well," he told her. "I'll get right on that in the morning."

He turned to the adjacent wall, where another bed sat. Emily was crouching beside it as she tucked Catherine into her blankets.

"Goodnight," she said to the elder daughter, planting a kiss on her forehead.

"Goodnight, Mama," the girl replied as Tomas lowered himself beside her. Emily crossed the room to repeat the ritual with Alice.

"Goodnight, my pretty girl," Tomas told his daughter.

"Good night, Papa," she smiled, exposing her upper gum where two teeth used to sit.

"Let's hope those teeth grow soon," he said, rising to his feet.

"Papa," she called to him quietly.

"Yes," he replied.

"Come closer," she instructed him.

He thought she might have wanted another hug, so he lowered himself to her level again.

"What is it, my princess?"

"Can you loosen my blanket?" she requested. "Mama has tucked me in too tightly again."

He chuckled softly as he reached around her to pull the blankets out a little from beneath her bedding.

"How is that?"

"Better," she replied. "Thank you."

He kissed her on the forehead. "Go to sleep."

Husband and wife walked along the hallway from the bedrooms to the living area of the house. It was a largish room with six deep, cushioned seats placed near a fireplace. A table for dining sat to one side of the room with a small kitchen equipped with a broad stove and benches.

Tomas was proud of his design, even prouder when the roof proved its worth during the first rain that they had experienced in the new house. Needing the bigger dwelling after Catherine's birth, and even more so with Alice's arrival, Tomas had busied himself with the construction of their new home and moved his family in only two years after returning from Blackrock Haven.

"Tea?" Emily asked as she moved into the kitchen.

"Please." Tomas yawned as he lowered himself into a soft chair by a window. Floral curtains, the material chosen by his wife when they visited Oldcastle long ago, hung neatly from a curtain rod that extended the window's length.

Tomas built the house, raised off the ground upon a platform, resting upon stone pillars that lay on their sides, allowing water to pass beneath the house without wetting the floorboards. It was a proud achievement for Tomas.

The decoration; the matching material of the furniture and complementary fabric of the curtains was all Emily's work. While he built the structure, with the help of his friends, she made it a home worth living in.

Others had seen what they could achieve and emulated it in their own houses. They had replaced several of the huts that they once lived in with more sophisticated, more civilised dwellings.

Woodmyst has come a long way, he thought.

"Here." Emily handed him a mug. The liquid was hot, steaming and sweet smelling. He sipped it as she sat in a chair beside him.

"Thank you," he told her. She was nursing her own cup, waiting for it to cool a little. She never could understand how he could drink it so hot.

"What are you going to do?" she asked him.

He looked over to her, not sure what she was referring to. They had just put the children to bed, which usually meant he was going to fall asleep in his chair soon. But something told him she didn't want to know about that.

"About the war?" She gave him a look that told him he was thicker than a tree trunk.

"Oh," he replied. "Well, first, we don't know if there is a war for certain. But I will talk with the council tomorrow."

"You're not going to try to work out defences for the town?"

"We haven't had to work out defences since the attack of the Night Demons," he told her. "And that didn't work out too well for us in the end."

She nodded, sipping her tea. It was still too hot.

"Your sister hates me, by the way," he said.

"What?"

"She won't look me in the eye," Tomas raised his eyebrows. "She watches me when she thinks I'm not looking and then, when I do, she turns away. She'll look at the ground, the sky, a pile of horseshit before she looks at me."

Emily giggled.

"What?" he asked.

She covered her mouth and shook her head.

"What?" he repeated. "Tell me, woman."

"She doesn't hate you, Tomas," she chuckled. "She's in love with you."

He almost spilled his tea.

No way.

She read the astonished look on his face.

"She's been in love with you for a long time," she told him, reaching out to his hand.

"She won't even speak to me unless you're there," he said. "How could you know? Did she tell you this?"

"No," Emily answered. "I just know."

"You sensed it?"

"I did." She nodded. "But I could see it when she sneaks a look at you. She admires you. She holds you deep in her thoughts and she even lusts after you."

"Oh, no." Tomas placed his mug upon a small table sitting between his and Emily's chair before rising to his feet. He placed a hand on his hip and the other on his forehead.

This is not good.

Emily giggled, obviously not feeling a tightness in the chest like he was experiencing. He shook his head as he lowered his hand to cover his mouth.

She put her cup down on the table next to his and stood behind him, wrapping her arms around his waist.

"It's all right," she assured him. "She's more embarrassed about it than you will be."

"I'm not going to be able to look at her the same ever again," he told his wife. "I wish I never knew."

"Why don't you wed her?" she asked him.

"Don't jest about this, Emily," he instructed her. "This isn't some little girl's infatuation. She's a woman."

"A woman with needs and desires," she said.

"She's your sister." He turned to face her, placing his hands on her shoulders.

"I know," Emily replied. "Which makes me more concerned for her than all other women in this village. She's family."

"So, let some other man marry her." He lowered his hands and walked across the room to the kitchen.

"No other man will have her, Tomas. Andris was the closest thing to a male companion for her. But duty only bound him to her, not love. And then he found love with Sevrina. She never admitted it, but that hurt her a little."

Tomas thought of the boys that were assigned to the Seven while they lived in Blackrock Castle. Andris had sworn to protect and serve Joanne, the Black Miss. After his liberation, he clung to that role for some time and found it hard to let it go. That was, until he met Sevrina Verney.

Sevrina was the sister of Lor, Tomas' childhood friend and a member of the council. The moment she laid eyes on Andris, she fell in love, as did he. It wasn't long before they married. He recalled the evening of the celebration and how Joanne hadn't attended. Tomas thought at the time it was so she could keep Lucy company, as the other was still wrestling with her fear towards others.

But Emily was right with what she had said. None of the men in Woodmyst had ever approached Joanne. He found this perplexing, as she was an exquisite woman and would have men fighting over her in normal circumstances.

He knew she was still without a husband because she possessed a power that they didn't understand. The other girls of the Seven had found their men, but they weren't like her. They weren't as powerful.

He leant his back against the kitchen bench, placing his hands upon its edge, by his sides. Looking at Emily, who moved towards him, he frowned as he gave thought to Joanne's plight.

"I love you," he told his wife. "And I love her because she's your sister and I love you."

She slid her arms around him.

"I know," she replied.

He embraced her and kissed her forehead.

"David has two wives," she said. "And they seem to be fine."

"David shares a bed with his two wives," Tomas informed her. "And they are fine with the arrangement."

She seemed to freeze, suddenly contemplating the living arrangements.

"Now, you're thinking about it a little more," he said. "Aren't you?"

"Well, I..." she started.

"You didn't consider where she will be if I want to lie with you," Tomas mentioned. "Nor did you consider where you will be if I want to lie with her. We only have two rooms and our daughters are in one of them."

She swallowed. It was loud.

"I'm fine with it," she told him.

"You're thinking about *her* welfare and not in the long term of how *you* will feel about it," he informed her.

"No," she said obstinately, "it's all right. We can make it work."

He breathed a sigh.

"All right," he reluctantly said. "I'll consider it a bit more. If I decide to ask her, the outcome will rely on her decision. She may not see this the way you do, Emily. She may say no."

Emily conceded and nodded. "You're right. She may say no. Considering that Lucy is in the picture as well."

"Well, of course," Tomas agreed. "She's living in the house with Joanne. It would be hard to leave her on her own like that."

"No," Emily said. "You really aren't that bright, are you? They're lovers."

Tomas was dumbstruck.

"Why?" he asked. But that wasn't right. His concern wasn't about who the women bedded with, but why his wife was pushing him to wed her sister. He moved away from her and back to the living room. "How do...?"

Stopping himself again, he still couldn't find the right words, so he sat down and stared at the rug.

"She doesn't need a husband if they have each other," Emily said. "That's what you're thinking."

He nodded.

"She loves you, Tomas," his wife told him, lowering to her knees before him. "She needs you."

"Lucy needs her," he replied. "She won't last without Joanne. And now you tell me they're lovers? They're as good as husband and wife, or wife and wife, or whatever it is called."

"She may need to move in with us too," Emily suggested. "We'll need a bigger house."

"Bigger...?" He shook his head in disbelief. "How will Lucy feel about this arrangement? I don't think you've thought this through.

"I'm not David. I have one wife whom I love very much." He leant forward and placed his hands gently on her cheeks. "Tonight, she is proving to be more than a handful. I don't think I'm able to cope with two, or potentially three grown women under the same roof."

She whimpered.

"No." He leant into her. "Don't cry."

"I know it's a silly idea," she blubbered.

"I will talk with her," he told her. "I will. But only about her feelings towards me. I don't think I could consider another marriage without consulting Richard, in any case. Given what you have told me, I'm not sure it would be wise."

"I'm just concerned for her," Emily said as Tomas wiped her tears with his thumbs.

"I know." He smiled.

"I want what's best for her."

"And that's me." He nodded. "I'm the best. But the best is yours."

She grinned.

"I'll talk to her," he assured her. "I'll talk to both of them, her and Lucy, and we'll see what they say about it. All right?"

She nodded. "All right."

"No more discussion about this until afterwards. Agreed?"

"Agreed," she replied.

He helped her to her feet and kissed her on her forehead.

"Now," he said. "Drink your tea before it gets too cold."

She sat back in her chair, wiping tears away as she retrieved her cup. There was still a thin vapour of steam rising from the surface as she lifted it to her lips.

Tomas swallowed his tea in three mouthfuls as he tried to get his head around what had just transpired.

Three

"I really don't have an answer for you, Tomas," Richard said, sitting on his porch to soak up the morning sun as it rose above the hill. "Marrying another woman is a big decision that I can't make for you. I agree with Emily, however. Joanne isn't going to find a man that will be willing to wed her. But the issue with Lucy, and your living arrangements; that's perplexing."

"I am really at a loss, Richard." Tomas looked towards the river.

"Just talk to them first," Becka told him. She was sitting beside her husband listening to the conversation as she darned a pair of Richard's trousers. "Joanne may not even want to marry you. Her loyalty to her sister might be enough to sway her away from you. That may be what she has been doing all this time. She loves you, but she could choose not to love you openly for yours and Emily's sake."

"But Emily knows," Tomas replied.

"Yes," Becka admitted. "But she doesn't know that you do. This could open a door that can never be closed."

Tomas sighed. He had hoped to get a straight answer. Instead, he ended up with more questions, more concerns and more troubles.

"You still need to talk to them," Richard told him. "It wouldn't be fair to you if you carry this with you for the rest of your life without letting it free. Yes, it may cause more concerns. But better for them to be in the open than to secretly harbour them where they will eat you away."

"What if she says yes?" Tomas asked.

"What if they both say yes?" Becka asked him. "Did you consider that? You may end up taking on two extra wives instead of one."

"Then your living conditions will certainly be inappropriate," Richard put in. "A house with two bedrooms will not be enough."

Tomas looked at the sky. "What will I do then?"

"I have an idea," Becka told him. "Why not build a new house? Build it as an additional part of your existing home. Join it by linking the porch to the other house."

"Two houses?" Richard asked her.

"Yes." She nodded. "Side by side. You and Emily will live in one. Joanne and Lucy will live in the other. Even if she doesn't want to wed you, at least you will have your family together. It's time that both those girls came into the fold instead of living out by the hill."

"That's something I'll need to talk with them about first," he replied. "I like the idea of having Catherine's and Alice's aunt close by. But they may want to remain on the outskirts."

Richard nodded.

"You should do what you think is best," the old man said. "Just know that both Becka and I will support you."

"Thank you both," Tomas said as he lifted himself to his feet. He kissed Becka on the cheek and clasped a hand on Richard's shoulder. "I'll see you at midday in the meeting hall for council?"

"You will," he replied.

Tomas made his way through the village, towards the hill. He guessed there was no time like the present to discuss his concerns with Joanne and Lucy. The conversation was inevitable and regardless of the outcome; it needed to be addressed.

The walk to their cottage by the hill didn't last as long as he would have liked it. His thoughts remained trapped in visions of what it would be like to have two, perhaps three, wives. He knew there were men who fantasised about lying with more than one woman, and others who had done so. But it had never crossed his mind to partake in such a fantasy himself.

He loved Emily, and from the moment he laid eyes on her, he knew he was in love. Even before they first lay with each other, he knew in his mind and his heart; she was the one.

Now he was standing on the grass outside the cottage where Joanne and Lucy dwelled. He stared at the door, mustering up the courage to knock on the door.

Forcing himself forward, he placed one foot softly on the porch and lifted himself to the level of the veranda. Another step forward put him directly in front of the thick timber door.

He took in a deep breath and let out a long exhale as he lifted his fist to rap against the wood.

The door opened.

Joanne stood in the doorway wearing her black robe.

"Good morning, Tomas," she said, looking at his chest. She was still avoiding his eyes. "I've made some tea. Please come in."

She moved to the side to allow him through. Lucy stood in the middle of the room and gestured to a chair for him to sit in as Joanne closed the door behind him, latching and locking it shut.

"We need to talk," he said as he lowered himself into the chair. It was comfortable and deep.

"I know," Joanne replied as she crossed the room and lifted two mugs. She handed one to Tomas before giving the other to Lucy, who seated herself slowly in a chair across from the visitor.

Tomas watched Joanne as she returned to their tiny kitchen to retrieve her own cup. It didn't surprise him she knew he was coming. She had shown a high level of intuition on many occasions.

"Do you know why I've come?"

"Yes," she replied as she took her seat beside Lucy. "We've been discussing it."

"You have?"

She nodded.

"Oh." He sipped his tea, feeling quite uncomfortable.

Joanne lifted her cup to her lips and moved her eyes to meet Tomas'. Her hazel eyes latched onto his. He couldn't remember if they had always been such a colour, but he was transfixed. It wasn't a spell that had captured him; it was her.

He suddenly felt shame as he thought of Emily, and he moved his eyes away.

"She wants this, Tomas," Joanne said. "We want this."

"I'm not sure that I'm capable," he replied. "How will this work? You two are... And we..."

He looked to Joanne. "How can we if you both are in love?"

"We're not in love, Tomas," Lucy told him. "We live with each other. We've found solace with each other many times. Winter gets cold and we crave human contact. But we each love another."

"I don't understand." Tomas moved his eyes between them, confused.

"I don't think I could ever let another man touch me," Lucy told him. "Except for you. You've shown kindness and love where others have been ignorant, pretending to not notice me. Besides David carrying me from my prison to the black ship, you were the first man to put his hand upon me. The only man. The others have kept their distance."

"When did I...?"

"It was just a hand on my shoulder as you handed me a cup of tea in your house," she told him. "Before you built the house you're in now. It was the first time I didn't feel afraid of a man."

Tomas rubbed his face as he tried to contemplate what was happening. The only thing to move through his head was how he had forgotten to shave as the stubble on his cheeks rustled against the palm of his hand.

"Here I was thinking we would have a much deeper and longer conversation about this," he said. "But it looks like the two of you have made up your minds before I arrived."

"We want you, Tomas," Joanne said. "We want to be your wives. The question is, do you want to be our husband?"

Three wives.

"How will we live?" he asked them, keeping Becka's proposition in the back of his mind.

"We could transport this cottage to join onto yours," Joanne proposed. "A few horses and some hard work..."

The concept sounded a lot like Becka's idea.

"Wait," Tomas interjected. "Did you speak to Becka about this before?"

"I may have put a suggestion into her head," she admitted.

"I didn't know you could do that." Tomas looked at her. "Never do that to me."

"I promise." She looked to the floor, a slight grin growing on her face.

"And look me in the eye more often," he instructed.

She lifted her gaze to his, sultry, captivating.

His heart almost stopped.

"All right." He nodded. "We can work out the house later. How do we want to do this?"

"I thought, considering you have two girls, that you would already know how to do this," Lucy said with a cheeky smile.

"I mean..." Tomas grinned. "Do we have a ceremony for everyone to attend? Do we keep it to a small few?"

"Or do we simply consummate, as some have done in this village?" Joanne added.

Tomas turned his head to the door, noticing the locked latch.

She had it planned.

She knew how this was going to play.

Joanne rose to her feet, placed her cup on the floor by her chair, and crossed the room to him. She held her hand out to him as Lucy moved towards the bedroom, untying the cords on her frock.

Tomas took Joanne's hand and lifted himself from his chair. She took the cup from his hand and placed it on the floor before leading him after Lucy.

The blonde woman let her garments fall to the floor as Joanne brought him closer to her. Lucy started on removing Tomas' clothing as Joanne slipped her robe off her shoulders and onto the floor.

Joanne slowly kissed his neck, his ear, his cheek, his lips. He responded by sliding his free hand around her waist, pulling her towards him. Her skin was smooth, warm as she pressed against his flesh.

He felt lips on his chest, and Lucy lifted herself to kiss his neck. His eyes met hers. She looked at him hungrily. He pulled her closer and kissed her hard.

Joanne pulled him towards the bed. She pushed him upon the mattress before lying beside him. Lucy crawled to his other side, running her lips over his skin on his shoulders.

Tomas closed his eyes as the two women embraced him.

Touched him.

Loved him.

***

His mind was still in that bedroom as he sat in the meeting hall with the other council members. He couldn't help picturing their faces, their legs, their breasts as Richard, seated upon a high-backed chair on the platform, called the meeting to order.

The sound of the man's voice snapped Tomas back to reality. He and the men of the council sat on the front benches in the room. There were others in rows behind them, lined up neatly on the dirt floor for other townsfolk to be seated upon during larger meetings.

This affair had only six men in total attending.

"This meeting is called," Richard began, "to decide what we are to do regarding a possible threat. In my opinion, and it is indeed an afterthought, we may be too late to construct adequate defences. That being said, we might consider the future and design fortifications for our expanding community."

"Are you suggesting another wall, Richard?" asked Lor.

"We saw haw that worked last time," Simon put in.

"Perhaps a fence," David suggested. "Like the one I hoisted you lot over at that fortress up north."

"Explain," Richard ordered.

"Well," David began, "they made the fence from logs that were standing on end. The tops had been sharpened to a point, and they had been joined together with beams on the inside of the fence and covered in something black and hard. It looked like dried syrup."

"I think it was tar," Oliver told him.

"It sounds like a lot of work," Tomas told them. "We would need to cut down quite a lot of trees, dig a great trench and do a significant amount of heavy lifting. I think it might be a worthwhile investment, but I don't know if we can get it done before war is at our front door."

"What do you suggest, Tomas?" Richard asked.

"I think we have several projects happening at once," he told them. "We need to set defences in the woods to the west. Not just on the paths, but among the wild growth. Traps. Pits. Things that will stall, if not completely stop anyone advancing that way. Things that would deter any man that would try to approach through the trees."

"What if they're not men?" David questioned. "The Night Demons were not men."

"We'll deal with that when it occurs," Tomas told him.

"What of the north and the east, Tomas?" Richard queried.

"The north can have similar traps to the west," he answered. "We use the grove to conceal them. The east is a little more difficult. There is a forest some distance away past the hill, but we can't see it. I suggest we build a watchtower on the hilltop and another where we used to hold Pyre, near the woods."

"That leaves the south open," Oliver said.

"If we can stop our enemies from attacking on these three fronts," Tomas said as he pointed to the west, north and east, "we funnel them through the valley to the south. We can see them coming. It will give us time to decide whether we stay and defend what is ours or, if there are too many, flee with our lives."

"Flee where?" Oliver asked.

"The caves," David suggested.

"That's one place I was thinking of," Tomas admitted.

"This is all speculative," Lor said. "We're basing this on the word of the Seven. Even then, they are uncertain that we will be attacked."

"You're right, my friend," Tomas replied. "We don't know for certain. But I was there when the green witch spoke her words. She said war will come. The Seven believe that time is here.

"They know of us. They know where we are. They know that the Seven killed their Sovereign. And they know that the Seven live amongst us. It only makes sense that they will come. We should prepare ourselves."

"Perhaps we should move the women to a more secure location," Lor suggested. "Somewhere like Oldcastle or Dweagan."

"They'll attack the coast first," David replied. "They already have agents on the coast and they have destroyed villages in many places where the land meets the water. People of the sea are a superstitious lot. Many are afraid of them. I don't know how secure such places really are."

"Inland is safe," Simon said. "They can't get their ships across mountains."

"We'll need a weapons check," Richard suggested. "We'll need to arm anyone who doesn't have a sword of their own."

"We still have quite a number of swords from old Woodmyst," Oliver informed them. "They're in boxes that we stored in the stable house. Most are dull and a little rusty. Nothing that a good whet stone can't clean up."

"That should take priority," Lor said. "Preparing the weapons."

"Agreed," Tomas nodded. "You should get to work on it."

"I'll help," Oliver volunteered. "We could get the Blackrock boys to help."

"You'll need more men," Richard told him.

"We should send a runner to Oldcastle and Dweagan for any news or strange happenings," Tomas recommended.

"I'll organise the riders," Simon replied.

"That leaves your towers and defences," Richard said.

"David and I will organise those," Tomas told him.

Four

The lumber mill was a large construction, positioned by the river's edge where the stream disappeared into the forest. It was merely a long and wide gable roof seated upon tall wooden beams, with one exception. They had built a large waterwheel to its side, turning as the flow of water pushed it around.

It connected to a number of rods and gears that pushed a large piston attached to a heavy blade. Tomas watched with interest as the machine sawed through the length of a broad log as two men pushed the timber along a bench and into the blade at the far end.

A marvellous contraption, he thought.

The sweet smell of sawdust hung heavily in the air. He found it a welcoming aroma. Besides his home and the stable house, this was his favourite place to spend his time.

"We'll need tall beams that need to be set into the ground," David said as he watched the long log being cut through. "Maybe a few of those when they're done."

"I didn't come here for the towers, David," Tomas informed the tall man. "You know this industry better than any of us, so I trust your decision. I'll simply help build the things when you've prepared the timber."

"All right," David replied, moving his eyes to his friend, surmising that the other wanted to talk about something closer to his chest. "What can I help you with?"

"I need to build a new house," Tomas told him. "An addition to the one I'm in now."

"Another baby?" The giant smiled.

"No," he replied. "But it is for additions to the family."

David furrowed his brow.

"I've wed Joanne and Lucy," he whispered.

David looked around to see if any of the men in the mill had heard. A couple of them were married to members of the Seven, and he didn't want them taking the news back to their wives. Others were husbands of renowned gossipers, and he didn't need the town to know this before Tomas explained himself.

He took Tomas by the arm, hard, and directed him to the open ground between the lumber mill and the woods, where an enormous pile of logs lay upon the grass.

"You're being unfaithful to Emily?" David asked, and the anger in his voice came through strongly.

"What?" Tomas looked at him wide-eyed. He thought David was about to knock his head off with the monstrous fist he had made with his other hand. "No. No. Nothing like that. It was her suggestion."

David let him go and stepped back, looking him up and down as he shook his head. "This makes no sense," he said finally. "It's so unlike you. Was..." He looked around to make sure that there were no ears listening. "Is she denying you? Are you getting bored with her?"

"No," Tomas replied. "I love her very much. We frequently, you know."

"How often is frequently?" he asked. "Once or twice a week?"

"Every evening," Tomas answered honestly.

That impressed David, a slight smile growing on his face.

"Then why would she suggest you marry two more girls?"

"She suggested I marry Joanne."

"Because no other men pay her any attention." David nodded understandingly. "They're frightened of her. The stories of Blackrock Haven scare them. The women too."

"I know," Tomas replied, peering into the water as it flowed noisily past the rotating wheel.

"I'm surprised to hear Lucy would give herself to you," David told him, remembering the silent, traumatised girl he carried from the warehouse in Blackrock Haven.

"Not as much as I," Tomas admitted.

David scrutinised the man.

"Not at the same time?"

Tomas nodded bashfully.

"You dirty dog," he said, chuckling, slapping the smaller man on the back.

Tomas felt as if he was about to go flying through the air.

"You have two wives," Tomas said, confused. "And you share a bed with both of them."

"Yes," David admitted. "But it took them some time to warm up to the idea. They slept in separate rooms for some time."

"I'm a degenerate." Tomas looked his friend in the eyes; the conviction was strong.

"No, Tomas." David put his hands on the man's shoulders. "You did a good thing. They would never have husbands if not for you. I'll help you with the house. We'll get the men to build the towers and we'll get to work on this. I'll call it a personal project for a friend.

"But know this," the big man continued. "This isn't a competition. I've got two wives, so now you think you've bested me with three? You may find that you've bitten off more than you can chew."

"I'm already thinking this," Tomas admitted.

David laughed as he wrapped a burly arm around his friend. "Congratulations, Tomas."

***

He spent the rest of the afternoon digging in the ground beside his house, trying to make the earth as level as he could for a few stone beams on which he intended to place the new house. Armed with only a shovel, the work was hard and laborious.

He had started his groundwork at the living room end of the existing structure, intending to set the foundation at a square edge to the end of his veranda. This way, the two houses would remain distinct, joined only by the porch.

If need be, he could build another house on the other side in the future. That way, they would have a small, square yard at the front of the three buildings; perhaps a place to let the children play, or a courtyard with a garden.

Emily rewarded him with water from a pitcher now and then as he continued to work until nightfall. With the job not quite complete, but too dark to see, Tomas stripped his clothing off, dropping it on his veranda before walking to the river behind his house to quickly wash the grime from his skin.

Emily was waiting for him behind the house when he returned, a large towel in her hands. He took it and dried himself off before wrapping the fabric around his waist.

Tomas was about to return to the front of the house, but Emily took his arm and held him in place with a gentle touch. She pulled him close and kissed him long and deep on the lips.

"Thank you," she told him.

"I've got three wives now," he told her. He didn't sound entirely happy about it.

She peered into his eyes and perceived his feelings.

"We'll make it work," she assured him.

"I'll need you," he said. He frowned and looked at her pleadingly.

"I'm here," she wrapped her arms around his shoulders. "I'm always with you."

Tears welled in his eyes. "I don't know what's wrong with me," he sobbed.

"You feel guilt," she said. "I can sense it. This is not a concept that you are comfortable with. But it will be fine, Tomas. I promise."

He placed his head on her shoulder and wept as she held him tightly.

***

With his daughters in bed asleep, and his ritual of drinking a cup of tea before bed completed, Tomas dropped his clothing on the bedroom floor and crawled into bed as Emily blew out the candles throughout the house. His body ached from the digging he had been doing.

When she entered the room, closing the door behind her, Emily found him lying on his stomach with his arms in an embrace around his pillow.

"How do you feel?" she said as she removed her garments.

"I'm so sore." His voice sounding muffled.

She straddled him, sitting on his rump as she moved her hands to his neck. Her fingers and thumbs rubbed him, massaging his muscles deeply. He moaned an appreciative sound.

"Better?"

"No," he said. "Keep going."

She smiled.

Moving her hands to his shoulder blades, then to his lower back, she closed her eyes to focus upon working the pain from his flesh.

"That's good," he told her. "Really good."

Her fingers moved along his spine, pushing, releasing, pushing, releasing.

He moaned with each impulse. His body relaxed and seemed to recuperate rapidly.

"You're using your tricks," he mumbled.

"Mm-hmm," she admitted.

"To what purpose?" he asked.

"I'm not done with you for the night," she told him.

He smiled and considered the day he had.

These women will be the death of me, he thought. *But it will be a good death.*

"How is that?" she asked.

"A little better," he answered.

"You're prolonging the inevitable," she told him as she continued to rub his skin.

"Just a little longer," he requested. "Please."

She smiled, running her hands over his hips and across the large muscles of his back.

"A little longer," she told him.

***

Sometime later, they rested in each other's arms, allowing sleep to overtake them. But Tomas was harbouring something he had discussed with his friends when the Seven had gathered by the oak tree in the ruins of the Great Hall.

"Emily," he whispered, hoping she was still awake.

"Mmm," she replied. Her tone informed her husband that she was nowhere near sleep yet.

"Why do you think that none of the Seven have had children?" he asked. "Could it be their abilities hindering them?"

"I don't know," she replied. "I doubt it's because of their abilities or powers."

"Why is that?" He stroked her shoulder, running his fingers along the smooth skin on her arm as she laid on her side, resting her head on his chest.

"You have two daughters," she told him. "That's why."

Tomas hadn't considered that. He took Emily's power for granted. It was a part of her that made her who she was.

"I don't understand it," he admitted. "Something must be preventing them from bearing children."

"Perhaps they are all barren?"

"All of them? It seems a little too coincidental for all seven to be barren. Well," he corrected himself, "the six that have been trying for some time."

"Perhaps the men have faulty seed?" she asked.

"Again," he said, "that seems a little too coincidental."

"Maybe." She paused. He waited for her to finish, but she remained silent.

"Maybe what?" he asked, urging her to continue.

"I don't want to say," she told him. "Just in case I make it happen."

"Just say it," he instructed her. "You can't make matters worse than they are."

"Maybe they're cursed," she said.

He sighed as he considered this. It had crossed his mind.

"Simon asked me that yesterday," he told her. "He obviously has concerns regarding this.

"Oliver told him that having children shouldn't matter as long as you are in love."

"He's right," Emily said.

"It's easy for a man with children to say something like that," Tomas said. "But for a man like Simon, who has seen the rest of his friends blessed with babies, it has got to be difficult."

Emily moved her fingers through the hair on her husband's chest.

"Do you think it could be Sumaiyya Tarkin?" she asked. "Maybe she has cursed the Seven."

"Maybe her offspring," he replied. "Ivo's child. *The Maji* is what that bitch in green called it. Maybe a curse comes from it."

"The Maji," Emily whispered. "I had forgotten about that."

"In your defence, it has been ten years." He squeezed her shoulders. "And they say that memory is the first thing to go in your old age."

She slapped his chest, causing a loud clap to resound through the room.

"You're older than me." She grinned.

"Yes, but..."

"But... What?"

"But I cannot remember what I was going to say," he chuckled.

She bit his nipple playfully.

"Ow," he blurted. "What was that for?"

"So, you don't forget," she told him.

"Forget what?"

"Not to make fun of me when we get older." She ran her finger across where she had bitten him. "Otherwise, I'll chew this off."

"Oh, really?" He laughed.

"Mm-hmm." She nodded.

"Not if I bite yours off first," he said, rolling her onto her back as he moved onto her, pulling the covers over their heads.

Five

Far to the west, upon the edge of the Sea of Solace, the population of a small township busied themselves with packing carts and loading their horses with as much as they could carry. Word had made its way around the shore about the closure of the Griralith Pass, causing widespread panic.

"Make haste, people," called a broad man upon a horse, trotting along the main road to the northern end of the small community. "We've received word of a large force heading this way from Meadowmoor."

Gasps spread across the town like wildfire as they repeated the name of a port town to the south, on the shore of the western sea.

"How long do we have?" called a woman, lifting a small girl onto a cart.

"Not long," the man on the steed answered. "Meadowmoor is about three days' march from here. I was told they have horses."

"By the gods," she breathed as she hoisted a small boy onto the wagon, placing him next to the girl.

"Where are we going, Mama?" the girl asked. There was fear in her voice, not because she understood their plight, but because she could see it in the eyes of her mother and every other adult that passed by.

"We're going to Redloch," she told the children.

"Why?" the boy whined.

"I need to…" she stopped trying to explain. "We just do."

She climbed onto the cart and took the reins in her hands. With a flick of the leather, the horses started forward. Directing the horses carefully, she merged with others who were already on the move. Like all of them, she hoped to make a lot of ground. Redloch was at least a five-day journey around the shoreline of the inland sea.

"Where's Papa?" the boy asked.

"He's with the other men," she told him.

"Why?" he pressed.

"They need to stay back to make sure everyone is moving safely away from Clearfog."

"Why is everyone leaving Clearfog, Mama?" the girl questioned.

The woman almost cried, but managed to control her emotions as she followed a long line of wagons and riders. The vast majority of the travellers were women and children. Their husbands, fathers and some of the older boys remained in Clearfog with swords in their hands.

"We're all going on a trip for a while," she finally answered. "That's all. It will be an adventure."

The caravan moved away from the water's edge in order to evade the sandy shore and take to solid ground near the trees. Carts and horses wound through a thin forest, keeping the coast of the Sea of Solace in sight as they moved north.

They would need to circumnavigate the sea, moving from the western edge to the north-eastern side where their nearest neighbours lived. The problem that they faced was with the towns on the shore of the western sea.

Rumours of black ships moored on wharves at Blackshore, and Erimoor had many of the older people in the caravan concerned, including the young woman with her two children.

Travellers that had passed through Clearfog had shared tales of black ships visiting the coast of the Western Sea many years before. The tales told of men and young boys being wiped out and women being taken along with other spoils.

It was enough to cause night terrors and sleepless nights.

Her hope, at the time of hearing the stories, was their intended to simply scare children. She was only a child herself when she had first been told the tales. Now, as an adult, they all came flooding back and the same dread she felt as an infant returned.

To save her children from the rumours, and to escape impending doom, she had loaded the wagon with bedding, blankets, and food. Her husband had told her he would stay to protect the town for as long as he could. She made him promise to run if the enemy numbered too many.

They climbed a ridge that followed the western shore for some distance. Looking to her right as they plodded along, she could see the inland sea stretching into the distance towards the east. It was an impressive view where, on a clear day, they could see the land on the far side.

Today was not quite such a day.

While the sun shone brightly in the clear morning sky, a low cloud had covered the eastern shore and spread across the water, almost reaching the western edge. Still, she thought, it was beautiful. Under different circumstances, she might have stopped to admire it some more.

By midmorning, the sun was high in the sky and the two little siblings had grown tired of travel, opting to climb into the back of the wagon with the supplies. They found a place large enough amongst the cargo to lie down and fall asleep.

Some riders dropped by as they travelled to check up on her and her children, staying long enough for some general conversation before moving on to the next in line. Those moments were welcome as young children couldn't keep a pleasant discussion going and, now that they were sleeping, she didn't have anyone to talk to.

The caravan reached the highest peak of the ridge by noon. A rider, a girl of about sixteen, stopped to look back towards where they had come from.

The woman watched as the girl pointed, her eyes wide and filled with tears.

Pulling on the reins, she stopped the cart and followed the girl's stare.

The sea filled most of her view. The clouds covering the eastern shore had dispersed, revealing some of the land on the far side. The contours of the land behind the travellers obscured most of their path, but she knew exactly where Clearfog was located.

Smoke rose in a thick column from a section of the shoreline that she couldn't see. The shoreline bent out of their view to the west.

She silently prayed for her husband's safety as she wept.

Her daughter chose that very moment to wake up. Seeing her mother crying made her upset.

"What's wrong, Mama?" she asked. Her eyes moved along the line of carts in front of them where she could see other travellers looking back, tears streaming down their faces. Her head turned to the south. More carts and riders had stopped to look over their shoulders.

She didn't understand.

"What are they looking at?" She wiped her eyes, still sleepy. The black smoke caught her eye. She watched it for a while with interest. "Where's Papa?"

***

The caravan moved back to lower ground as the sun slowly sank towards the west. They drew closer to the water's edge as they searched for a suitable place to set up camp. As long shadows formed across the sea, their desperation to rest increased. The children became restless and hungry and the mothers grew tired.

A natural cleft formation between rocky outcrops gave them some shelter for the night. Large enough to fit the horses and wagons, as well as tents and fires, the travellers settled down and took rest.

Knowing that their homes were probably ash, many spent the night either weeping or in deep thought as they considered their husbands, fathers and sons who had remained behind.

***

The morning light didn't bring any good omens with it. The woman looked at all the forlorn faces of those around her as they prepared to move onwards. They were all sluggish and miserable. Even the children.

Driving the cart forwards, she followed several others out of the rocky ground and towards the shore again.

Before long, the ground opened out into a wide grassland. The forest moved off to their left, disappearing behind a hill to the north as the shore took a sharp turn to the right. The water's edge would eventually turn north again. It was still a long way before they would get to the northern shore of the Sea of Solace.

The caravan made its course across the open ground, keeping the forest to the left as they all started up the embankment.

It was an easy climb, but long. As the ground rose gradually before them, it dropped away increasingly to their right, where the water lapped against the land.

The cart tilted at an odd angle to where the boy and girl worried they would all fall out.

"We'll be fine," the woman assured them. "It won't be long before we reach the top now."

"I can see the land way on the other side, Mama." The boy pointed across the sea.

"That's where we are going," she told him.

"All the way over there?" the girl squeaked.

"Mm-hmm," she replied as she steered the horses carefully behind another cart. "It will take some days, but we'll get there."

"Will Papa find us?" the boy questioned.

She hoped he was still alive and making his way to them.

"He knows where to find us," the woman answered.

She saw some movement ahead. A single rider took a wide run to the right, and a cart halted at the very top of the hill.

The rider on horseback started back towards them at high speed.

"What is she doing, Mama?" the boy asked, watching the rider approaching from the distance.

"I don't know," the woman replied.

She could hear the girl on the horse yelling something over and over, but she was too far to discern her words.

To her horror, she saw several men on horseback surround the wagon on top of the hill. They hacked into the travellers on board with their swords and axes, sending a spray of blood into the air.

"Turn around," the girl on the horse called frantically. Her voice grew louder and louder as she drew nearer, racing as fast as she could. "Turn around."

One attacker on the hill pulled a bow from his back and loaded an arrow.

"Turn around," the girl screamed.

The woman felt her heart pounding wildly in her chest.

The attacker loosed his arrow.

"Turn around. Turn around."

The shaft whistled through the air as it sped like the wind.

"Turn aragh." The rider fell from her horse and crumpled onto the grass beside the cart where the woman and her children sat. The little girl screamed as the boy sat motionless, in shock.

The woman grabbed the reins and pulled the steeds to the right, intending to turn the wagon around and run away.

In the corner of her eye, she saw dozens of men on horseback appear on the hilltop, one of them carrying a large jade banner as they made their advance upon the caravan.

The horses had finally turned the cart around to face the way they had come from. The woman was about to flick the reins to get the horses running when she saw something that made her stop in her tracks.

"Mama," the girl cried as dozens of other riders made their way up the hill towards the caravan. A gold banner waved proudly from one of the new arrivals.

The attack intensified at both ends of the caravan. There was no-where to run except downhill.

Several of the girls on horseback had started down the slope. Not seeing an alternative, except for the blades of the men with axes and swords, she turned the wagon towards the sea and flicked the reins.

"Mama," the little girl screamed again. The boy remained silent, wide-eyed, scared.

Some men from both the gold and jade groups gave chase as she bolted away. The cart bounced wildly, some of their cargo falling on the ground. Her heart pounded in her chest, throat and head as she screamed frantically.

They were catching her, weapons held high as they drew alongside the wagon.

"No, no, no, no," she hollered.

A rider reached over to the cart and caught the little girl in his hand.

"Mama," she cried again.

Before the woman could react, the man heaved the little girl out of the cart and callously let her drop to the ground, where she fell under the wheels.

The wagon rocked and bounced.

The boy screamed.

The woman lost all control.

She no longer heard her own cries.

She didn't see the steep slope before her.

She felt numb.

One rider, grimacing madly, raced to the side of the horses, pulling the cart. With a thrust of his sword, he plunged the blade into the ribs of a steed, retrieving it instantly and pulling his own charger away.

The wounded horse fell, causing the other to trip and crash into the dirt.

The cart smashed into the back of the steeds, its shafts pierced into the ground and sent the bulk of the cart into the sky. It catapulted over the fallen horses with the woman and her boy inside before plummeting to the ground, where it smashed into pieces.

The men gave a cheer before they turned their attention to the attack farther up the hill.

Her head swam with colours as she looked to her boy. His eyes were open, but he didn't move, didn't breathe.

She was gasping in short, sharp breaths. Her chest hurt, as if a thousand daggers had pierced her through.

Her legs wouldn't work.

Her arms couldn't move.

She tried to pray, but her voice made no sound.

She wanted to cry for her children, but no tears came.

Darkness filled her vision, making her think that the sun was setting, and the night was coming fast.

Six

She was once the daughter of the village chief who dwelt in the upper quarters of the Great Hall. The village once gave privilege and respect to her family, much more than any other inhabitant of Wood-myst. She was Isabel Shelley, with no need of want or desire as the serves would get the things she required at a whim. And now, she stood on her veranda, scraping a blade across her husband's scalp as she kept a watchful eye on her seven-year-old boy who sat on the grass with his face buried in a book.

She couldn't be any happier.

"Papa," the boy called.

"Yes, Arthur," David answered from his chair as Isabel wet his head with water from a bucket by his feet.

"Did you know that there were dragons in these parts nearly five-hundred years ago?"

"No, I did not," David replied.

"Mama, did you know that there are records of them having lairs and nests in the mountains, right here?"

"Perhaps they once lived in the caverns?" Isabel said.

His eyes lit up.

"Could we visit the caverns, Papa?" he asked eagerly. "Perhaps we will find the remains of a dragon."

"I don't think that you'll find any remains of dragons, son," David told him. "I've been there many times, and I have seen nothing like that. But yes, one day soon I will take you."

Arthur smiled as he returned to the pages of the book.

The boy's fascination with dragons was only natural. Living in an area that dragon fire had desolated would do that. Every child in Woodmyst harboured some curiosity about the strange creatures.

But Arthur had taken to books to find his answers. Both Isabel and Martha, also David's wife, had spent much of their time teaching Arthur to read. He displayed a love for words at the young age of three and was reading fluently before his fifth birthday.

David was the proudest father in Woodmyst. At least, his face said so as Isabel looked at him. He watched the boy dotingly as she removed the stubble from his head.

"What is he reading?" David asked.

"A realm history book that I picked up in Oldcastle some time ago," she told him. "I bought an incomplete set, three of four volumes. He's reading number two, I think."

"Has he read them before?"

"I think so," she replied. "He likes that one because..."

"It has dragons in it," he blurted. "Why not the volume one? Surely that would have plenty of tales about dragons."

"That's the one that is missing," she said. "I was also able to haggle it at a more reasonable price because of that."

"I care not about expenditure," he said. "As long as he's content."

She bent down and kissed his scalp.

"Perhaps I should keep an eye out to see if I can find the first volume?"

He nodded.

"Head still," she commanded.

"I wish I could read at his age," he told her.

"You can read now," she replied.

"Because of you and Martha," he said. "But I'll never be as good as him. He corrects me when I still get my words muddled." A smile crept on his face.

"Good morning," groaned a heavily pregnant woman as she shuffled out of the house's door and onto the porch.

"Good morning," Isabel replied.

"Morning," David said, keeping his eyes on his son so as not to get nicked by the blade in his wife's hand.

Martha lowered herself carefully, slowly, into a cushioned chair that her husband had moved out of the house for her so she could sit on the veranda when she wished. She grunted and breathed a sigh of relief when she was finally in place.

"Hurry and get out of me," she said to the large bump on her front. Isabel grinned, remembering her time of carrying Arthur in her belly.

She didn't miss the aching back, throbbing ankles, or the incredible pain that followed.

"She'll be here soon," Isabel told her.

"Could be a boy," David told her.

"Her belly is in the wrong place for a boy," she said.

"Could be one of each," Martha put in as she rubbed the mountain below her enlarging breasts. "And what is it with these milk sacks?"

David shook as he stifled a laugh.

"Hold still," Isabel told him, "or you'll lose an ear."

"What have you learnt this morning, Arthur?" Martha called to the boy on the grass.

"Hmm?" He looked up from his book to see her sitting in the chair behind his mother.

"Good morning, Mama." He smiled before putting his head back into his book.

She shook her head, raising her brow. He was so engrossed that he hadn't even heard her question.

"Good morning, Arthur," she replied with a grin.

"He loves to read, Martha," Isabel told her.

"I know," she said as she looked at the little boy lovingly. "He'll grow to be a scholar."

"That would be grand," David admitted. "My boy, a philosopher or a lecturer in the halls of the citadel in Strongholdt or Oldcastle."

"Perhaps," Isabel said, glancing towards the lad. "He may choose to use his gained wisdom to further the development of this village. We shouldn't put our own hopes and dreams upon him."

"We choose our own destiny in Woodmyst," Tomas called from beside the house.

"Morning, Tomas," Arthur called.

"Good morning, Arthur," Tomas returned. "Are you reading about dragons again?"

"Yes," the boy replied. "And something called the Agrodien. It says that they killed all the dragons in these parts."

"Ah yes." Tomas nodded. "The Agrodien. They wanted to live here, before Woodmyst existed. They were a vile, disgusting, ugly, brutish group of beings with dark skin and spikes sticking out of their backs. Claws as long as your body and teeth even longer.

"After they killed all the dragons, the men of the surrounding regions moved in to destroy the Agrodien, because they knew the Agrodien wouldn't just stop here. They would try to take all the lands. And if they were strong enough to destroy the dragons, then what chance did small villages of men have, do you think?"

"None," the boy answered, listening intently to Tomas' tale.

Isabel towelled David's head dry, completing the task of shaving his scalp.

"That's correct," Tomas acknowledged. "None whatsoever. So, the men of all the villages to the south, the east and the west banded together and struck first.

"Now, I don't know whether it was right here, where Woodmyst now sits, or if it was over the hill, or on the southern side of the river, but the attack took place nearby. The men swept in under the cover of darkness, armed with farming tools and nothing more.

"They killed the adult males, and only the adult males, or so the story is told, driving the females and children away to the north. Some say that the Agrodien live today in the middle of all lands. Away from men and out of sight."

"Only the males?" the boy asked.

"That's what they say," Tomas said as he walked slowly along the veranda towards David, who was kissing Isabel on the cheek.

"But the victors write history," Arthur informed him.

Tomas raised his eyebrows and stopped in his tracks.

"You believe the story is made up?"

"Perhaps, parts of it," the boy replied as David stooped down to kiss Martha on her forehead and rub her enormous belly.

"Explain," Tomas grinned.

"Papa told me of the tale involving the Night Demons," Arthur started. "He said that they let some of the younger women survive with the children, possibly to help raise the younglings. This, as far as I can tell, is the only time when any conquering force has allowed survivors to carry on."

"Go on," Tomas urged.

"Well, the Night Demons destroyed old Woodmyst and all the men who fought on the walls. They still killed women and feeble who were unarmed and seeking refuge in the Great Hall. After reading many books on history, I believe conquering forces don't differentiate their victims. They kill and destroy in order to control. The Night Demons are the only exception.

"Perhaps the Agrodien who live today are simply the linage of those who managed to escape. The males that were killed remained behind to allow their females and offspring to flee.

"Neat history only exists in tales and books. Genuine history needs to be found in between the lines that are written. They didn't survive because they were allowed to. They survived because they fled."

"You're very wise for a seven-year-old boy, Arthur." Tomas frowned, moving to the boy and crouching by his side. "And you are correct. Real history is terrible and ghastly. But sometimes we need the tales, and the words in books to give us hope. Sometimes we need to believe that humanity and goodness exist whereas sometimes it does not. Do you understand?"

The boy nodded.

"I would ask that you keep this conversation quiet," Tomas instructed. "Your parents and I are the only ones that you can discuss this with further."

"Yes, Tomas," Arthur agreed.

***

"The boy displays intelligence beyond his years," Tomas said to David as they crossed the village.

"I have to admit," David replied, "I've not heard words like that come from him before."

"I've not heard words like that come from anyone before," Tomas stated. "There is a depth of knowledge and understanding that surpasses any scholar that I've ever met."

"I don't know who it is that he takes after, Tomas. It's definitely not me. I cut lumber and raise cattle. I never opened a book until after I wed Isabel and Martha."

"Perhaps he takes after Isabel," Tomas suggested.

"She likes to read," David acknowledged. "But she prefers poetry and stories of love and romance. He reads books of scholarly content. A seven-year-old boy who delves into philosophy and history, economics and things that my head just cannot fathom."

"He's his own person then," Tomas returned. "He neither takes after his mother or father. He's discovered his interests on his own. Either that, or you're not the father."

"Don't jest about such things," David grumbled.

Tomas laughed.

"Don't worry." He clasped his hand on his friend's shoulder. "There isn't another man in Woodmyst that shares the level of intelligence that the boy possesses. No one else could have sired him and Isabel is not the kind of woman to do that to you. Besides, his features are yours."

"I know," the big man nodded. "I just wonder where he gets it from. My father wasn't a bright man. He was a smith who hit a hammer against iron. And Isabel's father..."

"Barnard Shelley," Tomas smiled wryly. "Definitely not a scholar."

"I guess that makes him the first of his kind." David cocked his head.

"Well," Tomas continued with a grin, "you could always look at it like this. Perhaps Arthur's offspring will be as dumb as that wood you have in your mill, thus completing the cycle."

"Bastard." The giant shook his head. He moved his eyes to the hill-top where the base frame of the tower stood. The platform was under construction, leaving the shelter to be put in place once they completed the deck. "The watchtower looks to be coming along well."

"Much quicker than I expected," Tomas admitted. "I'm thinking that if the men build the other just as speedily, we may place another two along the edge of the village, facing the grove and then maybe one to the side of each bridge."

"Are you thinking of building a wall?" David asked.

"No," Tomas replied. "I think fleeing is a better defence against some enemies."

David remembered the rubble of iron and stone that remained after the attack on Woodmyst when he was a child. The thick walls may as well have been constructed of twigs and grass for all that it was worth against dragon fire.

They arrived at Tomas' house where Emily, Joanne and Lucy sat together on the veranda drinking tea as Catherine and Alice played on the grass before them.

"Good morning, ladies," David called as they approached. They returned the greeting as the two men made their way to the construction site of the new house being built beside the existing home.

The frame rested upon long foundation stones that lifted the floor from off the ground. They had nailed floorboards in place and wooden planks fixed to the external walls of the house.

Today's task was to shingle the gabled roof and, if time permitted, start on covering the internal walls.

"Have you considered what type of shutters that you want to cover the windows with yet?" David asked Tomas.

"That's for them to decide." The other pointed to Lucy and Joanne.

"We," said Lucy as she moved her eyes to Joanne, "want it to look exactly like this house. It should match."

"We want the same shutters, the same doors, the same curtains," Joanne listed off.

"Curtains are your problem," David replied. "I deal with lumber and carpentry. Decorations are in your hands."

"You'll be wanting glass on the windows next," Tomas muttered as he moved a ladder into place.

"Well, now that you mention it," Emily said.

"No," Tomas glared at her. "Glass is expensive and we can make do with wooden shutters, just like everyone else."

"See," David said to Tomas, "I told you that having more than one wife is wonderful. It's why I shave my head."

"I thought you shaved because you preferred the way it feels," Tomas replied.

"I did," David acknowledged. "That was before I married. Now it's to hide the grey of worry. Wait until they start ganging up on you."

"I wish you told me this before."

"The benefits are worth it, my friend." He smiled cheekily. "Oh yes. The benefits."

The women overheard and giggled.

Seven

"It has begun, Mistress." A deep, gravelly voice thundered through the throne room where Sumaiyya rested upon a high-backed marble seat. She measured the being that stood below her, just a few paces away from the platform where she sat.

The speaker was immensely tall; a giant that stood at least twice her height. His shoulders were broad and his stature was indeed menacing.

So tall was he, that she had to look up to him to meet his eyes. Despite that, she could not see them.

His face hid behind an impressive helmet made of thick iron. A dark shadow lay beneath the eyelets and the grill over his mouth. Armour covered his entire body, without an ounce of flesh to be seen.

This was the only way that he presented himself. This was the only way that he could present himself.

"Report," she commanded.

"The Gold Mistress' forces have combined with those of the Jade Mistress," he started.

"They have desolated Clearfog and any who have attempted to flee. There are no survivors. They make their way to Redloch as we speak.

"The fleet awaits your command in Erimoor. They can sail immediately and destroy all vessels and major ports between Blackshore and Oldcastle without need to resupply."

"Send the frigates," she told him. "The rest of the fleet will wait for the Maji. We will sail to Dweagan to join the march north."

"Yes Mistress," he replied.

"Is the Maji ready?"

"I have watched over him as you commanded, Mistress," the monstrosity replied. "He shows signs of trepidation."

"Trepidation?" Her eyes flared. "He is the Maji. The Heir of Darkness. The Ruler of All. How could he have trepidations?"

"Forgive me, Mistress," the armoured giant bowed his head. "But he spends more time watching the trees and the birds on the branches than he does honing his skills."

"Birds on branches?" She rose to her feet and walked down the steps slowly towards him, holding her hand toward his chest like a claw. "You wait until now, the dawn of his victory, to tell me of this."

Several guards that were positioned at intervals along the wall tensed. They had seen this before.

She tightened her fingers slowly, bringing them together.

He lifted his gauntlet to his breast, shaking as pain flowed over him, through him.

"Apologies, Mistress," he said.

"Have I not been kind to you and your kin, Vonavo?"

"You have, Mistress." He fell to his knees. The sound of iron clanging against the marble floor was deafening.

"Did I not give you purpose instead of leaving you to wander the deadlands of the Core?"

"You did, Mistress."

"I entrusted you to watch my son. Is this not a privilege?"

"It is, Mistress," he replied, struggling to get the words out.

She released her hold on him.

"Send your messengers to the Mistresses," she commanded. "I want all cities and all villages, big and small, to be destroyed. Everything between them and the Black Miss must burn to ash. No one is to be left alive. No armies, no men, no women, no children."

"Yes, Mistress," he replied as he lifted himself back to his feet.

"Inform the Haigok and Agrodien that their services are required. It's time for them to reclaim their lands," she continued.

"And prepare my son to travel," she continued. "We make for Erimoor."

"It will be done." He bowed before turning towards a large arch at the far end of the room. His footfalls shook the floor as he moved away.

She climbed the steps and resumed her place on the throne.

She rested her elbows on the arms of the chair and placed her forehead in her hand as she gave thought to her son.

The Great Maji.

It was almost laughable.

He had displayed immense power at a young age, causing objects to move with his abilities. But he had never shown the desire to bring harm. He had only done so because she wanted it from him.

He is still young; she thought. *Only nine.*

Perhaps she was moving too early. Perhaps she should have waited a little longer before seeking her revenge.

No. The time is now.

He would rule the world.

He would take it all.

She had the Coven of Mirikin on her side. She had their forces on the move.

She would have her victory.

The Black Miss and her little band of bitches would die.

For ten long years, she had waited.

He would fulfil his destiny and take his rightful place as the Maji.

"For you, my Sovereign." She wept. "I do this for you, my love."

***

The boy was sitting in his room, a book in his hands, but his face staring out of the window at a large oak tree. He heard Vonavo approaching, as everyone could.

"Good morning, Vonavo," the boy said.

"A good morning to you, Maji," the giant replied.

"I don't like that name," the boy told him.

"Apologies, Master Takmel," the being said. "But your mother insists and I must obey her."

"Of course, you must." The boy sounded sad. "We all must. Why did she send you to me now? Am I to practise my skills by drowning kittens or torture some poor girl my age, as she so pressures me to do?" He shook his head as he spoke the words.

The armoured one looked at the boy for what seemed a long time. Takmel turned to him, standing in the doorway, unable to read any expression because of the armour cage over his face.

"She commands you to prepare for a journey," the giant said finally. "We make for the fleet in Erimoor."

"So, it begins." Takmel closed his book and rose to his feet. "We go to war."

"You are going to be victorious, Maj..." The beast stopped himself. "Master Takmel."

"My mother is the one who wants victory, Vonavo. This has been in her heart since the time before I was born."

"She seeks vengeance," Vonavo stated.

The lad stared at the giant. It was a rarity to hear him speak freely. Fear had suppressed his liberty. Now, he was only a slave to the White Mistress.

"Forgive me, Master Takmel." He bowed. "I speak out of turn."

"I am not my mother, Vonavo. You may speak."

"I know she wants revenge," he continued. "Perhaps for a loved one."

"Yes," the boy replied.

"Your father?"

"No." Takmel shook his head as he opened his closet. "She killed my father."

Vonavo was silent, cocking his head slightly to the side.

"You've not heard this story?"

"No, Master Takmel. I have not."

"Well, then." The boy lifted some clothing out of the closet and placed it on his bed. "She lured my father to his death. The complete plan was to use him for his seed. I'm the product of manipulation, Vonavo. Nothing more."

"You're to be the Maji," the beast reminded him.

"A label found in a prophecy written by members of a coven," Takmel replied. "Wishful thinking."

"But you show incredible power. The first male to possess such abilities."

"My mother is a witch," the boy said as he lifted more items out of the closet. "There was a good chance that I would show some capability."

"So, if not your father," the giant asked, "for whom does she seek revenge?"

"The Green Mistress," Takmel told him. "Yasmeen Svoboda. A great woman, according to my mother. You may have known her by another title. The Sovereign."

"The Sovereign," Vonavo nodded. "Yes, I know this name."

"She meant a great deal to my mother," Takmel said.

"The head of the Coven of Mirikin. A role that the White Mistress assumed."

"Yes, but it was a much closer relationship than that, Vonavo." The boy opened a large wooden chest that was positioned at the base of his bed.

"They were in love?"

The boy nodded.

"How do you know all of this?" Vonavo asked.

"I can read her thoughts," he replied casually.

The giant stared at him for a moment.

"No," the boy told him. "I can't read yours. There is something mystical about you Vonavo. But I can sense your feelings. You long to be free."

"I live to serve the White Mistress, Master Takmel," he said, standing to full height.

"Of course, you do," Takmel nodded as he loaded his clothing into the open chest.

***

Vonavo carried the last of the fully-laden wooden chests down the main steps to the foyer of the castle. Two men stood by the large doors waiting for him, opening them as he drew closer. He stepped through, towering far above the men so high that he needed to duck slightly so he could pass through the entry.

A black carriage adorned with silver trimming awaited. They had loaded it with several other trunks and chests that belonged to the White Mistress and her son. Vonavo placed the trunk in his grasp on a rack on top of the roof, where the driver stood with ropes, ready to strap the cargo down.

The giant then moved to another wagon with six wheels, hitched to two large draught horses farther down the line. He climbed atop, seating himself on an oversized seat, where he waited for the command to move out.

In front of him, fifty horsemen dressed for battle waited patiently for their Mistress. Behind were several hundred more.

Many wagons with supplies were behind the warriors, carrying tents and food for the journey. But Vonavo knew the White Mistress too well.

The supplies were secondary.

If she could, she would order her men to take a village or town, using their supplies and their food before she used her own. Considering there were many settlements between Wintermarsh and Erimoor, where the fleet anchored, Vonavo didn't see the need for so many wagons at the rear of the company.

But a command from the White Mistress was a command that must be obeyed.

It wasn't too long before she moved through the doors, surrounded by several guards, with Takmel walking behind her. He clutched a book in his hand and peered across the yard to Vonavo, who kept his face forward, appearing not to see the boy.

Draped in white from head to toe, Sumaiyya pulled her hood over her head and rested a silver crown on top. She appeared as royalty; her garments hemmed in silver that sparkled in the sunlight.

The boy dressed more simply in a grey tunic over a black shirt and dark trousers. Vonavo had noticed him and knew the boy didn't agree with the luxurious life that his mother had brought him into. She appeared regal while he dressed as a commoner.

She had called him the *Heir of Darkness* and the *Ruler of All*. But the beast couldn't see it.

He saw a young boy who preferred books over sorcery.

He knew a lad who thought deeply about life, not one who would bring destruction and desolation.

He recognised Takmel Tarkin, the son of a father that he never knew. This was not the Maji, the son of the White Mistress foretold in prophecy.

Could the prophecy be wrong?

Could young Master Takmel be right?

Was the prophecy simply written by the coven of old because they wanted to believe in something unobtainable?

Vonavo believed the boy was in danger. He surmised that his own mother may lead him to impending doom, dragging the young lad into a war that she had put him in peril.

Vonavo understood Takmel well enough to know that violence had never coursed through his veins. He had never shown that he shared his mother's lust for blood and death.

The beast believed that the boy, like him, was bound to serve the White Mistress, fulfilling her wishes, acting on her behalf.

Perhaps, instead of the incredible pain that held the giant under her sway, it was simple love for a mother that kept him in place.

The boy had no choice.

At least, none that Vonavo could see.

The carriage door closed behind Takmel as he moved to his seat beside his mother.

"Move out," called an officer upon his steed, standing beside the White Mistress' carriage.

Someone repeated farther the command along the line in front of them.

The soldiers urged their horses forward. The driver of the carriage cracked his whip, causing the four chargers to pull the carriage away.

Vonavo waited for the soldiers behind the White Mistress' transport to follow on before snapping the lines to his own horses.

The procession moved through the gates of the castle's grounds and onto the wide road that stretched through the city of Wintermarsh.

Soon, Vonavo thought, they would leave the city limits and be in the wild between the city that he had called home for ten years and the large town of Ironfields to the south.

As they drove, he gave thought to the boy.

Even with his distaste towards violence, there was no doubting that he was going to be exposed to it.

Vonavo hoped it wouldn't change the boy's character. But he had seen many a good man become a monster after seeing blood flow.

He would try to keep close to the lad. Try to protect him from seeing too much.

But there was the White Mistress to contend with.

She wanted her son involved.

She wanted the boy to utilise his abilities for destruction.

She hoped to make him a bringer of death.

Her dream was to make him a conqueror of all.

The White Witch wanted the Maji to go to war.

Eight

Standing tall, above all the other ships about her, the *Adelandria* waited at the wharves of Oldcastle as some of her crew went ashore in order to appease their personal appetites. The rest remained on board to see to minor maintenance.

"She's got a lot of guns for a cargo ship," said the dock manager, a scrawny old man with a leathery face. Captain Jeremy Schoenbach could tell that the individual had spent many a year on the seas. "I hope none are loaded. We don't want any mishaps while she's moored here."

"They're safe." Jeremy smiled. "How long since you've been out there, my friend?"

"Too long." The man nodded. "My knees won't let me anymore."

"What did you do?" the captain questioned. "Navy? Merchant?"

"Fish for most of it. I worked mostly out of Byview and moved here with my family about seven years ago. My son got work as a magistrate," the elder replied as the two men strolled along the dock towards the Adelandria. "But back in Byview, I had to partake in some merchant work when the pot ran low, if you know what I mean."

Jeremy knew all too well what the gentleman meant.

For many years, under the leadership of Captain Dakmel Tarkin, they had searched for the black ship that had stolen his commander's life; his wife and son slaughtered before him, before they raped his daughter and stole her away.

When their supplies ran low on the *Adelandria*, and the search couldn't be continued, they took work as a merchant vessel. It was the only way the ship could keep afloat and the men on board could continue the hunt.

Most of the crew had faced a similar fate as Tarkin. They had suffered significant loss at the hands of those that were referred to as the *Prophets of the Sovereign*, the crew of the black ship.

Some had lost their farms and livestock by fire, others had lost their families by sword. They had desolated entire villages, such as the island settlements of Erilia, in the south. Then there was his own story, where his dreams and heart had been shattered when they attacked his homeland.

Jeremy still remembered her face so clearly in his mind. She was beyond stunning. More than that, she possessed a beautiful soul. Kind. Loving.

Meaghan.

What they did to her was something that only wild animals could do; tormenting her; molesting her before they tore her limb from limb.

The hunt may have started with Tarkin, but it had become the legacy of the *Adelandria*. With the untimely death of his beloved captain, murdered by his own daughter, the responsibility fell upon him.

With their new friends from Woodmyst, and after facing many trials along their path, they vanquished the Sovereign and the crew of the black ship. The liberation of Blackrock Haven had ended in blood and fire; a just ending for the monsters who had given much worse upon innocent people from all lands.

"So." Jeremy returned his attention to the old man. "You now take care of the docks to stay by the sea?"

"One dock," the man replied. "Just this one. When there are no ships to harbour, I drop a line in at the end of the dock and spend my day in ecstasy."

Jeremy smiled. "Sounds like paradise."

"Would be." The other pointed to the city full of hustle and bustle behind them. "If it wasn't for that pile of shit."

"That's precisely why I stay on board my vessel instead of staying in town."

"So?" The dock manager smiled. "No visiting the brothel? No woman to help satisfy certain urges?"

The captain looked at the ship as Karlena walked down the gangplank to the dock.

"I've no need for any women on shore when I have the best with me," Jeremy replied.

She had her curved sword strapped over her back and a dagger sheathed to her thigh.

"What a dish!" the old man breathed as he watched her intently. She tied her dark hair back in a braid. Her sultry eyes looked directly at her captain. Her cleavage exposed at the top of her leather vest showing smooth skin.

"Careful, old man," Jeremy warned. "That's my wife."

"Apologies," the dock manager said. "My word, you are a lucky man. The sea, this ship and such a woman. She is a goddess."

"You've no idea." The captain smiled, stepping towards the Erilian warrior. "Excuse me."

"Of course." The old man stepped away to allow the captain and his wife a moment.

Jeremy wrapped his arms around Karlena, pressing his forehead to hers.

"I'll miss you," she told him.

"I don't want you to leave," he said. "But they must be told. Ride as fast as you can. Keep a watchful eye out."

"Come as soon as you can," she told him.

"I will," he replied. "Be safe."

She touched her lips to his and held him for a long moment before letting him go, turning away to join the other three Erilian women waiting for her. They sat on horses, purchased from a local stable.

As soon as Karlena was in her saddle, the four warriors raced away, keeping to the edge of town. Jeremy watched them for as long as he could as they bolted past the wharves, disappearing behind some large warehouses.

"Are they sisters?" the old man asked. "They all appear similar."

"Sisters…" Jeremy nodded. "But not by blood. They all come from Erilia."

"Erilia!" the dock manager gasped. "I thought none survived of Erilia."

"There were five," the captain told him. "One perished on the plains near Blackrock Haven ten years ago."

"Ten years, you say?" The old man looked at Jeremy for a long time. The captain of the *Adelandria* felt uncomfortable under the other's stare. "You destroyed them?"

"I was there," Jeremy admitted.

The old man wrapped his arms around the captain.

"I nullify your fee, good captain," the dock manager said, tears streaming down his face.

Jeremy placed a hand on the man's back. "Thank you. But why?"

The elderly man stepped back, keeping his hands on Jeremy's shoulders.

"They kept my granddaughter in a cage in that place," he sobbed. "To this day, she won't talk about what they did to her. But she tells us of the women and men who rescued her."

The old man turned to look to the far end of the dock, trying to see through the warehouses.

"Were they…?"

"They were there too," Jeremy informed him. "They had more of a direct hand in releasing your daughter than I did."

"They have business here?"

"Not here," Jeremy replied. "They go to Woodmyst."

"Why Woodmyst?" the dock manager asked. "Farmers and hunters."

"If it were not for Woodmyst," the captain told him, "your daughter may have perished in that prison. They had a man who led us to that place. We are bound to them with friendship and brotherhood."

"Then I am in debt to them and you both, Captain." The old man extended his hand. "My name is Ewan Cunningham and I am at your service."

"Captain Jeremy Schoenbach." He took the dock manager's hand.

"So," said the old man when they had released their grasp, "if they are heading to Woodmyst, why do they travel to the south?"

"What do you mean?" Jeremy asked, his brow furrowed.

"Well, the river that passes through Woodmyst empties into the Sea of Lunkhul, just a short distance to the west of here. They could have simply crossed the bridge and followed the road all the way."

***

The streets were tough to navigate with tight corners and the occasional person who didn't look before crossing the road. They were thankful once the area opened up around them. The structures thinned, becoming sparser and sparser as they ventured farther away from the port city of Oldcastle.

Running the horses at a rapid pace, they intended to cover as much ground as they could before the sun made its way to the western plateau and disappeared from the sky. For now, the glowing orb was hanging high above them. They still had a few hours of light left and intended to make as much ground as they could while it still illuminated their way.

Keeping to the coastline, they knew they would eventually come to the edge of the Lunkhul Forest. From there, they would head north, keeping the woods to their right until they found the road to Woodmyst. They assumed it to be a well-worn road, as Tomas had spoken of horses and carts using the trail to travel to Oldcastle for trade.

They started across an open plain where several farmhouses dotted the area, distanced to within eyesight of each other, livestock grazing on the grassland between each property. The sheep and goats scurried away from the charging riders. The cattle were stubborn, waiting to see how close the horses would come before deciding whether to move or to stand their ground.

The forest fast approached, thick with pine and oak, stretching from the edge of a steep, rocky bluff where waves exploded into white spray, to as far as the eye could see to the north. It was still a few leagues away from them, but Karlena gestured for them to turn to their left so they could cut across the open plain before reaching the forest's edge.

By mid-afternoon, after the steeds had taken rest, the Erilian women walked their horses for a time. They had raced them and ridden them for a great distance. Now, led by the reins, the warriors took time to rest the horses' backs and also stretch their own legs.

"We need to consider camp soon," Akasati suggested.

Karlena looked at the sun.

"We still have some daylight left."

"Are you considering camping on this side of the wood," Akasati said, "or finding a place in the trees?"

"I think inside is best," she replied. "Jeremy believes there may be eyes upon our friends, watching the comings and goings to their lands."

"You're inclined to agree?" Sharek asked.

"I'm inclined to keep us safe," Karlena replied.

"The woods would supply shelter from prying eyes," Rhydra said. "But they would also prevent us from seeing if anyone approaches."

"The woods themselves will help with that," Akasati told her. "Twigs cracking under footfalls. Rustling leaves as they pass by a brush. I think the forest is a safer option."

"As do I," Karlena told them. "We will stay in the forest."

"We should probably find the road first," Sharek mentioned.

Karlena stroked her horse's nose. It gave a soft nicker in reply.

"All right," she said. "Time to resume riding."

They mounted their steeds and charged ahead, racing along the edge of the woods. Karlena, the first mate of the *Adelandria*, wanted to be in the forest and on the road to Woodmyst before nightfall. The problem was, as Sharek had pointed out, they needed to find the road first.

The land rose and fell in a few places, where small streams flowed towards the west and out of view.

"I've just realised how we can find the road," Sharek called as they raced their steeds through a tiny creek.

"How?" Akasati asked.

"The river," the other replied.

Karlena could have smacked herself in the head. *The river.* She had totally forgotten about it. They all had.

It has been ten years. You can't expect to remember every conversation that you had with the men of Woodmyst.

Still, she felt inept for not remembering something as significant as a river that passed by their village.

She recalled Tomas' tale that involved the dragons burning pasture lands on the southern side of the broad stream. She remembered Simon telling some men by the fire of how he would fish in the water for trout.

How could you forget the river?

She shook her head slightly.

Too much salty air affecting the brain, perhaps.

"I can't believe I forgot about the river," Rhydra called.

"We all forgot about it," Karlena replied. "Let's just find it and the road to Woodmyst."

Slowly, the sun descended to the horizon. They would need to consider making camp soon before the light vanished.

The river was wide and fast flowing. Standing upon the southern shore, the women could see a well-worn road that followed the northern edge of the stream.

They all felt ashamed, unwise.

Had they remembered the river, they would have followed it all the way from Oldcastle upon the very road they needed to be on. The women peered up and down along the stream for a suitable place to cross.

There was no bridge or shallow place. Not even a sign of rapids to show higher ground below the surface.

The water was deep.

"I believe there would be a bridge back along the way somewhere," Sharek said. "There would have to be, considering the farmhouses we could see before."

"If we double back and follow the river downstream," Akasati objected, "we may end up in Oldcastle again before seeing a bridge. I say we cross here."

"It runs swiftly by," Sharek returned.

"Not so much that it would be dangerous," Rhydra told her.

"We cross here," Karlena told them. "The worst that could happen is that we will get wet. As soon as we find suitable ground to camp on, we'll make a fire and dry our clothing out. We have blankets to keep warm. We'll be fine."

"Famous last words," Sharek quipped.

"I'll go first," Karlena announced as she urged her steed towards the water. It hesitated, not wanting to enter the deep stream.

With a hard kick from its rider, it stepped down off the bank and into the flow.

Its hooves left the ground beneath the surface as it moved on into the wide waterway. They drifted downstream some way as the horse swam for dear life.

Water flowed over its back and up to Karlena's waist as she wrapped her arms around the beast's neck and tightened her legs around its flanks. The current was stronger than she'd expected.

The other women gasped as they watched their friend and her charger struggle against the flow of the river. They followed by the water's edge as Karlena drifted farther and farther downstream.

Keeping its head above the surface, the horse kicked rhythmically, moving towards the northern shore.

Eventually, it touched earth and found its grip. Pulling itself forward, the steed moved to the northern bank of the river with Karlena on its back.

Water fell loudly to the surface, and then the horse raced up the embankment to safer ground.

Karlena breathed a sigh of relief as she stroked the horse on the neck.

"Good girl," she said.

The horse snorted loudly, not happy about the experience.

"All right," Karlena called out once she had composed herself. "Easy. Who's next?"

Nine

Robed in lilac and standing upon a hill with several guards about her, the dark-haired woman watched the large seaside town below her suffer at her hand.

One hundred of her troopers stormed the village from all sides, preventing any from escaping the wrath of the Lilac Mistress.

She observed from the peak as her men forced men, women, and children into the open market square in the town centre. Once the citizens were herded like cattle, pressing against each other, struggling to be free, her soldiers acted.

Swords and spears plunged into flesh. As the people fell to the ground, the soldiers stepped forward, striking the next villager, then the next.

The troopers' boots became marred with blood, tissue, and grime as they stepped onto the fallen bodies of fathers, mothers, brothers, sisters, adults, and babies.

They silenced cries with a heel to one's head, movement stilled with a spear through the back.

The Lilac Mistress' instructions were complete once the square was awash with blood.

"Wine," she commanded her cupbearer. An adolescent girl, wearing little more than a sheer white garment and sandals, moved to her side with her head bowed. She carefully carried a silver goblet in her hands, raising it to the woman in lilac.

The Mistress took it without looking at the girl, fixating upon the scene below her. She took a mouthful of the red liquid and swirled it around before swallowing with a loud gulp.

Her soldiers in the town set torches to the buildings as they progressed back towards the edge of the community.

As the houses and hovels took to the flame, they could hear several screams from people who attempted to hide from the invading forces.

She observed one man burst through the door of his burning house, flames covering him from head to toe. He dropped onto the ground close to his dwelling and remained still as the fire continued to burn.

Such a waste of effort, she thought.

She sculled the rest of the goblet's contents and held the cup out to her side, giving it a slight shake.

The cupbearer took a pitcher of wine from the hands of an older uniformed man standing by the Mistress' carriage and carried it to her woman's side, where she filled the goblet. The Lilac Mistress returned the cup to her lips before the girl had completed the pour. A drop or two of wine dropped to the grass near her feet.

The Lilac Mistress didn't appear to notice, keeping her eyes on the village.

Behind her, a soldier rode up to the cart where he dismounted his steed. He raced over to the woman's side, where he dropped to a knee and waited to be acknowledged.

"Take this." She handed the goblet to the girl. "Place the cup and vessel in the cart and return to me."

"Yes, Mistress." The girl bowed before carrying the goblet and pitcher of wine away.

"Speak," the Lilac Mistress commanded the soldier.

"Mistress," the man began. "The Scarlet Mistress sends her salutations on your victory here at Grassbeach. Her forces have closed the Griralith Pass by joining with those of the Gold Mistress. The fortresses along the channel burn all the way to Starrybourne. She has sacked Dellmoor. Its streets overflow with the blood of man and beast alike.

She has split her forces as she moves to the east. They intend to take Melamwed and Kailibard at the same time."

"They are small and have no chance of victory against her." The Lilac Mistress smiled before glancing over her shoulder to the older guard standing near her carriage. "Summon the troops. We camp here for the night and move on at first light."

"Yes, Mistress," the guard responded, waving another soldier forward.

The soldier had a horn strapped to his side. He walked a few paces and blew the trumpet loudly. The sound pierced the air, causing all the men in the village to look towards the hill.

Without hesitation, the troopers left the streets of the town in haste and formed into two lines. As a unit, they marched towards the hill, leaving the town to burn behind them.

As this transpired, the Lilac Mistress continued her conversation with the man on his knee.

"What other news?" she inquired.

"The Gomatha report that the Gold Mistress' forces have joined with those of the Jade Mistress," he told her. "They now surround Redloch and intend to move south to join with the Pearl Mistress in Mallowhill. From there..."

"From there," she interrupted, "they will take Strongholdt and Havencrest. It seems everything is in motion."

"Yes, Mistress," the soldier replied.

"Join the ranks and set up camp," she ordered.

"Yes, Mistress," he said again as he rose to his feet and moved behind her, beyond the carriage.

"Come," the woman in lilac called to her cupbearer.

The girl ran to her Mistress' side and bowed.

"Yes, Mistress?"

"Stand straight," the woman commanded.

The girl did so. Her shoulders were back and her head high.

"Yes, Mistress."

Without warning, the Lilac Mistress swung her hand back and smacked the young girl across the jaw. The cupbearer fell to the ground, her face felt numb as white spots appeared before her eyes.

"If you ever cause any of my wine to fall again..." The woman bored into the girl with a fiery glare, "I will pluck your eyes from your head and drink your blood through the sockets."

The girl sobbed.

"Now, pick yourself up and pour me more wine."

"Yes, Mistress." The girl got to her feet, holding her hand to her face. She stumbled slightly as she moved towards the carriage.

The uniformed man by the carriage poured the wine into the goblet as she approached. The girl's hand shook as she reached out to take it. He lowered the pitcher and goblet to the driver's seat of the carriage and took both of her small hands in his.

She looked into his eyes. Peering back to her, he took a deep breath and exhaled slowly.

Following his lead, she inhaled, exhaled and stopped shaking. She took the cup and returned to the Lilac Mistress, who continued to watch the Grassbeach and its inhabitants burn.

***

The sun had fallen below the trees of the woods, and the two men barely able to stand after a full day of hard labour. They had spent most of the morning nailing long wooden planks over the roof beams and sealing the joins with a thick mixture that David had created from tree-sap and bees' wax. It set hard like rock and stopped water from seeping between the pieces of timber.

They attached the shingles next, starting from the bottom of the roof and working their way towards the apex. They had covered the façade of the new house, but the rear was a little less than three quarters done.

They spent the last moments of their time on the ladders draping a canvas tarpaulin over the top of the house, promising Tomas' new wives that they would have it all done by the next day.

"We could move in," Lucy suggested, sitting on the grass with Catherine and Alice.

"Let's wait until we get the shingles on," David told her. "We'll be hammering away up there.

You don't want dirt, sawdust or anything like that on your nice furniture."

"Or even worse," Tomas said. "David could fall through and land on your pretty head."

She laughed.

"Could happen," David added.

"Besides," Emily interjected. "We will need to give it a good clean out and the shutters are yet to be attached."

"I haven't started your shutters yet," David admitted. "But I have a few spares from other projects. "They are mismatched, and probably a little oversized for your windows. But they will offer some protection from the weather until I finish yours. I hope that is all right?"

"It will be fine, David." Joanne smiled, sitting on the edge of her new veranda, her side resting against a support beam. She turned to face her sister, who sat in a chair on the other veranda perpendicular to her own. "It's perfect."

"Almost," Tomas told her. "We just need to join that little corner to make the two porches meet together, put a cover over the top and we're done."

"Until you need the third house built," David chuckled.

"Third house?" Lucy asked.

"Well, when you have children," he said before turning to Joanne, "and you have children, you won't be able to all fit in there. "You'll need another one of these over there."

He pointed directly across from the new house to the far side of the older one.

"Three houses?" Lucy questioned. "Won't that get tongues wagging?"

"They already are," Emily told her. "I've talked to Tomas regarding this and it will be done.

But it can wait for now."

Tomas nodded.

"Well," David said, stepping down from the veranda and starting across the grass. "I'll see you tomorrow. I'll come to you Tomas. I might be a little late. I've got a feeling that one of my wives needs a good..."

He stopped and remembered the two young girls sitting on the grass.

"Need a good what, Uncle David?" Alice, the younger, called.

"Meal," he replied. "She needs a good meal and I intend to cook for her."

Tomas laughed as the big man waved and moved off.

"It's nice that he would cook for his wives," Catherine said to Lucy.

"Maybe you could cook for me tonight?" Joanne asked Tomas.

"Not tonight," he replied. "I am too sore."

Emily giggled.

"What's so funny?" he asked.

"She's better with her hands than I am."

He remembered her massage that had reinvigorated him and put him in the mood to embrace her.

"How do you know this?" He looked back and forth at the two women. "Do you talk about this behind my back?"

"We always do," Lucy told him.

Tomas ran his hand down his face as he exhaled a long sigh.

"Joanne taught me the trick," Emily told him. "My back hurt a lot when I was carrying Catherine. She showed me how to relieve the aching. Only, she is far better at it than I."

This intrigued Tomas.

They could all read his face as he raised his eyebrows and pondered the concept.

Why not? She is your wife.

"You could go to the old house tonight," Emily told him, referring to her father's house by the hill, "grab a horse and wagon in the morning and bring back some of the furniture before you get started on the rest of those shingles."

"Yes, master." He smiled. "All right. I'll do it, because I need some magic fingers." Tomas rubbed his neck.

"As am I," Joanne whispered just loud enough for him to hear, smiling cheekily.

**

They set a small fire and laid down bedding nearby. The horses, tethered to some trees, happily munched upon the growth by their feet as the women sat by the hearth.

They wrapped themselves in blankets to keep the chill of the night air off their bare backs as their garments hung on crude clotheslines they had made from their steeds' harnesses tied from a tree at one side of their camp to another on the other side.

"I hope they dry by morning," Akasati said, directing her angry words to Karlena. "There is nothing worse than soggy trousers for riding in."

"I can only apologise so much," Karlena replied.

"Please, Akasati," said Rhydra. "Enough is enough. It was only water, and we have spent our whole lives around water."

The other threw a small twig into the fire, still feeling a slight temper as she peered into the flames.

"They'll dry," Sharek told her. "You fret over nothing."

"I fret because I wonder what we do if someone finds us here," she replied. "We've no clothes on."

"We can still use our swords without apparel, Akasati," Rhydra told her.

"But we will be naked."

"That could work to our advantage." Karlena smiled. "It might put our enemies off and they grab for the wrong swords instead."

The other two laughed. Anger wandered from Akasati as a smile grew on her face.

She looked at Karlena, her demeanour changing to a more pleasant one. "I'm sorry, sister," she said. "I don't know why I got so upset."

"I'm sorry too," the other replied. "I should have asked for directions before leading us across the plain."

"I would embrace you," Akasati told her. "But I don't want to drop my blanket."

"I understand." Karlena smiled.

A soft, brief breeze blew through the camp, seeming to dampen the flames momentarily.

"What was that?" Sharek hissed.

The Erilian warriors stood, blades in hands and blankets fallen to the ground.

"That was no ordinary wind," Karlena said. "There was a presence."

"A spectre?" Rhydra asked.

"I don't know," she replied as they turned their backs to the flames.

The woods were dark as the shadow of night covered all within view.

The leaves rustled to the north of their camp as something unseen moved around them, circling.

"What are you?" Karlena called.

A soft, deep whisper like a sigh resonated from the darkness before the thing rustled through the forest, speeding towards the east.

"What was that?" Sharek repeated.

Karlena stared into the darkness after the visitor with steely eyes. A thing with no form yet tangible... With no words to describe it, she said the first thing that entered her mind.

"A shadow demon."

Ten

Waking before sunlight, his arm draped over his young wife's body, Tomas believed that his back had never felt better. He would have loved to remain with her like this all day, but there were chores to be done and other projects in the township that he needed to check on.

It had been two days since he went to inspect the progress of the towers and the traps being set in the woods to the west and grove to the north. He felt he was neglecting his village in favour of his three wives and their needs.

Still, he had grown to love them all, each differently, each just as much as the other.

Joanne, whom he lay with, doted on him. She poured his tea and put food on his plate, brought it to him and cleaned his mess. He had never asked her to and was quite willing to do the same for her. But she was quick to the task and would have it fulfilled before he had time to consider it.

Her enchanted hands had done wonders for his muscles, far more than Emily could with her abilities. But Joanne hadn't stopped there. She saw scratches and bruises on his skin and rubbed brown vinegar over his wounds with her warm fingers.

Joanne was more upfront about her needs as well. She was more adventurous than Emily and Lucy, particularly in bed. He tried his best to accommodate her, but he was getting older and she was still young. Sometimes, her plan didn't always come to fruition, ending in riotous laughter. Such as it was during the night.

He tried to move away from her so he could dress and get busy with preparing a cart for their furniture. She stirred, sensing his movement.

"Where are you going?" she asked, reaching behind her and gripping his rump.

"I need to get working," he replied before kissing her neck. "The shingles need to be fixed and you're moving."

"It's still dark," she told him. "The stars are out. Stay a little longer."

He hesitated. It was going to be a long day's work and he should start before the sun breached the horizon.

"Please?" she begged.

He smiled and pressed himself against her again, resting his head on the pillow and moving his arm over her waist.

She moved her hand to lace her fingers with his.

"Where was Lucy last night?" he asked.

"You desired her also?" Joanne turned her head slightly.

Tomas couldn't tell if his question offended her.

"I desire all of you," he said. "Last night, I wanted to be with you and just you."

She seemed to accept his words.

"Lucy slept in her room," she told him. "We thought you didn't enjoy the experience with both of us as much as we thought you would have. So we discussed our future engagements with you and decided we would keep it like this."

"That I lie with only you?"

"No, silly." She rolled over to face him. "Last night, you were with me. Tonight, you may be with her. But never with the two of us together."

"I *enjoyed* it," he admitted. Her eyes lit up a little. "But it is not for me. I honestly didn't know which one of you I should have met eyes with, touched or kissed. It was confusing for me."

She nodded, running her fingers over his chest.

"I like this," he told her. "Two of us alone. I can hold you and talk with you and learn more about you."

She reached to his face and kissed him long on his lips.

"I love you, Tomas Warde."

"I love you, Joanne Warde," he replied.

***

With the cart loaded with all the furniture from the house and a hearty breakfast of sausage and eggs in the belly, Tomas led the steed tethered to the wagon, holding its bridle in his hand as he walked by its side. Both Lucy and Joanne strolled together near him as they made their way along the riverbank towards the new house at the edge of the township.

The sky was a pale blue, but the sun had not risen above the mountains far to the east yet. As much as Tomas wanted to get an earlier start on his set tasks, he was glad at the opportunity of spending time with his two wives for breakfast.

Lucy slaved over the stove for the three of them while Joanne doted on him once again. He thought that if he was to let her, she would have carved his food up and fed it to him as well.

"I just thought of something," Lucy said, turning to look back at the house by the hill.

Tomas stopped the horse and looked at her. "What is it?"

"The hives," she said. "Should we consider moving the hives?"

Tomas shook his head.

"They're fine where they are," he assured her. "You can still see them from your new home."

"What about the men on the tower?" she said. "Will they hurt the bees?"

Tomas recognised her anxiety. It was something she had suffered from since her treatment in the prison of Blackrock Haven. Most of the time she was fine, but now and then, when something new or strange reached into her mind and heart, she panicked.

Moving to a new house, he guessed, was the trigger for this attack. He frowned, feeling helpless and not knowing how to comfort his wife. All he understood was that this was not about the bees. It was about her.

Letting go of the horse, he went to her and wrapped his arms around her.

"No one will hurt the bees," he told her. His voice was gentle. "They are safe. You are safe. I won't let any harm come to you. I love you, Lucy Warde."

She moved her eyes away from the hilltop to meet his. They were full of tears that teetered on her eyelashes, building before they would fall upon her cheeks.

He kissed her forehead.

"I love you," he told her again.

She buried her head into his chest and broke down. Joanne couldn't contain herself, letting herself cry as she moved to Lucy's back, wrapping her arms around them both.

***

The sound of hammering echoed across the village, emitting from several places.

Echoing thuds resonated from within the tree line of the woods and the grove as several men dug trenches and positioned large timber pikes into the ground at the base of dugouts and deep pits. The towers were having their viewing platforms and rooves constructed with several men working on each.

Lor and his crew were continuing to sharpen the dull blades stored in the stables. Some were remnants of the Realm War; others made in haste for the conflict with the Night Demons.

Meanwhile, David and Tomas worked their way along the rear side of the new house's roof, tacking shingles carefully into place. By mid-morning, the men expected to have the task completed by midday.

"When we get to the top," Tomas asked, "do we bend the shingles over to cap it off?"

"No," the big man told him. "The shingles will snap. "I've had the lads make some capping shingles for the ridge. We will gather them from the mill later and have it all done by sunset."

"You're a good man, David," Tomas said as he hammered another tack into a shingle.

"I know," he replied. "And humble, too."

Tomas lifted himself slightly to see over the apex of the roof and down to the grass in front of his two houses. There he could see Joanne running around with his two daughters, playing some chasing game. The feet of his other two wives were just visible on the veranda of the older dwelling. They were sitting side by side, probably drinking tea as they observed the others at play.

My happy family, he thought before returning to his task.

David lifted his upper body and twisted to the left, then the right.

"A little tight in the muscles," he said.

Tomas simply smiled, silently thankful that he could choose between two women that could relieve his aches with a simple touch.

A horn blew from the west, reverberating across the village. Tomas lifted himself over the apex of the roof and shouted down to those below.

"Inside," he commanded.

Joanne ushered her nieces to their mother, who took them all inside, closing the door behind them.

David and Tomas dropped their hammers and descended the ladder. Both men bolted around the side of the house, past the cart laden with furniture and through the township, making their way towards the new tower being constructed near the edge of the woods.

People scurried through the streets as they passed them by. Women and children disappeared into their dwellings as men gathered weapons before falling in line behind Tomas and the giant.

The horn blew again as the men drew nearer to the tower. They heard the piercing sound of a horse squealing from deep within the trees.

"What is it?" Tomas called to the men on the tower.

"We're uncertain," one of them replied as he pointed to the road through the forest. "The trumpet call came from in there."

He started for the road.

"Tomas," David called.

The other stopped to face his friend.

"You're not armed," the giant reminded him.

A horse squealed again. The trumpet call repeated.

Tomas looked at the gathering crowd of men. Lor, Oliver, and Simon pushed their way to the front, and Richard followed. Everyone was armed except for David and himself.

He approached Richard with his hand outstretched.

"You stay here," he said, relieving the older man of his weapon and handing it to David.

"If I don't come back, they'll look to you."

Richard nodded, his eyes sad to not be a member of the party, but thankful that he didn't have to be.

"The rest of you, with me," Tomas commanded.

"You're still without a sword, Tomas," David said again.

"Then you will need to watch over me, my friend," he replied. "Otherwise, you'll have three women after your head and two of them are witches."

"Then don't run too far from my side," David told him as they ran, following the road into the woods. "I'm getting slower in my old age."

"You're not thirty yet," Oliver quipped. "And you're complaining of old age."

"Too many wives for you to handle," Simon put in as they ran. "I am thirty and feel like a young bull."

"Look like one too," David told him.

They moved around a bend in the road and saw several men surrounding four riders. The riders held curved swords high above their heads while the men pointed their own blades at the steeds.

"By the gods," David breathed upon seeing the sight.

"Lower your weapons," Tomas ordered.

"Tomas," Lor started. "They're armed."

"They're friends," Simon assured him.

"Lower them, now," Tomas barked.

The men complied, stepping away from the riders, placing their swords in sheaths strapped to their backs.

"Tomas," said the lead rider, lowering her blade.

"Karlena." He smiled. "Apologies for the welcome."

"No apology necessary," she replied. "We must take certain measures at such a time as this."

"You have news?"

"I do," she told him. "I must speak to Emily and the potentials."

"Come," he told her. "You are welcome in Woodmyst."

***

"We've been sensing something building for some time," she told the council. "But a shadow has also befallen the lands and prevented us from being able to focus on the source of this change."

The Erilians sat in the front row of benches in the meeting hall. Richard sat on the platform with the members of the council on either side of him, listening intently to Karlena's story.

Emily and the Seven positioned themselves next to the women warriors invited to partake in the meeting, along with the council members.

Other villagers gathered to listen to the proceedings; so many that Tomas had ordered the walls opened so that when the benches had filled, other people could gather at the edges of the hall.

"Do you know what this shadow is?" Richard asked.

"We believe the White Mistress had returned," Karlena told him. "We believe that the war, promised by the Sovereign, has begun."

"We saw the closing of the Griralith Pass," Akasati added.

"The way to Strongholdt?" Richard queried.

"Yes," Karlena replied. "We were on our way there to offload our cargo. The fortresses turned to fire and smoke before the walls of the passage fell to the sea."

"Why would they close the Pass?" Tomas asked.

"During the Realm War," Richard told him, "Strongholdt had a great navy. They kept all of her ships in the Sea of Solace."

"It is still so today," Karlena said. "By closing the Pass, no ships can enter."

"And none can leave," Tomas nodded. "Including the fleet."

"Clever move." Richard scratched his beard.

"It implies that the enemy must have a fleet of their own," Lor put in. "Why else would you prevent armed ships from sailing through the Griralith Pass?"

"There have been reports of a fleet massing farther north of the Pass, at Erimoor," Karlena told them.

"She is there," Joanne blurted. All eyes moved to her. "I can feel it. Sumaiyya is in the north."

"And the other Mistresses?" Oliver asked.

"They're everywhere," Isabel, the White Miss, answered. "Far away but all around."

Tomas sighed as he looked at David, Simon, and Oliver.

"They've taken the coast," Simon said. "And the coast wasn't ready."

"Their next course of action will be to destroy all who stand in their way," Richard announced with sadness in his voice.

It reminded him of certain tactics used during the Realm War where armies destroyed villages and massacred people for simply not standing under the banner of their rulers. Farmers and fishmongers, men with no knowledge of battle, burned alive because they wouldn't, couldn't fight.

"They will make their way inland," he said. "I've the feeling that this White Mistress intends to take it all."

"She will," Joanne said. "Her mind is twisted and after what we did to the Green Mistress, she will come for us. Woodmyst is in danger."

"We should leave," Tricia, the Scarlet Miss, suggested. The rest of the Seven moved their eyes to her. "Woodmyst will be safer without us."

"No," Simon, her husband, objected. "She will destroy Woodmyst because it suits her to do so. She won't come here just for you, my love. She will come here simply because we are here."

"Simon is right," Tomas said. "By fleeing, all you will do is give her something to chase. She will come for you, but she will strike the village first. She knows us, despises us. Her focus will be upon us, eventually.

"Richard has told us they will move inland," he continued. "Then we proceed with fortifying Woodmyst as best we can. She may work her way to us, destroying everything between here and the coast, or she may send her forces beforehand.

"In any case, every man and woman who can fight must carry a weapon from this day forth. We must be prepared."

"Captain Schoenbach will be with us as soon as he is able," Karlena announced. "May I request you grant he and his men permission to enter Woodmyst?"

"No request needed," Tomas told her. "All friends of Woodmyst are welcome."

He stood on the platform to address the villagers gathered about the hall.

"These are the Erilian warriors you have all heard so much about," he announced. "They liberated Blackrock Haven and helped to rescue the women that some of you call your wives. They are as much a part of Woodmyst as I am. Tonight, we will feast in their honour."

He turned to Karlena, who still stood before the assembly. Lowering himself from the platform, he took her hands and kissed her cheek.

"Welcome home," he told her.

Applause erupted through the room as Emily and the Seven embraced the Erilians. More and more people stepped forward to clasp hands or wrap arms around the warriors. They shed tears as familiar faces from Blackrock Haven welcomed the women.

Eleven

Work resumed on the towers and the traps in the woods.

David and Tomas completed the tacking of the shingles. They fixed the capping in place and the roof was done.

By nightfall, they moved all the furniture inside the house, and some of it was in place. The rest sat on the floor of the living quarters awaiting organisation. It would stay there until after the feast. Both Joanne and Lucy had spent most of the afternoon preparing food while Emily caught up with her adopted sisters.

The meeting hall had its seating arranged into three sections where long trestle tables, merely wide planks of timber resting upon saw horses, stretched from one end of the structure to the other. The women and adolescent daughters of the village placed steaming roast lamb and chicken upon large metal plates carved ready to serve.

As people filled the seats, they kept the positions near the front of the room for their esteemed guests, the Erilian warriors. Some attempted to take and maintain places near to the visitors' seats, but this proved difficult as chores called people away and others would then claim the seats for themselves.

Unlike the days of old Woodmyst, when the council members sat upon a high and lofty platform, Tomas and the current members sat amongst the people instead. He introduced this idea when they first constructed the meeting hall, not wanting to give any opportunity for someone to feel lower than another in his village. Everyone was equal, man and woman.

However, he wished he had made an exception to the rule for this night and ordered the townsmen to reserve some seats for him.

He found a spot at the rear of the room for his family, all five of them. There was no seat for him.

"You can have my seat, Papa," Alice told him from her place at the end of a bench.

"No." He smiled, standing at the end of the table. "It's all right. I'll be fine."

"Good," she said, swinging her legs back and forth. Emily, sitting across the table from the young girl, chuckled and took his hand.

"Why don't you grab one of our chairs from the veranda?" she told him. "I'll mind your place."

"No," David called from the table behind her. "Don't go all the way back to your house for a lousy chair. Go to mine, it's closer. I have a chair on my veranda. You could take that."

"The big cushioned thing?" Tomas queried.

"No, the one from the table," the giant told him. "I was on it the other morning when you came over. I keep forgetting to take it inside."

Tomas recalled the conversation he had with little Arthur Gyfford while Isabel scraped his father's scalp clean with a blade. David had been sitting in a wooden chair that morning.

"I pushed against the wall by the door," Martha told him.

"All right," Tomas nodded. "Thank you."

She waved her hand and shot him a smile as she rubbed her bulging belly with her other hand.

"I'll be right back," he said to Emily.

Tomas left the noise of chatter and the smell of roast meat as he moved towards David's house, past a few dwellings to the west of the meeting hall. He ventured beyond the circle of light from the lanterns hung about the central building and the hearth on the open ground where the spit once turned.

Now in shadow, guided by the light of the moon, he navigated through the village to his friend's house. The chair was indeed sitting by the door.

It almost appeared as if made of silver in the light from the sky. Almost everything did.

Tomas looked towards the lumber mill, and the apex of its roof silhouetted against a star-filled sky. The shadows of the woods behind it were thick and ominous.

Reaching for the wooden seat, he moved his eyes to the southern plantations. The crops had taken well to the warm season, and the cornstalks had grown quite tall. They had taken well, stretching along the riverside and far back into the vale.

Too bad we may need to burn them all, he thought.

His mind had moved to strategizing for the impending war. To him, the corn offered an excellent food source for his people. It also offered suitable cover for an enemy.

Just when he thought everything was working in their favour, and his village might live peacefully once again, news of war had come. He knew this would not be a repeat of the assault from the Night Demons.

It would be worse.

They had no walls to offer protection and not near the number of men that old Woodmyst had. The township was nothing more than a bunch of rough individuals who were attempting to make something of nothing.

He admired his people, though. They were a proud community who had seen some of the worst atrocities children should never have to face. Slavery, abuse, murder had forced them to become orphans.

Now, so many of them had children of their own, and he feared that the white witch was not simply going to take them from their sons and daughters, but that she would subjugate the younglings to pain and suffering before death.

How could they defend against such a force?

A wisp of wind blew past him.

Sudden.

There was a thickness to it.

An essence. Almost tangible.

It moved by the front of the house, towards the grove.

He moved his eyes to follow it, feeling confused why he would try to view a force that was invisible.

But it wasn't invisible.

It was a shadow.

A vapour.

"What are you?" he hissed after it, remembering he was armed with only a wooden chair. Something told him that chair or not, weapons would not work on a being such as this.

It stopped in place, its form shimmering, flowing like smoke or water. Darkness was its form, Tomas thought. It seemed to draw the light into it, consuming it.

Hovering above the ground at the end of the veranda, its bulk appearing as the height of a large man, it seemed to measure Tomas.

"What are you?" he repeated, stepping towards it.

Slowly, it floated towards him, edging towards the house.

Tomas did not know of how he should fight such a thing. He supposed that if the being wanted to end his life, it would. He asked again.

"What are you? Speak."

"Gomatha," it whispered. Its voice was both deep and soft, reminding Tomas of a breeze rustling through the leaves as thunder rolled in the distance.

"What is your purpose, Gomatha?"

"Eyes," it replied.

"Eyes?" Tomas repeated. "You're a spy. Who do you work for?"

"Work, no," it answered. "Slave. All Gomatha slaves."

Tomas took a deep breath.

"Which Mistress controls you, Gomatha?"

"The White is Mistress."

The White.

"You are to report on what you see, yes?"

"Yes," it hissed.

"Not on what you do?"

"If asked, I speak," it told him.

Tomas nodded, understanding that the creature only told what it had to.

"If I ask?"

"I speak," it replied.

"Good." Tomas frowned. "How many witches are there?"

"Nine," it whispered.

"Is the war about to begin?"

"War is," it replied. "War is now."

"What does she want to achieve from this?"

It didn't answer. Tomas tried a different angle.

"Do you know what her plans are?"

"To destroy," it replied.

Tomas suddenly remembered Ivo, lying on the floor of the white witch's lair.

"Did she have a child?"

"Yes."

"A son?"

"Yes."

"Is he the Maji?"

"She claims so."

"Do you believe he is?" Tomas asked, sensing doubt in the creature.

It didn't respond. Tomas decided not to press. He still wasn't sure what the being was capable of, so he intended to not offend it.

"Why did you stop when I called you?" Tomas asked.

Again, it didn't reply. It moved away slowly.

"Slaves can be free, Gomatha," Tomas said.

It paused again, seeming to soak in the man's words for a moment.

"A dream," it argued.

"Not a dream." Tomas pointed to the village. "You tell Sumaiyya Tarkin that Woodmyst is free and we will not be slaves to her or her kind. You tell her the men and women of Woodmyst will always be free."

"Free," it repeated.

"There are no slaves here, Gomatha." Tomas stepped toward the shadow, hoping to sow a seed. "You tell your kind that there are no slaves here."

It hovered a moment longer, as if to consider what Tomas had said. Then, in a gust, it vanished into the darkness.

Tomas stood for what seemed a very long time, staring towards the grove. His heart throbbed and his breathing became shallow. Suddenly, his legs became weak, making him glad he had a chair in his hands.

He sat down, placing his elbows on his knees and lowering his head as he took in some deep breaths to calm his nerves.

"There you are," David called, appearing from behind a neighbour's house. "Your wives are getting worried. They thought you might have gotten lost. Why are you sitting down?"

"I've just spoken with a shadow demon," Tomas informed him.

David could see from the expression on his friend's face that he wasn't speaking in jest. Something very real had transpired, and it clearly upset Tomas.

"What did it say?" the giant asked, standing on the grass in front of his house.

"It told me it came here to spy for the white witch," Tomas replied.

"Did you have it in a hold at the time?"

"It spoke on its own," the other told him. "I just asked it questions."

"Why would a spy tell you who it was working for of its own free will?"

"I think you have just answered your own question," Tomas replied, taking in another deep breath. "It's a slave to her and I think it wants to be free."

"So," David leant against a support beam that held up the awning over his porch. "It answered your questions because it wants to be free?"

"I think it believes that's as close to freedom as it could get," Tomas said.

"You're shaking," the bald man stated. "Did it threaten you?"

"No." He shook his head. "I just spoke to a shadow demon. You'd be shaking too."

"I would have shit in my trousers," David confessed.

Tomas took another deep breath and shook his head. "I think I may have hastened our part in this war," Tomas said.

"What do you mean?"

"I told it to send the white witch a message," he admitted.

"What message?"

"That Woodmyst will always be free."

"Suits me fine." The giant nodded.

"She'll be angry at that, I suppose." Tomas frowned.

"She will come regardless, my friend. Your words won't change her mind as to what she has planned for us. Besides, we have the Seven."

"She has nine," the other informed him.

"Oh, yeah." David stood upright. "We also have the Erilian sisterhood. So shove that where the sun can't shine."

Tomas chuckled.

"Look," David said. "What if we set more men on the watch? They could keep an eye out for this shadow demon and report to us if they see it again."

"No," Tomas answered, rising to his feet and lifting the chair from the decking. "Spotting shadows in the night is tough enough. I don't think there is a way to hinder them without some mystical ability. Besides, if it intended harm, it had ample opportunity to kill me just now."

"It could be here to report on the layout of the land for an impending attack," David suggested as they walked towards the centre of the village.

"I think that's exactly why it is here," Tomas agreed. "We need to get our defences in order and prepare the people for the worst."

"Will you make an announcement tonight?" David asked.

Tomas shook his head. "Let's wait until tomorrow. Tonight we dine and celebrate the arrival of our friends."

"Will you be all right?" the big man asked, noticing a tremor in his friend's voice.

"I'll talk with Emily and Joanne when we return home," he replied. "Maybe they have felt the presence of the shadow. I would like to know if it is inherently evil."

"It's a shadow," David told him. "It's unnatural. It must be evil."

"Remember the deeds of my father and the other members of the council during the Realm War," Tomas retorted. "We believed them all to be good men, but they harboured a secret so vile that it came back to affect us all.

"The idea of someone or something being good or evil depends upon the perspective of the individual," he continued. "We believe ourselves to be good. But the men in the white witch's army might see us as evil."

"That's why you spoke to this thing about being free," David said. "You're hoping that it perceives its enslavement as oppressive."

"Hoping, yes," Tomas replied.

"Perhaps an uprising?"

"I don't know what kind of hold she has over the shadow demon," Tomas admitted. "It may be dangerous for it. Otherwise, why hasn't it freed itself from her bondage already?"

"Well," David said as they entered the circle of light, "let's hope she doesn't command them to fight for her. I don't know of a way to slay shadows."

"Me either," Tomas replied.

David clasped a hand on his friend's shoulder. "Leave the chair when you're done. I'll grab it tomorrow."

"You're a good friend, David," Tomas replied.

"The best." He smiled as he slipped into his space at the table between his two wives.

Twelve

It was late and a thin cloud had risen from the ocean, covering the stars with a fine, misty veil. The moon penetrated the haze, sending its silver glow over the ebbing waves.

Lighting his pipe as he sat on a stool, his back against the wall of the warehouse, Reynard Merys, the dock manager of Oakbeach, considered a night of fishing. The only thing to cause him to reassess the option was the bright orb in the sky.

Light seemed to scare fish away and there was just too much of it tonight. The clouds could provide the dulling effect he needed, but the cover wasn't thick enough.

Inhaling through his pipe, the tobacco crackling softly as it burned; he looked to the stars and listened to the waves breaking against the shore beneath the wharf. It was soothing, and he believed that if he stayed long enough, it would cause him to drift to sleep.

An unexpected sound grabbed his attention.

A rustling.

He listened intently, trying to determine what the noise was.

Silence.

Wind in the trees, he thought. *Just wind in the trees.*

He moved his eyes towards the town to his right and could see the lights still burning in the Halle's inn. Several of the seafarers whose ships moored at the docks nearby frequented the tavern every night.

Reynard squinted his leathery face as he saw shadows moving by the windows of the establishment. There was still a sizable crowd inside.

If he couldn't fish, he might as well have a drink.

After lifting himself from his seat, he sauntered to the end of the platform and carefully stepped down to the ground. His old legs felt stiff. His knees ached as he moved along the road that bridged the divide between the docks and the township of Oakbeach.

The gravel crunched loudly under his feet as he continued to puff on his pipe and shuffle along, gradually building his speed up to a slow walk.

The rustling started again to his right.

He turned his head instinctively but saw nothing.

Just the wind in the trees, he assured himself.

Continuing to move along the well-worn road and his slow and steady pace, he wondered if he would make it to the inn before it closed for the night.

He took another long drag through his pipe and received nothing but air.

As he tapped the bowl against his belt buckle, some ash and dottle fell from the pipe and upon the ground. He pulled a small pouch from his tobacco pocket and loaded the chamber with a fine shag, pressing it in deep so he could fit more into the top.

After placing the pipe in his mouth, he patted his pockets, searching for his tiny flint rocks.

They were not there.

In his mind's eye, he could picture the small stones sitting by his chair by the wall of the warehouse.

He turned to face the warehouse.

It was a fair distance away. The area between the inn and himself was much less.

They have candles; he thought. *I'll light this bugger once I'm there.*

So, onwards he went, shuffling his feet once again to build the momentum before progressing into a walk of sorts.

The rustling came from behind him.

This time, he ignored it. He wanted a drink and a good smoke.

Wind in the trees could go unnoticed.

The gravel crunched as his knees ached.

His legs burned as something bit him in the small of his back.

He took a few more paces before the pain registered.

Something didn't feel right. Tremors moved up and down his legs before he dropped to his knees.

The pain in his back throbbed. Reaching with his hand, he tried to feel for the cause of the problem. His old bones wouldn't let him.

He heard the rustling again, louder, closer.

Turning his head, he saw several men in dark clothing.

Reynard was confused. He still wasn't sure what had bitten him.

"I'm hurt," he told the men, dropping his pipe to the ground.

One man reached behind Reynard and retrieved the knife he had flung into the old man. The blade was long and smeared with dark blood.

With a quick thrust, the uniformed man dug the blade into Reynard's chin and pushed it in deep, up to the hilt.

The old man felt relief as a great crunching sound filled his ears.

His legs didn't burn.

His knees didn't ache.

He could feel nothing.

The uniformed man retrieved his knife from the old man's head and wiped the blade on his victim's shirt before sheathing it and allowing the body to fall to the road.

With a wave of the hand, he signalled for others dressed as he, hiding in the shadows of the tree line, to step into the light and advance.

***

Raucous laughter and lewd conversation filled the room, almost as thick as the smell of smoke, mead, and wine. With so many men filling the tavern, and all chairs occupied, a number stood in any place they could find space. James Halle and his wife had not seen this many in their establishment at such a late hour since the liberation of Blackrock Haven.

"More mead, my good man," a tall individual with a long beard and wild hair hollered.

"We might need to make this the last round, Captain," James replied. "My supplies are getting low."

"I'll purchase it all," the man replied. "We sail for Dendadia tomorrow. So tonight we get pissed."

The innkeeper chuckled.

I'm glad I'm not sailing with you, Halle thought. *You drunken bastard.*

"More mead coming up," he replied, turning to the kitchen where Anya, his wife, shook her head as she hammered a tap into another barrel.

"They're going to drink us dry," she told her husband as he entered the kitchen.

"Their coin is paying for it," he informed her. "I'll put in another order with Reynard in the morning."

"It could take a week before it gets to us," she said.

"Then I'll visit the other taverns in town and see if they will sell me a barrel or two." He kissed her cheek. "We'll be fine, my love."

A great crash from the main room caused the two of them to jump.

"By the gods," Anya cried. "Now they're destroying the place."

James Halle stormed from the kitchen and back to the bar.

All the men in the tavern stood silently, staring at the floor by the window. Smashed glass lay upon the floor at their feet.

"What in the blazes is going on in here?" hollered James.

The captain saw the disappointed look on the innkeeper's face.

"It wasn't us, my good man," the rough individual told him before turning to his men.

"Move out of the way. Let the innkeeper see."

The men parted, allowing the space between the bar and the broken window to open.

There were sharp shards of glass on the floor, stained with blood. Lying on top was a round object, spherical in appearance.

It took James Halle a moment to realise that he was looking at a severed head. A moment after that, he recognised the leathery face of his friend, the dock manager.

"What is going on?" Anya called as she moved towards her husband.

"Stay in the kitchen," he ordered her abruptly. "Don't come out here."

"Why?" she asked, stopping in her tracks. She wrung her hands nervously as she peered at her husband for an answer. "What is it?"

"Reynard is dead," he told her.

"What?" She reached for a hold on the kitchen bench as her knees gave way.

A flare outside caught the men's attention. Someone had lit a torch.

"The killer is still in our midst," one man called.

"Then let's get the bastard," another shouted as he drew his sword, almost falling over from his drunken state.

More torches flickered to life outside the inn. A long line of light stretched along the road in both directions.

"There are too many." The captain frowned. "And we are too drunk."

One of the flaming torches smashed through another window, sending glass and flames across the room.

Tongues of fire hit several men, their clothing catching light. Others quickly doused the flames by patting their friend's garments with open hands.

The torch rested on the floor by the fireplace.

"Put that out," the captain commanded. A man quickly stomped the fire out with his boot.

"Oh no," another called from by the newly broken window.

Dozens of flaming torches were arcing through the air towards the tavern; too many for the men to stop.

Some landed on the thatched roof, while others entered the room via the windows. Still more found a way into the front bedroom across the hall from the bar.

Anya screamed.

"We need to get out of here," called a man.

"That's what they want," another replied. "They'll cut us down once we're outside."

"We can't stay here," James Halle called. "I'm taking my wife outside."

The captain nodded. "We fight."

As the innkeeper gathered his wife to her feet and ushered her through the kitchen and into the corridor of the inn, the captain led his wild-looking crew through the front door and towards the blades of the awaiting troopers.

Swords clashed in the front yard of the establishment as James and Anya moved through the door. Thick black smoke filled the inn as flames engulfed the front rooms and the roof.

James admired the drunken men who fought bravely, considering their state of being. But they were at a loss. Too intoxicated to respond to the soldiers' blows, many of the sailors were on the ground and bleeding out before the innkeeper and his wife were clear of their burning home.

He moved his eyes to his left, towards the township of Oakbeach. Tall flames flared across the village as over one hundred soldiers moved through the streets. The sound of screaming women and crying children echoed across the air in his ears.

His barn in the yard to the side of the tavern had smoke billowing out of it. The screams of horses and calls from his milking cow blared into the night as the straw inside blazed.

On the open ground, near the base of the hills that climbed to the mountains to the west, a multitude, an army, awaited. Before them, seated upon a tall horse, was a woman dressed in pink. Two riders, positioned on either side of her, carried pink banners that wafted in the breeze.

It all suddenly came back to James Halle.

The story of the White Mistress and the Sovereign.

He remembered the young girls, *potentials*, wearing clothing of a variety of colours. One in lilac, one in scarlet, another in black. There was something similar with this woman to how the young girls had dressed.

They had gone to Woodmyst; he recollected. And, although it had been ten years since he had seen them last, he did not believe this woman to be one of them.

This was one of the Mistresses he had heard about.

As his wife gripped him tightly, standing in front of their burning home, he wished he could fly away with her, escaping what he knew to be inevitable.

The captain had put two of the enemy soldiers down, but there were too many to hold back.

He had fought bravely.

He had fought well.

He had fallen from a wound in the back.

A coward's attack was the only way they could defeat him, the innkeeper thought as he held his sobbing wife against him.

With the sailors slain and lying in pools of blood across the yard, the soldiers turned their attention to the innkeeper and his wife.

"I love you, Anya," he told her.

"I love you, too," she sobbed.

***

"Oakbeach has fallen, Mistress," a soldier on foot announced to the woman in pink.

"I can see," she told him. "Any losses to our men?"

"None to report," he told her. "Oakbeach had no defences so resistance is limited."

"Survivors?"

"None, Mistress," he replied, a hint of sorrow in his voice.

She considered that for a moment. *No survivors.*

"A shame, really," she said. "We should have allowed the women and children to live."

"Perhaps the next target, Mistress?"

She looked at the soldier, her eyebrows lifted high.

"Sadly," she told him, "I have my instructions to follow just as you do yours."

He lowered his head, but she perceived his thoughts.

"She is powerful, Jonathon," she reminded him. "They all are. What can I do?"

"There are rumours," he started, "of the potentials. Perhaps..."

"Stop," she commanded him. "I know of the potentials and I know where they are. The White Mistress has informed us of them."

"We go to destroy them?"

"It must be done," she replied, peering with sad eyes at the sight before her.

"You could join with them," he told her. "We would all support you, my love."

She shot him a look of contention.

"Mistress." He bowed.

She winced, a slight heartache as she watched him bowing to her.

Mistress. She hated the term.

It implied that she was lord over them, over him. She didn't want to be, but it was a requirement.

"I can't," she told him. "I am of the Coven of Mirikin. I made a vow to the Sovereign that when this day would come, I would stand with my sisters."

He came closer to her side, whispering. "I beg of you, Amicia. Please reconsider. I can't do this. None of these men can." He gestured to the soldiers standing behind her. "These people are supposed to be under our protection. That's why you've resorted to sending in those thugs. Prisoners, murderers, not soldiers. Please, Amicia."

Her eyes glistened in the moonlight as tears welled.

"Ready the men to return home," she commanded him. "We will resupply before moving on to Belburn."

He bowed his head like a faithful servant.

"Yes, my Mistress."

A lone tear streaked across her cheek as she watched him walk away into the darkness.

Thirteen

"You have two daughters!" Emily appeared furious as she yelled at her husband. He knew her too well and understood that she was frightened more than angry. "How can you put yourself at such a risk? It could've killed you."

"It didn't," he told her as he placed his hands on her shoulders. "I'm still here. I'm all right."

Lucy smacked him on the shoulder so hard that it stung.

"You fool," she sobbed. "You damned fool."

He shook his head and looked at Joanne, who stood with her arms crossed by Catherine's and Alice's closed bedroom door.

"Don't look at me for help," she told him. "I'd hit you myself if I were any closer."

His eyes moved to Erilian women sitting around the room, their bedrolls laid out on the floor.

"At least we had weapons when we saw this thing," Karlena said.

"Excellent," he said. "I'm outnumbered on all sides."

"What were you thinking?" Emily asked him. "Asking it questions and waiting for replies. Why didn't you just run?"

"I don't know," he answered honestly. "I just thought... I really don't know."

She hugged him tightly. He wrapped his arms around her and held her for a long moment before she suddenly pulled away and punched his chest. She turned and stormed away to the bedroom, slamming the door behind her.

Tomas stood with his palms facing the air.

What just happened?

"Time, Tomas," Akasati told him. "She just needs some."

"I know." He nodded.

Lucy hit him again before plonking herself down in a chair, crossing her arms and scowling at him.

"You're thinking," Sharek suggested, "what's one shadow demon matter when the entire world is about to burn?"

"I am," he admitted. "I think this is a slight overreaction, considering the bigger picture."

His wives glared at him.

"To them, Tomas," Sharek replied, "you are the bigger picture. Just as Dakmel was for us. His blind fury, his mission in life to destroy the Sovereign, it often got between us and there were many a night when we would react to his actions much like this.

"At the risk of receiving your wives' wrath, and for what it's worth, I think you were right to question the shadow."

All the women moved their eyes to her, Joanne and Lucy holding their temper strongly.

"If you hadn't," Sharek continued. "We wouldn't know of the nine Mistresses and we wouldn't know that Sumaiyya had a son. These are important pieces of knowledge that could help the Seven focus their abilities. Perhaps a weakness can be found."

"We could have lost our husband," Joanne told her.

"But you didn't," she replied. "Instead, you got some valuable information."

Lucy took a deep breath and looked at Tomas.

"Promise me something," she said to him.

"Anything," he replied, turning to her.

"Promise me you won't approach anyone or anything like that again. No asking questions. No trying to make friends. Just run or make sure you have adequate support."

He didn't know what adequate support against a shadow would look like, so he saw no point in arguing the facts with her.

"I promise," he told her, taking her face in his hands and crouching to her level. "I promise with all of my heart."

She reached out to him, wrapping her arms around his neck, placing a kiss upon his lips.

"I'm still angry at you," she said.

Joanne sat down and rubbed her eyes, pinching the bridge of her nose with her thumb and forefinger. Tomas turned his gaze to her.

"What's the matter?"

"Nothing," she said, lying. She didn't want to talk to him because of her mood.

"You can stay angry at me for the rest of your days if you wish," he told her. "But I can't stop feeling the way I do for you. I'm your husband and I can tell that there is something wrong. Talk to me."

She opened her eyes and looked into his. "We'll need arrows and fire," she told him. "I don't know why. I just saw a vision of our own people setting flames to the plantations."

"Why would we do that?" Lucy asked.

Tomas recalled he had been considering burning the fields to prevent the enemy from using them as ground cover. Could this be what Joanne had seen?

"I don't know," she replied. "But I know it will be done. We need to prepare for it."

Tomas nodded.

"We'll take care of it tomorrow," he told her. "Right now, it's getting late. I think it would be best for everyone to sleep."

Joanne stood up and walked to the door, giving Tomas the cold shoulder as she left the dwelling and moved along the veranda to the new house.

She still hadn't quite forgiven him for risking his life with the Gomatha.

He felt something wrap itself around his fingers. Looking down, he saw Lucy's hand gripping his.

"I'm still angry at you too," she told him. "But I'm more glad to have you with me."

She stood to her feet and led him out of the house. Tomas turned to close the door behind him. The Erilian women gave him a cheeky smile and a wave as he pulled it shut.

***

Ruttger, personal guard to the Lilac Mistress, quietly clothed himself in the darkness of his lover's tent. She slept soundly, peacefully as he pulled on his trousers on before sitting on the edge of her bed to lace his boots.

He didn't know what she saw in him, a much older man who was well past his prime. She was beautiful and young. She could have any man in the land if she were not a slave to the Lilac Mistress.

In any other situation, she would have been esteemed, looked up to. Men would have gladly fought and died for her. But here she was, a cupbearer.

He stood and lifted his shirt from the back of a chair and slipped into it, buttoning it hastily so he could be out of her tent before sunrise. Tucking his shirt into his pants, he moved his gaze over her.

Her skin was smooth, young, soft, like silk. She lay upon her side facing him, allowing him to trace the curves of her legs, her thighs, her waist, her breasts.

How could she love an old man like him?

He pulled a sheet gently over her body and kissed her forehead, taking one last admiring look, soaking her in with his eyes before leaving the tent.

Once outside, he checked his sword and strapped his belt securely. He assured that his pouch, slung over his shoulder, was within easy reach. On opening it, he checked its contents; a bandage, two flint rocks, a small whetstone and a tiny vial.

He held the tiny bottle up to the moonlight. It was cylindrical with a small cork sealing it shut. The liquid inside was clear, meaning it would mix well.

Placing it back into his pouch, he strolled across the camp to a fire where four men sat, keeping warm from the night chill.

"Ruttger," one of them called softly with a smile.

"Commander to you," he replied. "You're on duty."

"Apologies," the other replied, remembering his place.

"We can't afford to appear undisciplined in the open," he reminded. "She may have eyes watching."

"Understood, sir," the soldier replied.

"How long must we..." one sitting by the fire began.

"Shhh," Ruttger hissed as he glanced around to see if anyone was nearby.

The older man reached out towards the fire and rubbed his hands together, peering around the hearth to his most trusted soldiers; the four he could rely upon the most.

Each of them was a lieutenant in his army, and had been so before the arrival of the Lilac Mistress. Forced to obey, they had all become slaves because of a general that negotiated a deal that couldn't be refused.

"We'll strike soon," he whispered, barely audible over the crackling fire.

"That fat shit General Vandran should have shown more clout," said one man.

"He was afraid," Ruttger told him. "She had his family and threatened his life. What would you have done in his place?"

"I would have used my sword," he replied.

"You've had plenty of opportunities since," another said. "What stopped you?"

He didn't reply. Instead, he fell silent and peered into the flames.

"Exactly," the other pointed to him. "You're scared shitless, just like the rest of us. Just as the general was."

"Yeah," the first replied. "Well, his deal didn't help him much, did it? The bastard and his family are dead."

"And so shall we be if she fulfils her goal," Ruttger told them. "We leave for Greyrose at first light. She intends for us to be there by nightfall. Ready the men you trust and be careful. She still has many who are loyal to her."

***

By first light, the Lilac Mistress' force was on the move, heading east towards her next intended target, Greyrose.

They marched along the coast, keeping within sight of the vast horizon where the ocean met the sky.

The ground trembled as over five hundred men marched in unison across the open ground. They passed an isolated farmhouse or two every few miles. The Lilac Mistress would command them to be destroyed, forcing Ruttger to order a few of his riders to kill any inside and burn the structures to the ground.

Minor victories for the Coven, he thought. *Poor peasants who were probably oblivious to what was happening in the world.*

For most of the day, this was how it played out.

Then, in mid-afternoon, they came within eyesight of Greyrose, a tiny hamlet that sat neatly in a tiny bay. It was nothing more than a fishing village with twenty or so houses.

Some inhabitants saw the approaching army and fled on foot across the plain, away to the east.

"Send horses to take them down," the Lilac Mistress commanded from her carriage.

"Move one hundred men into the village. I want it burning now."

"Yes, Mistress," Ruttger replied from his steed. He looked to his lover, the cupbearer, who sat across from the woman inside the carriage. She pretended not to see him, not wanting the lady in lilac to notice them.

Ruttger moved away to relay her commands as she called for her driver to open the door to the transport.

Before long, fifty men on horseback were racing across the land towards the fleeing peasants as one hundred men on foot marched towards the township.

She moved some distance to the side of the vehicle, pulling her hood over her head. Four guards, assigned to keeping her safe, moved into place by her side. They held long spears in their hands and sheathed swords at their sides.

The Lilac Mistress observed the riders as they caught up to the fleeing villagers. Men, women and children; the horsemen mowed them over, sending the runners to the ground as they ran over the top.

A few of the peasants stopped running, their life expired. Others crawled, obviously injured, while more regained their footing and continued to run.

The horsemen chased after those on foot, planting them onto the ground one by one with steed and sword. Ruttger felt a lump in his throat growing as the riders returned to finish off the injured.

"Wine," the Lilac Mistress commanded, ready to celebrate her victory over unarmed people once again.

Ruttger moved his steed to the rear of the wagon and tethered it there before moving to his regular position by the carriage door.

The cupbearer stepped to the door, and he offered his hand to her as she climbed down. She poured some wine from the pitcher that sat on a small table inside the transport and carried the goblet to the woman.

Ruttger saw his chance.

The Lilac Mistress faced away from him, as did her guards. The cupbearer had no clue of his plan, so she could not give an accidental sign to the woman when she took the drink.

He hastily opened his pouch and lifted the vial from inside as stealthily as he could. Carefully, he plucked the cork from its top before reaching for the pitcher.

The Lilac Mistress took the goblet from the young girl, with their backs still towards him.

He poured the entire contents of the vial into the pitcher and put it back in place on the table.

Ruttger dropped the empty vial back into his pouch as he scanned around to see who had noticed.

There were no eyes upon him. Even the driver was too transfixed on the view ahead as the riders returned and the men on foot reached the township.

The woman held the cup out to the girl.

"Another," she instructed, handing the cup over.

"Yes, Mistress," the cupbearer replied, returning to the carriage so she could fill the goblet again.

Ruttger smiled to her as she brushed by him. She shot him a small grin as she reached to the table and poured from the vessel.

Watching her return to the Lilac Mistress, he felt an icy trickle of sweat slide along his backbone.

"Mistress." The cupbearer bowed as she handed the goblet to the woman.

She grasped the cup in her hands as she kept her eyes on the township of Greyrose. Flames rose from buildings towards the edge of the village. Screams resounded from inside the structures.

It was the same old, ghastly story.

Drink, he urged her.

Boots smashed into infants' faces as swords slid through mothers' necks.

Drink, you bitch, so that this can be over.

Men cried in pain as soldiers plucked their intestines from their abdomens.

She lifted the cup to her lips as she giggled with her mouth closed.

Yes.

Tipping the goblet high, tilting her head back, she gulped it down.

Yes.

He placed a hand on the hilt of his sword, ready to act.

She lowered the goblet and laughed out loud as the cries from the peasant village grew louder and louder and the flames flared higher and higher.

Come on, he urged.

"Wine," the woman commanded again.

"Yes, Mistress," the girl replied, retrieving the goblet and returning to the carriage.

The Lilac Mistress laughed loudly, drunkenly, as she observed the massacre.

The cupbearer poured another measure of wine into the vessel and returned it to the woman.

The witch took it and swallowed it in a matter of moments.

That's it. Drink it all.

She waved her arms open, laughing hysterically, dropping the goblet to the ground.

The young girl stooped to pick it up.

"What did you do to me?" The Lilac Mistress giggled.

"Mistress?" The cupbearer rose to her feet, clutching the goblet in her hands.

"I'm not right." The woman breathed shallowly and swayed. "You did something to my wine."

"No, Mistress." The young cupbearer shook her head and backed away.

The woman in lilac dribbled blood from her mouth and nose.

"What is this?" She giggled.

Ruttger moved forward, slowly and quietly lifting his sword from its sheath.

"You little whore," the witch hollered as blood streamed from her eyes. She reached her hand to the girl, squeezing her fingers together.

The cupbearer felt her ribs tightening, immense pain building inside her.

She couldn't scream or call out. She couldn't even breathe.

Ruttger moved with swiftness and accuracy.

Four heads rolled upon the ground as he moved like the wind. The lifeless bodies of her guards dropped to the soil, twitching as pinched nerves reacted to the attack.

He lunged and brought his weapon down across the Lilac Mistress' head, planting it so deeply that the blade touched the tips of both ears.

The cupbearer fell to the ground, regaining control. She breathed in, filling her lungs.

The witch toppled to the ground as Ruttger retrieved his blade from her corpse.

"Courtney," he called, dropping his weapon and racing to the cupbearer's side. He lifted her into his arms and cradled her.

She wept, reaching to his face. "Are we free?"

He nodded.

"We are free."

Ruttger's four men held their swords aloft.

"We are free," one of them called.

The men gave a mighty cheer.

"Sound the trumpet and recall our men. We no longer slay the innocent," he continued.

The horn blew, long and loud, signalling the men in the town to return to their ranks.

Ruttger stood to his feet, helping Courtney to hers.

"We don't need to be afraid," he called to the soldiers. "The Mistresses can be defeated. Look." He pointed to the carcass of the woman in lilac with her head split almost in two.

"I ride to Oldcastle," he announced. "I choose to fight against the Coven of Mirikin. Who will join me?"

They all gave a great cry, raising their swords high.

Fourteen

Black ships, frigates, sailed past the closed Griralith Pass where waves crashed violently upon the toppled rubble, sending white spray into the air.

The fleet numbered twenty, all armed with ten canons, ready for battle.

They tacked to the starboard, keeping their sails at beam reaching as they forced their way south through a westerly wind.

The next leg of the voyage, once they were clear of the Pass, would take them on a south-westerly course. They would increase speed then, having the wind to their backs.

On the deck of the lead ship, standing by a young man operating the wheel, was a broad, well-dressed man. His uniform, as with the other men on deck, was dark with brass buttons and buckles.

A heavy, curved sword was slung upon his waist and two thick gold aiguillettes, decorative braided cords, were slung from two buttons on his chest to the strap on his right shoulder, allowing them to dangle in long curves across his breast. Gold epaulettes with trimmings made of the same material as his braids decorated the shoulders of his coat.

A wide black tricorn sat upon his head. Sticking up from this hat, tethered to a gold buckle on the black band that encompassed the crown, was a long white feather; a symbol for the Mistress he served.

"Make the turn," he commanded the young man as he scratched his well-groomed beard. His voice was deep and raspy.

"Aye, Admiral Dzeiks," the young man replied, turning the wheel to redirect the ship slightly to its left.

The frigate turned to port, smashing through high waves and sending a spray across the deck.

"Broad reaching," the admiral called.

"Broad reaching," another older man, dressed similarly to the admiral, and standing a short distance from him, echoed loudly.

Several others repeated the command as the crew adjusted the jib, rotating the sails as the vessel turned so they filled with as much wind as possible.

The ship picked up speed and cut through the water with haste.

Dzeiks nodded, pleased with the manoeuvre.

"Good job, gentlemen," he said before turning to the older officer. "Maintain this heading. Notify me when Dellmoor is in sight, Coster."

"Aye, Admiral," the officer replied.

Dzeiks descended a set of steps to the port side of the upper deck before turning to his right, into his quarters.

He entered the room, closing the door behind him where he removed his hat and scratched his short-cropped hair, placing the tricorn on a dresser by the door. He slung his sword upon a hook that jutted from a support beam in the centre of the room as he moved his eyes to his bed, resting against the aft wall.

Curled up under the covers was a young lady, sleeping soundly.

Removing his coat, draping it over a chair near the dresser, he kept his gaze fixed on her. He could see her dark curls spread across the pillow and nothing more. The covers pulled over her so high they almost hid her face from view.

After removing his clothing and placing it neatly over the chair that held his jacket, he reached to the door and latched it before moving to the bed. She murmured and stirred as he slid in between the sheets behind her.

"I'm sorry," he told her. "I didn't mean to wake you."

She turned over to face him, smiling as she slipped her arm around his waist.

"I fell asleep waiting for you," she told him.

"Well," he said, and smiled, "you can return to your slumber. I need to rest and I think you took all of my energy already."

She slid her fingers down his body to his member.

"You still have some," she told him as she took him in her hand.

"I need to sleep, Leona," he replied. "I really do."

"Fine," she said, disappointed, and rolling back to face the other way. "I'll do my slave duty and lie here until you desire to have me, Admiral Dzeiks."

"I do desire you." He moved his arm over her. "Always. But I am just a man and I need to rest. The White Mistress would want me at my best."

She stared at the wall beside the bed, thinking about the two of them and their bonds to their Mistress as the ship lolled over the waves.

"Will I ever be set free, Isak?" she asked him, taking his hand in hers and moving it to her chest.

"When the White Mistress has achieved victory," he replied, "I will seek an audience with her and request permission for you to be my wife. That is the only way she will grant your freedom, my love."

"Why can't we just flee?" she asked. "We could run away and be together. Both of us free."

"I am free," he told her. "All the men in this fleet are free. I told you this."

She turned to him, her eyes watering.

"I don't understand this," she said. "How you could serve her freely. She is cruel and wicked."

"Shhh," he warned her. "You will not speak of the Mistress like that again. She is the Prime Mistress of the Coven of Mirikin, and I serve the Prime Mistress. I served the Sovereign before her and I will serve her until another claims her place. I choose to do so, not because they frighten me, but because I believe in the cause.

"Their plan is for a better world with control, organisation, laws. Right now, there is chaos. There is no control. Each city, tribe and creature does as it will with no structure or consequences to their decision making. The Sovereign saw the fault with this, as does the White Mistress. As do I."

"But she kills innocent people and," she let her tears fall, "takes young girls to be slaves."

"Do I treat you as the other slave girls are treated?"

She shook her head.

"Then, they are simply collateral," he told her. "Some things need to be broken and cleaned away for the sake of order. And that is what she brings, what we bring. A new world with order."

He kissed her cheek.

"You have a place in the new world, my love," he told her, resting his head against his pillow and closing his eyes. "It will be with me. When I speak to the White Mistress, she will decide to grant me your hand in marriage or not. In either case, you will always be my property. My gift from my Mistress."

So, she thought. *I'm to remain a slave forever.*

***

"I still can't believe you took two more wives, Tomas," Lor said as the two men sat side by side in the stable house, scraping whetstones along the edges of dull blades.

"Neither can I," he replied.

"I find it hard enough with your sister," the other continued. "If I upset her, she gives me silence for days. She'll smile at you and everyone else and pretend everything is fine, even hugging and kissing me in the eyes of all around. But as soon as we get home, it's like I don't exist."

"I know what you mean," Tomas said. "Lucy came around quicker than the other two, letting me sleep in her bed. Emily and Joanne would have rather me sleep here with the horses. Joanne has forgiven me, but Emily holds disappointment in me still. At least she's let me back into bed."

Lor smiled.

"I don't know how you manage it." The man shook his head.

Tomas glanced at him.

"Manage what?"

"Well," Lor started, sliding the stone along the blade slowly, causing it to emit a soft, metallic ringing sound. "Three wives would be difficult enough, in my mind. But to have two of them sisters! I wonder what they must discuss. And with both of them possessing mystical abilities, it makes me wonder."

Tomas furrowed his brow as he placed the sword upon a small pile of ones he had completed sharpening, rising to his feet to grab another dull one from a crate against the rear wall.

"Wonder what?"

"Hmm?" Lor shook his head. "Nothing. Don't worry."

"He's going to want to know, now," David said, sliding his own whetstone along a blade.

"Know what?" Tomas asked. "Have you two been talking behind my back?"

"The whole village talks behind each other's back," Simon put in. "Why should we treat you any differently?"

"So," Tomas said, sitting on his stool beside Lor once again. "It makes you wonder?"

Lor looked at the other men gathered near to them.

"You need to tell him now, Lor," Oliver said.

"They are both witches," Lor said. "I know we don't like to use that word, but let's face it, that is what they are."

Tomas nodded. "I'll agree. They are witches. So, what of it?"

"We know witches can be manipulative," he continued. "They can put suggestions into our minds and use their tricks to make us do things that we usually would think twice about. Take Ivo, for example. There was no way that he would have ventured into the woods if it weren't for the white witch. You said that yourself."

Tomas looked to the three men who had been with him on the expedition to Blackrock Haven. They supported his views concerning Ivo's demise. It now appeared that they supported Lor's position concerning something else; something to do with his wives.

"Go on," he told his friend, a slight heat building on his neck as he attempted to suppress his temper.

"What if they banded together in order to manipulate you?"

"Emily and Joanne?"

"Yes," Lor replied.

"For what purpose?" Tomas asked.

"To make Joanne your wife," Lor told him. "Think about it. *You* would never have married more than one woman. It just isn't you. One of *them* suggested it to you, didn't they?"

It was true. Emily had put the idea to him.

"And Joanne was ready for you when you went to talk with her," David put in.

"So was Lucy," Tomas replied. "She has no abilities such as they do."

"Joanne spoke to her, Tomas," Simon added. "You told us that."

Tomas pondered this for a moment.

"So," he started. "I am being used?"

"No," Lor answered him. "They love you and dearly so. You're lucky to have such fine wives. Both Linet and I love them like sisters. We just don't believe that you would have agreed to wed them without a little coaxing."

"I..." he began, thinking of his words carefully, doubting his facilities. "If the ones that I love can manipulate me in such a way, how can I resist the powers of the enemy?"

"They protect you, Tomas," Simon informed him. "Just as Tricia protects me. Just as the Seven protect our home. They have no malice towards you. Only love. I think that's why they may have done what we think they have done; because they love you.

"Joanne has admired you from the moment Andris fell in love with Sevrina Verney," he continued. "Perhaps before that. We all could see it. She looked at you like the sun shone from your arse. You just didn't notice her."

"She was a kid back then," Tomas said.

"Yes," Simon continued, "but she still kept her eyes upon you well after she became an adult. Something that you only just realised."

"Who else was going to look at her the way she looked at you?" David said, scraping his whetstone along a blade. "And who else is there that she would look to? It had to be you, my friend."

"I shouldn't have mentioned anything," Lor said, wishing that he hadn't started the conversation. "I apologise, Tomas. Forget I said anything."

"No," Tomas frowned. "I think you are all correct. They manipulated me. I think Emily intended for me to marry Joanne. Lucy was a tag along because she wouldn't let another near her. But I don't regret what has happened. I admit I had trepidations at first, but I think it's worked out for us."

"I think so, too," Lor said.

"You're suited for each other," David told him. "Go home tonight and lie with all three of them together."

"We don't do that." Tomas smiled.

"*You* don't do that," the big man corrected him. "They simply respect your wishes concerning your sleeping arrangements."

"We will not be discussing my nocturnal activities, David." The other smiled.

"What?" Oliver looked confused. "You lot only meet with your wives at night? You don't know what you're missing."

The others chuckled.

"What's so humorous?" said a woman by the stable door. The men turned their faces to the new arrival, as did a few of the steeds standing in their pens.

Linet Verney, Lor's wife and Tomas' sister, was holding hands with a small boy that toddled beside her. Her other arm cradled a basket.

"Hullo Alan." Oliver waved to the lad. The boy stuck a finger in his mouth and moved behind his mother's dress to hide.

Lor put his whetstone down and placed the sword he had been working on upon the ground. He moved across the room to his wife and kissed her on the cheek before lowering himself to his son and taking him into his arms.

"What's going on?" he asked her as he lifted the boy up to his chest, returning to his feet.

"I'm just on my way home after helping the Wardes with the new house," she told him. "How long will you be? The sun is getting low."

"Give me a moment and I'll join you," Lor told her as he placed Alan back on the ground.

Oliver tried again now that the lad was in the open.

"Hullo Alan." He waved.

The boy returned the finger to his mouth and ran back to his mother, burying his face into her dress.

"I don't get why he's so scared of me," the blond man said. "I'm much better looking than any of you, but I'm the only one he's frightened of."

"How old is he now?" David asked.

"About to turn three," Linet told him.

Lor retrieved his whetstone, placing it into his trousers' pocket, and clasped a hand on Tomas' shoulder.

"They love you, Tomas," he said. "Even if they were a little sneaky. But they suit you, and you suit them. Be good to them. Particularly Emily. Remember, she has been with you longer and knows you better than anyone."

"You think she may be jealous?" Tomas asked him earnestly.

"Maybe," he replied. "She is competing with two younger ladies for your affection."

"It's not a competition," he said.

"You know that." Lor smiled, agreeing with his friend. "And I'm sure she has that in her mind also, but something inside of her probably doesn't. Part of her is possibly a little confused. This did all occur rather quickly.

"Put yourself in her situation. If she had three husbands, and you were but only one of them, how would you feel? It may not be that difficult to understand why she is still a little angry with you."

Tomas nodded as he absorbed the words. He hadn't thought of things from Emily's perspective.

"Thank you, Lor," Tomas replied.

Little Alan turned towards them. Tomas waved to the lad, who responded in kind before Lor picked the boy off the ground and carried him away.

"Did you see that?" Oliver shook his head. "He did that out of spite."

The others chuckled as they tidied up, preparing to go home.

Fifteen

With the children in bed, and the nightly chores complete, Tomas settled back in his chair as his routine demanded. Joanne and Lucy had organised bedding for the Erilian warriors in the old house by the hill before retiring to their own dwelling, leaving him and Emily alone.

She moved from the kitchen, a cup of steaming tea in her hand, and lowered herself into a seat across the room from him. He looked at her for a short time, gathering that the reason she hadn't brought him a cup was because of her continuing anger towards him.

Emily would usually sit by him, where she would talk to him for some time before they retreated to the bedroom. But not tonight.

Ever since his confrontation with the Gomatha, she had been giving him the silent treatment. She would sit and prefer to stare at the wall than to acknowledge his existence.

He rubbed his brow before moving a finger to his temple.

Rising to his feet, he crossed the room, passing her as he entered the bedroom. She looked after him as he disappeared from view. Some rummaging noises travelled down the short hall to her as she nursed her cup, wondering what he was doing.

Moments later, he emerged with a pack slung over his shoulders and his saddle gear in his hands. He walked across the room and opened the door to leave.

"Where are you going?" she asked.

"So, you *can* speak." He raised his eyebrows. "I thought you must have forgotten how."

She stood up, still holding the cup, peering at the riding equipment.

"I don't understand," she said. "Why are you leaving?"

He took a deep breath and turned to face her.

"It's obvious to me you don't want me here any longer," he told her. "I think your concern regarding my conversation with the shadow demon is one thing. But this, whatever you harbour in your heart, has moved beyond that. You won't even look at me anymore, Emily.

"I think you are envious of your sister and Lucy, and I understand that. But I've never shown them favouritism over you. I love you all. I married you first and I will always love you. But I don't know if you love me anymore. I think you see me as nothing more than a belonging. Something that you own.

"I do not want to be a wedge between you and your sister. I don't want you to treat her how you've been treating me. This silence is killing me.

"I am sorry for what I've done to you, and perhaps I should have been stronger and said no when you suggested I wed Joanne. Perhaps then, we wouldn't be in this situation.

"I feel I've exposed a weakness through all of this. I don't know what to do to make this right." He wept.

"Don't leave us." She shook her head.

"I'm leaving for the caverns," he told her. "I need to be alone. I need time to think. I think you do too."

Her hands shook, and her chin trembled as tears streamed down her face.

"Please." She lost control, dropping the teacup and falling to her knees.

"Tell the girls I love them." He turned and walked into the night air, closing the door behind him.

She stared at the door for a long time, mouth agape and eyes streaming. Her throat burnt, wanting to scream after him, but no sound came out.

Her body forced her to take in loud gusts of air, still not allowing her to call.

Then gradually, as more air went in, small whimpers escaped, building, building until she cried out, bawling upon the floor uncontrollably, staring at the door that she could no longer see through the tears.

She wanted him back.

She needed him back.

"Mama," Catherine called, running across the floor to her. She wrapped her slender arms around her mother's neck. The sight of Emily's state was enough to set the young girl into a crying fit. "Mama? Mama?"

Alice stood in the hallway, confused and crying.

The door opened, and Joanne and Lucy came tearing in, stopping only to assess the scene in front of them.

"What's going on?" Lucy called out, racing across the room to hold Alice.

"He, he, he," Emily tried as Joanne kneeled on the floor before her, wrapping her arms around her sister.

"It's all right," she said.

Emily shook her head, her breaths short.

"He left us," she managed. "He left us."

Joanne quickly shot back to her feet, looked at the shocked faces of all inside the room before quickly dashing back out through the door.

She knew there would be only one place he would go, so she ran across the ground with bare feet, wondering what she was going to say to Tomas when she found him. Her anger took precedence for the moment, but her love for him told her to be easy on him. Men were a strange creature, and she was sure that this one had his reasons for walking away, and that they made perfect sense to him.

She navigated through the village, crossing to the far side where the stable house stood. The doors were closed, but that could mean he was inside. She continued to run for the building and was about to open the door when she heard hooves beating on the ground.

She turned towards the hill, seeing the silhouette of the tower standing on top, and two men standing guard inside. The sound of a galloping horse growing fainter as it crossed the pasture drew her attention to the meadow.

There, she saw him, racing away to the hill. He was too far for her to call, and too quick to run after.

She dropped to her knees and cried.

All she could do was watch him race over the hill and vanish into the darkness.

***

The Fuchsia Mistress slept restlessly in her soft bed with her lover by her side. He watched her as she twitched, dreaming of the things she had done, wishing that she had not.

Like him, he knew she longed for a way out, but they were both slaves to the Coven of Mirikin; bound to the cause.

The Fuchsia Mistress, Amicia, had told him of how she was in the Sovereign's service. They had taken her from her homeland as a child, forced to lie with men before the Green Mistress showed her the meaning of power.

She confessed she had enjoyed it, taking her manservant's innocence before taking his life. The rush that ran through her body was indescribable.

But as the years passed by, long after she swore to submit to the Coven of Mirikin, she had doubts. Her heart had softened.

He knew she wanted to be free, but she didn't have the urgency to do so. Fear of the other Mistresses prevented her from breaking away.

Jonathon ran his fingers through her hair. She seemed to calm a little at his touch.

He loved her and wanted nothing more than to be with her.

That would only happen if they were both free of the coven. Free of this war that the white witch waged upon all lands.

War, he thought. *Slaughter, more like it.*

Villagers, farmers, peasants and innocents were the only people that he had seen come under their blades.

This was not war. It was an extermination.

He had forged a plan to force his beloved's hand to decide regarding her loyalties.

She had told him she loved him, and her eyes informed him she despised the actions the Mirikin expected her to fulfil. Yet she claimed she must obey the coven's demands and follow the White Mistress' orders.

He leant into her and kissed her forehead.

"I'm sorry, my love," he whispered.

Rising carefully, so as not to wake her, he dressed quietly and left a note on the bedside table for her to find when she woke. After leaving her chamber, he walked along the corridor between her room to a large stairwell, passing several guards that lined the walls on either side of the passage. They acknowledged his superiority by standing at attention as he passed them by, falling back into a more relaxed posture once he had moved on.

He descended the stairs, carrying his helmet under his arm. More guards stood stolidly in the foyer as he approached, and two of them opened the doors for him.

Once outside, he passed more guards as he walked along a gravel yard towards the stables to the side of the castle. Apart from the men standing on duty, there was no one else to be seen. The barracks were dark, as was the city of Newholt below in the valley.

It was past midnight, meaning most people would be fast asleep.

But not him.

He had been thinking of this for such a long time.

He hoped she wouldn't be angry.

Saddling his horse, strapping a bedroll behind the seat, he prepared to leave. The horse seemed eager to go. He rubbed the beast's nose to calm her down.

"Soon, feisty one," he told the mare.

Reaching behind a pile of straw, he retrieved some supplies he had placed there earlier. There was a large satchel of dried food, including fish wrapped in brown paper and some bread, two canteens of water and an old tattered cloak with a hood.

The satchel and canteens were slung over the saddle where he could reach them while he rode the steed. He folded the cloak into a tight bundle and slipped it into the bedroll.

He retrieved his helmet from the floor and mounted the mare. Taking a deep breath, he urged the beast forward. She bolted through the stable doors and across the gravel yard, passing by all the guards outside the castle before speeding through the open gates.

Following the road down the hill, he detoured around the township of Newholt and turned towards the south. His next stop was Belburn, the intended target for the Fuchsia Mistress.

He hoped she found his letter.

He believed it explained his intensions clearly enough.

He prayed to the gods that they had forbidden him to pray to, that she would see his heart and soften towards it.

If she didn't, he knew what his fate would be.

But he had hope.

***

Vonavo stared towards the horizon where the stars touched the surface of the water to the west. He considered the message that he had received from his spy in the east, overlooking the little village where the potentials lived.

Uncertain as to whether he should relay the message from the man or hide it from his Mistress was his primary concern. But he was bound to do her will.

If she asked, he would tell.

He hoped she would not ask.

The man's words would only enrage her, and knowing her as he did, she would bring pain to him again.

Woodmyst is free, he had been told to tell her.

Free.

How he liked the sound of that. So much he said it out loud.

"Free." His voice rumbled like gentle thunder.

"What did you say, Vonavo?" a tiny voice asked from behind him.

The monstrosity in armour turned to see the son of the White Mistress standing before him.

"Master Takmel." Vonavo bowed. "It's late and you should be resting. The deck of a ship is no place to be at night for a boy your age."

"I couldn't sleep," the lad replied, moving to the banister beside the being. He rested his arms on the rail and stared towards the sea. "What was it you said?"

"Free," he replied, answering only because the boy had asked, wishing he didn't need to.

"Do you wish this?"

"Master?" Vonavo asked, not understanding the question.

"To be free?" Takmel elaborated.

"Yes," he replied.

The boy nodded.

"So do I."

"You are the son of the White Mistress," the being told him. "You *are* free."

"I'm anything but free, Vonavo," he said. "I'm expected to be something I don't want to be. Do things I don't want to do. These men revere me because of fear. As do you."

For Vonavo, this was true. His fear of the white witch had placed him in the boy's service. If he was free, if his kind were free, they would have nothing to do with her and her child.

"She has built a cage for me," Takmel continued. "One that I do not know how to escape from. I want to be free too."

Vonavo considered his words and wanted to tell the boy that he could do as he willed. But he also knew that the White Mistress held her anger deep and would punish him extensively if he were to whisper ideas into her son's head.

"You have a destiny," he said instead, turning his head to face the boy. "You are to be ruler of all. You are to be the Maji. You *will* be free."

"I don't like that name," Takmel replied.

"When you are the Maji," Vonavo said again, "you *will* be free."

The lad turned to face the being, the message sinking in.

The boy nodded.

"If my mother asks about our conversations," he told the armoured giant, "you can tell her we discussed my becoming the Maji, and how I will reign over all the lands and decide how to best rule it all. Understand?"

"I do," Vonavo answered, "Maji."

***

Sumaiyya Tarkin had taken to staying in her cabin during the voyage. They had been at sea for three days with constant rocking and swaying as the ship rolled and rocked over what she perceived as steep waves.

Travelling by ship did not agree with her.

The last time she had been on an ocean vessel was when the black ship had taken her from her homelands, away from her family. Her memory of it had been all but blocked out.

Now, as she sat cross-legged on her bed, it had all come back to her.

The ugly head of the ship's commander, freshly wounded across his face from her father's blade, breathing on her. His hands touching her. His sweat rubbing on her.

The entire memory made her feel nauseous.

She closed her eyes and tried to breathe deeply, steadily, calming her nerves and body. Several times, she had reached for the bucket the captain had given to her. Several times she had handed it to the men standing outside of her door to empty it overboard, demanding a new one, a clean one, to be brought to her.

Sitting on the bed, inhaling deep and blowing her exhales long, she reached for a large satchel she had brought with her luggage. She emptied some contents onto her bedspread in front of her legs.

Straw.

From beside her bed, on a small table, she retrieved some twine and a small paring knife. She cut a length of the twine with the blade and bound a handful of hay together, forming a bundle. With more twine, she forged the stubble into a familiar form.

Her eyes stayed closed.

Her breathing continued in long, controlled inhales and exhales.

She was not feeling any better, but her work needed to continue.

Before long, she had manipulated the small bundle of straw into the shape of a man. Her eyes opened so she could inspect the doll.

She smiled, happy with the way it appeared, and tossed indifferently upon the floor.

It landed on its side and bounced, finally settling on a patch of bare floor between another five straw dolls. Surrounding these were another twenty. Around them lay another fifty.

Hundreds of the little figurines almost covered the floor.

But she was not done. She cut some more twine and created a new straw doll.

There was still so much more to do yet.

Sixteen

Tomas sat on a small boulder by a tidy fire with kindling piled upon the cave floor within reach.

He stared blankly into the flames, watched by his steed, who moved her head to scrutinise him closely.

"What?" he said the beast, a hint of annoyance in his voice.

She snorted her reply and turned her nose towards the mouth of the cave.

The morning light was building outside. He guessed the horse wanted to return home. Not ready to leave, nor wanting to, he threw another piece of wood on the hearth and went back to staring at the flames.

The horse clopped towards the opening and stared outside.

"Go then," Tomas told it, peering across the fire to where he had laid his bedroll down, positioning his saddle for a pillow. He hadn't slept in it; instead, he had sat all night to think.

He believed Emily no longer wanted him and had stewed this thought over and over in his mind until it made him sick. In the early hours of the morning, well before first light, he had found a tree outside to lean against as he vomited.

It didn't make him feel any better.

The horse watched him, waiting for him to saddle her. But he didn't move. She hung her head and stepped onto the grass, where she grazed, leaving him to his thoughts.

Tomas cried again.

He couldn't return like this.

***

By mid-morning, and with no sign of Tomas, people in Woodmyst grew concerned. Talk of the Night Demons returning started amongst those who remembered the days of old. Others believed that the white witch had sent someone to take him.

David and Simon, upon hearing such words from certain individuals, instructed them to keep their talk behind closed lips, as it didn't help anyone. Both men paid Tomas' house a visit, hoping to find him in bed, perhaps ill or tired.

Seeing all three women and his two daughters on the veranda crying, the Erilian warriors consoling them, the men feared the worse.

"Where is he?" David asked.

"He left," Emily replied, Karlena beside her, arms around her shoulders.

"Why would he leave?" Simon asked. "What happened?"

"I was angry at him," she told them.

"So?" Simon shook his head. "You've had disagreements before."

"I wouldn't speak to him," she sobbed.

"I don't understand," the stocky man said to the bald giant.

"She has been keeping silent towards Tomas since the night of the shadow demon," Akasati informed them.

"Oh." Simon lifted his eyebrows. "And I guess he had enough."

Emily nodded.

"Why didn't he just come and stay with one of you?" David asked Joanne and Lucy, who were sitting on their porch weeping.

"He told Emily that he didn't want to get in the way of their relationship." Lucy pointed to the two sisters, Rhydra rubbing her shoulders. "He said he should have been stronger and said *no* to marrying us."

David felt heartbroken. "I'm sure that he didn't mean it the way it sounded," he said. "Where did he go?"

"He said the caverns," Emily blubbered.

"I'll come with you," Joanne said, standing up, with Akasati about to follow.

"No," he replied. "You'll stay here with your family. I'll talk to him. Find out what's in his head. But Emily..." he looked at the auburn-haired woman. "It maybe *you* that needs to see him and talk to him."

"I know," she sobbed. "I've done nothing like this before. I don't know why I hurt him."

David nodded. "I'll try to persuade him to come home."

"Tell him I love him and I'm sorry."

"I will," he replied, turning away to cross through the village to the stable house.

"Do you want me to accompany you?" Simon asked.

"I think he would feel crowded if too many of us go to him," the other replied. "I'll go to Tomas. You might like to tell Richard of what has happened."

***

"Perhaps I was wrong about him," Richard said as he sat in a chair on his front porch. Becka sat on the edge of the platform with her back against a support beam, saddened by the news Simon had just shared.

"I had hoped for him to be the leader this village needs," the old man said. "But if he can't manage a situation like this..."

"With all due respect, Richard," Simon interjected. "The man is under pressure at the moment. This village doesn't require one individual leader. It needs a council, and the council has been lacking, putting too much on Tomas' shoulders when news of this impending war reached our ears. It was only going to be a matter of time before he would break."

Richard rubbed the stubble on his chin as he absorbed Simon's words.

There had indeed been a mass of weight laid upon Tomas. The villagers placed a heavy burden on his shoulders; expecting him, not asking him to fulfil the role of a leader.

Even when they once had a chief, they still had a council that shared the load. Simon was right with what he had said. They hadn't been sharing. They had been dumping the village problems onto Tomas since he returned from Blackrock Haven. A communal belief that the hero who had returned with the Seven could take on all of their problems emerged.

Meanwhile, he had nobody to help him with his own.

"I should go to the girls," Becka said, lifting herself from the edge of the veranda.

Richard nodded. "Give them my best wishes and prayers."

She walked away, towards the river as Simon sat against the wall of the house.

"It'll work out," Richard said out loud, more to himself than to the man sitting nearby. "He just needs time. *They* just need time together. To talk."

"There may not be enough time," Simon told him. "This darkness surrounding us is closing in. Right upon us. Without him, we will be weak. Perhaps the enemy knows this and has brought about an early wound, striking at us where it hurts the most. From the inside."

Richard nodded. "You could be right. There's no guarantee that he will return. Others will need to step up if that's the case."

"Others *need* to step up regardless," Simon replied.

***

David moved into the highlands beyond the hill, circling a jagged ridge to find the yawning mouths of the caverns.

Smoke drifted from an opening as a dark mare munched quietly on the green fodder close by.

David dropped from his steed and wrapped the reins loosely around a low branch on a small pine tree, leaving enough slack for the horse to chew the grass.

He walked to the cave where he could see Tomas peering into the fire, moving inside to crouch across the flames from the other.

"Good morning, Tomas," he said.

Tomas nodded; his eyes sad.

"I could tell you that your kids need you," David started. "I could tell you that Joanne and Lucy are at home crying. I could tell you that Emily is a mess. I've never seen her like that, Tomas. It's breaking my heart.

"She loves you Tomas," he told him. "She needs you to come back. She needs to talk to you."

"She's had plenty of time before now to do just that," Tomas replied. "My walking away from her caused her to realise that she needs to talk to me when I had been sitting there, each and every night, waiting for her to say something.

"She preferred the company of the floorboards to that of her own husband," he said, his eyes watering up.

"So, what are you going to do?" David asked him. "Stay here like a hermit? Live off the land? Leave your two daughters and three wives and roam the wilds?"

Tomas moved his eyes back to the flames, frowning.

"Fine, then." David nodded. He rose to his feet. "Move your gear over. I need space for my bedroll."

Tomas looked up at him. "What do you mean?"

"You're my friend, Tomas," the big man replied. "I'll go where you go. Besides, you didn't bring your sword. I did. Now we have a weapon we can hunt with."

"You can't," Tomas stood to his feet. "You have a son and another child on the way."

"So?" David asked. "Isabel has an intellect that I'll never be able to match, so she can teach the children more than I ever could. Martha is loving and caring, more in touch with her emotions than I'll ever be. She will nurture the younglings just fine. They don't need me. You do, however. We'll watch each other's back. Hunt deer in winter and Qedia in the warmer seasons. It'll be grand."

"But..." Tomas furrowed his brow.

"I'll be back," David told him, moving towards the mouth of the cave. "I'll just get my belongings."

"Wait," the other shouted.

David stopped and turned to face his friend.

"You can't leave them," he told the giant. "Not like that. They need you."

"So do your family, Tomas," David responded. "What's the difference between what you're doing out here and if I decide to join you?"

"You bastard." Tomas shook his head.

David walked towards him.

"Even if Emily didn't want you or love you any longer," he said. "Those two little girls do. And if Joanne and Lucy decide to walk away from you, Catherine and Alice should never be put in a situation where they may wish to do the same. You're their father. Their papa. How dare you leave them, Tomas!

Tomas lowered his eyes in shame. Tears streaked over his cheeks as he realised how much hurt he had caused by walking away.

"Now!" David grabbed him by the shoulders. "Pack your gear, load up your horse and accompany me back to town before I flatten your nose for putting me in this situation."

Tomas nodded, suddenly embracing the big man. David placed his giant hand on the other's back and let him have his moment.

**

Amicia sat on the edge of her bed, reading the note again for the third, then fourth time. She couldn't believe he would do such a thing to her, force her to decide between him and the White Mistress.

She scrunched the parchment in her fist, angry at her lover, Jonathon. He knew her vows bound her to the will of the coven, that she had sworn her allegiance to the White Mistress. How could she stand against such power?

She thought of him, on his own, without her. She couldn't bear it. Amicia opened the letter out again, just to see his handwriting, wanting him here with her.

Amicia,

Don't be angry, but I have gone to warn the people of Belburn of your approach.

Afterwards, I intend to ride to Woodmyst where I will offer my services to assist them or tender my surrender. Whichever they will accept first.

Please consider leaving this gruesome cause and join me.

We could fight against them, or their enemies may imprison us. In either case, we would be together. We would be free.

I cannot be a puppet any longer.

I would rather you with me in my arms, my love.

Jonathon.

She sobbed, holding the note to her chest.

What choice did she really have?

He had turned from her, turned from the coven, choosing to become their enemy.

Choosing to become her enemy.

She rose to her feet and crossed the room, dropping the parchment to the floor as tears rolled over her face. Opening the closet, she glared at the clothes hung upon racks and folded neatly on shelves.

Fuchsia dresses, fuchsia robes.

Fuchsia, fuchsia, fuchsia.

She grabbed the articles and pulled them out violently, grunting and snorting angrily as she tossed them all onto the floor, onto the bed, everywhere.

At last, with her closet all but empty, she stared at the only articles left folded, tucked away behind everything.

A plain dress with a brown and white checked pattern. A white blouse folded on top and a grey cloak rolled up to the side.

Simple clothing.

Clothing not fit for a Mistress belonging to the Coven of Mirikin.

Clothing that cost a soldier a year's wages.

Clothing that Jonathon had purchased for her.

Her eyes welled up again as she carefully lifted the clothes from the closet and placed them delicately on the bed.

She ran her hands over them, feeling their coarse material against her fingertips.

He had forced her hand.

She dropped her nightclothes to the floor and dressed.

Moments later, she exited her chamber and started along the corridor to the stairwell.

"Call the troopers," she commanded the guard nearest to her door.

"Mistress?" he sounded puzzled, looking at her apparel. She appeared as a commoner, not a witch of the coven.

"Am I not your Mistress?" She glared at him.

He looked along the hallway to see other guards shooting sideways glances.

"Yes, Mistress," he replied.

"Then gather the troops," she ordered. "I want all troops, all guards at assembly before the castle. Place the mercenaries to the front. Make sure all enlisted men are armed and take all weapons from the mercenaries."

He gave her a curious look.

She shot him a sharp glare.

"Yes, Mistress," he replied before turning away and racing in front of her down the corridor.

She started after him, passing the other guards that were posted in the passageway.

"This means you also," she barked. "Move it."

They immediately hastened away from her.

She moved to the top of the stairs outside the main door of the building, ordering two guards to remain by her side.

The soldiers rallied in neat lines and rows in the large gravel yard, numbering five hundred men. The mercenaries took their time taking their position, shooting looks of disdain towards the woman in front of them.

"Where are our weapons and who's this, then?" called one of them, scratching his crotch as he moved directly in front of Amicia. "Are you the Pink Lady's chamber pot emptier?"

The other mercenaries laughed.

"I am Amicia Elynbrigge," she called out, loud enough for all to hear. "I am the Fuchsia Mistress. I am a member of the Coven of Mirikin and servant to the White Mistress. As you know, the coven has declared a great war and many lands are falling. It would seem that inevitable victory is in the grasp of the White Mistress as she forges a way for the Maji.

"It is your duty to see to the destruction of all her enemies, who are also my enemies between here and Dweagan, before the last assault upon Woodmyst occurs. For that is where her most powerful foes dwell."

She looked to the mercenary, who was continuing to play with his crotch, flicking his tongue out at her.

"These men are not honourable men," she announced. "I paid them to do what you prefer not to do. I understand that you honourable soldiers find this cause questionable, if not deplorable. I, too, do not wish to bring harm to innocent lives. It took someone close to me to realise just how much.

"I am Amicia Elynbrigge," she announced, "and the reign of the Fuchsia Mistress is complete. I will go to Woodmyst and offer myself to them. They can choose to accept me as an ally or take me prisoner. I would ask that you join me to aid them in their fight. I ask, not command. You are free men."

The soldiers turned to one another, not sure if they had heard correctly.

"Free," she called again. "It also means that these men before me will not be paid for their services and they will no longer be required.

"You can't do that, bitch." One of them stepped forward.

One of her guards stepped forward to block the individual.

"I think I'm owed some compensation for my time," the crotch scratcher called out as he pulled down his trousers to reveal himself to her. "How's about putting yourself on this?"

She reached her hand out to him and squeezed her fingers. His ribs cracked loudly as they broke beneath her power.

He screamed as excruciating pain swept over him. Blood seeped from his tear ducts and dripped from his nose as she brought her fingers closer and closer together.

"Kill the mercenaries," a guard called.

The troopers lifted swords and spears, moving into the unarmed men and placed them all onto the gravel beneath their feet. There was not much more to the struggle except cowardly pleas for mercy, which went unheard as the troopers hacked and gored all one hundred mercenaries to death.

The crotch scratcher fell in a writhing, twisted, bleeding lump as Amicia released him.

With blood spread from one side of the yard to the other, she met the eyes of every soldier before her.

"You are free," she told them. "But I would be thankful if you would join me."

"I serve you, Mistress," a guard said, stepping forward.

"As do I," called another.

"And I," said yet another.

Before long, they had all pledged their allegiance to her.

"Thank you," she called to them. "I am Amicia. I am no longer your Mistress."

"My lady," announced a guard.

The troopers repeated the salutation.

She nodded, wishing Jonathon was here to see what had transpired, feeling a warmth in her heart she had not felt since childhood.

"Your orders, my lady?" the guard asked.

"Fetch the catapults," she instructed. "I intend to make them a gift to Woodmyst."

Seventeen

David strolled across the grass in front of the Wardes' house. He noticed the women had moved inside Emily's dwelling where the Erilian girls played the hosts, serving tea and continuing to offer comfort to the distressed wives.

Shaking his head as he ascended the step to the platform, he couldn't believe that the three of them were still sobbing as much as they had been before he left. Then again, he thought, perhaps he would too if he were a woman whose husband left in the middle of the night.

Rapping on the door, he hoped that this would all be over soon.

Karlena opened the door to him, allowing him inside.

"Did you find him?" Emily asked, holding a kerchief to her nose.

He nodded.

"Where is he?"

"He waits for you in your father's house," David told her.

Joanne and Lucy stood to leave.

"No," David said to them before pointing to Emily. "Just you."

She sat in her seat, staring at the floor as Karlena returned to her side.

"What are you waiting for?" the Erilian woman said to her. "Go to him."

"I—" She shook her head. Something prevented her from standing.

"Then I shall tell him to leave and be on his way," David informed them.

"Why?" Joanne asked him. "Why would you do that? We still love him, even if she does not."

Emily shot her a glance, full of disdain.

"There," David said, pointing to Emily again. "That's why. He doesn't want to bring a wedge between you and your sister. He loves you all so much that he would rather be with none of you than to see you hate one another or fight for his attention or even feel jealousy towards each other. You two are sisters, and one of you is not behaving so.

"If you," David turned his attention to Emily, who stared at the floor, "his first wife, cannot swallow your pride and see him, then he *will* leave. I will see to it myself."

He turned and walked back to the door.

"Where are you going?" Lucy looked worried.

"I will walk back to the cottage by the hill to help my friend on his way," he told her. "If Emily reaches him before me, I will turn around and go to my wives and son."

And with that, he left.

All eyes fell upon her, waiting for her to respond.

She didn't move.

"You are a fool, Emily," Joanne told her. "If he leaves, I *will* follow him. You will lose a husband and a sister."

Emily sobbed.

"Get up," Lucy hollered.

"I can't," Emily said, shaking her head.

"You stubborn cow!" Lucy stood up, crying. She stormed from the house, and her heavy footfalls trailed across the veranda to the new cottage before the sound of a slamming door shook the room.

"Why, Emily?" Joanne glared at her sister. "He's the father of your children."

"Then he should come home," she spat.

Joanne shook her head.

"*You* did this," she responded. "*You* need to fix it."

Joanne followed Lucy's trail to the other house and disappeared from view.

Some silence passed before Akasati spoke to her.

"You need to go to him," she said. "Otherwise, you let the darkness win. You let it linger too long and now you don't want to let it go. You've let it become a part of you.

"Go to him," she urged. "Or you lose it all."

Emily moved her eyes to her daughters, sitting on the floor, looking at her with sad, pleading eyes.

She heard the door of the nearby cottage open, some footfalls moving as the door closed.

It grabbed her curiosity, causing her to peer through the window towards the other house by tilting her head.

Joanne and Lucy had packs on their backs. They were leaving too.

This set Emily into another crying fit.

***

Joanne and Lucy started towards the hill, noticing David dawdling through the grass not too far from their home.

"Where are you off to?" he asked them.

"To be with our husband," Lucy replied.

"I told you it was only Emily that is meant to go to him."

"We know," Joanne replied. "But we will not lose him because of her stubbornness. We will follow him wherever he would take us, David. All the way back to Blackrock Haven if that is where he wishes to go."

"You would leave your own sister?" he asked.

"For Tomas…" She wiped a tear from her eye. "Yes."

He turned to the houses and breathed a deep sigh.

"I thought she would have run past me and all the way to the cottage," he told them, sounding disappointed. "I really thought their love was as deep as the ocean and as tall as the sky. It appears that I was wrong."

He turned towards the hill and walked at a more natural pace. The two women kept to his side.

"I'll take you to him and then I will prepare three horses," David said. "He won't want to stay here without her by his side.

"He was hoping she would meet him halfway. He rode back from the caves. She only needed to come from the house," he told them. "Maybe he was expecting too much from her."

"I don't think so," Joanne put in. "I would have run all the way to the caverns for him. She would rather sit in her chair and feel sorry for herself. He deserves better than that, David."

"This is a sad day indeed," David muttered. "It would probably be best to leave the village. But I hope, I pray, that they reconcile."

"Those poor little girls," Lucy sobbed. "Shouldn't we take them with us?"

"No," David responded. "To lose a husband is one thing, but to have your children taken would tear her soul apart. You are right, though. They will have a hard time ahead of them.

"So will he." David gestured to the cottage by the hill. "He will miss them for a long, long time and then some more. He will need you the most when he thinks about them."

"I never would have thought something such as this to happen," Lucy said. "Not between Emily and Tomas."

David nodded. "It is odd, indeed. But we seem to be here, like travelling on a road too narrow to turn upon."

"It's the white witch who is behind all of this," Joanne told them. "She sends a veil over us. Emily has given herself to it, letting the darkness in. That is why she behaves as she does."

"Then perhaps you and the others of the Seven can do something to set her free?" David asked.

"She needs to decide to be free," Joanne replied. "Each of us had to decide to not let our doubts and fears get the better of us ever since this began. Emily lowered her guard and let it in. What's worse is that she knows it, and she is still unwilling to fight it."

David nodded. "Then I guess the Seven becomes the Six."

"They are strong," Joanne informed him.

"Yes," he replied. "But you are stronger, and you strengthen them when you unite with them."

"Are you trying to persuade me to stay, David?"

"Perhaps," he confessed.

"My husband comes first," she replied. "He completes me."

David felt himself choking up. Joanne was truly madly in love with Tomas. Perhaps even more than his other two wives combined. Definitely, it would appear more than Emily for the moment.

They were about halfway between the cottage by the hill and the edge of the village when they saw the door open and Tomas step upon the veranda. He was peering towards them, his hands by his sides.

"Tomas," Joanne whispered, a magnificent smile spreading across her face.

Stepping off the porch, he walked towards them as they picked up pace, closing the distance between them.

"He comes to meet us," Lucy said.

David grinned.

Suddenly, another woman overtook them, swiftly moving through the tall grass.

It was Emily.

Her auburn hair trailed behind her as she lifted her dress, allowing her legs to run. Like the wind, she moved to him.

As she drew near, he opened his arms and took her to his chest, swinging her around in a circle.

David stopped walking, as did the two women by his side. They watched for a long time as both Tomas and Emily embraced. Eventually, they pulled apart and, holding hands, moved into the cabin, closing the door behind them.

"Well," Joanne said, sounding saddened, "I don't believe we will be leaving Woodmyst."

"Your sister and her husband have reunited," David said. "We need to give them some space. This is a time to celebrate."

"I know," she replied. "I was just hoping to..."

"Spend some time with him?"

She nodded.

"You too?" he said to Lucy.

"I want to spend all my time with him," she admitted.

He nodded as he turned back towards the village.

"Come along," he said. "You have two little girls at home who will need you to take care of them tonight. I don't expect that they will see their mother and father until tomorrow."

***

"You two will sleep in my bed," Joanne told her two nieces.

"Why can't we sleep in our own beds?" Alice asked as she shovelled a forkful of mashed potato into her mouth.

"Because Akasati is sleeping in your bed tonight," Joanne told her, sitting by her side at the table.

"And where will you sleep?" the little girl questioned; her mouth still full.

"I'll sleep with Lucy."

"And Karlena?"

"She will sleep in your parents' bed with Sharek."

"And Rhydra?"

"In my bed, silly," Catherine told her.

"And where will Mama and Papa sleep?"

"Auntie Joanne told you already," Catherine huffed. "They're staying at the hill cottage tonight."

"Why?"

"Because..." Joanne looked at the other adults in the room for help.

"Because your mama and papa need some time to be alone," Lucy told Alice.

"Why?"

"Because they had a big fight and your mama and papa were both very sad," Lucy frowned.

"And Papa left," the little girl put in.

"Yes, he did." Lucy nodded. "For a little while. But he came back, and he needs time to help your mama feel happy again."

"Why don't you tell her how he intends to make Mama happy?" Catherine asked, a cheeky grin growing on her face.

Lucy and Joanne shot the elder girl a stern glare. The Erilian women stifled their laughter.

"How?" Alice asked, shovelling more potato past her lips.

"He..." Lucy turned to the little girl, creeping across the room with her fingers like claws, "is going to sneak up on your mama and tickle her like this."

Lucy dug her fingertips into Alice's ribs. The little girl laughed and twisted violently, causing potato to explode from her mouth, onto the table and across her sister's blouse.

"Yuck," Catherine hollered.

Joanne erupted in laughter, pointing to the mess on her niece's dress.

"Not funny," the elder girl objected, a slight smile working its way onto her.

Lucy and Alice chuckled as Joanne reached for a cloth. One was always sitting on the back of a chair by the table, as Alice had proven to be a messy eater, even at the ripe age of seven. She dabbed at the mess on Catherine's blouse as the laughter subsided.

"Do you think they will stay together?" the older girl asked.

"I think so," Joanne answered. "Yes."

"I was so scared, Auntie Joanne." Catherine locked eyes with her aunt.

"Me too, sweetie." She ran her fingers through the girl's long auburn hair.

"I don't want my papa to ever leave again," she said, a tear growing in her eye. "You and Mama could make it so that he never leaves."

"Your mama is working on that right now," Joanne told her earnestly.

"With a tickle game," Alice added matter-of-factly.

"Right." Joanne nodded.

"No," Catherine said. "I mean, you and Mama could *make* him believe he wants to stay."

Joanne frowned and kissed the girl on the forehead.

"We don't use our powers like that. Not on the ones we love," she explained. "Think of it like this. What if I put you in a cage and told you to sit in one place, never to move? Never going outside to play. Never to see your friends again. Never hiding in the grove forever. Would you like that?"

"No," she replied.

"It would make you sad, right?"

"Yes." She nodded.

"That's what it would be like for your papa if I made him believe he wanted to stay," Joanne explained. "He would be in an invisible cage and part of him would know it, but wouldn't be able to get free. I can never do that to your papa."

"Because you love him?"

"Because I love him," she answered the girl.

Catherine moved to her auntie's lap and placed her arms around her.

"I love you, Auntie Joanne," she said.

Joanne wrapped her arms around the little girl tightly. "I love you too."

Eighteen

Strongholdt burned.

Smoke and flames veiled the citadel, and the wharves had melted into the Sea of Solace.

The soldiers slaughtered the scholars and sacked the government.

With three forces approaching from all sides, the armed forces had no chance of victory. Still, they tried, fighting valiantly until the last man stood alone.

Brick and mortar cracked and crumbled.

Pillars smashed and toppled.

Buildings that once stood proud and lofty turned to rubble as Strongholdt's people roasted in the flames.

Archers from the Jade Mistress' force took to shooting fiery arrows into the navy ships anchored off the coast. Two hundred vessels smouldered as the heat built inside. Soon after, they erupted into orange balls of flame as the black powder meant for the cannons caught fire.

The Pearl Mistress, after joining with the others at Mallowhill to the north, concentrated her troopers on the gates through the city walls. There, they prevented every man, woman and child from fleeing the burning city. The soldiers constructed great barricades across each exit using overturned carts and bodies of the fallen. If any navigated over the blockades, armed men were waiting for them with spears, arrows, or blades.

By late afternoon, there was not a place within the city that fire hadn't kissed.

Screams of pain faded.

Cries for help fell silent.

The Mistresses commanded their forces to march on, for their next target was far, far away. They would pass through the Core, the lands of the Agrodien and the Haigok, as they progressed to their enemies beyond the Lunkhul Forest, Woodmyst.

The smoke rising from the city of Strongholdt was thick and wide, appearing as storm clouds spreading across the sky.

The three Mistresses combined their forces into one massive army, two thousand strong. As they marched into the evening, the Gold Mistress sent a platoon of twenty riders in search of settlers and farmers in the area. They investigated every dot of flickering light in the distance, resulting in many farmhouses being burnt to the ground and their inhabitants coming under the sword.

They marched well into the night before the three witches called for the soldiers to stop and set up camp. By midnight, the Mistresses and their troopers, apart from the night guards, were sleeping on the border of the Core Lands.

***

Jonathon, upon his steed, led the people of Belburn away from their small township after convincing their chief that the Fuchsia Mistress was on her way. They moved to the north, making for the mountain pass that wound its way over the ridge to the plantations of Woodmyst.

"We need to move in haste," he called over his shoulder. "If the gear you lug is too heavy, leave it. Your lives are far more important than equipment."

"What if Woodmyst can't cater for us?" the chief, a scrawny old man with snow-white hair, asked.

"We'll make do," Jonathon told him. "Woodmyst has found her way through the darkest of times. I'm sure she can handle a few hundred souls."

They had been on the move for several hours. Most of the people were on foot and growing tired.

"When will we stop, Mama?" a small girl called.

Jonathon heard the question and wanted to tell her they would stop soon. But they wouldn't.

They had only just climbed into the mountains and the land still spread wide and open on all sides. He wanted to get higher, where the road was thinner and bordered by tall cliffs.

If Amicia had followed her coven rather than her heart, he knew she would send men after him.

He needed a place where he could defend against them, and where they were, on the steep slopes leading to the mountain range, was not the place to be.

"We need to get higher into the mountains," he called back to the people. "It's not safe here."

"We make for the twisted road," the chief yelled. "It will be safer there."

Jonathon listened to the conversation between mother and daughter travelling behind him.

"Is the twisted road far?" the girl asked.

"It is still a way from here," the woman replied. "But Chief Harling is correct; it will be safer than here. We can rest then."

"I'm sleepy," the girl complained.

Jonathon had to admit that the hour was late. They had been travelling under the cover of darkness and he calculated that morning light was only a couple of hours away.

They would need to rest during daylight. There would be no other chance for them to relax. This would force them to continue travelling during the night hours again.

It was not ideal, Jonathon thought, but what other option did he have?

"When we are safe, sweetie," he said to the girl, "you can use my bedding to sleep in. It comes from a royal castle and is filled with the soft down of swans from Havencrest. They're the softest swans of all the lands."

"Is that true, Mama?" the girl asked.

"It must be," she replied, holding her daughter's hand and smiling at the rider. A silent *thank you* passed from one to the other.

Jonathon replied with a nod and a smile.

"You're a good man, Commander," the chief said.

"Jonathon, please," he replied. "I deserted my post. I command no one any longer. In fact, I'm without a home at the moment."

"What made you desert?" Harling asked. "Considering that the Mistresses have such powers, how did you gather such courage to come to us and give warning?"

"I did it because I could not watch innocent lives be destroyed all for the cause of absolute power," he answered. "I couldn't bear to hear another infant suddenly stop crying because some soldier put a boot to its head, or a mother screaming at such a sight.

"But most of all," he continued, "I did it for love."

"I don't understand," the chief said.

"I was in love," Jonathon stated. "I *am* in love with the Fuchsia Mistress."

"How could you be?" Harling asked. "She's a... a..."

"A witch?"

The chief nodded.

"That she is," Jonathon replied. "But she has a good heart. She is trapped, a slave to the coven. I simply couldn't bear to watch her become a monster. So I ran, hoping she would reconsider her role."

"You hope she would choose you over them?" Chief Harling questioned.

"I do," the other replied. "But she has been a part of them for so long. She could send someone to take my life right at this moment. Even so, I still love her."

The chief nodded, understanding situations of the heart.

"My wife passed away some time ago," Harling said. "Several years, in fact. Most of the people in Belburn would have me take another wife, but I can't."

"You still love her," Jonathon said.

"Today, as much as I did the first day," he replied. "I remember she was fair and beautiful, like the morning sun when she was young. And even with the lines of age and her golden hair turning grey, she became lovelier to me every minute.

"Oh, I miss her so much," he admitted as his eyes welled with tears. "I can't remember her face too well now. But I remember her here," and he pointed to his heart. "I remember her ways and her essence. I carry that as some people would carry a lock of their loved one's hair."

Jonathon wiped his eyes on his sleeve.

"That's what I want for Amicia and myself," he told the older man. "A love like that."

"Pray to the gods for it," the chief told him. "We all will. Perhaps she won't pursue you with ill intent. Perhaps she will come to you with open arms."

"It would be a dream come true," Jonathon said.

***

Joanne jumped out of bed and raced through the house, thumping into the front door before she could open it. She pulled the door open, holding her belly with one hand. Taking two steps across the veranda, she dropped to her knees and opened her mouth, vomiting on the grass by the house.

Lucy was right behind her, being woken suddenly and full of fright. She had practically chased the other through their dwelling, reaching her just in time to see her retch all over the lawn.

"What's wrong?" Lucy asked.

"I feel nauseous," Joanne told her before losing some more of her stomach's contents.

"Maybe something you ate didn't agree?" the other suggested as she crouched beside her, placing her arm around Joanne's shoulders.

The auburn woman clutched at the floorboards of the porch as she hung her head over the side. Lucy pulled her hair back, away from receiving any splashback.

"I ate the same as you and the girls," Joanne told her.

"Should I get you some water?"

Joanne shook her head. "I think I'm fine."

Karlena stepped onto the veranda of the house next to theirs. She wiped her eyes and staggered from still being half asleep.

"What's going on?" she asked. "I heard thumping."

"Joanne isn't well," Lucy told her.

"I think I'm better," the auburn girl replied, keeping her head over the grass, peering at the puddle of regurgitated food.

"Let me see." Karlena crossed the porch and crouched at her side.

She put her hand on Joanne's forehead.

It felt cool to the touch, nothing unusual.

"No fever."

Her fingers pressed and wriggled against the woman's neck, just below the jaw.

Joanne could feel a strange sensation like spider's legs creeping across her throat.

"No swelling."

Her palm moved to Joanne's belly.

Karlena closed her eyes and focused on her power.

She breathed deep and deliberate.

"Close your eyes and breathe," she told Joanne. "Sit up straight."

Joanne remained on her knees, straightened her back and placed her hands on her lap.

She closed her eyes and breathed deeply, copying Karlena.

Lucy inhaled and exhaled with the two others. She didn't know why she did so. It just seemed like the right thing to do at that moment.

"You're with child," Karlena said suddenly.

Lucy fell to her rump as Joanne shook her head. Her eyes spoke disbelief towards the news.

"I can ask the others to join us," Karlena suggested. "Maybe with more of us we can know for sure, but I think I'm correct."

"But..." Joanne continued shaking her head, "none of the Seven has been with child."

"Well," Karlena said, and smiled. "Now one is. Congratulations."

Nineteen

The Fuchsia Mistress, now dressed in simple clothing, rode a black mare as her forces followed her. They had made their way along the eastern slopes that led into the mountains, intending to bypass Belburn and make for the pass through the ranges and on to Woodmyst.

Her men numbered six hundred strong. Some had returned to their families, unable to muster the nerve to continue spilling blood for any cause. They preferred to return to their ploughs or fishing boats rather than hold a sword again.

She let them go with her blessing. Those who stayed with her had witnessed their colleagues' release, becoming convinced that their Mistress had turned a new leaf. They instantly renewed their loyalty to her and decided that a fight against the witches was a far better cause than the one for which they had been a part.

Now, marching on the slopes beside the mountains as the sun rose gradually in the sky, the men shared a determination to see their world freed from the tyranny of Mirikin.

The mountain range turned slowly to the west and the terrain gradually become rougher. The massive draught horses in teams of four struggled as they pulled the partially constructed catapults behind them.

The weapons were made of thick, strong timber and were held together by large iron bolts. They sat upon specially constructed carts with three iron axels and six enormous wheels.

Amicia, the Fuchsia Mistress, observed the catapult drivers when she noticed the terrain becoming more rough and uneven. They navigated over the land with minimal disruptions.

Once in a while, a few troopers on foot would file in behind a cart to push it over a boulder or through a divot.

It was slow-moving; tedious and tiring for the men and horses.

A rider appeared before her, making his way rapidly towards them.

He pulled alongside of Amicia's horse before acknowledging her.

"Mistress," he began.

"Not anymore," she reminded him.

"Begging pardon, my lady," he corrected himself. "Lord Brondt is high upon the pass."

"Were you seen?"

"No, my lady," the soldier replied.

"Is he alone?" Amicia asked.

"No, my lady," he answered. "The citizens of Belburn travel with him. They were resting in a narrow section they call the—"

"The Twisted Road," she interjected. "I know it. I've had it on my mind for most of this journey. Do you think we will safely take the catapults through without too much trouble?"

"I believe we can," he said. "The road isn't all that narrow. The turns might be tight, but they should fit."

She nodded.

"What more of Lord Brondt?"

"They left their camp about an hour or so ago, my lady," he replied. "They are not that far ahead. But they move a little more hastily than us."

"They've rested," she said to herself. "That's good. He's going to need it before I catch up to him."

The soldier wasn't able to tell if she meant her words to reflect anger or something else. Then he noticed the tiny smile on her face and knew.

"Shall I join the ranks, my lady?" he asked.

"Do as you wish," she told him. "You're a free man now."

"Yes, my lady," he nodded before dropping back to the other men.

Amicia rode quietly, thinking of Lord Brondt, her Jonathon. She was glad to hear that he was fine and safe for the time being.

Her thoughts moved to the villagers that travelled with her beloved and suddenly, desperation and desire to protect them flooded over her. A nearby threat made its way into her mind, reminding her that there wasn't just the White Mistress in the west to deal with, but both the Lavender and Violet Mistresses were making their way towards them from the southern peninsular.

She was meant to meet them both and combine forces with them in Dweagan the day after the next, where they would await their coven's Prime, the White Mistress.

How disappointed they will be, Amicia thought as she turned her steed towards the slopes, following a well-worn path into the mountains.

***

The people of Belburn made their way steadily down the road that took them through the pass in the mountains. They could see the vast plantations before them as they closed the distance between themselves and Woodmyst.

Sounds of joy and elation resounded throughout the travellers as they realised, they had almost reached their intended goal. Most of them had not slept during the early hours of the morning because of their anxieties and concerns about what was to come. They had stayed on the Twisted Road for an hour or two before opting to move on with their expedition.

Jonathon urged them to rest a little more, but they were adamant and pressed him to lead them on. Having compassion upon them, he submitted and now directed them towards the floor of the valley.

The morning sun had breached the mountains to the east, illuminating the small village to the north with a bright radiance. Smoke wafted from chimneys and they could see some movement as people busied themselves.

It appeared welcoming.

But Jonathon knew looks could be deceiving.

"Continue on the road," he told Chief Harling, who rode by his side.

"Why?" the chief asked. "Where are you going?"

"I'll ride ahead and tell them of our approach," he replied.

"They look friendly enough from here," Harling replied, waving his hand towards the village.

"This is Woodmyst," Jonathon informed him. "They've had to deal with dragons and invaders. I don't think they have a high level of trust after that experience."

"Good point," the chief agreed. "We'll be with you momentarily."

Jonathon kicked his feet and urged his steed to race forwards. Following the road, and trying to keep in plain view, he galloped his horse through the corn and wheat fields that lined the road on either side.

There were wooden bridges along the road that crossed thin channels where water moved between the fields. The hooves of his steed made a loud clatter as he crossed each one. He thought the sound would definitely apprise the people of his approach.

This, he believed, could be a good thing if they looked to see who was coming along the road, or a bad thing if they shot arrows before asking questions.

Ahead of him, he saw a stone bridge that crossed a wide river.

On the far side of the bridge stood a giant, bald-headed man holding a long sword.

Jonathon slowed his approach and pulled his steed to a stop on the edge of the overpass, where he dismounted and walked slowly onto the bridge. The soldier removed his helmet and dropped it onto the road as he approached. He then unbuckled his sheath and let it fall before retrieving his dagger and tossing it to the dirt as well.

Holding his arms out to the sides, he slowly turned to show the large man that he had no ill intentions or weapons to perform such schemes.

"Approach slowly," the man bellowed.

Jonathon took a quick look at the scenery before him.

He saw several houses, well-constructed and several men with blades in their hands, watching him intently. Behind the bald man were four dark-haired women with curved blades and dressed like guerrilla warriors. Another seven women, younger in age, stood attentively. One of them with auburn hair wore black, reminding Jonathon of the pink garments Amicia wore.

Is she one of them? One that I've not heard of?

He looked to his right and saw a man and woman holding hands as they approached the village from a cottage by a hill. The man let go of the woman's hand upon seeing Jonathon on the bridge and started running.

"I mean no harm," Jonathon announced for all to hear as he returned his eyes to the bald man. "My name is Jonathon Brondt. I was commander of the Fuchsia Mistress' forces. I have deserted my post to offer my surrender to the people of Woodmyst."

"Fuchsia?" The bald man turned to the woman in black and those around her. They shook their head. They had never heard of the Mistress that Jonathon spoke about.

"She serves the White Mistress," the soldier called.

"We know *her*," the giant replied. "Walk towards me slowly."

The running man arrived at the side of the bridge.

The woman in black took a step forward, her body tensing as the newcomer drew closer to Jonathon.

The soldier, knowing what the Mistresses were capable of, stopped walking.

"Who is this man?" the new arrival asked.

"Get back, Tomas," the big man instructed. "You've no sword."

Tomas stepped away, keeping his eyes on the soldier.

"Tomas," the woman in black hissed.

He moved to her side and took her hand.

Jonathon noted that this man had just been with another woman who also had auburn hair. He had heard stories told by Amicia that an auburn-haired girl was responsible for the death of the Sovereign. Looking at the two women with red hair, he could see similar features.

He could see they were related, and both shared the same man. But only one of them dressed like a Mistress.

Could it be that they intend to fight one of their own?

"There are others behind me," Jonathon announced as he closed the distance between himself and the giant. "People from Belburn. They were to be wiped out by an impending attack. I brought them here in hope to seek sanctuary."

"Sanctuary will be given to them," Tomas announced. "If they are who you say they are."

"Their chief rides with them," Jonathon told him. "There are women and children. They need much rest. We travelled for most of the night."

"And you?" Tomas asked.

"I am your prisoner," he replied. "If I can aid you, then I will do so gladly."

The bald man looked towards Tomas.

"We chain him to a beam in the meeting hall for now and give him some food," Tomas instructed. "I want to question him some more with the Seven. Put men on the bridge to await our new guests. We'll need food and water for the women and children first."

The big man nodded.

"I'll get on it," he replied. "It's good to see you two back together."

Tomas smiled as the other auburn woman took his free hand.

Several men surrounded Jonathon, ushering him through the village towards its centre. His eyes kept moving to the young woman in black, wondering if she was indeed a Mistress or something else.

She was ready to leap in when she believed her man was in danger. This gave Jonathon the distinct feeling that she possessed some power that could have rendered him useless if she felt inclined to use it.

As the big man walked ahead of him, leading his guards away, he observed the woman in black and the other auburn lady wrap their arms around the man as they wandered to another place in the village. Another woman, with lighter hair, ran to the man named Tomas, wrapped her arms around his neck and planted a kiss on his lips.

It would appear that things were done very differently in Woodmyst than they are at home, Jonathan supposed.

***

"How is this possible?" Tomas asked Joanne, surprised.

She looked at him confusedly, uncertain whether he had received joyful news.

Emily smiled from ear to ear and hurried to embrace her sister. "I'm so happy for you," she told Joanne.

"What do you mean, *how is this possible?*" Lucy questioned her husband. "You know how this works."

"I didn't mean that, silly girl," he replied. "I just mean that none of the Seven have children. How is it that Joanne can be with child?"

"I don't know," she replied as Emily released her. Tomas moved to her and wrapped his arms around her, a broad smile expanding on his face.

"I hope it's a son," she said. "You already have two daughters."

"It matters not," he told her. "I'll not be displeased with another daughter."

"What if that's all we can ever provide for you?" Lucy asked him.

"I'm fine with that," he replied honestly.

Holding Joanne's hands in his own, he stepped back from her and looked at each one of them, admiring them.

"I'm happy to be back with you," he told them. "And I'm sorry for the pain I've caused you all."

He held his right arm out to Lucy, who moved into him. With his left hand, he pulled Joanne towards him. She moved her arms around his waist before he stretched his arm to Emily, bringing her into the hug.

"I won't leave like that again," he said. "I promise. I don't know why I did that."

"It was them," Joanne said. "The Mistresses. They send a darkness this way to put us in a state of disunity."

"Then," Tomas stated, "we need to ensure that we are united."

Lucy tilted her head so that she could look him squarely in the eyes.

"You're not suggesting that the four of us...?"

"No, woman," he scolded with a smile. "I'm talking about the village. United as a community."

"Oh." She looked away, embarrassed.

The others laughed softly.

"I already told Tomas that I won't behave in such a manner again," Emily told the other wives. "And if I do, I expect you two to chastise me and bring me to correction."

"I won't hold back if there is a next time," Joanne told her sister.

Tomas moved his eyes between Lucy and Joanne.

"So!" He smiled. "You were both willing to follow me if I left?"

"You're my husband," Lucy replied. "I would follow you into the deadlands of the Core if that's where you intended to go."

"As would I," Joanne added.

"The three of you..." He shook his head. "You're really something."

***

Jonathon sat perched on a bench positioned by one of the support beams in the meeting hall. They had bound his hands in front of him, locked in shackles connected by a short chain. Another chain ran from one link attached to the restraints, down to another set of manacles around his ankles.

He chewed on some fresh bread and drank water from a cup placed on the bench by his side. He was grateful for the food and drink as his supplies were running low and turning stale. The bread he placed in his mouth was still warm, fresh from the oven, and he believed he had tasted nothing any better.

"Enjoying your meal?" the man he had seen with three women asked him.

"Yes, thank you," Jonathon replied as Tomas dragged a bench over the floor before sitting across from the prisoner. "You were not lying about the people following you. I spotted them at the far end of the valley and sent a rider to greet them, and our people are preparing food for them as we speak.

"If they vouch for you, I will consider removing the restraints. But you must answer a few questions that we have. Understood?"

"Yes," Jonathon replied as he placed the warm bread on the bench beside him, giving his full attention to his host.

"My name is Tomas Warde," said the man. "The big man watching you is David Gyfford. The reason I tell you our names is so that you can refer to us correctly. Also, you need to know that David and I will be the men to execute you if you prove to be our enemy."

Jonathon nodded understandingly.

Seven women, including the one in black, entered the building and sat behind Tomas, watching the man closely. David moved to the platform and sat on a chair to watch the interrogation.

"My name is Jonathon Brondt. I'm the commander of the Fuchsia Mistress' forces." He stopped and shook his head. "I *was* the commander of the Fuchsia Mistress' forces."

"Who is the Fuchsia Mistress?" Tomas asked. "Her name and location."

"Her name is Amicia Elynbrigge," Jonathon replied. He suddenly felt as if he was betraying her. His eyes welled up with water as he spoke. "She is based in Newholt. She is probably marching this way as we speak and I love her with all of my heart."

"Then you are loyal to your Mistress," Tomas stated.

"No," the soldier replied. "I am loyal to Amicia. She is a kind-hearted woman, but she is held in bonds of her own." He lifted his arms to jingle his chains. "Ones that the White Mistress, the Prime of her coven, has placed over all the Mirikin."

"Mirikin?" Tomas asked.

"We know this name," one of the Seven told him.

Tomas nodded. He noticed Jonathon looking at them, curiosity clearly on his face.

"These women were once in the house of Yasmeen Svoboda," Tomas told him. "Do you know this name?"

Jonathon nodded. "The Sovereign."

"They were to be trained to become like your beloved Fuchsia Mistress," Tomas informed him.

"The last of the potentials?" the captive asked.

"Yes."

"Then, this one is not a Mistress?" the soldier questioned, glancing towards the woman in black.

"This one is my wife, Joanne," Tomas replied. "And right now, she is no concern of yours."

"Apologies." Jonathon looked at the floor.

"Why did you desert your post?"

"I couldn't stand by and just watch innocent people perish any longer," he replied. "I know Amicia feels the same as I, but the White Mistress and the other members of her coven force her hand. I hoped that by running away, I might have been able to persuade her to leave their cause and follow her heart. I still hope for this."

Tomas nodded.

"Are your men loyal to you or her?"

"Her," Jonathon answered. "But only through fear."

"Fear of her?" Tomas asked.

"And of the coven," the prisoner replied. "Have you seen what a Mistress can do?"

"I've seen," Tomas informed him. "What is their strategy?"

Jonathon moved his sleeve over his eyes to brush the tears away. The chains jingled softly as he lowered his hands back to his lap.

"She was to march to Belburn today and lay it to waste," he explained. "After that, she was to move to Dweagan where she would meet up with the Lavender Mistress and the Violet Mistress."

"Lavender and Violet?" Tomas turned to the Seven. "Isn't that the same thing?"

"A slight difference, my love," Joanne replied.

Tomas frowned, tilting his head as he turned to face the captive again.

"Numbers?"

"Our forces numbered around eight hundred with the mercenaries," Jonathon told him. "Seven hundred trained military personnel. You could assume that the other Mistresses have similar numbers supporting them."

"So, they meet at Dweagan," Tomas confirmed. "What is the next move?"

"Amicia told me that the White Mistress will arrive with her fleet. They will then march north and take Woodmyst."

"We could run," David suggested.

"No, you can't," the prisoner replied. "The other Mirikin come from the west and north. They hem you in. This will be the last stand."

"We could cross the mountains to Oakbeach and hope to find ships to take us," Tomas put to the others.

"Oakbeach is gone," Jonathon told him. "The mercenaries burned it to the ground. I saw it with my own eyes. It was because of what I witnessed at Oakbeach that I sit here before you now."

"Were there any survivors?" Tomas asked.

"None survived," the captive answered. "The buildings burned, and they scuttled the ships. There is nothing left but ash."

Tomas stood and walked slowly towards David, rubbing his brow as he shook his head.

"We had friends in Oakbeach," Joanne told the prisoner.

"I am sorry," Jonathon told her. "I truly am. But every man, woman and child everywhere are facing the same fate. The Mirikin are destroying everything in their path, saving you until last."

Tomas turned to face the man in chains. "Have you any news of Oldcastle?"

"Oldcastle is to be desolated by sea and land," he replied. "The White Mistress' fleet approaches on the sea and the Scarlet Mistress will join forces with the Jade Mistress to attack the city from the land. Eventually, every city, town and settlement will be annihilated."

"For what purpose?" David asked. "Why destroy everyone?"

"It's a new beginning," Tomas answered. "Sumaiyya intends for the entire world to be what Blackrock Haven once was. Women as a mere means to reproduce. Men to fulfil the manual labour. Slaves on all levels."

"That's their cause," Jonathon added. "It has always been their plan."

"David." Tomas turned to his friend. "I need a ground runner to fly to Oldcastle. They need to be warned that forces are coming to destroy them."

The big man lifted himself from his seat and exited the meeting hall, moving towards the stable house.

Tomas turned towards the prisoner.

"I will talk with those from Belburn," Tomas told Jonathon. "If they speak well of you, I will remove your chains will. If not, you will remain shackled until I decide how best to deal with you. Until then, if there is anything you require, speak to the men watching over you."

Twenty

Smoke billowed from the seaside township of Rededge. With the Lavender and Violet Mistresses' forces now combined with two thousand men, there was little chance of victory for the little fishing village. They desolated its meagre population of fewer than one thousand people within a matter of minutes.

With the destruction of all settlements and communities on the peninsula between Freymoor, the land that the Lavender Mistress called home far to the south, and the lair of the violet witch in Linport, there were only two targets of interest left before they would reach Dweagan. One of these burned before them.

Both the Mistresses watched with anticipation as they listened to screams suddenly silenced by a slash of a sword, waiting for their men to regroup on the far side of the township as they completed their gruesome task. With their guards flanking them, they moved around the outskirts of the town upon their steeds, taking to a ridge that encircled the hamlet.

"There," the Lavender Mistress said to the other. "Do you see? Some children are trying to flee towards the forest."

"Where?" the other asked, standing in her stirrups to get a better view. "I can't see anything through this ghastly smoke."

"See where the trees make a sort of gap where the hills meet?"

"Yes," the violet witch replied.

"Watch there," the woman in lavender told her. "You'll see them soon enough."

She watched for some time. Sure enough, a small group of children ranging from toddlers to older younglings just big enough to carry the smaller ones ran into view, making for the forest to their right.

"Why aren't the men chasing them?" the Violet Mistress asked her guards.

"They may not see them from their positions, Mistress," a guard replied.

"Why don't we have some fun?" Lavender suggested. "It's been so long since I've played with any children."

"We are making good time," Violet agreed. "We can take Barrow-field on the morrow. Let's play."

Giggling like giddy little girls, the two witches urged their horses forward in haste. They raced along the edge of the woods, laughing madly as they closed on the area where the children had entered the trees. Their guards raced after them, trying to keep up with their Mistresses.

Both Lavender and Violet entered the forest upon seeing the children moving amongst the brush a short distance beyond the tree line. They slowed their horses to a trot as they navigated around bushes and trunks, ducking beneath low limbs and climbing over fallen logs.

"Hello," Lavender called. "Hello, boys and girls. Do you need help?"

Violet giggled wildly.

The children saw the approaching women dressed in their colours and felt afraid. Several cried as they tried to move faster, attempting to move farther into the trees.

"Did mother and father die?" she called. "Are you all alone with no one to look after you?"

"I'll tell you what," Lavender called to them. "We'll play a game. If we can't catch you by the time I count to ten, we won't eat you. All right?"

The younglings felt their hearts racing as their breathing grew into rapid gasps.

"One."

They moved their little legs as quickly as they could, stepping over logs and running through thick, thorny scrub.

"Two."

Some had their clothes rent as they caught sleeves on sharp branches that protruded from the undergrowth.

"Three."

Several scratches and shallow cuts appeared on their skin as they desperately moved to save their lives.

"Four."

Tears streamed across their faces, mixing with ash and snot as fear gripped hold of them.

"Five."

Her voice sounded close, as if the numbers were being called from within their heads.

"Six."

Moans emitted from the older children as they panted and struggled, holding on to the smaller ones tightly as they ran.

"Seven."

The Lavender Mistress suddenly appeared in front of them, the woman in violet behind.

"I found you." Lavender smiled wickedly, stretching her hand towards the escapees. She slowly brought her fingers together, savouring the screams of pain from the young ones as their intestine pushed inwards, causing her victims' internal organs to implode.

Violet clapped her hands delightedly before joining the massacre. One by one, the children fell, spewing blood from their mouths and noses onto the forest floor.

"What do we do now?" Violet asked when the last of the younglings stopped moving.

"Well, I said that if we couldn't catch them by the time I counted to ten, we wouldn't eat them," Lavender replied.

Violet laughed hysterically.

"Guard," she called over her shoulder.

"Yes, Mistress," a uniformed man on horseback replied from behind her. He moved his eyes across the scenery between the two witches. There were nine youthful faces smeared with blood, staring blankly up at the sky with mouths agape.

A strong sting of bile reached his throat.

"Have someone filet the kill and broil the portions," she commanded.

The guard turned a pale white, using what energy he had remaining to hold the contents of his stomach in place.

"Yes, Mistress," he replied, turning his horse back towards the open ground.

***

Vonavo stood sentry over Takmel, watching the boy from the fore-deck as he sat closer to the bow, reading his book. He had been sitting there for a very long time, acting against the wishes of the White Mistress. The armoured being had suggested to the lad that he needed to hone his skills, as his mother had directed. Takmel had responded with a remark about how his mother was too ill to come up on deck to make herself known, so it didn't matter what he did or didn't do.

Not in a position to argue, Vonavo fulfilled his duty by standing watch, assuring the boy's safety.

"Leave us," he heard a voice to his side. He turned his head to see the white witch standing beside him. Her skin colour was off white and she did not appear entirely well.

"Yes, Mistress." He bowed before walking away. His feet thudded against the wooden deck loudly with each stride.

She watched him move to the mid-deck, where he stopped and turned to keep watch of the lad from a distance. The guard she had placed over her son was vigilant, a reason she had chosen him for the duty. She also knew he was much quicker than he appeared, which made her uneasy, untrusting towards the monster. For this reason, she kept him on a tight leash and locked in his armour prison.

"Are you hungry?" she asked the boy.

"Hello, Mama," he said, looking up from his book and smiling. "You don't look well." He crossed the deck to her and wrapped his arms around her waist.

She hesitated and placed a hand on his back before lowering her cheek against the crown of his head. It had been a very long time since she had touched him. She didn't realise that she had missed him so much.

"Hello, Takmel," she replied, kissing his head. "Are you hungry?"

"No," he replied. "Vonavo watched me eat about an hour ago. I had a pork sandwich that the chef made for me in the galley. He then watched my take a piss before coming out here to watch me read my book. Vonavo watches everything that I do."

She took the hint.

"You are important," she told him. "I need for him to keep an eye on you at all times. Particularly now I am busy with our cause. It will be all over soon and you will be in your rightful place of power."

"I don't want power," he told her.

She furrowed her brow, not understanding how he couldn't want the very things that she sought for him.

"Why can't we just go home and stay there?" he asked.

"You want to reign only over Wintermarsh when you can rule the entire world?"

"I don't want to rule anything," he told her. "I just want to go home with you."

She continued to look confused.

"This is your destiny, Takmel," Sumaiyya told him. "This is what you were born to do. You are the Heir of Darkness. The Maji."

The boy realised he wasn't getting through to her. As with many similar conversations with his mother before, this one had reverted to the prophecy about his birth.

What if the prophecy is wrong?

He wanted to shout the words, but knew it would be pointless.

"Yes, Mama," he replied instead, lowering his head disappointedly.

"I'm going back to my room," she told him before kissing his forehead. "Don't stay out too long. The sun sinks into the waves. It will be dark soon."

But I'm the Heir of Darkness, he felt like saying.

"I won't, Mama," he told her.

"I've got something to do and will be preoccupied," she said, pulling away. "Will you be fine on your own with Vonavo?"

I have been for the past few months.

"Yes, Mama."

"Good boy," she said, turning away.

He watched her leave as tears welled in his eyes. When she had gone, he dropped to the deck and crossed his legs, lowering his face into his hands.

The armoured being returned to his side.

"Stand to your feet, Takmel," he said in a low voice.

The boy looked at him. It was the first time that Vonavo had given an instruction. Usually, his words came as suggestions.

"The men of the fleet are loyal to your mother," the being explained. "They are not slaves like the men of the land. If they see you behaving so, they may inform her. Stand to your feet and act like the Maji she believes you are."

Takmel wiped his eyes, picked his book up from the deck and lifted himself to stand alongside the monstrosity.

"Compose yourself," Vonavo commanded.

The boy took some deep breaths.

"Did anyone notice?" he asked.

"Only I," he replied.

"She won't even listen to me, Vonavo," Takmel told the other.

"This isn't the place to discuss such things," the giant replied. "But you must understand that her rage blinds her."

"You speak of Woodmyst."

"I do," he replied. "Perhaps when they meet with their destruction, she will pay more attention to you?"

"No," Takmel answered. "She has a lust for death. This will never end, Vonavo. It will go on and on."

***

Sumaiyya sat on her bed with her legs crossed, her hands on her knees and her eyes rolled back in her head. Across her floor, lying in neat rows covering the cabin, were hundreds of straw dolls.

She rocked back and forth, singing ancient words, a tune like a child's song.

Her mind was upon several women that had been plaguing her thoughts for the past ten years and who were now all in one place. Woodmyst.

She focused her efforts there.

All of her hatred and anger.

She willed her vengeance into that single location.

It was time to strike.

The first attack was about to begin.

***

They had erected tents along the northern bank of the river between the edge of the village and the cottage by the hill. Several campfires allowed families to enjoy a warm fire through the night, and some hot water for tea.

The cattle and sheep had moved closer to the grove, away from the newcomers to graze as the sun disappeared behind the trees of the forest. A red glow covered the sky as twilight approached.

"Could I have a cup of tea, Mama?" a little girl asked as her mother made a brew for her man sitting beside her by the firelight.

"All right," the woman answered. "But not a big one like your papa and me."

The girl, only five, nodded with a huge grin. It was her first cup of tea, an adult drink.

The woman handed a small cup of tea to the girl.

"Mind it," she warned. "It's very hot."

"I will," she replied before sipping. It burned her tongue and tasted bitter. She started breathing rapidly through her mouth, attempting to cool down.

Her father laughed.

"Not funny," the little girl retorted.

"Of course, it isn't." He continued to chuckle.

"I don't like it." She handed the cup to her mother, who poured the contents into her own mug before topping it up with the brew she had made.

"Do you want some cool water instead?" the woman asked.

"Mmmm." The girl nodded as her mother passed a canteen over.

The girl popped the cork from the top and sculled it down rapidly.

"Slowly," her dad instructed.

The girl lowered the canteen, moving her eyes across the far bank of the river.

"Why are the farmers still in the corn when it's getting dark?" she asked.

"What are you talking about?" Her father looked at her.

"There are farmers in the corn," she said, pointing across the wide river.

The man and his wife peered across the water and saw the tall stalks of corn waving gently in the breeze. The shadows between the crops were growing darker and darker as the sunlight diminished and the stars winked to life in the sky above.

Between the corn stalks stood the forms of men.

They stretched their arms straight out to their sides.

They hid their faces beneath wide-brimmed hats.

They covered their bodies in long, dark, tattered coats.

"No sweetie," the man told his daughter. "They're not farmers. They're scarecrows. The farmers make those to scare birds away."

"I know what a scarecrow is, Papa," she replied. "Those ones are moving."

"Scarecrows can't moo…," he began. His eyes locked onto one figure as its arms lowered slowly to its sides. "By the gods," he gasped.

The woman screamed.

Her shrill cry echoed across the valley.

Twenty-One

"What was that?" Lucy called, getting to her feet.

They were gathered in the living quarters of Emily's house. Both Emily and Joanne were sitting still in their deep-cushioned chairs. Tomas moved his eyes from them to his daughters sitting at the table, behaving as their mother and aunt. Calm and unperturbed.

The only ones to appear overtly alarmed to the scream were Lucy and himself.

Something mystical was occurring.

A horn blew from the watchtower on the hill, followed immediately by another trumpet call from the tower near the woods.

Tomas lifted himself from his seat and moved to the bedroom.

"Where are you going?" Lucy called, standing in the middle of the room.

"Quiet, please," Catherine said as she adjusted her head slightly, appearing to listen to something that the other could not hear.

"I'm getting my sword," Tomas told Lucy. "We're about to be attacked."

"How do you know?" she asked as he moved back into the living quarters, holding his sword. He gestured to the women sitting about the room.

"Does this look normal to you?" he said. "They hear or sense something."

"What do we do?" Lucy sobbed. She shook uncontrollably.

Tomas moved to her and placed his arm around her waist. He kissed her forehead before pressing his brow to hers.

"Gather my daughters and take them to my sister's," he instructed her.

"And them?" Lucy pointed to Joanne and Emily.

"Emily!" he exclaimed. She snapped out of her trance-like state and looked at him.

"Yes?" she answered.

"Grab your sword," he told her. "We have a fight to attend."

He then touched Joanne on the shoulder. She gazed up at him and nodded.

"I'll gather the others." She stood and made her way to the door.

He placed his attention back to Lucy, who was watching the entire exchange in awe. He kissed her again.

"Go to Linet," he instructed her one more time.

"Yes," she replied. Hastily, she took Alice and Catherine by the hands. They both turned their faces to her and smiled, seemingly oblivious to the danger.

"Could you hear the singing?" Alice asked.

"There was no one singing," Lucy said, pulling them after her.

"Go quickly," Tomas ordered them.

"Where are we going?" Catherine questioned as they neared the door.

"To your Aunty Linet's," Lucy replied, before turning her attention to both Emily and Tomas. "Be careful."

Tomas was strapping his leather breastplate over his torso. "You too."

Emily raced over to kiss both of her daughters on the forehead. "Be good for Lucy."

The horns blew again.

Lucy dragged the girls outside and started running across the village.

"Are you ready?" Tomas asked his wife.

"Almost," Emily replied, pulling a pair of trousers over her legs before removing her long dress.

"What was that about *singing?*"

"Singing?" she asked.

"Alice said she could hear singing," Tomas elaborated as he watched Emily lacing her trousers up in haste.

"I could hear it too," she answered. "It was very soft. Distant. I couldn't understand the words. I think I've heard it before. Maybe back when we first met, on our way to Blackrock Haven."

Sumaiyya, Tomas thought. *It has to be.*

Emily laced her boots quickly and took her curved sword from the top of a closet near the bed.

"I'm ready," she announced.

They ran outside, intending to rendezvous with others at the meeting hall, as was the plan, but David stopped them, who was dashing towards them with his long sword in his hand.

"They're across the river," the giant hollered.

"Who?" Tomas called as his friend passed by.

"Straw men," came the response.

Straw men.

Emily and Tomas looked at one another for a fleeting moment.

She was back.

They turned and followed David past their house and to the river bank. Peering across the river, they could see the neat rows of crops standing taller than their giant friend. The unmistakable forms of men stood between each neat line of vegetation. But these were indeed not men.

"They won't cross here," Tomas told them. "They'll make for the bridges. That's where we need to focus our attention."

David looked along the bank in both directions.

"Not all of our men are here," he said. "And the people of Belburn are unarmed."

"We move them back to the grove," Tomas suggested. He turned his attention to David.

"Take the western bridge with as many of our men as you can and hold it."

"What about me?" Emily asked.

"I would have you by my side," he said. "But I need you at the eastern bridge. Take the Erilian warriors with you and have them fire flaming arrows into the crops."

"We'll lose our harvest, Tomas," David called to him.

"It's either that or our village," he replied before pointing into the cornfield. "Look."

David moved his eyes across the river and into the plantation, where he could see a multitude of straw men standing inside the fields. There were hundreds of them.

"By the gods," David hissed as he moved away.

***

Emily raced away towards the cottage by the hill, where the Erilian women were dwelling.

Three of them were already in the meadow, ushering people away from the riverbank.

Frantically, the refugees from Belburn raced across the pastureland, juggling their belongings and herding their children towards the grove on the far side of the open ground.

"Arrows," she called as she drew closer to the women. "We need arrows."

"Akasati is already on it," Karlena called back.

"Then we need to keep the bridge," Emily instructed. "The straw men won't cross the water. The current is too strong."

The refugees continued moving away to the northern side of the grassed area, scaring cattle and sheep that were grazing peacefully by the trees.

Emily jogged to the bridge and stood at the edge, sword at the ready. Across the wide stream, she could see dozens of wide-brimmed hats at the edge of the field.

Karlena came to her side, her curved blade in her hand.

"The white witch is back," she said. "Isn't she?"

"It would appear so," Emily replied. "It started like this last time."

"Not like this," Sharek put in. "She didn't present us with this many. Her powers have grown."

"Perhaps," Emily said. "Or maybe she taps into the power of her sisters."

"Or maybe this is the work of the Maji," Rhydra suggested.

"No," Emily told her. "This is Sumaiyya. I heard a woman's voice singing."

"I told you I wasn't going mad," Rhydra said to the other two Erilians. "I heard it too."

"Nobody said you were going mad." Karlena smiled. "We said you were already so."

The straw men moved slowly, pushing their way through the cornstalks, making their way towards the far side of the bridge. The plants shook and trembled as the scarecrows toppled and crushed the stalks before crowding near the crossing.

Six armed men, husbands of the potentials, ran from the village and joined the women.

"Our wives told us to join with you," Simon called as they drew near.

"Where are your wives?" Emily asked him, placing her eyes back on the enemy across the way.

"The Seven gather in the meeting hall," he replied. "We were going to stand watch over them, but they told us we're needed in the fight. We need more men," he gasped as he glanced at the number of straw men moving through the cornfields to gather by the bridge.

"The bridge will be a channel," Emily said. "They can't all cross at once. We can drop them into the water during the fight."

"The water will soak into the straw?" asked one man.

"No," Simon replied. "Straw floats, Gilbert. But if we hack these bastards up and drop them piece by piece, the water will disperse them, and they won't be able to reform."

"Reform?" asked another.

"The straw men can gather their pieces back together," Karlena told him. "You don't want to give them that opportunity."

"Next time you go on an expedition to rescue people," another said, "can you please try to make more friends instead of enemies that can do shit like this?"

**

David gathered with ten other men. Amongst them were Oliver and Andris, who was once the servant of the Black Miss, Joanne.

"What are they waiting for?" Oliver called.

The straw men seemed to stare with their eyeless sockets towards the men waiting for them on the bridge. Their hessian faces grimaced. Their wooden claws stretched and flexed.

David wondered if the action was intimidation or a reaction of nervous anticipation on the scarecrows' part.

One of the straw men suddenly lurched forwards and bolted directly for the bald giant. Its boots flapped loudly against the stone surface of the bridge as it increased its speed.

David swung his blade upward in a long arc, sliding through the air with a loud whoosh.

The sword slid through the creature's chest, spilling straw and wood onto the stone surface. It peered down at the mess as its dry intestines dropped from beneath its tattered coat.

The giant brought the blade around in a horizontal slice, taking the head and its brimmed hat from the shoulders of the straw man.

The hessian head fell into the stream with a soft splash.

Still standing, the straw man's body thrashed out towards David with its sharp claws. The big man blocked the attack and used his boot to push the creature away.

It stumbled back, but regained its balance before lunging for the man again.

David thrust his sword into the straw man's chest and lifted it into the air. He directed the blade's tip over the side of the bridge and, with a flick of the wrist, dropped the creature into the water below.

He turned to face the gathering foes at the far end of the overpass.

As one, they began filing onto the crossing, speeding towards him.

The other men ran onto the bridge to support him.

"I'll take left, you take right," he said to Oliver. "The rest of you get whatever makes it past us.

Iron and wood collided. Straw and splinters dropped upon the ground.

One after another, the men cut the straw men apart and dropped their pieces into the rushing water. The chaff and timber drifted far downstream, churned and taken by the current and dispersing the portions upon the river bed or thinly along the shores.

The scarecrows continued their assault.

Relentless.

Unfeeling.

Fearless.

***

"Where are those arrows?" Tomas bellowed.

Lor stood by his side, fending the straw men back with blocks and parries.

"Don't fight them like men," Richard called from behind them. "They're not alive. They don't feel pain."

"Hack them to pieces," Tomas reminded the other as he removed an arm from one creature. It continued to reach for him with its remaining arm, scratching his chest plate deeply enough to leave a long score.

Tomas chopped with his sword, well into the shoulder of the scarecrow, lopping its other arm from its torso. Continuing to hack into the creature, he broke the straw man into a dozen or more pieces. Straw, wood and hessian sack pieces covered the surface of the bridge.

Lor stepped back as he witnessed several pieces of discarded scarecrows link together on the ground.

"What devilry is this?" he spat. "They reform."

"Where are those bloody arrows?" Tomas called again.

"I've sent a man," Richard replied as he slid his blade into a straw man that crawled along the ground. Its legs and one arm removed, but it was still intent on crossing the bridge.

Now, on the end of Richard's blade, it dangled precariously over the side of the bridge. The old man shook his sword to drop the creature to the water below them, but it gripped the blade with its sharp, wooden fingers.

It wasn't going anywhere.

Richard continued to shake the sword, hoping the straw man would dislodge from it.

Instead, the creature pulled itself along the blade towards the man.

Reaching out with its claws, it wrapped its hand around Richard's throat and squeezed.

Glaring into its eyeless face, the old man continued to push the sword as far away from himself as he could, attempting to force the scarecrow to let go.

It wouldn't.

Its long, slender arm kept a firm hold on his neck.

Richard realised that there was no victory to be had here. The creature had the upper hand. The only option he had was to release his sword and remove the creature's hand from his throat with his own.

Suddenly, a flaming arrow stuck into the straw man's shoulder. The flames took to it in an instant. Its torso filled with fire, causing it to fall away from the blade in pieces.

The claw continued to grip at Richard's neck, but with so little of the straw man left on the blade, the old man used one of his own hands to pry the creature's claws away.

Richard glanced around to see where the arrow had originated. There was nobody near to him with fire or archery equipment.

He moved his eyes along the river bank to the east. At a point half the distance between the bridge by the cottage near the hill and the crossing that he was upon, Akasati stood by one of the Belburn camp-fires with bow in hand.

"How could she make such a shot from that distance?" he breathed.

"You can thank her later, Richard," Tomas told him. "We have more straw men to fight."

***

Looking along the river, Akasati could see throngs of scarecrows emerging from deep within the neat rows of crops. Knowing that the people of the village relied on the vegetation for food and trade played heavily on her mind.

But there really was no other option.

If she tried to save the harvest, the people would tire and the straw men would prevail.

She lifted an arrow from her quiver and doused its tip in the flames of the fire by her feet.

Taking aim, long and high, she loosed the shaft into the field across the stream. It flew through the sky like a shooting star, arching far across the cornstalks.

Before it landed, she had fired off another five fiery arrows to different locations across the river.

Flames took hold of the dry leaves that had fallen on the ground at the feet of the cornstalks. It wasn't long before tall flames rose in the fields and started feeding on the crops.

With a heavy heart, she fired more arrows into the region.

Twenty-Two

"Mama." Alan buried his face into his mother's chest as she cradled him tightly. She was sitting in a deep chair with three other women and her two nieces nearby.

"It's all right," she lied, feeling as frightened as he did as the sounds of battle making their way from the river to their ears inside the cottage far to the north-western edge of the village.

Lucy hummed a soothing tune as she held Alice on her lap, and the small girl took to sticking her thumb into her mouth.

"I like your song better than hers," Catherine said.

"Who?" Sevrina, Andris' wife and Lor's sister asked.

"The lady," Catherine told her.

"I don't like her," Alice mumbled over her thumb.

"What lady, Catherine?" Becka said from another chair close by.

"The one that doesn't like Aunty Joanne," she replied.

"Is she still singing now?"

Catherine nodded.

"Do you know it?" Sevrina asked. "Could you sing it to us?"

The girl shook her head.

"It keeps changing," she told them. "And the words are funny. Alice is right, your song is better. Please sing it."

"I was just humming a tune," Lucy said. "There are no words."

"But it's nicer," Catherine said. "I don't like the lady's song."

Lucy started humming her tune. The young girls listened to it, trying to drown out the song in their heads. Even Alan moved his eyes from his mother to the fair-haired woman who held his cousin.

He closed his eyes as he listened to Lucy's voice. Slowly, he drifted to sleep as the din of battle continued outside.

***

Joanne led the six other women through the village to the river's edge behind her house. Across the stream, they could see the corn stalks moving back and forth wildly as a multitude of straw men made their way to the roads at the sides of the fields.

The Seven scanned the edge of the watercourse, where their own people fought bravely. But with limited numbers in Woodmyst, they would soon tire and the straw men would come.

The song of Sumaiyya echoed like a distant voice in their heads. To them, it was as if an itch that they couldn't scratch continuously aggravated them.

Tall tongues of fire stretched from the roof of the crops, but it had not caught quickly enough. The vegetation was green and struggled to burn, enabling the straw men to navigate around the flames.

Linking hands and focusing upon the fire in the fields, the Seven closed their eyes and acted as one.

"Breathe," Joanne said, her voice expressionless, even without pitch.

The flames in the middle of the cornfield erupted into giant fire-balls, expanding in all directions with fervency. Light and immense heat engulfed large patches of ground, so intense that they could feel it from across the river.

"Wind," she muttered.

The air above the cornfields swirled, building a strong breeze that pushed the flames wider and wider, burning further into the crops and destroying many scarecrows in one sweep.

"Fly."

The flames lifted into the air, forming spirals and twisters of orange and red light. Snaking this way and that, the thick threads of fire bent over the plantation, lighting all the crops from the river's edge to the far end of the valley ablaze.

"By the gods," David gasped as he watched the spectacle unfold. The behaviour of the fire reminded him of a creature from the deep, with its many arms reaching in different directions.

"They truly are powerful," Karlena muttered to Emily.

"I don't think she even knows what she is capable of," the other replied.

"Fall."

The spires of fire crashed to the surface with a loud sound that was like thunder or a million trees being felled at once. The flames expanded outwards, pushed by the force of the falling tendrils of light.

A great cloud of heat swept from the centre of the plantations in all directions. The Seven raised their hands as the wall of fire drew closer and closer. It hit an invisible barrier when it met the river's edge, reaching high into the sky.

"Keep fighting," Tomas barked. The others watched in awe as the fire dance before them.

Straw men, set ablaze, continued to run onto the bridge. Their wooden bones protruded through their clothing and hessian skin as the fire consumed them.

Tomas hacked through the blazing scarecrows with his blade, lopping limbs and ribs from the creatures before kicking their pieces back into the wall of fire on the other side of the bridge.

More straw men, not more than timber skeletons, ran upon the bridge. Their sharp claws stretched towards the men fighting on the bridges. Tongues of fire lapped along their scrawny arms and legs.

The creatures scratched and clawed frantically as swords tore them apart.

"Smother," said Joanne as the Seven lowered their arms.

The wall of fire withdrew, dragging any straw man remaining upon the bridges after it. The flames pulled away, all towards a central point over the plantations. The stupendous ball of heat enfolded upon itself, growing smaller and smaller, leaving ash and blackened earth in its wake.

The flames continued to shrink into themselves; the fireball retreating to a tiny spot of light above the valley.

It hung there, a bright intensity that was difficult to look at.

Many upon the bridges and those who gathered by the grove needed to shield their eyes from the brilliance.

Suddenly, with a resounding clap, it vanished into a ring of flames that spread across the sky. The circle of fire diminished before it reached the river and the night returned.

Thick clouds of smoke lingered in the air, swirling above the valley.

"Rain," Joanne muttered.

Instantly, a downpour fell from the sky over the valley and the village.

The Seven released their hands and toppled to the ground, their energy spent.

Tomas scanned the landscape carefully.

It was bleak.

Blackened, smoking ground extending away to the south as far as he could see. Where crops once stood, tall and green, now replaced by dead land. All their hard work or sowing and toiling washed away in the rain as ash.

The straw men had been defeated, and the village was safe for now.

But it was at a significant cost. Winter would be a tough one without wheat, oats, and corn.

"Tomas," a voice called from behind him. It was Lor. "You are being called."

He moved away from the bridge and made his way towards the village, making his way to the assembly hall.

"Tomas," a man called. "They need you at your home."

He nodded to the other and redirected his approach.

Crossing the grass to his door, he could see several men gathered inside his dwelling. It was unusual to have so many people in his house at one time, and he grew curious.

He raced onto the veranda and through the door.

"What is it?" he asked aloud.

"The Seven have fainted," a man informed him.

Tomas noticed they had placed the women into the cushioned chairs about the room, including Joanne. He raced to her side and dropped to his knees. Taking her hand in his, he felt her cold, clammy skin with his fingers.

"Thank you all for bringing them here, but I need everyone out," he commanded. "And someone, find the husbands of these women."

The men filed out silently, leaving Tomas in the room alone with the Seven. He reached over to a dark-haired woman who sat beside Joanne. Tricia, Simon's wife.

Taking her hand in his, he felt the same coldness in her flesh.

They were all wet through, soaked from the rain that teemed down outside.

He rose to his feet and raced to the fireplace to stoke the hearth back to life. After placing a log on top, he moved into the kitchen area and did the same with the stove.

Tomas then moved into the bedrooms and grabbed every blanket he could find and placed them in the middle of the floor in the living quarters.

Starting with his wife, Joanne, he removed her wet clothing, tossing the garments aside. She groaned as he handled her roughly, but he was acting in haste.

He grabbed a blanket and draped it over her, tucking it around her shoulders and body, covering her from neck to toe. Attempting to warm her, he rubbed her arms. Again, she groaned, as if protesting.

"Wake up," he whispered into her ear before kissing her forehead.

He moved to Tricia and unlaced her blouse.

Before long, he had three women covered in blankets. The room was heating rapidly, and he felt sweat trickling down his back as he hastily undressed another of the Seven.

Emily burst in through the door with six men following her into the house.

"What are you doing?" She glared at him.

"Help me," he called to them. "They're all cold and wet. We need to get them dry and warm."

"Go to your wives," Emily ordered the men, ushering them into the room. "And do as Tomas says."

It wasn't too long before blankets covered all the women. Both Emily and Tomas crouched beside Joanne, rubbing their hands against her covers to warm her body.

"Thirsty," she groaned finally.

Emily smiled as a tear rolled over her cheek.

"Of course, you are," Tomas replied. "I'll get you some water."

"Not too much," Emily told him as he moved to the kitchen.

He found a mug and took some water from a pot that sat on the bench. Returning to his wives, he handed to mug to Emily, who then rested the rim of the cup gently against her sister's lips.

"Take it slowly," she said.

Joanne didn't listen. After a sip, she burst into a coughing fit.

"Sorry," she whispered when she had regained composure.

"How do you feel?" Tomas asked her.

"Tired," she replied.

"Do you know what happened to you?" Emily queried.

"We used too much power," Joanne replied. She dug her hand out from beneath the blanket, causing it to fall away from her breasts as she wiped her eyes. "It drained us. How are the others?"

Tomas quickly put the cover back over her. "They're all here. But they haven't woken yet."

Joanne peered around to see the other six women seated around the room with their husbands by their sides.

She moved her eyes down to her belly and rubbed it with her hand, which was still beneath the blanket.

"What's wrong?" Emily asked, noticing her sister's change in temperament. "Is the child fine?"

Joanne nodded slowly.

"There is a presence there that lives," she replied. "The child is strong. I can feel it."

Tomas furrowed his brow, considering her words.

"Could the child be a factor in why your energy... drained?" he asked her.

"I think so," Joanne nodded. "Yes. I must have drawn too much from the others so that the child could keep what it needed. How is she?" Joanne looked over at Tricia sitting beside her. She had groaned as Simon spoke softly to her, rubbing her shoulders.

"She's coming around," Simon replied. "She'll be fine, Joanne. They all will. You did well out there tonight."

"I think I'll boil some water," Emily said. "There'll be a few cups of tea to make."

Tomas nodded as Emily got to her feet and crossed the room.

"Help her," Joanne said to him, looking deep into his eyes.

"I want to be by your side in case you need me again," he told her.

"I'll be fine," she assured him. She pulled him into her with her free hand and kissed him.

"Don't go anywhere," he told her. She smiled as he moved away.

She closed her eyes and saw fire. The insides of her eyelids burned.

Apart from the image of flames, which she thought would last for some time yet, her mind was calm.

Sumaiyya's song had been silenced.

***

Sitting on her bed, her legs crossed and her eyes wide open, confused by what had occurred.

Her straw dolls sat charred and smoking upon the floor. Destroyed by the auburn bitch and her six dogs.

They pose a genuine threat to the Coven of Mirikin; she thought.

They pose a threat to my son.

They pose a threat to me.

Sumaiyya ran her fingers through her long blonde hair and took a deep breath.

"Guard," she called.

The door opened, and a uniformed man stepped into the room. His eyes fell upon the smouldering dolls on the floor.

"Yes, Mistress?" he said.

"Clean this mess up," she commanded.

"Yes, Mistress." He stooped down and collected the dolls into his arms. There were too many to collect, and they fell from his grasp and back onto the floor.

"Get a box to put them in, you fool," she barked.

"Yes, Mistress," he replied, turning to leave the room.

"And be quick about it," she ordered.

He left the room quickly, closing the door behind him.

Sumaiyya gritted her teeth so hard she tasted blood. Her hands turned into tightly balled fists and her knuckles changed to a milky white.

She shook uncontrollably as energy formed in the pit of her stomach, building to her chest and rising in her throat.

She screamed a shrill cry of frustration that echoed throughout the entire ship.

"Mama," Takmel gasped, starting towards his cabin door.

Vonavo placed his massive hand across the boy's chest, preventing him from advancing.

"I don't think that would be wise," he said to the lad.

"She's upset," the boy replied. "I should go to her."

"When she is upset," the armoured giant started, "I've found the best place to be is as far from the White Mistress as you can be."

Twenty-Three

Amicia paused on the road that led into the valley, moving her eyes across the scorched earth that stretched away from her. Her lip quivered as she wondered what might have happened, particularly to a certain soldier to whom her heart belonged.

"My lady," a soldier said from beside her. "We cannot stop here. The horses can't hold the weight of the catapults on the steep gradient."

"What do you think happened here?" she asked him.

"I couldn't say, my lady," he replied. "But the far side of the river appears green and teeming with life."

She moved her eyes across the watercourse and saw the village with houses, people, and livestock. Her heart pounded excitedly.

"My lady," the soldier said. "We need to move on."

"Of course." She nodded and urged her horse forward.

Before long, they were upon the road crossing the plains with smouldering fields on either side of them. Puddles spread across the path here and there.

"I don't recall any rain last night," one soldier said to another behind her.

"That's because it didn't rain," the other soldier replied.

"It was induced," she told them. "A coven caused this."

"The Mirikin?" asked the soldier to her side.

"I don't think so," she said, covering her face with a cloth as the powerful stench of wet, steaming ash and cinders made its way to her nostrils.

***

"Who is this, now?" David asked, standing on the centre bridge with Tomas as they viewed the damage on the valley in the morning light.

"Get the soldier," Tomas called to some young men nearby. "Commander Brondt."

The men raced away towards the town centre.

"You think this is the Mistress he warned about?" David asked.

"I'm not sure," he replied. "But there is a sizable force travelling down from the mountain and onto the road."

David squinted, peering to the far end of the vale.

"What are those?" he asked, referring to the large carriages being drawn behind teams of horses.

"I don't know."

"I count seven," David said. "No, eight."

"Let's assume that they are weapons," Tomas said as he repositioned his sheath from his hip to his back so that the hilt of his sword stuck above his shoulder.

"What?" the big man looked at him. "Are you planning to face them?"

"We'll get our people on the shore here," he said. "A show of numbers. They don't know we're down on weapons. I'll go out there and demand their surrender with a threat of arrows or something."

"Sounds like a grand plan," David replied sarcastically.

"Your people will perish if you do, Tomas," a voice called from behind him.

The two men turned to see Jonathon Brondt approaching.

"Those things out there being driven by horses are catapults," he told them. "They have a long enough range to flatten your village from about half the distance of that valley there."

"Wonderful," the giant breathed.

"Let me go out to them," he said. "Perhaps I could persuade them to join with you."

"No," Tomas replied. "You're a traitor, so they'll probably kill you."

"If they do, you can prepare yourselves for battle before they have a chance to construct those weapons," Jonathon told him.

"You could still be lying to me," Tomas said. "If I let you go back to them, you could join with them."

"I understand your doubts," the soldier replied. "I truly do. But I had a chance to take up a sword and take out some of your people last night when you were engaged with those things. I even considered finding a sword so that I could join with you. But I honoured our agreement. I have not touched a blade, not even to cut my food, since our conversation. I am on your side, Tomas."

Tomas looked at the man for a long time before moving his eyes to the encroaching force. They were roughly a quarter of the distance across the vale, moving at a slow pace.

He took a deep breath as he peered at the leader of the multitude.

It was a woman dressed in simple clothing. This wasn't how he had pictured the Mistresses after engaging with both the white and green witches.

"Who is that before them?" he asked the soldier.

Jonathon looked towards the woman for a long time. Tears welled in his eyes as his hand covered his mouth.

"What's wrong?" David asked, his brow creased.

"It's her," he replied. "It's Amicia. She wears the clothes I bought for her. She has never worn them before."

Tomas felt a lump in his throat.

"Fetch a horse," he ordered the young men nearby.

One man ran towards the stable house, disappearing into the village.

"She would always wear that sickening pink garb," Jonathon told them. "Never, not even once, did she ever look upon those clothes. I saved for over a year and gave them to her as a gift. She told me I was a fool for buying them. She was one of the Mirikin and required to wear the attire of the coven. I thought she must have thrown them away, but look."

David put his hand on the man's shoulder.

"Women, huh?"

"She looks beautiful," Jonathon muttered as a young man led a horseback across the village by the reins.

"Sorry, Tomas," the young man said. "I didn't know if you wanted me to bother with a saddle or not. So, I only fitted the bridle."

"You did well," the other replied, taking the reins from the man. He then handed them to the soldier.

Jonathon looked at him questionably.

"Go to her," Tomas told him.

Jonathon took the reins, keeping his eyes on the other.

Tomas nodded, "Go on."

In one swift leap, Jonathon was astride the steed and racing along the road towards the approaching army. He was about halfway to them when Tomas noticed the woman race her horse forwards as well.

The two bolted across the valley towards each other at an incredible speed. The wind tossed the woman's long dark hair about wildly as she drew nearer to Jonathon.

Pulling up within arm's reach of each other, they both dropped to the road and fell into each other's embrace.

Even from the distance of the bridge, Tomas could tell that the two embraced with a kiss as they fell to the surface of the road.

"You're taking a risk," David told him, observing the two lovers reacquainting themselves.

"I don't think so," Tomas told him as he let a smile creep across his face.

***

Dust wafted through the air, collecting where two winds collided, turning into spiralling twisters that scattered loose shrubbery and silt across the sparse landscape before dissipating and falling back to the earth. The heat rising from the pale, sandy surface was intense, almost feeling like a wave that pushed with a tangible force behind it.

Blackbirds circled far above, riding the thermal winds that rose from the sand. They watched many men moving below with interest, waiting for them to drop one by one.

"Any man who lags," the Gold Mistress called, "will watch as I remove his intestines and feed them to the crows."

The foot soldiers of three armies, combined as one force, marched across the wasteland, urged onwards by the cruel words of the woman.

Flat, bleak ground surrounded them in all directions. Any trees offering shade seemed to be miles away to the north and south of them. Nothing that offered shelter was ahead to the east; only more flat land and towers of rock in the far distance.

Dark wisps of cloud formed on the horizon to the east. Gradually, as the day developed, the tiny puffs of vapour grew into a steady grey band that stretched across the landscape before them.

But that was where the clouds stayed.

The wind didn't send the dark band towards them to offer any reprieve from the burning orb in the sky. Instead, it remained above the horizon, lingering just beyond the stone towers.

By mid-morning, the sun glared down upon the men in their dark uniforms. Their packs and weapons weighed heavy and their armour even more so as they trudged onwards, churning sand and dust into small clouds that hung around their feet.

Sweat trickled down their backs, poured from their brows and dribbled off their chins.

"How long must we endure this heat?" the Jade Mistress asked the other two witches.

They rode slowly, surrounded by several guards upon horses, padding themselves with kerchiefs as they perspired in the heat.

"There is water beyond the spires," the woman in pearl told her, referring to the towers of stone far away on the horizon. "The land becomes green again where streams flow down from the mountains."

"Yes," Jade said. "But how long?"

"A day or two," Gold replied. "As long as these imbeciles don't slow us down." She turned in her saddle to face the multitude of men marching sluggishly behind the steeds. "Keep up, you dogs."

A sudden powerful hot gust blew the dust around them into the air.

The women squinted as they shielded their faces from the flying grit.

Within moments, the dust settled to the floor again.

The Gold Mistress dusted her garments with her hands.

"Disgusting place," she said. "Why didn't we go around and stick to the southern borders of the Core instead of attempting to cross it?"

"The Prime commanded it," Pearl informed her. "We will come out of these lands near the western region of the Forest of Khun and attack Woodmyst from the north."

"Have you been this way before?" Gold asked her, slapping her palms against her lap, making small dust clouds explode from the fabric.

"The Sovereign wanted me to be posted on the western slopes of the mountains before she moved me to Mallowhill."

"So, you spied out the land." Jade ran her cloth over the back of her neck.

"Of course, I did," she said.

"And what did you find there?" Gold queried as she turned to see how the troopers were managing. She slipped a little in her saddle as she noticed a few stumbling, exhausted and over-heated. "Move, you bastards."

"Nothing," Pearl replied. "Trees, rivers, snow, and that was all. There was not even one measly farmhouse anywhere between the mountain range to the borders of these forsaken lands. At least in Mallowhill I could find a half-decent man or two to pass the time with."

"Some of this lot came from there," Gold grunted, "and I wouldn't call them half-decent. They can't even walk on the ground in the daylight without tripping over themselves."

"You're letting the heat get to you," the Jade Mistress told her. "Calm down and have some water."

"I'm fine," she snapped, turning her attention to the marching soldiers. "Quicken your pace."

She swayed back and forth, round and round.

"We need to rest," Pearl told her.

"I'm fine, I said," she barked as her eyes spun in their sockets.

"Stop," the Pearl Mistress commanded. "We take rest."

"What do you think you are..." the woman in gold slurred before slipping from her steed's back, thudding hard against the ground.

"Stupid woman," the Jade Mistress snorted, dismounting from her horse. "Water, now."

A guard leapt from his charger and brought a canteen to the lady in jade.

"Mistress." He bowed, handing the vessel over.

She took it, cradling the Gold Mistress' head, and poured a small amount of water over the fallen woman's lips.

The woman in gold stirred.

"How did I...?"

"From now on," Jade told her, "when one of us tells you to calm down and have water, you do so."

"I'm fine," the woman in gold replied sluggishly.

"And that's why you're lying in the dust," Pearl told her. "We stay until you can climb back upon your steed. Agreed?"

The Gold Mistress blushed from embarrassment.

"Agreed," she said bashfully.

Twenty-Four

"These men have given their allegiance to me," Amicia told Tomas. "I have arranged with them to follow your orders and the catapults are my gift to you, no matter what fate you have in store for me."

They sat in the meeting hall, facing each other on two benches by the platform where the council members observed from their chairs. Tomas hadn't worried about placing the woman in chains. He didn't believe they would prove any worth considering she was a witch.

"You will lead them," Tomas said to Jonathon, who sat beside the Mistress.

The other nodded as he held the woman's hand, lacing his fingers with hers.

The Seven had gathered nearby, resting on some benches to the side of the room. Their husbands were standing behind them, still concerned for their wellbeing after the battle with the straw men. With Tomas questioning the Fuchsia Mistress, and Simon seated with the council, Emily had positioned herself behind Joanne, and Lucy behind Tricia.

The women still appeared weak, exhausted, and desperately needed rest. But with the arrival of the Mistress, they had all felt the need to sit in on the interrogation, wanting to know if one of the Mirikin could really turn from their cause.

Amicia moved her face to them, fear in her eyes as she sensed their power. The Seven glared towards her, trying to get a reading of her emotions and thoughts.

"I really mean no harm," she told them before turning her attention back to Tomas. "I'm here to help."

"We heard of your assault upon Oakbeach." Tomas felt the emotion rising in his voice. "We had friends there."

The woman's face winced as tears streamed down her face.

"I had no choice," she whimpered.

"Of course, you did," David said. "You chose to come to us now. You brought these impressive weapons with you. Why couldn't you have chosen this path before you killed my friends?"

She broke down, placing her face against Jonathon's chest. He wrapped his arms around her, shooting a disapproving look at the bald giant on the platform.

David shook his head and turned his palms towards the sky as he shrugged his shoulders.

What?

"Perhaps," Tomas began, scratching his chin as he considered his words, "the assault on Oakbeach was the turning point for you. Perhaps you have turned a new leaf and wish to fight alongside us. But you must understand why we may be hesitant towards simply accepting you into our fold.

"We have seen what the Mirikin are capable of. We have faced the Sovereign and defeated her and her prophets. The question we are asking ourselves is why we should treat you any differently to how we treated them?"

"I understand," she blubbered. "I have done some terrible things for the sake of the coven. But I believed that if I had not, then I too would lose my life. The White Mistress is not a forgiving woman, and to go against her means death. I am so afraid of her."

Tomas nodded, seeing the terror on Amicia's face.

"It is Sumaiyya Tarkin who is truly afraid," Simon announced. The assembly moved their eyes to him. Amicia's expression turned to one of confusion.

How could the White Mistress be afraid?

"She has been so since the downfall of Blackrock Haven," continued Simon. "She knows that the Seven wield a power that she cannot match. A power that vanquished the Green Mistress. She knows the strength that lives inside our Joanne, the Black Miss, and it frightens her.

"That is why she comes here. She sets her bitches to destroy everything around us, hoping to produce fear within us so that we feel useless, helpless, unable to stand against her.

"There was a darkness that fell over this village, causing my wife and the other women of the Seven to question their abilities. It forged a rift between you and Emily that you've only just remedied," he said to Tomas.

"Perhaps this woman, breaking away from the claws of the Mirikin, was the reason we regain some control," suggested the burly man. "Perhaps the Mirikin is broken."

"I have sensed a change," Amicia told them. "Something is different."

"Joanne," Richard called. He had been watching the Seven intently during the meeting. The auburn woman, now dressed in one of her sister's dresses, moved her eyes to the old man on the platform. "What does the Seven think of all this?"

"They have been weakened," she replied. "But not enough to stop them from advancing. It feels like..."

"An injured animal," Isabel Barnes, the White Miss, interjected. "Wounded, but more dangerous. Desperate and willing to do anything to survive."

Joanne nodded, as did the rest of The Seven, agreeing with the analogy.

"We can't hold you," Tomas told Amicia. "We can't keep you as our prisoner. There are a few in this village who I know that could stop you if you tried to act against us, and I will leave it up to them to decide your fate if that be the case.

"Until then, you are free to roam. But we will watch you. I am not setting a guard to accompany you. Just know that eyes will be upon you."

"I will earn your trust," she assured him. "I will prove my worth to you and your village. You can rely on me to serve you."

"We have no servants," Tomas told her. "We are all free here."

He stood to his feet, ending the meeting between himself and the Fuchsia Mistress.

"Now," he said to her, "if you don't mind, these men and I would like to get our wives home so they can rest."

She nodded, turning towards the Seven who were being helped to their feet by their spouses. As they moved away, she turned her face to Jonathan, who held her in his arms.

"What happened to them?"

"Woodmyst was attacked last night," he told her.

"By whom?"

"Creatures of straw and wood," Jonathon replied.

"The White Mistress." Amicia frowned. "Did she set the valley ablaze?"

"No." He shook his head. "Those girls did that. I have seen nothing like it before. They made the fire dance. It was both terrifying and beautiful."

Terrifying and beautiful, she thought. *Just like the Seven.*

"They *terrify* me," she admitted.

"Who?" asked Jonathon. "The Seven?"

"That man was right when he said that those women wield a power that the White Mistress cannot match. There is great energy in them. Especially the one with red hair. Something grows inside of her. Something formidable."

"You don't need to fear them, Amicia," he told her. "You are not a slave to the White Mistress any longer. They are good people here. Join with them. Help them. "

She nodded before placing her head against his chest.

"I'm so happy to be with you again," she said.

He smiled and kissed the top of her head.

"Me too."

***

Over five hundred men marched and rode from the west towards Oldcastle. They closed on the city slowly, intending to give the men upon the many watchtowers a chance to see them approach.

Ruttger rode at the head of the company with Courtney, his young lover, pressed against his back. She wrapped her arms around his waist, her head resting on his shoulder.

They moved closer to the outskirts of the city where some people lived in small houses with well-kept gardens that mainly grew things like lettuce, tomatoes, and carrots. Some people dwelling inside the huts had seen the approaching army and dashed to the city to hide behind the reach of the towers' arrows.

"Hold here," Ruttger called.

The men pulled to a stop and took rest. Many plonked themselves onto the ground to rest their legs after a long march. Others dismounted to stretch their muscles after hours of riding.

The old man dropped from his steed and lowered the young woman to the ground by putting his hands on her hips, lifting her from the horse's back.

"How do you feel?" he asked her.

"Very sore," she replied.

He smiled. "You've been riding in carriages for too long. You need to toughen up."

"You want my rump to be tough?" She grinned.

"Cheeky," Ruttger winked at her as a soldier stepped to his side.

"Riders approach," the man told him.

Ruttger looked towards the city where he saw a group of twenty men on horseback galloping towards them.

"That was fast," he said, dropping his sheath and sword to the ground. "Wait here and tell the men to remain at ease. We want to make friends, not enemies."

"Yes, Commander," the soldier replied before moving away.

"You wish for me to remain here also?" Courtney asked him.

"No." He shook his head. "I want you to hold my hand and stand by my side."

She took his hand in hers. "Lead the way."

Together, they walked towards the approaching riders, who slowed their approach as they drew near.

"Stand where you are," one rider called a short distance away from the old man. "Who are you and what is your business with Oldcastle?"

"I am Ruttger Harrow, Commander of the Lilac Mistress' ground forces," he began. "I am also the vanquisher of the Lilac Mistress and now command free men. We offer our help to Oldcastle."

"For what do we need help?" the man on horseback asked.

"Another Mistress is bringing her army from the north," Ruttger told him. "We need to evacuate your people before she arrives."

"Oldcastle can defend herself against one woman and a force of this size." The man waved his hand to Ruttger's troops.

"Have you ever faced a Mistress in battle?" the old man questioned.

"No." The rider laughed. "How hard could it be? You're an old man and you say you vanquished one."

"I used poison," Ruttger informed him. "An assassin's method. Sneaky. Cowardly. I admit and confess to that openly. If I, or any of my men, had attempted a front-on attack, we would be dead.

"I have only ever heard of one time when a Mistress was killed by an oncoming enemy. Only one. And the victor of that battle dwells in Woodmyst.

"If you won't heed our warning, we will carry on and offer our help to them."

The rider turned to his men and spoke with them, keeping his voice low so that neither Ruttger nor Courtney could hear what they said.

"You may go no closer to the city," the rider told him after some time. "You can rest here and set up camp if you wish. I need to take this news to my superior. If we require your help, a rider will return to let you know."

"Fair enough." Ruttger nodded.

The riders turned their steeds and hastily made their way back to the city as Ruttger and Courtney watched them ride away.

"Do you think they'll take you up on your offer?" she asked him.

"I don't know," he replied. "One thing is for certain. You will go to Woodmyst in either case. I don't want you here when the Scarlett Mistress arrives."

"I don't want to leave you," she argued. "My place is with you."

"Your place is to be free," he told her. "And that is as far away from danger as I can get you."

"Woodmyst is no safer than Oldcastle," she said. "You and I both know that."

He frowned, holding her against him.

"I don't want to lose you," Ruttger whispered into her ear as he embraced her tightly.

"Then I should stay with you, right by your side."

He knew he would not win the argument.

She was adamant, stubborn, and free.

He wanted nothing more than for her to be who she wanted to be, and now she was. It was not his place to tell her to be something or someone else.

As much as he didn't like the idea of her being near a battle, she had chosen to be by his side. He didn't want to be away from her ever again, either.

"Then you shall remain by my side," he told her before kissing her softly on the mouth.

"Black ships on the horizon," one of his men called.

Ruttger peered into the sea, scanning the horizon for any sign of approaching vessels.

"Where?" he called.

"To the west," the man called, pointing along the coastline. All five hundred men stood to their feet and stared at where the soldier gestured.

Sure enough, twenty ships with sails full of wind raced across the waves towards the east. Their course would lead them straight past the wharves of Oldcastle.

The inhabitants of the city did not know what they were in for.

Not only was there a Mistress encroaching from the north, but they were about to get hammered from the sea by cannon fire.

Ruttger noticed the white banners flying high upon the masts above the black sails of the vessels.

"Frigates of the White Mistress," he called. "Loyal bastards, every man on board."

"What do we do?" a soldier asked him.

"Nothing we can do," he replied. "Nothing."

"Those poor people." Courtney shook her head.

"May the gods protect them," a soldier said as they watched the ship approach.

The sound of bells pealing rang out from the city.

Twenty-Five

Ewan Cunningham, the dock manager, ran as fast as his old legs could carry him. The ringing of the temple bells chimed across the city, announcing danger.

"Something approaches," he called to the men on board the *Adelandria*.

"Twenty black frigates," Captain Jeremy Schoenbach returned. "I see five vessels departing from the other wharves nearby."

"Our only defence against approaching enemies from the sea," the old man replied. "We don't stand a chance."

"Cast off," Jeremy bellowed to his men.

"You're leaving?"

"I'm joining the fight," he answered.

"Permission to board, Captain," Ewan requested.

"You have family here," the captain reminded him.

"One last turn upon the waves," he pleaded. "I beg of you, Jeremy."

"It may be your last," he said, waving the dock manager up the gangplank.

"Thank you, Captain," he replied, hobbling up the bridge between the wharf and the main deck entry port.

"You man the wheel, Ewan," Jeremy told him. "I will be in the wheelhouse with you."

"Captain," Gustav Steinman, a tall, burly man called. "We are missing five men."

"Probably in a brothel," the captain chortled. "Stand on the Quarter Deck. I need your eyes and voice up top. We'll make do with what we have. Spare what men you can to Baldwyn and Jeff for cannon duty."

"Aye, sir," the other called before turning and pointing to his men. "You, you, you and you. Get below deck and report to Chief Palmer. You five, to Chief Hudon. The rest of you, get on the ropes. This ship should have been out there already."

The sails opened.

The gangplank retracted.

They tossed aside the mooring ropes as the massive vessel moved slowly away from the wharf.

Wind filled the giant canvas sheets, pushing the ship away from Oldcastle and into the open sea.

Steering towards the southwest, Ewan Cunningham grinned from ear to ear. He didn't care that he may head for certain death. He was on board a ship again. He was where he belonged.

"Prepare starboard cannons!" Jeremy called from a small platform beside the enclosed wheelhouse.

"Prepare starboard cannons," Gustav repeated, facing a trap door amid deck.

The two chiefs of the lower decks repeated the order. Fifteen men, seven on the lower, eight on the mid, scrambled to the right side of the ship and started frantically loading black powder and iron projectiles into the snout of twenty-four guns.

"Canons ready," a voice called from below.

"Canons ready, Captain," Gustav called from the quarterdeck.

Jeremy took a deep breath, feeling his heart race from the excitement. It had been some time since he felt such exhilaration.

The city's ships turned to face the enemy vessels head-on. They were much smaller than the *Adelandria* and posed no threat to such a formidable force. Still, their men showed a stoic character, willing to confront such odds to save their friends and families from impending doom.

The enemy was still a fair distance from the *Adelandria*. Jeremy seized the opportunity to get all guns on board loaded.

"Prepare port canons," he commanded.

Once again, the order echoed down the line.

The sight of smoke puffing from the sides of the vessels pierced the hearts of the men on deck. Splinters of wood and tongues of fire flew in all directions as the sound of cracking thunder reached their ears moments later.

The enemy had fired first, using their bow canons, striking one of the Oldcastle ships in the nose.

"Do we fire, Captain?" Gustave asked. "They are in range of our cannons."

"No," Jeremy replied. "We could hit friendly ships. We need to close the distance."

"Port cannons ready, Captain," the call came back from the quarter-deck.

Jeremy observed as they exchanged more cannon fire, more fire leapt into the air and more timber splintered and sprayed from the vessels. The smoke grew thicker with each blast, causing a cloud to form around the vessels.

Eventually, the flash of orange blasts and the noise of rapid explosions were the only sign that a battle was taking place.

"I hope the city is taking this opportunity to evacuate," Ewan muttered from behind the wheel.

"I'm sure they have that under control," Jeremy replied. "Take her out wide and keep our starboard side towards the smoke cloud. I want to get around behind them."

"Aye, Captain," the old man said.

"We're going to circle," the captain called to Gustav.

The other nodded. "Into the wind then?"

"Into the wind and around that cloud," he replied.

"Aye." Gustav turned to the deck crew. "Beam reaching, into the wind."

Leona held her hands over her ears as the ship rocked violently. Several loud blasts had erupted beside the cabin, shattering the window into tiny shards of glass that fell across the floor. Smoke poured into the room as she screamed in terror.

With nowhere to run or hide, she cowered beside the bed with a blanket over her head.

"Fire again," Admiral Isak Dzeiks bellowed. "I want these bastards on the bottom of the ocean."

The order ran down the line and the cannons roared a terrible cry, spitting more smoke into the air and biting deep into the ship beside the frigate.

Splinters of wood, iron, fire and flesh fell onto the deck beside the admiral as he peered through the thick cloud of smoke towards his enemy's vessel beside his.

They fired back, thrusting steel projectiles into his frigate. Again, the ship rocked violently as the sails ripped; the hull tore open and men fell to the sea.

"I need those cannons firing more quickly," Dzeiks hollered. "Rapid firing. Load the cannons faster and fire."

"You heard the admiral," Coster Yadley, the first officer, called. "Work harder you shits."

The *Adelandria* moved at a snail's pace as she headed into the wind. The men watched in silence as the hulls of two ships disappeared beneath the waves at the edge of the smoke cloud.

The rest of the vessels were deep inside, exchanging blast after blast.

Smoke and ship drifted towards the east, carried by the westerly wind, while the *Adelandria* allowed the cloud to pass by.

"Wait a moment longer," Jeremy called. "We'll let the smoke pass before turning back towards the shore. I want to be behind it when we open fire."

"Aye, Captain," Ewan replied.

"Aye, sir," Gustav called from the quarterdeck.

The thunderous explosions dwindled as the battle between the vessels from Oldcastle and the west ended.

Jeremy could only assume that the enemy scuttled the ships from the city. The *Adelandria* was the only hope left for the Oldcastle.

"Bring her around to starboard," Captain Schoenbach commanded.

Ewan turned the wheel.

The massive ship turned towards the shore, coming about behind the enemy vessels that were veiled behind the thick smoke.

The captain of the *Adelandria* silently prayed that they remained unseen.

"Starboard cannons ready to fire," he called.

"Starboard cannons ready," Gustav relayed.

The ship moved steadily, silently, straightening its approach to the shore and placing the cloud to their side.

"Fire," Jeremy commanded.

"Fire," hollered Gustav, not caring if the enemy heard.

The cannons erupted in sequence as the men raced from one gun to the next, triggering the flintlock mechanisms by pulling small levers attached to the sides of the weapons.

"Reload starboard and ready to fire port," the captain barked. "Tack hard to starboard, I want the port guns on them."

"Aye, Captain," the old man replied, spinning the wheel as hard to the right as he could.

Dzeiks was face down on the deck. A large chunk of wood stuck through his shoulder.

"Where did that come from?" he called.

"We can't see a thing, Admiral," Yardley replied. "The smoke is too thick."

"Fan out," the admiral ordered. "Get the ships apart from each other."

Leona lay on the floor, crumpled on her side.

Her face had torn open from above the right eye to her top lip, a large flap of skin folding over and touching the boards on the floor as blood pooled around her.

She couldn't move.

Her legs were twisted awkwardly beneath her.

She couldn't breathe.

Air refused to fill her lungs as she stared at the expanding red puddle before her.

All she could do was think of what it would have been like to be free.

The room exploded into splinters of wood, shards of glass, and slithers of iron as it became cannon fodder.

"We are sinking, Admiral," Coster Yardley, the First Officer called.

"Fire the aft canons," he ordered. "Keep firing until we can fire no more."

"Shouldn't we abandon ship?"

"Fire the fucking canons," the admiral hollered. "Fire! Fire! Fire!"

"Reload port canons and ready to fire starboard," Jeremy commanded. "Tack to port."

"They're spreading the fleet," Gustav informed his captain.

"How many do we see?"

"Numbers?" the man on the quarterdeck called to another high on the mainmast.

A moment of silence followed as the man above counted the enemy vessels in sight.

"Nine," the man yelled back. "They lost eleven."

"Let's finish them off," Jeremy called.

Water splashed about the ship as cannon fire erupted from within the cloud.

The *Adelandria* rocked slightly from an impact against her bow.

"We're hit," a crewman called from the front of the ship.

"How bad?" asked Gustav.

"We take water," the other replied.

"Captain," the man on the quarterdeck began.

"I heard," he replied. "We'll take as many of them before we go under. That bastard with the aft canons goes first."

"Get us out of this cloud," Dzeiks ordered. "And keep firing."

The cannons fired one after the other, pausing only to reload.

"Admiral," Yardley called. "What of the cabin girl. She is down below and the water rises."

"Fire the cannons," the other commanded. "Destroy the enemy. We can replace slave girls."

"Aye, sir," replied the First Officer.

The boards of the deck lifted, bowing in the centre as cannon fire found the black powder stored below deck.

Whitewash exploded all around as the blast lifted water, wood, and flesh into the air. Dzeiks felt immense heat surrounding him as his uniform melted from his body and his flesh bubbled like boiling water.

He saw nothing but blinding light as fire lapped his skin, peeling his eyelids open and melting the gelatinous orbs in their sockets.

Screaming a shrill cry as the heat tore through his cheeks, burning his hair and roasting his organs, he flailed wildly to avoid the flames.

Falling to through the deck as it disintegrated beneath him, he hit the large beams of the ship's skeleton.

Falling.

Falling.

Into the sea he sank, the saltwater stinging his body as there were no outer skin layers left to shield him from the pain. He screamed in agony, blowing bubbles into the ocean until his lungs emptied of oxygen.

Inhaling a deep breath, he took in water.

His body convulsed and tried to expunge the seawater before attempting to take in more air. Only water was available, filling his lungs even more.

Slowly, painfully, Admiral Isak Dzeiks sank farther and farther into the dark void of the sea.

"By the gods," Ewan Cunningham breathed as a great fireball appeared to his right.

"That's one," Jeremy called. "Eight more to go."

"Six," the man up the mast called back. "That blast took out two others besides. They both sink fast."

"Where is the next closest to us?" Gustav called.

The man pointed to out to the starboard bow.

Seeing the man's gesture, Ewan turned the wheel.

One by one, the enemy ships sank beneath the waves as the *Adelandria* found each one of them and filled their hulks with iron and fire.

Lower and lower, the great ship sank into the sea as she manoeuvred to intercept the black ships.

With the last of the White Mistress' vessels below the surface, Jeremy took one last look around the deck.

The *Adelandria* had been his home for almost two decades. Now, as he saw the water rising around her, he knew it was time to say goodbye.

"Lower the sails," he told Gustav, his voice shaking with sadness, "and call all the men onto the quarterdeck. It's time to abandon ship."

Twenty-Six

The crewmen of the *Adelandria* swam towards a rocky outcrop where white spray exploded on dark, smooth stone. The tide pushed the men violently against the hard surface as they attempted to find a grip, trying desperately to climb ashore.

Abrasions appeared on their skin as they clawed at the rocks, finding no hold. With their wounds stinging as saltwater washed over them, all experienced a feeling of frustration.

They had just won the battle against the fleet of black ships. Now they were losing another with nature, tossed around like toys on the sea.

Jeremy swore several times as his hands grasped at the stone when the rising water drew him nearer to the land, only to slip back to the liquid as the tide pulled away.

His hands were bloodied.

His sleeves shredded.

His arms grazed.

The tide pushed him towards the black rock again.

If I miss it this time, he thought, *I'll swim all the way back to the bloody wharf.*

Reaching with his arms, stretching out his fingers, Jeremy attempted to grip the stone. The tide pulled away again as white foam filled his view.

He missed and fell.

Something grabbed his wrist.

A hand.

He looked up to see a blurry shape of a man.

"Come on," the figure groaned as he pulled the captain from the water.

Jeremy crawled up the smooth surface until he found the level area that the man stood upon. He wiped his eyes, removing the burning salt liquid, and turned to the other.

"Thank you," he said. "I've more men in the water."

"We're getting them, Commander," the other replied.

"Jeremy," he said, as he lifted himself to his feet, blood dripping from his fingers.

"Ruttger," the other introduced himself. "We'll need to patch you and your men up. It looks as though most of you have sustained injuries."

"From the bloody rocks," Jeremy told him. "Not from the battle."

"If it's any consolation, you saved the city," Ruttger told him. "For now."

"For now?" the captain asked. "What do you mean, for now?"

"A Mistress makes her way to Oldcastle," the other informed him.

"The white witch comes here?"

"No," Ruttger answered, looking at him with interest. "The Scarlet Mistress. You know the White Mistress, though. I can hear it in your voice."

"I knew her father," Jeremy replied, turning to face the sea where the *Adelandria* slowly sank. Her bow was below the surface, and large white plumes of foam erupted through her windows and canon ports as she descended. "He was once my commander. Captain of that vessel."

"Was he on board?" Ruttger turned his face to the ship, a concerned expression on his face.

"No," the captain replied, looking to his side and noticing that his sword was missing from his side. "I inherited his command about ten years ago, after she murdered him. Her own father." Jeremy shook his head and sat down on the rocks, still exhausted from the swim and heartbroken at the scene before him. "And now I have let him down. I have destroyed his vessel, my home. I am so sorry, Captain."

Ruttger moved his eyes to the wounded man and lowered himself beside him.

"This is not your fault," the older man told him. "Your men are ashore, alive, and with you. Look."

Jeremy moved his eyes around where he saw a great number of men dressed similarly to Ruttger, attending to the crewmen of the *Adelandria*. All of them shared his pain as they watched in awe as their ship sat halfway out of the sea, the water touching the quarterdeck.

Sinking.

Sinking.

"She may have been your home until today," Ruttger said. "To-morrow, you will find a new one."

"I think we already know where our future lies," Jeremy told him. "When we have rested, we'll make for Woodmyst."

"Woodmyst?"

"You know it?" Jeremy asked as he kept his eyes on the *Adelandria*.

"Yes," Ruttger answered. "I intend to go there myself once I face the Scarlet Mistress. But you must know that the plan is for all the Mirikin to advance on Woodmyst."

The captain nodded.

"We thought she would plan this," he told the older man. "I have friends there. And family. I will stand with them at the end."

"Then let us bandage you up." Ruttger gestured for one of his men to approach. "You'll need water and some food before you leave."

"Thank you again," Jeremy said as the stern of the *Adelandria* disappeared beneath the waves, leaving a foaming, bubbling wake on the surface.

***

Bandaged, watered and fed, the crewmen of the *Adelandria* hobbled to the city with Ruttger and his men in tow. Some troops on horseback rode out to meet them, intent on preventing the army of darkly clad men from passing into Oldcastle.

"Halt," one of them called. "We have refused those men entry until told otherwise."

"Those men," Jeremy said, "bandaged our wounds and gave us their provisions while you bastards cowered away in your hovels. My men and I just lost our ship defending you lot. Now move aside. We need to speak to the magistrate."

"We can't let you do that," the soldier replied. "Besides, you would need an appointment to speak to any of the magistrates."

"My son works in the magistrate's office," Ewan Cunningham informed the other. "And not you or anyone in your army can stop me from seeing him."

The troops held their ground.

"How about this." Jeremy smiled. "Move out of my way, or I'll give the command for my men to cut you down. I'm not in the mood for this kind of treatment. There are five hundred behind me and seven of you. What do you say?"

"All right," the soldier replied, realising he had no chance of keeping the men out of the city. "But we will escort you."

"Fine," Jeremy agreed, waving the man on. "Lead the way."

The riders turned their steeds and slowly rode back the way they had come from. Jeremy limped behind them, with Ruttger and Courtney by his side.

"You should have had him with you when we first arrived," she whispered to her lover.

"Perhaps I should have channelled my sailor's manners," he said. "I think I'll be more forceful next time."

"It wouldn't suit you," she said, wrapping her arm around his. "Besides, I prefer you the way you are."

People scurried to the left and to the right, darting for doors and closing the window shutters as the army made its way through the streets of Oldcastle. After winding through several narrow avenues past small markets and villas, they entered a wide, straight road that stretched through the middle of the city from the south where the wharves lay to the centre of the metropolis where a great citadel stood.

The tall white walls of the structure seemed to shine like a beacon as the sun's reflected light reflected into the city. Large, golden domes rested upon the tops of the four spires that stood at each corner of the main building. Its roof, tiled with dark slate, met at an apex adorned with golden leaves and floral arrangements upon twisting vines that hemmed the gable.

"Beautiful," Courtney breathed as they made their way towards the structure. "I've seen nothing like it in my life."

"My son works in there," Ewan told her proudly.

The party stopped at the base of a great stone stair.

"You will need to venture the rest of the way on your own," the rider told them. "Your men can wait here with us."

"Baldwyn," Jeremy called.

"Sir," answered a well-built man with an advanced receding hairline.

"Whistle if you notice any trouble," the captain said, keeping his eye on the horsemen.

"Aye," Baldwyn replied.

Jeremy started up the stairs with Ewan, Ruttger, and Courtney.

It was a long climb for both the captain and the dock manager. Both had sustained several minor injuries on their knees and shins from their struggle with the rocks by the sea.

At the top of the stairs, with some relief to the injured men, the ground levelled out to a wide path with neat gardens of hedges and flowers bordering each side. A large arched door stood before them, open and inviting them into a huge open area inside the building.

Light streamed in through skylights and reflected through the room by large mirrors angled to distribute the rays throughout the interior. People bustled about with scrolls and parchments conducting work about which that none of the four visitors had a clue.

"State your business," a guard wearing a blue uniform with gold trimmings and buttons ordered as they entered the arch.

"We're here to speak to a magistrate," Ewan told him.

"Do you have an appointment?"

"Well..." The old man moved his eyes between the guard and those who had come with him. "No. But my son works for Magistrate Dennison."

"No appointment," the guard replied. "No seeing the magistrate."

"You know what?" Jeremy shook his head. "The pompous attitude of this city is giving me a migraine. Let's get your son and his family and go. Let Oldcastle burn to the ground."

The guard moved his eyes to the captain.

"Are you threatening Oldcastle?" he asked.

"I don't need to," Jeremy replied. "Your complacency will see you dead, and everyone in this wretched city will join you. All we need to do is simply leave."

"What do you mean?"

"We just destroyed an enemy fleet," Jeremy said loudly, attracting the attention of a growing crowd. "That was just the beginning. Now you have an army, here in your precious city, offering to help you against another approaching force. But you bastards are too busy writing on parchment to give a damn. Your city is about to be destroyed. Your people are about to die and you don't seem to care.

"Bugger this, Ewan. I lost my ship for this? I should have just kept sailing south instead of turning to face the enemy. I'm going to Woodmyst." He turned and headed back towards the arch.

"Wait," a burly man with a white beard called from farther inside the room.

"What?" The captain turned, tired and angry.

"That was your vessel we saw destroying the black ships?"

"What of it?"

"I would like to thank you." He reached his hand out to Jeremy. "I am Magistrate Dennison."

The captain took the other's hand half-heartedly and shook it.

Dennison acknowledged each of them by taking their hands as well. "Please," he said. "Come this way. I would like to speak to you."

He led them through the open area to a small alcove where a desk and some seating awaited. Gesturing, he offered them each a seat before taking his place behind his desk.

"Please tell me," he asked. "Why have you come here so soon after such a great battle?"

"We came here," Jeremy replied, "because not one of your people came to us to see if we needed help. Instead, this man and his troops aided us and their treatment from your people was far less hospitable than what we received."

"I apologise," Dennison said before turning to Ruttger. "And how do you fit into this tale?"

"My men, this lady and I were in the service of the Lilac Mistress who was on her way here to destroy your city."

"Has she arrived with you?" Dennison appeared agitated.

"I killed her and set my men free," the soldier replied. "We are here to aid you against the Scarlet Mistress who approaches from the north with seven hundred men."

"Seven hundred?" Dennison shook his head. "We don't have even a quarter of that in our combined forces."

"You lost your fighting ships out there," Jeremy told him. "You don't have those men anymore either."

"What do you suggest we do?" the magistrate asked. "We are not equipped to fight. We are a merchant city. We deal with trade. That's all we do."

"Evacuate the women and children to Woodmyst," Ewan told him. "Put swords in the hands of the men and fight."

"Fight?" the burly man questioned. "We'll perish."

"It appears you were right, Captain," Ewan said to Jeremy. "My people, the men in particular, are all cowardly bastards."

"Excuse me?" Dennison raised his eyebrows.

"If you don't mind, Magistrate Dennison," the old man said, lifting himself from his chair. "I'd like to take my son, Henry Cunningham, and leave. I have no intention of letting him die in a city full of people that are unwilling to stand up for themselves."

Jeremy stood with the dock manager, preparing to leave. Both Ruttger and Courtney were a little hesitant at first. After giving each other a quick glance, they too stood.

"Wait!" Magistrate Dennison held up his hands. "Please, sit. Please."

The four visitors returned to their chairs slowly.

"We'll evacuate the women and children," he said. "That I can assure you. But you are right about our attitude. No one, not even our soldiers, has ever seen battle. Not since the days of the Realm War. The best I can offer is that our armed forces will remain behind and any man who will volunteer to assist. But we don't force our people to take up arms. It just isn't the Oldcastle way."

"I don't care what you do," Jeremy replied before turning to Ruttger. "I'm leaving. My crewmen are free to decide whether they want to fight here or join me in Woodmyst. You decide what's best for you. But I urge you, young miss, to join me. I believe Woodmyst would be safer than staying here."

"I'll stay with Ruttger," Courtney replied.

"And I will stay to fight the Scarlet Mistress," the old soldier told the captain.

Magistrate Dennison stared at his desk, reflecting upon the words of those around him.

He looked to Ruttger and Courtney and frowned.

"I feel I need to prove my worth," he said. "So, I will join you here."

Twenty-Seven

Magistrate Dennison stood upon the northern platform of the citadel, overlooking the city and the farmlands beyond. The river snaked away to the north before turning slowly to the east.

He felt a sadness growing in his heart as hundreds of women and children, along with the elderly and feeble, made their way along the western bank of the wide stream, following the road to Woodmyst. Horses carrying riders, carriages transporting passengers, hand-carts laden with supplies and pedestrians moved as a crowd with Jeremy and his crewmen riding at the head of the mob.

Dennison would have liked the brave men to stay and help defend their city some more, but they had sacrificed so much already. Their ship, their home, the *Adelandria*, rested at the bottom of the Sea of Lunkhul. He couldn't dare approach them about assisting Oldcastle any more than they had.

Turning to Ruttger, standing beside him with Courtney, he measured the man with his eyes and wondered why he had remained behind.

"How old are you, Commander?"

"Why?" the other replied, slightly offended by the question. "Do you think me too old to battle?"

"No," Dennison replied defensively. "And yes. I just don't understand why you would want to remain here and battle when you have such a lovely young woman by your side. If I were in your position, I would have found some quiet place to wait this out and lived happily ever after."

Ruttger thought about that for a while, looking at Courtney with loving eyes.

"A pleasant dream to have, Magistrate," he said. "But if these Mistresses win, there will be no place to wait anything out and there most definitely won't be a *happily ever after*. They will reign with iron fists and terrible wrath."

He took Courtney's hand in his. "I admit I am old enough to be her father," he said to the other man, who was looking at the mismatched pair. "Perhaps even her grandfather. But we are in love, and I would do anything to assure that she is free. Right now, that means destroying the Scarlet Mistress. After, if we survive, it will mean moving on to Woodmyst."

"That's where the other Mistresses move to?" Dennison asked.

"There is such a hatred for that place that I can't explain," Ruttger told him. "The Lilac Mistress spoke the name of Woodmyst as if it were bile in her mouth.

"I have heard rumours that they have witches there who vanquished the Sovereign. I never heard the Lilac Mistress talk of such things herself, but the way she said the name of that place makes me believe it to be true. I only hope they are not bent on domination like the Mistresses."

"The Seven," Magistrate Dennison told him. "That's what we call them."

"You have seen them?" Courtney asked eagerly. "I've heard they are beautiful."

"Oh, yes." Dennison nodded. "I have seen them and they are lovely. All of them are good-hearted souls. Kind and simple, as all from Woodmyst are."

"But they are witches?" the girl queried. "There are no good witches."

"I never said they were good," the magistrate replied. "I said they were kind. There is a story that the Seven, as little girls, were hurt in ways unimaginable. Things that children should never be subjected to. How anyone could come away from such treatment and be considered good, I do not know.

"Perhaps that is why they have chosen to dwell in such a place as Woodmyst," he continued. "The population is small. It's far away from any other settlement, isolated and closed off."

"How did you see them if they live so privately?" she asked.

"They have come to Oldcastle from time to time," he replied. "I have never spoken to them directly, but they are hard to miss. It's as if you are drawn to them."

"And in that time," Ruttger put in, "you have never heard of the Mistresses?"

"We have heard of the white witch and the Sovereign," Dennison replied, moving his eyes to the evacuees moving along the riverbank in the distance. "The captain was correct about the people of this city. We are a fickle bunch. Commerce and philosophising are the two consuming passions of the people who dwell here. Stories of magic, demons, witches and dragons are simply tales that we tell our children.

"Even after the attack of the Night Demons upon Woodmyst," he continued, "so long ago now, we didn't want to believe. Some of us had gone to see the aftermath of that, offering help. The walls were fallen. The village was burned. They killed everyone but the children and one man. But we didn't want to believe.

"But now, you say a witch comes for us." Dennison quickly glanced at Ruttger. "After seeing the Seven, only for the brief moments that I have, I am willing to believe you, Commander. But I think it may be too late.

"We have never concerned ourselves with the things of conflict. Not since the Realm War. Therefore, our armed forces have dwindled through the years as we became complacent. You saw our navy fall. Five ships. That was all we had. Now they are but wrecks beneath the waves.

"You have seven hundred men, you say." He looked at the old soldier, who nodded a reply. "I think we would be lucky to have fifty."

"Then we will need to draw the Scarlet Mistress and her forces into the city and fight them in the streets," Ruttger told him. "We can force them into thin alleys and lanes where their numbers can't build up and overwhelm our men."

"Pick them off one by one?" the magistrate asked.

"We won't win on the open ground," the commander told him. "They will surround us and cut us down. Bringing them into the city is our best option, but it will also mean that the city itself could still fall."

"You mean the structures may be destroyed?"

"Exactly," Ruttger answered. "They will set torches to the homes and try to topple this building. Oldcastle may not be, once this is over."

Magistrate Dennison peered around the city from the platform. He could see many homes and stores stretching out in all directions from the citadel. Places where people traded and bartered for goods. Homes where families dwelt and children were born.

"This city is just a shell that we can rebuild," Dennison said. "Our people are Oldcastle. We will live on."

***

The evacuees from Oldcastle had trekked along the road for several hours and moved into the Lunkhul forest, where the trees formed a natural arch over the road. The sun streamed through the canopy, forming soft beams of light that dotted the road, moving this way and that as a gentle breeze passed through the leaves.

Jeremy, riding at the lead of the procession, tried to keep a watchful eye on their surroundings but was finding it difficult to keep alert. His body ached from bruising and he felt drained of all energy.

He was ready to set up camp and rest.

The people behind him were the only reason that he continued to press on. He knew there was an urgency to get them all to a place of safety.

Safety, he thought. *All the Mistresses are moving towards Woodmyst. How could anyone be truly safe there?*

It was late in the afternoon, and as they progressed farther into the woods, it became darker. The canopy of the trees blocked a great deal of light from the sun and the lower the glowing orb sank in the west, the duller their path grew.

The captain felt uneasy. The hairs on his neck prickled and paranoia swept over him. Was something watching them in the forest?

"Gustav," he said. "Keep watch to the left. Something doesn't feel right."

"I've noticed it also," Baldwyn informed them, riding to Jeremy's right. "The forest is silent."

Jeremy listened carefully, intently.

Jingling fasteners and chains on wagons, grinding wheels, clopping hooves, chorused along the road. Rustling leaves, driven by the wind and soft creaking of limbs moving, resounded through the dark woods.

But no birds sang.

The captain put a hand on the hilt of his sword. It was larger and heavier than his own, which now lay on the floor of the Sea of Lunkhul. The magistrate had given him permission to rearm himself and his men before attempting the journey to Woodmyst.

"What do we do?" Gustav asked quietly.

"We should keep moving," Jeremy told him. "We need to get these people to our friends. But I am weary and in need of rest."

"Might I suggest we set up camp soon?" Ewan Cunningham proposed. "We can work out a duty roster and keep watch through the night. Perhaps what we fear is only a creature that dwells in these woods and means us no ill. A fire would be enough to discourage it from venturing too close."

"Perhaps," Baldwyn acknowledged. "But we have seen creatures that would brave danger because they are driven be desperation or by the will of another."

"Still," Jeremy put in, "we could defend ourselves and these people better on the ground, gathered nearer to each other. At the moment, those at the rear are unprotected. It grows dark and they would be the first to be attacked."

"So, the next clearing, then?" Baldwyn asked, pointing to a place further into the woods to their right where a large patch of open ground sat by the river. "We should set up camp there."

"How far to Woodmyst?" Jeremy asked Ewan.

"I'm uncertain," the old man replied. "I could ask one of the others who travel with us."

"Please," the captain requested.

Ewan turned his horse and rode back along the path to the nearest group of people from Oldcastle. It wasn't long before he returned to Jeremy's side.

"We are less than halfway," he informed the captain. "One of the older women told me we won't make the journey tonight."

"Then we set up camp," Jeremy informed his men. "Pass the word down the line. We will need to leave the wagons and the carts on the road. The trees are too thick to get them through. Bring the horses and what supplies we might need for the night only. Leave the rest behind."

***

Seated around several campfires, the evacuees consisting mainly of women, children and the elderly ate a meal of bread, salted meat and potatoes that were heated directly in the coals of the hearth. They had erected tents nearby, and several old men and a few of the *Adelandria's* crewmen stood watch at the fringes of the clearing. Small fires had been lit at intervals around the outside of the campsite, hoping to deter any creatures that posed a threat to the refugees.

"Let's hope there are only animals in those woods," Ewan Cunningham said to Jeremy. A woman and two children, one adolescent boy and one little girl, sat by the old man's side. "I don't like our chances with only wounded sailors and old men guarding us."

"Have you eaten enough, Mercy?" Jeremy asked the little girl, offering some bread, turning the conversation to another topic.

She nodded, peering into the fire.

"How about you, Ronald?" he questioned the boy.

"Yes, thank you, Captain Schoenbach," the lad replied politely.

"You have very well-mannered children, Mrs Cunningham," Jeremy told the woman.

"Thank you, Captain," she replied. "Please call me Laila."

"I can't do that," he replied. "It would be disrespectful to your husband, especially in his absence."

She nodded, accepting his words as she wrapped her arms around her daughter.

"Well," the captain said, lifting himself to his feet, groaning all the way. His legs ached and his arms throbbed where the many cuts from his clambering over the stone by the sea had left their marks. "I need some rest. I'll see you all in the morning."

"Good night, Captain." Ewan waved.

"Night," Jeremy replied as he moved away from the hearth and towards a group of tents in the centre of the clearing.

They tethered the horses he and his crewmen rode to a fallen log next to his shelter. One steed nodded its head as he approached. He rubbed its long nose as it gave a soft nicker.

Without undressing, the captain crawled into his bedding and closed his eyes. He drifted to sleep almost instantly, falling into a deep slumber.

His eyes flickered open as he felt someone shaking him.

"Captain," a voice called. "Captain. We're under attack."

The sound of screaming and calling resounded from outside the tent.

Baldwyn leant over Jeremy, shaking him.

"Captain. Wake up!"

Jeremy sat upright, suddenly, too quickly. His head spun.

"How could you sleep so deeply through this din?" Baldwyn questioned.

"What's happening?"

"We're under attack," he informed the captain. "Some strange creatures have entered the camp."

Jeremy jumped to his feet and reached for the sword by his bedding.

"What are they?"

"It would be easier to see for yourself," Baldwyn replied as he moved outside the tent with his own blade in his hand.

Jeremy followed the other outside and saw people running to the left and to the right, pursued by large beings with leathery skin and hulking frames.

The beasts had scales and spikes across their shoulders and massive arms, brandishing axes and swords. Their faces reminded Jeremy of lizards with glaring red eyes and long, yellow teeth.

Several women and old men were fighting back by hitting the creatures with flaming lumps of wood they had pulled from the hearths.

The attackers responded by plunging blades deep into those who dared to defend themselves, hacking the bodies into pieces before stuffing their mouths full with portions of their victim's flesh.

The captain peered quickly around the camp, noting many dead women and children, as well as some remains that he could not define as either.

Finding the nearest invader, dashing towards the horses from across the clearing, Jeremy darted to meet the creature.

The beast raised its axe above its head before bringing it down towards the captain. Jeremy darted to the side, dodging the blow. The creature planted his axe's blade into the turf.

Stomping his foot onto the handle of the weapon, preventing the beast from retrieving the axe, Jeremy slid his sword deep into the creature's chest. A dark liquid oozed out slowly, reminding the captain of syrup.

Jeremy pulled his sword from the beast and hacked into its neck, causing the attacker's head to loll to the side, attached only by a thin slither of muscle.

It fell.

The captain glanced around again and noticed that he had lost many of his fellow travellers. Many civilians lay dead or dying on the grass.

Most of the creatures were engaged in battle with the crewmen of the *Adelandria* and several old men who were barely holding their own.

Some beasts had their noses buried in the flesh of the fallen and were feasting on both the lifeless and those who were still breathing their last breath.

"Help me get those bastards," Jeremy called to Baldwyn, who was pulling his blade from a scaly head that he had split in half.

Both men moved about the campsite, hacking their weapons into the bodies of the creatures that feasted upon the dead and injured.

The battle continued for some time until the creatures found their numbers were dwindling. Eventually, they were out-manned and were being overwhelmed by the campers.

Twenty beasts fled into the woods, escaping the angry blades of the men. Several of the women were so enraged during the attack that they wanted to pursue their attackers and finish them.

"Bring them back before they get themselves killed," Jeremy commanded his men.

Gustav hacked the legs from one beast, preventing it from running. He secured it to a tree with rope, wrapping its arms around the trunk behind it. Dark, oozing syrup dribbled from the stumps where its legs once were.

"Who are you?" he asked, holding a dagger to its throat.

It grimaced, flicking its thin, forked tongue out as it moved its deep, red eyes over the interrogator.

"Not talking?" Gustav said as he moved the blade to the creature's left eye. "Start talking or I remove more pieces from you."

"The Maji comes," it hissed. "You will all die."

Gustav dug his knife into the beast's eye and twisted, feeling the blade scrape against bone.

The prisoner groaned.

"A man would scream," Baldwyn said as they approached.

"This is no man," Ewan Cunningham told him, watching a few paces away.

"Your family, Ewan?" Jeremy asked.

"They are safe," he replied. "I have put them in my tent. The children don't need to see this."

"Talk," Gustav barked.

"We are Agrodien," it answered. "The Mistress promised us our lands returned."

"What lands?" Jeremy asked, crouching by Gustav.

"These lands." Black liquid slowly dribbled from its eye socket. "Stolen by your kind a thousand years ago."

"And where did you come from, Agrodien?" Gustav said, holding his blade where the creature could see it.

"The Core," it hissed, wincing. "They drive us from our home. I hurt."

"I promise to end you quickly if you answer me correctly," Jeremy informed it. "Understand?"

"Yes!"

"Where were you heading?"

"A village," it replied. "Through the forest."

It has to be speaking of Woodmyst, the captain thought.

"What was the plan?"

"Destroy it all. Feast on the dead."

"One last question," the captain said. "No one dwells in the Core."

"Agrodien dwell in the Core," it replied. "Gomatha dwell in the Core."

"The Gomatha drive you from your home?"

"No." The creature rocked its head. "I hurt."

"Who drives you from your home?" Jeremy asked.

"Dragon keepers."

The Night Demons of Woodmyst, Jeremy supposed.

The captain stood up.

"I hurt," the creature hissed. "You promised."

He swung his sword into the Agrodien's neck, planting the blade into the trunk of the tree.

The creature's head rolled to the ground, its stumps twitching slightly, momentarily.

Baldwyn stared at the Agrodien's head resting on the grass, dark syrup-like liquid spilling from its wounds. Its eye moved upon him as its tongue continued to flick in and out a few times before falling still over its long yellow teeth.

"I don't think I'm going to sleep ever again after that," he said.

Twenty-Eight

The gold, jade and pearl banners continued to wave proudly in the dry wind that swept across the vast landscape of the Core. The great stone spires stretched into the sky, rising from a steep ridge ahead of the troops, almost touching the swirling clouds above them. Like spinning water, a turning whirlpool, the dark vapours churned above the combined forces as they continued to march towards the east.

The Mistresses pushed the armies to the brink of exhaustion, and then beyond. The men dragged their feet through the dust, knowing that if they were to stop and rest, they would feel the wrath of a witch. It would be better to fall down dead than to be subjected to the punishment of a Mistress.

"Do you think the wind causes such a phenomenon?" the Jade Mistress queried.

"It's not mystical," the woman in gold answered, peering up at the clouds spinning in the night sky. "But it's not natural either. Something stirs in the sky."

A terrible cry echoed over the air, rasping and deep.

"HALT!" it called.

The women pulled their steeds to a stop. The men almost fell over as they stilled themselves. Momentum nearly made them crash into each other.

Peering to the top of the ridge, they saw a lone figure cloaked in black, its hood pulled over the head.

"Trespassers," the figure hollered, pointing to the witches, holding a curved horn in its other clawed hand. Even from their distance, the men of the armies could see the bulbous, yellow eyes beneath the dark hood, glaring at the three women on horseback.

"Do you see what travels with us?" the Gold Mistress said calmly, her voice amplified with her power, boasting authority. "We are many. You are one."

"One," the figure bellowed. Suddenly, over a hundred other cloaked figures stepped into view atop of the rocky ridge. Each brandished a curved sword. "Yes. One. Together."

"Shoot an arrow at this imbecile," the Pearl Mistress instructed her guard.

"We still outnumber you," the woman in gold informed the figure, reaching her hand towards him.

The guard fired the arrow, penetrating deep into the figure's shoulder. He fell to his knees as he moved his clawed hand to the shaft, plucking it from his flesh before tossing it to the ground.

The other cloaked warriors changed their stances, preparing to attack.

"Turn around," the cloaked figure called. "Leave."

"Fool," the Gold Mistress replied, tightening her hand into a ball.

The cloaked figure dropped to his knees again, wincing in pain. The others by his side looked to him and back to the witch, understanding what was transpiring.

The figure buckled over and tried to raise the horn to his lips, but the pain was too much to bear.

The Gold Mistress grimaced as she held her victim in place, forcing his internal organs to press against each other, breaking open the lining of intestines and tissues.

One of the other cloaked figures lifted the horn from the crippled creature and placed it to his mouth.

The trumpet call was loud and long.

It echoed through the air and across the ground before silence filled the night once again.

"And just what was the purpose of that?" Pearl asked.

A guttural roar boomed like thunder from inside the cloud. Another echoed it, then another.

The ground seemed to tremble from the sound.

All eyes moved to the swirling clouds, the source of the cries.

Something large, dark and fast appeared through the vapours and vanished again. It looked leathery, membranous, like the wing of a bat.

The roar resounded again, causing the men on the ground to either freeze in fear or to flee back the way they had come. Suddenly, the soldiers forgot their weariness, turning their thoughts to survival.

The Gold Mistress lowered her hand and released the cloaked figure from her grasp as she looked at the sky, her stomach tightening with fear.

"It cannot be," she gasped.

They had heard stories of such things but had never seen them. These were the things of tales told to children at bedtime. They weren't things to be feared, for they were never really true.

At least that was what her father had told her before she was taken from her home.

Now she wished she was back there, lying in her bed with her father, tucking her in and kissing her goodnight.

Now she wished to wake up from the terrible dream.

Bursting from the clouds, the beast spread its great wings and dived towards the armies, swooping low enough so that the wind behind it knocked the men off their feet.

It rose again into the sky to circle back around.

As it did so, another flying monster emerged, and another.

Three great dragons circled the armies of the Mistresses.

The woman in jade shook with fear as her eyes widened and her heart raced.

The beasts were terrifying.

The horn blew again; a signal to the monsters.

They shot into the sky, flying back towards the clouds.

"They give us a chance." The Pearl Mistress breathed a sigh of relief, intending to turn and leave.

But she was mistaken.

Turning, just before their noses touched the dark vapours, the dragons dived towards the ground. Their mouths opened wide and a high-pitched whistle built in their throats as they took in air.

Just before they reached the ground, they levelled out and exhaled.

Long and wide jets of fire swept over the fleeing men as one dragon moved over them. Another made a pass by those who stood their ground, petrified by the vision before them. The last smothered the three Mistresses and their steeds in bright orange and yellow flames.

The shrill screams of burning men rose into the night sky with the smoke that lifted from their burning flesh.

The three witches felt their skin melting and peeling away as the flames penetrated deep into muscle and bone.

The horn sounded again, recalling the great monsters to complete the task.

Jets of scorching fire swept over the Mistresses and their combined forces again, roasting the men, women and steeds into charred piles of ash.

The cloaked figures gathered around their injured commander.

His body was limp; his yellow eyes lifeless.

***

The scarlet army marched across the plain, massing to the north of Oldcastle. The witch moved along the line of men, riding a steed in a thick, red caparison. Her eyes fixed upon the city.

It was silent.

It was still.

The metropolis was eerily quiet, even at such an early hour.

The sun was nowhere near the horizon, but a dull light was striking the area where the land met the sky. The day approached.

The farmhouses they had torched on their way past were empty.

The only blood spilt belonged to some livestock gathered near the houses and a few stray dogs that had taken the opportunity to rummage through food stores in the absence of people.

Tempted to pass by the city, the Scarlet Mistress glared at the citadel. Something drew her attention to the giant white structure in the centre of Oldcastle.

Movement.

An orange dot of light appeared through an arch in the side of the building. A lone flame, held by someone.

Soon, another joined it on a platform that hemmed the upper level of the citadel.

Then another.

"The battle will be in the city," she told her commander, riding by her side. "They invite us in."

"Forgive me, but this would be a tactical error, Mistress," the man informed her. "This won't be like the smaller communities such as Brookenesse or Melamwen. This is a large city with many places for their men to hide. They have the advantage. It would be best to draw them onto the plains."

"How do you propose we do that?" she asked. "They have the sea to their back and I can see vessels moored at the port. They don't need to come to us. We need to go to them."

"Yes, Mistress." He bowed his head.

"We follow the river down and enter the city from the west," she instructed. "Send one hundred men to burn the ships as the rest of our forces push through the streets and burn everything in our wake. Perhaps we can force them onto the open ground to the east. The river will limit their choices for escape. Once there, we can slaughter them all."

"And the Lilac Mistress?" the commander asked. "We were to join with her here."

"Do you see her anywhere?"

"No, Mistress," he replied.

"I don't intend to wait," she told him. "I don't sense her approach, which could mean only one thing. We are on our own."

More torches appeared on the platform surrounding the citadel. Numbering well over one hundred, they signalled defiance from the city that she intended to quash.

"Prepare for battle," she said.

The commander raised a horn to his lips and blew.

The first line, men on horseback, pulled their swords from sheathes. A loud ringing resonated as steel glided against steel.

"Advance," the commander called.

The army marched forwards with the Scarlet Mistress at the lead. They made their way to the road that snaked beside the river's edge.

The Mistress instructed a large portion of her men on horseback to move around the edge of the city towards the docks. Their task was to prevent the people of Oldcastle from using the ships as an escape.

The woman in scarlet moved into the streets of the metropolis with her force behind her.

Empty, silent alleys and lanes confronted her.

She continued to edge further and further into Oldcastle. The buildings became larger, and the streets grew longer the more she progressed into the city.

Gardens with budding flowers, with closed petals during the dark hours, hemmed the tight roads. Lampposts with lanterns swinging in the breeze upon tiny iron arms, illuminated by bright flames, poked from the garden beds on long stems.

Her eyes moved to the citadel, where the torches continued to burn.

They were watching her.

She could feel it.

But those in the citadel weren't the only ones watching her.

Others surrounded her.

With all of her men inside Oldcastle, she wondered if she had made a mistake.

Perhaps her commander was right.

The sense of confinement, of being surrounded, overwhelmed her.

The buildings were too high and too close to see their enemy until they would be too close to do anything about it.

Had she made a tactical error?

She considered turning around and fleeing back to the open plains. At least they could lob some flaming arrows into some buildings and watch the city burn from a safe distance.

She turned and could see several buildings in flames behind her forces. Her instructions had been to burn the city as they advanced, cutting off any feasible route for their enemy to escape through.

It was too late to run.

Flames flared to the south of the city.

The ships burned.

The Scarlet Mistress had no choice but to push on.

Something told her this was exactly what her enemy had intended.

***

Ruttger watched from his hiding position, tucked deep in a dark alley with Courtney and several of his best men.

They waited and willed their enemy to spill into the narrow streets of the city, the old soldier holding his horn tightly in his grasp.

He watched as the Scarlet Mistress directed men into several side streets in search of his men and those from Oldcastle who had enough courage to stand against the tyrannical force.

She was still a long distance from his position, at the far end of the narrow road to which the alley opened on. But she drew closer and closer with each step that her steed took.

Continuing to direct men into the side streets, she edged forwards with her commander by her side.

The old soldier, hiding in the darkness, needed her to come closer. He needed her to bring her army inside the city a little further.

Only when they had passed a certain point, a particular lamppost, would they give the signal.

The Scarlet Mistress moved to the right, heading along a road that would lead her to the primary artery that moved along the centre of Oldcastle towards the citadel.

The timing had to be right.

Ruttger couldn't let her get to the wide avenue. She needed to be trapped in the narrow access ways with the rest of her men.

The last of her men were taking too long to reach the lamppost.

They were continuing to check the side streets, lighting several buildings aflame as they moved after their comrades.

A few started towards his position, moving past the side street that the Scarlet Mistress had ventured down and towards him.

He had no choice.

He raised the trumpet and blew a long, loud call.

Twenty-Nine

"What is that light in the distance, Vonavo?"

The boy leant against the railing on the upper deck as they sailed towards the southeast.

"Oldcastle burns," the being answered, towering over the boy in his armour.

Takmel frowned as he thought about the great city falling far away on the horizon. His mind pictured men, women, and children caught in the flames.

Children, he thought, *like me.*

"I don't understand why my mother wishes to destroy everyone," he said, peering towards the faint orange glow.

"To make way for your reign," the giant answered. "If there is none to oppose you, the rest will fear you."

"I don't want to reign," he said.

"I know," the deep voice of the monstrosity rumbled.

Takmel watched in silence, keeping his eyes towards Oldcastle as the sun's first rays appeared on the horizon. Vonavo stood faithfully by his side.

"Do you truly believe that my mother does all of this for me, Vonavo?"

The giant turned his face mask towards the boy and considered the question for a time before returning his gaze to the pillar of smoke rising from far away.

"No, Takmel," he replied. "I do not."

***

Seated on the veranda, his children playing on the grass and his wives by his side as the morning sun beamed its radiance across the land, Tomas watched as Amicia strode across the village towards him. She was coming from the many tents set up along the edge of the grove where her men had set up camp.

Each day, she had sought him out to discuss tactics.

Each day, he grew to like her less and less.

He inwardly admitted her concern for Woodmyst. She reminded him several times about the lack of defensive structures. Occasionally, she would request moving the women and children to a safe place, until he asked for a suggestion; *where should they go?* Only then did she concede the Mistresses would indeed find any survivors after the battle was over. Hence, there were no safe places to hide.

Now, as she made her way towards him, he wondered what subject she wished to discuss today.

"Good morning," she said chirpily.

The Warde family acknowledged her with a chorused reply.

"Good morning, Amicia."

"I must apologise, ladies," she said as she pulled up at the edge of the grass. "But I was wondering if I may have a word with Tomas."

"If it's tactics you wish to discuss," he replied. "I am really unsure of what is left to converse about. We've constructed the catapults and have placed ample ammunitions near to each one. There is stone, timber and iron stacked in neat piles. We have swords and arrows and men willing to fight."

"The Mistresses," she stated.

"We've covered that too, Amicia," he reminded her. "We have the Seven, who defeated the Sovereign. There are also the Erilian warriors and my wife, Emily. Not to mention yourself."

"Well." She pursed her lips. "We haven't discussed the Maji."

"Girls," he called his two daughters. They both looked at him and smiled. The sight of Catherine's missing teeth made him grin. "Go and play on the grass behind the house. I'll be there to watch you in a moment."

"Yes, Papa," Catherine said, taking Alice's hand in hers and leading her younger sister away.

"I'll watch them," Lucy told him and Emily as she followed the two sisters around the house.

Tomas waited until the girls were out of listening distance.

"We won't be killing children," he told the woman standing before him.

"He is a danger," she argued. "The prophecy claims he is Heir of Darkness."

"Prophecy!" Tomas almost spat the word out of his mouth. "Some words that a witch made up to give your kind a purpose. The prophecy is false."

"And what if it isn't?" she asked. "What if he grows to be something terrible, something dangerous?"

"Then we'll deal with that when it happens," he replied. "The boy is the son of one of my friends. If anything, he needs to be rescued from his mother, not punished for what she does."

"So..." She shook her head. "You'll accept him into your fold? He's to become one of you? What if he sneaks around at night and slits every single one of your throats? What about your daughters?"

"Don't talk to me about the safety of my daughters." Tomas stood up. His anger caused his heart to feel as if it were about to explode through his ribs.

"Tomas," Joanne whispered. "She is only concerned. We all are."

"And I am not?" he said. "I remember what you said the Sovereign and her prophets did to you. And to you," he looked at the woman standing on the grass. "They molested you. Forced themselves upon you. Manipulated your minds by making you take power from others the way they took it from you.

"I will not let such a thing happen to my girls," he continued. "I would die for them. And I would kill every Mistress and bastard soldier they have enslaved if they ever try to take them from me. But I will not murder a child just because of some words that say he will become some evil overlord. That would make me no better than any of the witches that you were once like."

He stepped off the porch and made his way towards the edge of the house.

"Tomas," Emily called. "Where are you going?"

"To my girls," he replied as he disappeared around the corner of their dwelling.

"I'm sorry, Amicia," Joanne said. "I understand your opinion regarding this matter, but Tomas and any of the men that ventured with him to Blackrock Haven could harm no child, especially after what they saw there."

"His decision could bring ruin to us all," she said.

"Come," Emily told her. She poured a cup of steaming liquid from a teapot resting upon a small table between her seat and where Tomas had been. "Sit with us. Have some tea."

The woman accepted and sat in Tomas's chair.

"Thank you," she replied as she took the cup in both hands.

"I must say," Emily stated, "that I agree with him. The boy is only ten, and we could teach him to turn from such darkness."

"Not if it is inherited," Amicia suggested.

"If you're talking about Sumaiyya," Emily replied, "she was the daughter of a good man and woman. I only ever knew her father, but he spoke fondly of his departed wife.

"Sumaiyya's evil wasn't inherited. It was learned. She was taken from her family at around the age of what the boy is now.

"And even while *she* may be evil now," she continued. "His father was not. Ivo Hamond was a brave and stoic man, like most in this village. The Maji, if that is his title, has more in his favour of being good than he does of being evil."

"I can't help but to hear the words of the prophecy repeat over and over in my head," Amicia confessed. "Perhaps it is because it was engraved into me from the time I became the Fuchsia Miss."

"Did this prophecy say that the child would be from the womb of the White Mistress?" Joanne asked.

"No," she replied. "It said that the Maji would be the first and only child of any Mirikin."

"I am with child," Joanne told her.

"I have heard," Amicia said. "This is good news."

"It is." She smiled. "I was the first of my coven, the Seven. They have all been trying for so long and I have only realised just recently that it was I that was keeping them from bearing children of their own."

"I don't understand." Amicia furrowed her brow.

Behind her, Emily wore a confused look as she listened to her sister.

"I am the prime of the Seven," she informed them. "I did not intend to be so, but I am. I am the most powerful of them. I can channel them. I am, by all regards, their leader."

"I think Sumaiyya Tarkin is, and always has been, your prime. Even before the death of the Green Mistress. The Sovereign used fear to establish herself. Sumaiyya used her abilities.

"She could also accomplish something that the Sovereign was not," Joanne continued. "She gave birth. This alone may have been enough to break a cycle within the Mirikin. Have you tried for a child with Jonathon?"

"No," she replied. "Not exactly. I don't see how…"

"I met with the Seven in the evening before last," Joanne told the other two women. "We met by the young oak in the ruins of the Great Hall. There were seven of us. But I felt nine lives in our circle.

"One of them was the one I carry inside of me. The other…"

"Another of the Seven is with child?" Emily asked.

"I believe so." Joanne nodded. "But I do not know which one. What I am trying to say is that I broke something that I, as the prime, held over the others of my coven. Perhaps when we vanquish the White Mistress, the hold over the Mirikin will break also.

"The Maji is the son of the White Mistress," she continued, looking to Amicia. "I don't believe he is inherently evil. Anything he is, if it lines up with this prophecy, is because she taught it to him, or she uses her power to influence him. We destroy the White Mistress, we free the Maji."

Amicia looked over towards the blackened fields to the south as she absorbed Joanne's words.

"You may be right," she admitted. "But what if you're not? He is a child now, but children grow. If you take him in, he may grow like a worm that bores into crops, destroying it from the inside over time. He may not even know what he's doing, just following his nature, like a worm. Please heed my words and prepare yourselves for such a time if it arises."

***

Tomas sat on the bank of the river, watching the water flow by. He gave thought to Amicia's words as he observed some geese splashing in the reeds by the edge of the stream.

There was no way that he was going to slit a young boy's throat, no matter what he was capable of. He had seen enough tiny bodies left to burn because of a tyrant's expansion ten years earlier. Now there was another that made her way towards his homeland.

He would not lower himself to her standards and destroy the lives of innocent people, particularly that of a little boy.

Catherine moved to his side and snuggled against him. She peered up to his face and saw tears clinging to his eyelids.

He placed his broad arm around her and pulled her towards him tightly.

"Don't leave us, Papa," she said suddenly.

"Why would...?" He looked at her, confused by her words. "I'm not going anywhere."

"Yes, you are," she told him.

"Your mama and I had a disagreement," he told her, "but we've worked it all out. I won't leave you ever again. I love you too much."

"That's why you will leave," she told him, and a tear ran over her cheek. "Because you love us. But if you leave, you won't come back, Papa. I don't want you to go."

"All right," he replied. "I'll stay right here with you."

She shook her head. "No, you won't."

She buried her head in his chest and cried.

He still wasn't sure what she meant, so he wrapped his arm around her tighter and kissed the crown of her auburn head.

A horn trumpeted from the tower to the western edge of the community.

Tomas turned his head to see what the concern was, but he couldn't see past the houses of the village.

"Come," he said to Catherine, lifting himself to his feet. "Let's get you back to the house."

He looked over to Lucy, who was already moving towards the dwelling with Alice on her hip.

He led his elder daughter by the hand back to the veranda where Emily, Joanne and Amicia were waiting. They were standing on the platform, peering towards the western tower.

"There are people approaching," Emily told him.

"I want you all to wait here," he told them. "Stay inside until I return."

"I'll get your sword," said Emily as she darted inside.

"Girls," he said to his daughters, who were both craning their necks to see who was coming through the woods. "Inside."

His daughters moved away reluctantly as Emily emerged with his sword in her hands.

"I should come with you," she said.

"I need you to stay with the girls," he told her. "Catherine said something a little strange a moment ago."

"Perhaps I should come," Joanne offered.

"I need to know you are all going to stay here," he told his three wives before looking at Amicia. "That includes you."

They nodded.

He waited until they were all behind the closed door of the dwelling before turning to cross the village.

Passing by the meeting hall, he met up with Oliver, who was running the other way.

"It's Jeremy," he called. "I'm going to get the Erilian girls. He brings others with him."

"Jeremy?" Tomas quizzed as he turned to watch the other run across the field.

Continuing towards the tower, Tomas moved his eyes over the scene before him.

Several men rode into view. Behind them, many people walked slowly out of the woods and upon the open ground. Many amongst them appeared to be injured.

"Tomas?" a familiar voice called.

"Jeremy," he replied, running towards a man who was lowering himself from a steed. The two men embraced briefly.

"You look older," the captain said to the other, a slight grin on his face.

"As do you, my friend." Tomas smiled, glancing towards the people travelling with the crewmen. "What's with your companions?"

"They're from Oldcastle," Jeremy informed him. "Their city is due to be attacked by the Scarlet Mistress. We attempted to get here in one piece, but some strange creatures in the woods ambushed us.

"As you can see, we suffered some great losses." The captain pointed to some carts moving onto the grass, laden with bodies."

"How many?" Tomas questioned.

"Nearly four hundred," Jeremy replied.

"Four hundred!" he breathed as he watched more people leading more carts onto the open ground, laden with their dead. "Survivors?"

"Even fewer," the captain answered.

"Jeremy," a woman called from behind Tomas. He turned to see Karlena bolting from the village towards the captain of the *Adelandria*.

She practically leapt into his arms and slammed her lips against his.

"I missed you," she said.

"I missed you more," he replied before kissing her again.

Thirty

"We can't save the city," Magistrate Dennison called over the roar of the fire that streamed through the surrounding buildings. "She has only twenty men left standing with her and they're trapped. We should leave while we still have a chance."

"I need to see she is dead," Ruttger told him. Many of his men laid in the streets beside the bodies of their enemy. With only fifty men remaining, most were soldiers and only a few men of Oldcastle, he contemplated running to save Courtney from a terrible fate. But he needed to witness the demise of the Scarlet Mistress.

"We can't wait here," the magistrate said. "We'll be burned to death. The wind pushes the fire north. We must leave."

The old soldier held onto his lover's hand, peering into her eyes.

"I'll be with you whatever you decide," she told him.

"I need to," he said to her.

"I know," she replied, gripping his hand tightly, fear creeping over the both of them.

The flames parted before them as the woman in red waved her hands this way and that, making a path for herself and her guards to pass through. Her eyes, filled with hate, bore down upon Ruttger and his men who stood upon the primary avenue of Oldcastle.

"Arrows," the commander of the Lilac forces hollered as he raised his sword and pulled Courtney behind him. His men quickly loaded their bows, collected from the dead during the battle.

"You have put up a good fight, old warrior," the Scarlett Mistress called. "But you won't survive this."

269

With that, she waved her hand in a sweeping motion, causing the flames to twist into a spiral that stretched towards Ruttger and his men.

"Loose," he called.

The projectiles streaked through the air, through the tendril of fire, and into the men around the Scarlet Mistress. Her guards fell to the ground, writhing in pain or dead as long shafts poked from their flesh.

The woman stepped forward, stumbling as she approached her foes.

Her control of the flames lost, causing the passage she had made to close behind her and her spiral to vanish into the air.

Moving her gaze to her chest, she saw a rod sticking from her left breast. Her fingers touched the shaft where it met her flesh. Pulling her hand away, she saw crimson blood trickling across her palm.

She dropped to her knees and glowered at Ruttger as she made shallow, raspy breaths.

"This isn't the end, warrior," she grunted, blood spilling over her lips. "The Maji will come."

Ruttger walked to her and plunged his sword into her neck.

"It's over for you," he snarled before retrieving his blade.

She fell onto the street.

The battle was over.

The old soldier turned to the magistrate.

"Now, we can leave," he said, grabbing Courtney's hand and moving towards the direction of the citadel, away from the approaching flames.

***

They placed wood and kindling on the charred surface of the devastated cornfields. David guided the operation, instructing many men to gather all the timber from the lumber mill and still more to cut into the woods.

By late afternoon, they constructed a long pyre between the western and centre bridges. They placed the bodies of the fallen refugees on the heap as all the people of Woodmyst and their visitors gathered along the riverbank near the town to pay their respects to those across the way.

The council and several elderly people from Oldcastle gathered by the pyre, flaming torches in their hands. Richard stepped to the southern river bank, near the pile of timber, so he could address the gathering crowd on the opposite side of the stream.

"Our hearts are with the people of Oldcastle," he cried out. "They have lost many. Friends and family.

"We have much in common with Oldcastle," the old man continued. "We have a longstanding friendship with her people. We have many of the same customs. We believe in the same gods.

"I don't know the words to speak, nor do I have any that would bring comfort. What I have is an offering from the heart. My people and yours will be one people. United, not only as friends, but family. I extend this offer to all gathered tonight.

"Our home is your home," he said as he moved his gaze over soldiers, children, women, and witches alike. "We welcome you here, as we send these who sleep into what comes next.

"Pray your prayers. Offer your blessings. Let Gwendra release her hold on them. May Grolle lead them on their way."

The councilmen and the elderly gathered by the pyre lowered their torches to the kindling. The flames caught immediately, spreading across the base of the woodpile and snaking through the timber towards the bodies lying on top.

Tomas, positioned about halfway along the pyre, looked to his left where David stood. The bald man peered into the fire, silently mouthing words of prayer as flames lapped the dead. Not truly understanding how someone could believe in unseen entities, Tomas' mind moved towards imagining the last moments that these people experienced before falling victim to their fate.

Agrodien, Jeremy had said. Tomas had heard the word spoken as a child in stories his father told him. He recalled tales of brave men who battled against the terrible Agrodien, driving them away from the lands of men and into the dark lands to the north, beyond the mountains. He believed them to be nothing more than fables of adventure and excitement.

"Agrodien. Gomatha. The Mirikin. The Maji," he whispered, scowling at the fire. He would have encountered none of them if it were not for one. "The Sovereign," he spat.

In his mind, the Sovereign was responsible for everything that had happened. Even after her death, she was still having a significant influence upon the transpirations of all people.

Villages were being destroyed. Men, women and children murdered. Innocence stolen, and death crept over the lands.

It was the White Mistress at the helm of it all. Of that, Tomas knew. But if Yasmeen Svoboda, the Green Mistress, hadn't sent her prophets to steal young Sumaiyya Tarkin from her family, or any of the other members of the Mirikin, none of this would be happening.

If only someone had slaughtered her earlier.

If only someone had slit her throat before she realised what power she possessed.

The Maji will be the Heir of Darkness. You could stop him before he recognises his potential.

"No," Tomas said aloud, silencing the argumentative voice in his head.

David shot the man a quick glance.

Are you all right?

Tomas nodded, assuring his friend that he was fine.

Flames swept over the deceased from Oldcastle as the gathering across the flowing stream paid their respects in their own ways.

Emily moved her eyes to Catherine and Alice by her side. Alice watched the pyre in silence while her older sister wept bitterly.

Pulling the young girl to her tightly, Emily kissed her daughter's head and stroked her auburn hair.

"You cry for them?" Emily asked her.

"Yes," she replied. "And no. I also cry for Papa."

"Why Papa?" her mother questioned.

Catherine shook her head. She didn't want to say.

"You can tell me," Emily urged her. "Why do you cry for Papa? Is it because you think he will leave us?"

"He told you?" The girl looked up to her mother.

Emily nodded. "Of course. I'm your mama. He tells me everything and I tell him everything."

Wiping her eyes, Catherine returned her gaze to the pyre across the river. "He will leave," she said. "And he won't be able to come back to us."

"Why not?" Emily asked.

The girl shrugged.

"He won't leave us," said Emily, frowning as tears welled in her eyes. "Not again. Never again."

Catherine bit her tongue and pursed her lips as she continued to cry.

**

Several hours later, a gathering met in the meeting hall. The canvas walls lowered so the meeting could proceed without drawing unnecessary attention.

"We need to consider guarding the northern and western edges of the village," Lor said to the others.

They sat in a rough circle upon benches and chairs that they moved into place for the meeting. Besides the council members, their wives and the Seven, others attended the meeting to offer their opinions regarding preparations for the White Mistress' impending assault.

The Erilian warriors regrouped with the crewmen of the *Adelandria*. Karlena pressed to Jeremy's side as they listened to Lor's words.

"If the Agrodien return while we are focused on the white witch approaching from the south, they will take the village right from underneath us," he continued.

"We can concentrate our force on the south," Jonathon suggested. Amicia sat by his side, clasping his hand. Her nerves were on edge concerning the White Mistress and he could feel it in her grasp. "I will position our men on the southern bank with the catapults. If her forces make it past the barrage of rock iron, wood and arrows, then we will fight hand to hand. We won't let them pass by us. You could then concentrate your men on the woods and grove in case of an attack from the rear," he finished.

"You have six hundred men," Jeremy reminded him. "She meets with two other Mistresses to the south and will combine forces there. How many will that give her?"

"Close to three thousand," Amicia replied with a frown. "They will outnumber us."

Eyes lowered to the ground as hearts sank.

Tomas and David scanned the group, not believing what they were seeing.

"How could you lack confidence now?" David asked, turning to the crew of the *Adelandria*. "Do you not remember what we have faced together in the snow all those years ago? We liberated slaves and slew an entire town full of enemy soldiers. We emptied two outposts of their guards and destroyed the indestructible straw men of that bitch in white.

"And you, Richard!" He turned to the old man seated nearby. "You killed a dragon. A bloody dragon. All on your own.

"Look." He pointed beyond the village to the east, towards the rows of tents. "We have an army. If one man can slaughter a dragon, if a handful of us can kill the garrisons of the Sovereign, imagine what we would be capable of with what we have here.

"An army. The Seven. A Mistress. The sons of Woodmyst." He looked at each one of them in the circle. "That woman doesn't stand a chance."

"Well said." Tomas leaned past Lucy and Martha, sitting to his left to slap his hand on his friend's back. He then turned his attention to the others. "I won't have such a down look upon any of your faces." He stood. "Our people look to us. If they see fear in you, what hope do they have? We may as well spill each other's blood here and get it over and done with before the white witch makes her way over those mountains.

"We will win," he told them. "If you don't agree with me, take a horse and leave. I don't need any of you getting in my way with your cowardice. Fight or piss off."

David smiled wryly as Tomas resumed his seat.

"David and Tomas are right," Ewan Cunningham put in. He sat with the crewmen, listening to the discussion. "I don't think any of us are unwilling to fight. But complacency and doubt will set in if we lose faith in ourselves.

"I see doubt here in your faces and I find this perplexing, considering the tales I have heard of Woodmyst and the dragons, as well as the stories the crew told me of your trek to the north. Are you letting her darkness take hold again?

"I'm old and weary," he continued. "But I'm not dead yet. So, I only have one question to ask concerning what is to come. Where do you want me?"

"It's getting late," Richard informed them. "We have much to prepare tomorrow. We will place men on the north and west of the village. I will lead them myself."

Becka looked at him with a concerned expression. "Richard," she begged. "I don't want you to fight."

"Like Ewan, I am old," he told her. "But I'm not dead. I need you to keep inside with the wives and children of the councilmen. What sort of husband would I be if I hid with the women?"

She shook her head at him.

"Don't concern yourself," he told her. "With luck, the fighting will take place in the fields. Perhaps nothing will approach from the trees and I will end up being bored before the end."

She pressed her lips together tightly, clearly upset that he hadn't discussed this with her in private before the meeting.

"I'll join you," Lor volunteered. "We will need the others to protect the Seven."

"Do you intend to take us into the battle?" Sarah Fitzwillyam, the Lilac Miss, asked Tomas.

"No," he replied. "Depending upon what Joanne does, I intend to keep you on this side of the river."

"After seeing what you were capable of the other night with the firestorm," Simon put in, "there really isn't a need to take you across the water."

"I don't know if we could do that again," Joanne informed them. "That exhausted us and was only for a fleeting moment. This is a battle. We may need to be more cautious and try to keep our strength."

Tomas reached past Emily and took her hand. "We have faith in you." He looked to each of the other women of the Seven. "All of you." He got up. "We should get some rest," he said.

"Richard is right. It is late and we have much to do tomorrow."

Thirty-One

Fifty men on horseback tore along the road to Woodmyst. Courtney wrapped her arms tightly around Ruttger's waist as they galloped through the forest.

Far behind them, beyond their view, thick plumes of smoke wafted from Oldcastle and into the sky.

The riders entered the forest at full pace, driving their horses hard. Ruttger intended to be in Woodmyst before morning to offer his assistance to the village in their fight against the remaining Mistresses.

Exhausted and ready to collapse, the men fought the need to take a rest, knowing that time was running out. The only one who questioned the need to move in such haste was the magistrate.

"Forgive me, Commander," Dennison began. "But why the desperate flight to Woodmyst?"

"You saw what happened to your city?" the old warrior asked him.

"I did," he replied.

"That has happened to every other city, port and farmhouse from the Western Sea to Oldcastle," Ruttger informed the other. "I have no doubt that the same has happened along the shores of the Eastern Sea. The only place left for free men is Woodmyst."

"That doesn't mean there is safe refuge there," the magistrate argued.

"No," the old man retorted. "We don't go to Woodmyst to seek refuge. We go to help defend her."

"With so few men?"

"Where else would we go?" Courtney asked him. "Where else could we go? We should be with them. Even if it means our end. At least we will die free."

Ruttger put his hand on hers.

Good answer, he thought.

The dark road before them was barely visible. It was merely by the will of the horses that they continued to ride so quickly. The steeds could see the path where the men could not and sprinted persistently through the black night.

"Your people are there too," she continued. "You couldn't leave them, nor could you lead them to another place.

"There is nowhere that you could go that the Mistresses won't find you. Better to die facing your enemy than to feel a blade in your back," she finished.

"Fair enough." Dennison frowned. "But for your information, I had no intention of running away."

Ruttger sighed. "Knowing what the Mistresses are capable of," he told the magistrate, "no man amongst us would blame you if you tried to run. Believe me when I say that all of us have considered it at some time since the death of the lilac witch."

"But there is nowhere to hide."

"Exactly," the old warrior answered.

Magistrate Dennison shook his head.

What will become of this world in the aftermath of the Mistresses? Dennison thought. *Will we be able to rebuild and continue, or will we need to start all over again? And what if the Mistresses are victorious? Will they destroy all free people? Will they murder everyone? Or will they be enslaved?*

Dennison understood that regardless of whether they won or lost, the outcome of this conflict was going to be a restart for all people.

***

The fleet anchored off the shore of Dweagan, except for the vessel that carried the White Mistress and her son. She held his hand as they disembarked the ship and strode along the long jetty to where both the Lavender and Violet Mistresses awaited her.

The two women lowered their heads, bowing before their prime and the Maji. Their men, lined in rows and columns behind them, rested on one knee with their faces pointed to the ground.

"Mistress," both women said as she drew near to them.

"See to my men," Sumaiyya commanded. "They approach by long-boats and land upon the beaches to the south. I want them fed, pleasured and rested before sunrise."

"Pleasured?" the woman in violet asked.

"You left some females alive in your taking of this city?"

"Of course," the woman replied. "There are almost two thousand prisoners, all of whom are girls. But most are not much older than your son."

"And?" The White Mistress raised her eyebrows.

Takmel glanced at Vonavo, following close behind. The boy's eyes told the other the conversation alarmed him.

Vonavo gave a slight gesture with his fingers for the lad to turn around and place his attention on the Mistresses. Takmel complied, but didn't like what he was hearing from the three women.

"We just thought they may be too young," the Lavender Mistress informed their prime.

"Do you know how old I was when the prophets first had their way with me?" Sumaiyya asked them. "Nine years old. Why should we treat any of the females of this city any differently? The Sovereign established the way of the Mirikin. It is up to us to enforce it.

"Now, get your men to gather the girls and offer them to my men and give them a place to spend the night. Then find suitable accommodation for me and my son. Something regal."

"We have many dwellings to choose from," the Lavender Mistress replied. "We slaughtered all the boys, men, and elderly. Only the younger women and the girls remain. Every dwelling is empty. Your men and ours will have roofs over their heads tonight and beds to sleep in."

"We have also chosen suitable accommodation for you, Mistress," said the woman in violet. "A mansion sitting at the top of the hill to the east overlooking the city is yours. We believe it belonged to the magistrate of Dweagan."

Sumaiyya, still holding onto Takmel's hand, moved into the city, tailed closely by Vonavo and several guards.

"Did you have much opposition?" she asked the other two.

"Not really, Mistress," Violet answered. "Some rag-tag bands of resistance attempted to fight us in the alleys but we outnumbered them."

"And the bodies?" Sumaiyya questioned. "I do not want to be sleeping near carcases."

"Piled to the south of the city and burned," the Violet Mistress informed the other.

"Good," the woman in white replied.

They continued into the city that appeared silent and still. Their footfalls echoed from the walls of the emptied buildings and their voices reverberated along the streets.

The boy gave his mind to the plight of the captured girls. His heart pounded quickly in his chest as he tried to think of a way to change his mother's mind.

"How long shall we claim this city for before we move on to Woodmyst, Mistress?" Lavender asked.

"We move out at first light," she replied.

"This doesn't give us long to meet your requests regarding your men," Lavender pointed out.

"Then you had better get busy," Sumaiyya told her.

"Mother?" Takmel spoke up.

"Yes, my love," she replied, devoting her attention to him.

"I don't want the girls touched," he said with authority in his voice.

"What?" She stared at him with a quizzical look.

"I want them all," he told her. "For me."

"You're too young to..." she replied.

"This one," he interrupted, pointing to the violet women, "told you they were not much older than me. Would I be correct in saying there are some younger as well?" he asked the Violet Mistress.

She smiled. "Cute boy."

"I am the Maji." He glared at her. "You mock me?"

She flashed her eyes between the White Mistress and the woman in lavender.

"Answer my question or I'll pull your intestines out through your mouth," he said, trying to sound convincing.

"Yes," she replied. Her voice was shaking as fear gripped her. "There are some as young as six."

He moved his eyes to his mother, maintaining an expression of anger. "I want all the girls that are fifteen or younger placed under my care," he commanded. "They will be mine to do as I will with them."

Sumaiyya stared at her son, surprised. She had never heard him speak in such a manner.

"Forgive me, Maji," the woman in lavender said, bowing her head. "But if you take that many from us, we won't have enough to please your mother's forces."

"They are *my* forces," he corrected her. "The White Mistress has simply been my caretaker until I was ready to take control. I am starting now with building my own slave force. I want the females. They will come in useful and provide me with many heirs. Give them to me."

"Do you wish to stop the advance on Woodmyst also?" his mother asked.

His mind raced. She was probing him, testing to see if he was truly behaving as she believed the prophecy foretold.

"Warfare is your expertise, Mother," he replied. "I have no wish to control these men yet. But the men of the fleet will damage, or possibly kill, the females. What use is that to me when I can provide them with sons and daughters, children of power?

"Take your Woodmyst if that pleases you," he told her. "But giving me the girls will pleasure me. I demand that they be given to me."

"And if I refuse?" she asked. He sensed some trepidation in her voice.

"Do you wish to discover what I am capable of?" He locked eyes with her, letting go of her hand.

"Takmel!" Tears welled in her eyes. "I'm your mother."

"And I'm the Maji," he answered. He felt a great energy building in his stomach and burning in his chest. He reached his hand towards the Violet Mistress and made a fist.

Her body crumpled to the ground, inwards and upon itself. Her head burst open and grey matter spilt onto the street. Her intestines sprouted from her stomach and flung onto the road with copious amounts of blood splashing onto the cobblestones.

Both remaining Mistresses jumped backwards. Sumaiyya let out a sharp yelp.

The action was so fast, instant.

It even surprised Takmel at how quickly he could squish the woman. He felt horrible for doing it, but he was glad to be rid of the witch.

"Takmel!" his mother shrieked. The men nearby stood suddenly, staring at the mess that was once a Mistress.

Lavender breathed in sharp gasps as her stomach rose to her throat.

"What did you do?" she huffed. "What did you do? What did you do?"

"Silence, woman," Takmel barked. "Give me the females, or you will be next."

She bowed, her body convulsing.

The boy moved his eyes to his mother.

"You tell the men that they can use their hands for pleasure," he hissed. "All the women will be mine. None, not one, will be touched.

"That," he said, pointing to the pile of flesh and blood, "was just a fraction of what I am capable of. You do not know my full abilities.

"Don't trifle with me, Mother." He stepped towards her. "Your purpose is to serve me. Not the other way around."

Tears streamed down her face. She no longer recognised the boy before her. She bowed her head, submitting to him. "Maji," she sobbed.

**

"Your performance was truly remarkable," Vonavo told him.

The boy stood on a balcony in the mansion, looking over the city to the sea beyond where the many ships anchored.

"I truly didn't know that I was capable of such a thing," he informed the giant.

"Are you feeling all right?"

"My heart still races," Takmel replied. "I was frightened."

"You looked in control." Vonavo moved to his side. "Your mother fears you. Why didn't you command her to abandon the attack on Woodmyst?"

"I feared she would discover I was pretending," he answered. "If I told her to turn the forces around, she would have known that all I wanted the girls for was to save them from what the men would have done to them."

"What do you intend to do with the females?" Vonavo queried. "Will you breed with them all?"

"No," the boy said. "I intend to free them. But she could never know this."

"For that to happen, Takmel, she will need to perish. I know you don't wish to hear this, but it is the truth. She will oppose you if you dare try to set them free."

"I know," replied the lad. "There won't be any redemption for my mother. I sensed it a long time ago. She has become the White Mistress. Sumaiyya Tarkin died in the lair of the Yasmeen Svoboda when she was still a child."

"She loves you," the armoured monstrosity told him.

"My mother loves me," the boy corrected him. "That tiny part of her appeared briefly today. It was unexpected."

"Do you love her, Takmel?"

"Yes. Of course, I do. But she's determined to see the world burn and I can't let that happen, Vonavo."

Thirty-Two

Daybreak approached.

A deep crimson line expanded across the sky, extinguishing the stars one by one. A chill wind swept up from the seaside, over the city, chilling the boy's skin as he stood upon the stairs that led to the mansion's door.

Vonavo stood loyally by his side, constantly watching over the lad and keeping others at bay when they approached.

Standing at attention before him, the men of the Violet Mistress waited for instruction from the Maji. He had called them together to give them his personal instructions before his mother overrode them.

"You are all to remain here in Dweagan," he commanded. "Your orders are to watch over my property. Not one of you is to touch them, leer at them, or consider them as toys of pleasure.

"If any of you harm them or interfere with them in any way," he continued. "I will deal with you personally. You witnessed what I did to your Mistress. Imagine what I could do to you.

"The females are mine. I would have you care for them like daughters or sisters. Anything more, and you will feel my wrath.

"Commander," he called to a uniformed man standing before the men.

"Yes, Maji," the officer replied.

Sumaiyya appeared behind her son, moving through the open door of the mansion as she lifted her hood over her head. She wore a surprised expression as she moved her eyes across the assembled forces standing on the lawn in front of the house.

"Remove the females from their shackles and place them in the best dwellings in the city," Takmel ordered. "Keep them fed. Allow them access to the stores and give them what they desire. Clothing, linen, whatever they want. Be sure that your men keep them safe. I remind you; no hand is to be laid upon them."

"As you command, Maji." The commander bowed.

The commander faced his men and ordered them to march. Their footfalls were loud as they stepped across the loose gravel that lay on the road before the manor.

Sumaiyya moved to her son, watching the men disappear before placing her attention upon him.

"What are you doing?" she asked. "We need those men at Wood-myst."

"I need them here more," he replied, turning to enter the building.

"You can't just release my men for your own desires," she told him.

"Your men?" He glared at his mother before correcting her. "*My* men. *Mine.* I gave them an order. They will follow it. They know *me* as their master. Not *you.*"

"Takmel," she retorted. "I need them to help me destroy the women that killed the Sovereign."

"You will make do with what you have," he told her as he moved to the door.

She gripped his arm.

He turned to look at her sharply, maintaining his composure.

Vonavo stepped forward to intervene, but Takmel held up a hand that instructed him to stay where he was.

"You forget your place, White Mistress," he said calmly. "You may have given birth to me. But you were nothing more than a mere vessel.

"I am the Maji. I am the Heir of Darkness. I am the Ruler of all. What are you, but one of my servants? Release your hold or this will be your end."

She let him go. Her hands shook and her chin quivered.

"Now," he said. "Prepare yourself to journey north. If you wish to take Woodmyst so much, you will need to get there first."

The boy disappeared into the house, with Vonavo trailing behind. Sumaiyya stepped in his way.

"You were about to strike me," she scowled at the giant. "Do you forget what hold I have over you?"

"You instructed me to protect the Maji," he reminded her. "You threatened him, Mistress. I was merely fulfilling my duty. Now, if you'll excuse me, I should be by the Maji's side."

She continued to glare at the monstrosity, stepping aside to allow him to pass.

"Thank you, Mistress."

***

The procession made for the mountains to the north of Dweagan. They trekked along the foothills of the towering range towards the east, making their way towards the pass that would take them over the alps.

The Lavender Mistress constantly turned in her saddle, peering back to the armoured giant who rode a specially built wagon with six wheels.

"What is it that sparks your interest?" the woman in white asked her as they both led the forces on.

"That monster that travels with your son," she replied. "Who is he?"

"Vonavo is my servant," Sumaiyya replied. "He protects my son and is loyal to his duty."

A little too loyal, she thought, remembering he will come between her and her son.

"You let your son ride with him?"

"My son," the White Mistress started, "will do whatever he wishes. He is the Maji."

Lavender watched the woman in white for some time. She first noticed how young Sumaiyya was, how strikingly beautiful she appeared. But underneath it all, she noticed fear.

The woman in lavender considered that if the White Mistress was afraid, then perhaps she should be afraid as well.

"He scares you?"

Sumaiyya shot a glance at the other. *Be careful.*

"I apologise, Mistress." Lavender lowered her head.

"My son," she replied. "The Maji is proving to be stronger than I had expected. I thought he would support my actions, but he proves he has an agenda of his own. I only wish I knew what it was."

"Does he work with us or against us?" asked the Lavender Mistress.

"I'm uncertain," Sumaiyya replied. "Perhaps neither. Perhaps he works for himself."

***

The horn on the western tower blew. The men gathered on the edge of the village with swords in their hands. The sound of thundering hoofbeats resonated through the woods towards the gathering.

One by one, the horsemen filed upon the grassed area between the edge of the forest and the township. They filed as best as they could along the tree line, dropping their weapons to the ground.

"Who are you?" Tomas called.

"I am Magistrate Dennison from Oldcastle," one man called. "These men were under the command of the Lilac Mistress."

"And where is she?" asked the other suspiciously.

"She is dead," replied another man, much older, with a young woman seated behind him on his steed. "I killed her."

"Your name?"

"Ruttger Harrow," he answered. "Commander of the Lilac Mistress' forces."

"You don't seem to have too many with you," David hollered.

"Most lie in the streets of Oldcastle," Ruttger told them. "They burn with the men of the Scarlett Mistress."

"And she?" Tomas questioned.

"She is dead," the old soldier replied.

"What do you think, Tomas?" Simon asked quietly.

"I think we should give them the benefit of the doubt," he replied. "We let them stay. Give them some food and a place to rest their heads. They look exhausted."

"The woman?" David gestured by nodding towards the old man and the young lady.

"I'll speak to him," Tomas replied. "Perhaps that is his daughter. If so, he would not want to be far from her."

"Lower your weapons," David called to the men of Woodmyst.

They sheathed swords as the men relaxed their stance.

Tomas approached the new arrivals.

"Dismount and reclaim your weapons," he instructed. "Enemies of the Mistresses are welcome here."

"Thank you," Dennison said as he lowered himself from his horse. "I assume you are the Chief of Woodmyst."

"We have not had a Chief since the days of the Night Demons," he replied. "But I guess you can consider me a leader amongst my people. My name is Tomas Warde."

The two men shook hands.

"It appears you have quite a number of refugees here," the magistrate observed.

"We have people from Belburn," Tomas replied. "The Fuchsia Mistress' forces from Newholt and several people from your city also. There is plenty of space on the ground, but we are low on shelter, I'm afraid."

"We could fix the meeting hall for our visitors," Joanne said, approaching with the other six women of her coven.

Courtney slunk behind Ruttger, and his men tensed as the women drew nearer. The old soldier tightened his hand around the hilt of his sword as his eyes locked on Joanne.

She dressed in her black garments with her hood over her head. The resemblance of the clothing worn by the Mistresses was remarkable. So much so that they thought she might be one.

Tomas instantly placed his own hand upon his sword, ready to fight. Several men behind Tomas saw the quiet exchange and pulled their swords, alarming the rest of the men of Woodmyst, who brandished their weapons in response.

"This is my wife, old man," Tomas informed Ruttger. "She is not the enemy. These women were responsible for the death of the Sovereign."

Ruttger and his men moved their eyes away from Joanne and upon Tomas.

"I thought you may have heard of that," he continued. "How about you place your sword in its sheath and relax?"

The old man slid his blade into its casing and breathed a little easier. "These are the Seven?" he asked.

"They are," Tomas answered, still gripping his sword, ready to release it from the sheath strapped to his side. The men of Woodmyst behind him continued to hold their weapons in their hands, awaiting instructions to attack.

"My ladies." Ruttger dropped to one knee. Courtney continued to stand behind him, holding onto his shoulders as she stared fearfully at the women gathered by Tomas' side. The old commander's men bent their knees also, bowing to the Seven. "We are at your service."

Thirty-Three

"Just how many of these Mistresses are there?" Chief Harling asked after hearing both stories from Ruttger and Magistrate Dennison as they sat in a circle under the roof of the assembly hall.

"There were nine," Amicia replied. "Counting the White Mistress and myself. But I sense some are lost."

"There are two," Joanne informed her. "Not counting you."

"And you know this, how?" questioned Harling.

"The Seven met this morning before daybreak in the ruins of the Great Hall," Simon answered.

"Sumaiyya travels over the mountains with another of the Mirikin," a girl with golden hair informed them. "But there is another with significant power that journeys with them. I cannot focus on who or what it is."

"*You* could not?" the chief of Belburn quizzed. "I thought you worked as one."

"We do," Joanne told him. "Each of us has certain abilities in which we excel more than the others. I can manipulate matter. Tricia, we discovered, can influence others to her will, man and beast."

"That's why I wedded her," Simon put in. "She made me do it."

Tricia slapped him on the arm playfully.

"Gilda," Joanne continued, "can see beyond natural measures."

"You could see them?" Richard asked.

"Not the way I see you now," Gilda replied. "It's more like a feeling. I can sense a presence and whether they are familiar to me."

"Which is why she could recognise Sumaiyya approaching," Joanne said.

"How long have you been able to do this?" Becka, Richard's wife, queried.

"I've always been able to," Gilda said. "I just didn't understand what it was until we recently gathered by the oak tree in the ruins."

"So, where exactly is this Sumaiyya now?" asked Chief Harling.

"I don't know. I need the help of my sisters."

"We draw from each other," Joanne informed the chief. "We gather together, and focus our power on a particular purpose. Usually, I am the channel by which the power moves. But occasionally, like this morning, it will select one of us who is stronger at a specific ability than the others."

"Sounds complicated," remarked Magistrate Dennison. "Does it drain you of your energy?"

"Not so much when it chooses one of the others," Joanne told him. "But sometimes, when it channels me and we focus on a single purpose, we grow tired."

"One time, you passed out," Lor put in. "We will need to keep you guarded at all times during the battle just in case that happens again."

"What did you do to tire yourselves so?" Dennison asked.

"We're calling it the *Fire Dance*," Emily, seated by Tomas, told him. "The sky was ablaze as the Seven engulfed our enemy on the other side of the river."

"Took your crops out as well, I see," Ruttger commented.

"They were using the cornfields as cover," Tomas said. "From experience, fire is the only way to defeat walking straw men."

"Straw men?" Courtney quizzed.

"That," Tomas answered, "is a long story for another time. And Lor is right. We need to keep you safe during the battle. I don't want any of you on the southern side of the river."

"I would prefer if they didn't go near the river at all, Tomas," said Gilda's husband.

The men agreed.

"Fair call," Tomas nodded. "They remain here in the village."

"No," Tricia told them. "We gather by the oak tree in the ruins. That's our place."

The others of the Seven nodded.

"I don't like it," Richard told them. "It's too open between the stones of the Great Hall and the woods."

"My men will guard them," Ruttger told him. "I'm certain their husbands would want to be near also.

"You can keep your men in the fields over the river," he said to Amicia and Jonathon. "Mine can guard to the west with the men of Woodmyst and your people from Belburn and Oldcastle," he pointed casually to Magistrate Dennison and Chief Harling, "can watch the grove over yonder."

"And just what do the Seven do during this time?" Lucy asked from her seat on the other side of Emily.

Tomas scratched his cheek as he gave this some thought.

"Are you able to manipulate the shots from the catapults?" he asked Joanne.

"We made the fire dance," she replied.

"I'll need you to help reduce the numbers in the white witch's army that approaches," he told her.

"What have you got in mind?" David asked, recognising a glint in Tomas' eyes that he hadn't seen for ten years.

"I want the Seven to make the fire dance again," he replied with a wry grin.

***

"The third presence that Gilda sensed," Tomas said to Joanne as the Warde family strolled across the village towards their home near the river. "Do you think it could be this Maji?"

"We couldn't get a feeling for age or gender," she replied. "But who else could it be?"

She grabbed his elbow and pulled him towards her as she stopped walking, bringing his attention to her.

"He is powerful, Tomas," she told him. "More powerful than Sumaiyya. More powerful than the Seven. If we saw such magic as light; Sumaiyya, the Mistresses, and the Seven would appear as the brightest stars in the sky. He would be like the sun."

"Then he's dangerous," her husband said, turning to look at his two daughters, who held onto Emily's hands.

"He poses a threat," Joanne replied. "I fear Amicia may be right. He may need to be destroyed."

Tomas shook his head. "I won't hurt a child, Joanne."

"You could sense the darkness in Sumaiyya," Lucy said. "Couldn't you do the same for this boy?"

"It's different," she answered. "There is neither light nor darkness, just strength."

"Perhaps he hasn't chosen a side to fight on," Emily suggested.

"Perhaps he's struggling within," Lucy put in. "Maybe he is being pulled one way and the other at the same time."

"Maybe he just doesn't want to fight at all," Catherine added.

The adults moved their eyes to her, surprised by her words.

"What do you mean?" Tomas said, crouching beside her.

"Maybe he doesn't want to be the Maji," she elaborated. "Maybe he just wants to be a little boy. Maybe he doesn't even want to have abilities."

Tomas stared into her eyes. "You can feel him. Can't you?"

She frowned and nodded.

"What can you tell me?"

She shook her head. "They want to hurt him and it's not his fault."

It's not his fault. Tomas replayed her words in his head.

"The white witch brings him," he said to his daughter. "She must have a purpose for him.

Why does she bring him here?"

"I don't know." She sobbed.

"You're not in trouble, sweetie," he assured her, placing his hand gently upon her cheek.

"He's so sad, Papa," Catherine told her father. "So, so sad."

Tomas kissed her forehead and wiped her tears with his thumbs.

Rising to his feet, he turned back to Joanne. "I'm sure that Sumaiyya believes she loves her son and that what she is doing is all for him. But it would appear that if Catherine is correct, this boy needs rescuing, not death."

Joanne wiped her eyes on her sleeve. "We sensed power in both of them too," she said, looking at the two little girls. "Gilda's strongest ability is like that of Yasmeen Svoboda's. She could find others with abilities and strength that surpassed the natural. Gilda saw Catherine. She saw a power emerging and developing that has the potential to match this boy's."

"She will need training, Tomas," Emily informed him. "They both will. But Catherine shows abilities already."

"You knew about this?" he asked her.

"Joanne and I talked about it," she replied. "I think, deep inside, you knew as well."

He did. He had always known that his daughters, particularly Catherine, were different. He had hoped they wouldn't share certain abilities of their mother and aunt, but he realised a long time ago to not put much faith in hopes.

Catherine, he discerned, would be powerful, perhaps even more so than her aunt. It seemed that his daughter was moving into an age where she was realizing her abilities. He was excited, but increasingly concerned about what this would mean for her.

"And you?" He turned to Lucy.

She shook her head. "This is the first that I have heard of it," she told him.

"Are you angry?" Emily asked him.

He shook his head. "No. It makes sense that you both would discuss this first. You have something that neither Lucy nor I could truly understand. It would seem my daughters share this trait with you also.

"If they need training, then they should receive it. I would have them both learn to control this rather than allow it to control them," he told his wives.

"Can the Seven teach them?" he asked Joanne.

"We have discussed the possibility," she replied. "All have agreed to help."

"Will they join your coven?" he questioned.

"No." She shook her head. "They will be the beginning of a new era."

***

Marching up the steep incline, towering rocks on either side of them as they wound through tight turns in the mountains, the soldiers of the White and Lavender forces moved at a great pace. Almost five thousand men crunched gravel into dust as they followed their Mistresses over the range that separated the southern peninsula from the lands of the north.

Vonavo carefully steered his oversized cart through the turns of the road, trying desperately not to slow the advance of the men behind him. The boy sat beside him, soaking in the surroundings and exploring with his eyes as they moved through the unfamiliar landscape.

"And what is this place known as?" he asked.

"This is what people call the Twisted Road," the armoured giant replied.

"An apt name," Takmel admitted.

"Wait until you see what lies beyond the ridge," Vonavo told him. "Then you will really see why it is called twisted."

"You have been here before?"

"Yes," the being answered. "Many, many years ago. Long before the time of the Mistresses. Long before the Realm War."

"Before?" The boy furrowed his brow. "How old are you Vonavo?"

"My kind does not count their age," he answered. "I am uncertain how many years have passed since I came to be."

"But you are old?"

"I would use the word *ancient* to best describe myself and my kind," he said.

"Why haven't you told me about this before?" the boy asked.

"I am required to give only direct responses, Takmel," the giant answered as he yanked the reins to the right to drive the horses pulling his cart sharply around a bend in the road. "I have, at times, given you more. I don't know why I have done so. Perhaps I have told you too much."

Takmel looked at the monstrosity sitting beside him. He was fond of the being, but Vonavo's tone suggested that the giant didn't share the feeling.

"You don't trust me," the boy said. "Do you?"

"You are the son of the White Mistress," he replied.

"But I have defied her in Dweagan," Takmel reminded him. "I destroyed the Violet Mistress."

"So, you have," Vonavo replied.

"Then why do you question *my* motives?"

"Your mother still rides for Woodmyst," the giant told him.

"She's my mother," he said. "I can't destroy her."

"You could destroy everything," Vonavo informed him. "You *are* the Maji."

Takmel felt a lump form in his throat.

"I don't want to be." The boy looked to the front of the procession as the road opened up again. His mother rode beside the Lavender Mistress far ahead of him.

"You can't avoid being what you already are, Takmel," the being rumbled. "You proved to your mother and these men that you are the Maji when you crushed that woman with your will. None, not even the Sovereign, could act so quickly and precisely with their magic."

"I *am* the heir of darkness," the boy sobbed.

"Yes," Vonavo replied. "You are the heir. But that doesn't mean you have to be dark. Your choices define who you are.

"You are the Maji. This is a fact that you cannot escape. But you can choose what kind of man you become.

"Your mother was coerced and fed words that made her believe she needed to become what the Sovereign intended for her to be. Your father was lured and seduced and had no choice."

"They were both weak." The boy frowned.

"Weak?" the giant asked.

"Their will was not strong enough to overcome the sway of suggestion." He wiped his eyes.

"In your mother's defence," the being said, "she was only a child, younger than you. Your father was a young man who tempted by beauty and sorcery that he had no defences against."

"Why him?" the boy asked. "Why did she choose a man of Woodmyst? Why that man?"

"They were seeking to free prisoners taken by the Prophets of the Sovereign," Vonavo explained. "The White Mistress attempted to prevent their advance and found one innocent amongst the men. Untouched by a woman."

"My father," the boy said.

"That is correct," the giant replied. "She needed his seed to form you, and his blood for the sacrifice."

Takmel shook his head slowly as he considered such a thing.

"How do you know all of this, Vonavo?" he asked. "Were you there?"

"No," the being answered. "But one of my kind is almost always nearby, watching, witnessing and absorbing the events taking place."

"Why?"

"It is how we survive," he replied. "We share tales of what takes place. We absorb them. It's our way of living, our nourishment."

"You record the history of man?"

"More than man," he answered. "We record the history of everything. We remember mountains sprouting from the earth before the time of beasts. Trees and forests that no longer exist. There was even a time when birds and insects covered the skies like thick storm clouds.

"Other beings appeared, and we saw an age of dragons followed by territorial squabbles between species like the Haigok, the Khorlo and the Agrodien. Then came the time of man.

"More disputes escalated with the increase of knowledge and the improvement of weaponry, from stone and wood to steel and technology like black powder and catapults. One day, man will destroy himself and his day will pass. No creature in all the histories holds as much contempt and hatred such as that of a man.

"I long to see the days of birds and insects again." Vonavo sounded sad. "But I fear that man will destroy it all first."

As they started their descent, the boy's eyes moved over the road, cut into the side of the mountain, stretching ahead of them before it turned sharply to the left where it travelled back towards them to a point just below their position. It continued downwards where it curved sharply again to the right, almost upon itself to slope away.

Takmel stared in disbelief as he tried to count the enormous number of twists in the road that zig-zagged down the side of the alps.

"The Twisted Road," Vonavo announced as his cart bounced over the gravel.

Thirty-Four

Jeremy sat by the river, close to the cottage by the hill. He picked up stones on the bank beside him and plopped them into the water one by one as he watched the waterfowls play amongst the reeds.

"What are you thinking?" Karlena asked him, sitting beside her husband on the grass.

"This place," he answered. "It's nice."

"Except for the ash and black ground across the river," she replied.

"It'll grow back," he said, placing an arm around her shoulders.

"I can see your mind turning things over," she told him.

"What if we settle here?"

"Here?" She raised her eyebrows.

"Mm-hmm!" he nodded. "We could build a house here. Farm some crops. Contribute to this community. Raise children. We have friends here."

"Farm?" She smiled. "Children?"

"Why not?" he asked, giving her a quizzical look.

"Won't you miss the ocean?"

"The *Adelandria* is gone," he said. "She was my home, but now I have nowhere. I have nothing."

"You have me." She placed her head on his shoulder.

"And I won't last without you," he told her. "That's why I'm asking if you want to stay here."

"I can't see you behind a plough," she said. "But I don't want to leave. If we survive what is to come, I think we should plant roots."

"Good," he said. "We are home then."

They held each other tightly as the waterfowls continued to splash and dive below the surface.

"So." Jeremy smiled. "Should we get started on those children now?"

**

Rhydra, Sharek and Akasati sat on the veranda with the Warde women as Baldwyn, Gustav and Tomas prepared a lunch of roast meat sandwiches and tea for the ladies.

"I haven't set foot in a galley for some time," Baldwyn called to the women. "I hope what I've prepared is sufficient."

"I'm sure it will be," Emily replied as he stroked Alice's long, dark hair. The girl had her ear to her mother's stomach.

"Not in there," she said before standing up and moving to Joanne in the next seat to rest her head against her aunt's belly.

"All right," Tomas called. "The tea is ready thanks to Gustav."

"My first-time making tea in a teapot," he replied as he carried a wooden tray laden with Emily's tea set.

"I prepared the food," Baldwyn said as he brought another tray with a plate loaded with sandwiches cut into small triangles. "But Tomas cooked the meat. So, if it's bad, blame him."

"Thank you, Baldwyn," Tomas said, carrying another tray with a plate of food.

"One in there," Alice said as she lifted herself again and moved to Lucy, placing her ear to the woman's abdomen.

They placed the trays on the dining table, moved onto the veranda so that they could enjoy the warmth of the sunlight during lunch.

"I'll get the crockery," Tomas announced as he dashed inside for some plates.

Gustav poured the tea and handed it to the women, starting with Emily, then Joanne.

"What are you doing?" Akasati asked the little girl, who still had her ear pressed against Lucy's stomach.

"Shh," Alice hissed, holding a finger to her lips. Lucy smiled, shaking her head as she ran her fingers through the dark strands of the little girl's hair.

"I just thought she was moving along trying to get attention from each of us," Emily said, placing her cup on a small table between hers and Joanne's seat.

"She's listening for something," Rhydra told them.

"An empty belly," Lucy told them as she took a cup from Gustav. "I'm so hungry and those sandwiches look good."

"One in there," Alice said as she stood upright.

"One what?" Akasati asked.

"Baby," the little girl announced.

Joanne spat her tea.

Emily suddenly stood.

A loud crash resounded from inside the house as Tomas dropped the plates onto the floor.

"A baby?" Sharek asked, not sure if she had heard the child correctly.

"One in her." She pointed to Joanne. "And one in her. Mama doesn't have one."

"Are you certain?" Lucy asked.

The girl nodded.

Catherine smiled, happy with the news, while all the adults wore surprised stares.

Sharek moved to Lucy and placed her hand upon the woman's belly.

Closing her eyes, she focused upon the life force of the woman seated near her.

"I can sense something," Sharek told them. "It is small. Tiny. Have you been sick?"

"No," Lucy replied.

"When was the last time that you and Tomas were..." she moved her eyes to Alice, remembering that she was in the presence of children, "... together?"

"Two nights ago, was our last time," she replied.

"It could be." Sharek looked at the others. "It is very tiny."

Joanne laughed softly, tears welling in her eyes. Emily placed her hands over her mouth as elation flooded over her.

Tomas stood frozen as he stared through the door to the veranda where his wife was sitting.

"Papa." Alice moved to him, upset by the reaction of the grown-ups. "Did I do something wrong?"

"No, my baby." He bent down and picked her up before she stepped onto the broken crockery on the floor. "You did nothing wrong. This is good news that you have brought us today.

Tomas moved onto the veranda and put his daughter on the platform before lowering himself to Lucy. Tears streamed down her cheeks as she faced him. He kissed her forehead and lips before wiping her tears away.

"This is very good news," he said.

***

The sound of birds squawking and fluttering through the trees drew the attention of some men standing at the edge of the western road. The din came from farther inside the woods to their right.

One man looked up to the tower nearby, where two men stood watch. Both of them were peering into the trees to see what had caused the commotion.

"What do you see?" the man on the ground called.

"We can't see," one watcher responded. "The foliage is too thick."

"I think it came from one of the traps we built," another on the ground said.

The men, numbering five, moved into the tree line to investigate. With caution, they stepped over fallen branches and placed their feet carefully on the ground so as to not draw attention to themselves. Loud thumping and rustling came from an area behind some thick growth.

Pushing past the brushes, they saw a large hole in the ground. Something had fallen into a pit that had been dug by some men of Woodmyst.

Gradually, slowly, they crept to the edge of the pit and peered over the edge.

Long wooden spikes stuck from the ground at the bottom of the deep hole. Pierced in several places, and still moving, was the form of a creature resembling a reptile.

Its arms reached desperately for an axe that rested just beyond its reach as it glared at the men with angry, red eyes. It snarled, baring its long, yellow teeth as dark blood oozed from beneath its upturned lips.

One man pulled a bow from his shoulder and loaded an arrow.

The shaft found its target deep in the creature's eye socket.

Instantly, the beast fell silent and moved no more.

"We should take it back to Tomas," another man suggested. "Perhaps this is one of the Agrodien the seafarers mentioned."

"I'm not taking the whole thing back," said another as he pulled his dagger from his belt. "It looks heavy. Help me down. We'll take its head."

Moments later, the creature's face was being stared at by the village council and a few of the crewmen of the *Adelandria*. It rested on a plate that sat upon a table in the assembly hall.

"Is this the type of creature that attacked you in the forest?" David asked the captain.

"That's what they looked like," he replied, staring at the creature's yellow teeth and scaly skin. "You could guarantee that if there is one of them nearby, there will be others."

Tomas surveyed the head, making mental observations, admiring the beast. He ran a finger along its neck, just above the point of separation, and felt the thick tendrils and intertwining muscles beneath the surface.

"What are you doing, Tomas?" Oliver asked.

"This creature is very strong," he said. "The hide is thick, and the neck is solid with tissue, which would make it hard to slice through with a blade. Where would you say you could do the most damage?" Tomas asked Jeremy.

"We could penetrate through the abdomen easily enough," the captain informed him. "It took a few swipes at the neck to stop them. Their backs are even thicker, like hard leather."

Tomas felt under the creature's chin to a soft patch of skin.

"They are weak here also," he told the men around him. "A carefully placed strike might see a blade cut into the throat or even reach the brain."

"I don't see your point, Tomas," Oliver said.

"It's simple," David replied. "We have people who are not as skilful with a blade amongst us. If we issue them with swords, we tell them to strike the abdomen or under the chin. Anywhere else is useless."

"Just the belly," Tomas corrected him. "The soft spot under the chin is too small for a novice. It would be sheer luck if anyone could hit it. What is their arm's reach like, Jeremy?"

"Long," he replied. "They seem to prefer the axe over the sword, which means they recoil their arms to swing their weapons. It's about the only time you will get to strike in a skirmish with one of them."

Tomas turned to look at the faces of the councilmen.

"I trust you won't object if I place Ruttger's men on the western edge of the village?" he asked. "I want them posted on the other side of the ruins, where the wall once stood."

The men looked at one another, remaining silent. Tomas took that as support for his request.

"Jeremy," he turned to the captain. "Could you spare your crew to join Ruttger's men?"

"Consider it done," Jeremy replied. "And may I say congratulations?"

The councilmen exchanged curious glances before looking to Tomas.

"I was going to mention it to you, but I didn't think this moment was appropriate," he told them.

"I apologise, Tomas," Jeremy said. "Sharek told me and I thought you would have shared the news by now."

"Nothing to apologise for," he told the captain before facing the councilmen. "Lucy is with child."

David laughed out loud, jumping from his seat and wrapping his arms around his friend, "You busy bastard."

The horn trumpeted from the eastern tower, instantly echoed by the call from the tower on the western edge of the city.

David let go of Tomas and darted towards the river with the assembly in tow. He glanced to the western tower where the men pointed towards the burnt fields across the wide stream.

Continuing to the river's edge, Tomas stared over the blackened plantations and could see nothing. He squinted and moved his eyes towards the mountains to the south and noticed movement on the slopes.

Jeremy pulled alongside him and took his spyglass from his pocket. He extended the tube and scanned the lower region of the mountains.

"A large force approaches along the road," he said. "Their lead men carry a white banner and a purple banner."

"Purple?" Tomas questioned as Jonathon came rushing up to them.

"Not purple," he corrected them. "Lavender. Do you see Violet?"

"What's the difference?" Jeremy asked. "They're both purple."

"Lavender is lighter," he replied. "Violet will be much darker. Can you see her banner?"

"There are no other banners," Jeremy informed him. "There is only white and lavender."

"Two Mistresses approach," Jonathon said as he signalled his men to cross the river and prepare for battle. "We'll do our part, Tomas. I'm afraid that you have the biggest responsibility of all. Keep my Amicia safe."

With that, the soldier ran off towards the village. Tomas watched him as he stopped to speak to Amicia. He kept his eyes upon them as Jonathon kissed her long on the lips.

Suddenly, the weight of the world fell upon his shoulders.

Jonathon raced away to join his men, leaving Amicia alone in the middle of the village. Tomas moved away from the men on the riverbank.

"Where are you going, Tomas?" Lor asked.

"We need to get people in their places," Tomas said. "And I can't leave her standing there all day and night. She will stay with my wife and children in the meeting hall."

"You would trust a Mistress with your children?" he asked.

"She isn't a Mistress, Lor," he replied. "Look at her and how she watches him. She gave up being one of them a while ago. Now, go get your wife and bring her to the meeting hall. I want as many of my family together as possible."

Both men moved in separate directions as they tore through the village. Tomas took Amicia's hand without speaking and pulled her after him.

"What are you doing?" she asked.

He dragged her towards his house where Emily and Joanne were dressing his daughters in long clothing, ready for a night away from home. Lucy was packing food into three baskets so they could share it with others at the meeting hall.

"Help her," Tomas pointed to his wife in the kitchen before turning to the others. "Are you two ready?"

"Your sword, breastplate, and belt are waiting for you on the bed," Emily told him. "I'll be in to put mine on once Lucy takes the girls to the meeting hall."

"And you?" he said to Joanne.

"Will you take me to the oak tree?" she asked.

"We both will," he told her.

"I think we're ready," Lucy called. "I'll need some help to carry these baskets."

Catherine was crying as she looked at her father.

"I need you to be good for Lucy," he said to both the girls.

"I will, Papa," Alice replied before he kissed her cheek.

"I love you, Papa," Catherine sobbed. "I'll miss you."

"I'll be back." He pressed his lips to her forehead. "And I love you too. Now, go help Lucy with those baskets."

Tomas kissed Lucy for a long time before letting her go. He then stood between the two sisters as they watched their family move away, disappearing into the village towards the meeting hall.

I hope someone took the Agrodien's head away, was all he could think as his eyes watched his daughters.

Joanne suddenly gripped his arm tightly.

"I'm scared," she confessed.

"They are two," he told her. "You are Seven. They fear you more. That's why they come. Remember that. They fear you more."

"They fear us more," she said to herself as she breathed deeply. "They fear us more."

Tomas moved inside the house to find his breastplate and weapons waiting for him where Emily had told him they were. She joined him and dressed for battle.

Both re-emerged on the veranda, where Joanne was continuing to chant the four words over and over. "They fear us more. They fear us more."

Tomas took her hand in his before reaching for Emily's.

Together, they moved to the west, towards the ruins of old Woodmyst.

The sun was making its way towards the treetops of the forest, and the shadows were growing long.

It was going to be a long night.

Thirty-Five

"So, this is Woodmyst," Sumaiyya said as she rode onto the plain.

"Rather unimpressive," the Lavender Mistress observed. "Don't you think?"

"Don't be fooled," her prime told her. "Sometimes the smallest of things can be the deadliest."

"Why do you suppose the ground is scorched?"

"Because they burnt it," Sumaiyya replied, remembering her attack upon the town with her straw men.

"Mistress," a man called from in front of her. "There are catapults at the far end of the plain."

"Fuchsia's treachery," the woman in white commented.

"So," Lavender said, "we are all that remain."

"It would appear so," she replied.

"Your son?" The other turned to face her. "He could end this now before it begins."

"He is the Maji." Sumaiyya shot the woman an angry glare. "Remember your place."

She suddenly recalled her own son telling her those very words.

Remember your place.

"Apologies, Mistress." Lavender bowed her head.

"Move your men into position, Commander," the white witch ordered.

"Yes, Mistress," said a uniformed man riding by her side.

He directed his horse onwards and started barking orders to the men as they descended upon the road, mustering them this way and that to form rows and columns on the level surface of the plain.

Sumaiyya moved her steed to the side of the raised land near the feet of the mountains, stopping near a rocky outcrop that looked over the blackened fields all the way to the village over the river. The Lavender Mistress followed her, pulling her horse alongside.

"Exciting," she giggled. "Isn't it?"

"Silence," Sumaiyya commanded as she observed the formation of the troops.

Vonavo pulled his cart to a stop at the top of a low rise that extended from the side of the mountains, stretching into the forest to his left. The soldiers and men of the fleet moved past him to join the ranks of the forces before him on the plain.

"It's so small, Vonavo," the boy commented. "They don't stand a chance against such an army."

"Perhaps," the armoured giant replied.

"I can feel them," he said. "They are frightened. But they stand strong. Why don't they run?"

"Where could they go?"

"Anywhere," Takmel answered. "They could go to the west."

"Your mother would pursue them," the being told him. "There is nowhere left that doesn't burn. Look at the village below and tell me how many people you think are down there."

"There are many," he replied. "Over a thousand. Most are women and children."

"More than that little village can cater for," Vonavo informed the boy. "Where do you think they came from?"

"The west." The boy frowned.

"And the east," the giant said. "There is nowhere to run. Others have escaped to this place instead. This is the last refuge of freemen."

Takmel turned to look at the armoured giant, but something drew his attention away.

Something that moved amongst the trees.

It was dark, like a shadow. It reminded the boy of black smoke, only it moved against the breeze.

"What was that?" he asked.

"An observer," the being replied. "It bears no threat to you."

Takmel stared at the giant, expecting more to the explanation, but received none. He peered towards the woods for a moment longer, not finding the shadow anywhere. Gradually, the boy moved his eyes back to the fields where the army formed up.

He wanted to ask Vonavo more about the shadow creature, but he knew the being would tell him only the most basic of information. The tone in the giant's answer informed the boy that there was no desire to answer questions concerning such a creature.

Instead, not wanting to press, Takmel kept his tongue still. The being seated beside him proved to be neither friend nor enemy. He was a slave under the White Mistress' control.

"If I freed you, Vonavo," the boy started, "would you be my friend?"

The giant turned his caged face towards the lad.

"I would be lying if I said I wasn't fond of you, Takmel," he replied. "But you are the Maji. You are the White Mistress' son. I cannot truthfully answer your question as I do not know what I may do if I were to be freed."

The Seven sat on the ground in a circle by the oak tree that grew in the centre of the Great Hall's ruins. Their legs crossed, eyes closed, and hands joined, creating a ring.

Tomas glanced around the grassed area where old Woodmyst once stood. Inside the toppled stone walls of the hall stood eleven other individuals who guarded the Seven. Emily had positioned herself near to his side on the western edge of the ruins. The Erilian warriors stood beside her, with Simon on his other side. Positioned to the north and south were the other five husbands of the women in the circle.

"They're united," Emily said to him. "I can feel a change in them."

"Then it begins," he whispered.

Jonathon instructed torches to be lit and the catapults to be loaded.

"Stone won't burn, Commander," one soldier reported as he moved along the line on horseback.

"We have the Seven on our side," he informed the soldier. "Who knows what they are capable of? Be ready to light your payload."

Rustling leaves and breaking wood resounded from the grove as something approached from deep beyond the tree line.

"Do you hear that?" Magistrate Dennison questioned.

"Our first visitors for the evening." Chief Harling smiled, brandishing his sword high so his men could see his signal.

Becka Dering, Martha Gyfford and Amicia Elynbrigge moved around the edge of the meeting hall, lowering the canvas walls using the rope and pulley system that resembled the sail rigging on a ship. They fixed the walls to the lower sections of the beams between each sail so they didn't move in the breeze.

Linet and Lucy lit a fire in a circle of stones on the floor.

"Who's hungry?" Becka asked, trying to keep the children focused on anything but what was happening outside.

Several of the younglings answered in the affirmative.

They set a metal tripod over the flames so an iron plate could sit above the hearth. Two large pots of water placed onto the plate would slowly heat while the children fed upon some dried fish and bread.

"My go home," Alan, Linet's three-year-old son, mumbled.

"Not tonight," his mother told him. "We're going to camp here."

"Camping, Alan," Alice said to her cousin excitedly.

The toddler shook his head, giving a great frown in response. "My go home."

A great crash exploded deep in the woods to the west. Some birds responded with an alarming call, objecting to the disturbance.

"The enemy has discovered one of our traps." Richard smiled.

"I hope you have more," Jeremy replied. "I don't think there will be only one of those bastards out there."

Another enormous crash to their left informed them of another trap being triggered. A roar emitted from the same direction, slowly dissipating in a gurgle before silence ensued.

"We have more." Richard nodded.

"Advance," the commander of the Mistress' forces shouted.

The army started its march across the charred fields. Their footfalls sounded like repetitive thunder as they stepped upon loose gravel, hardened ground and burnt chaff.

Gradually, as the sun made its way below the canopy of the forest, the uniformed men encroached towards the middle of the plain, drawing nearer and nearer to the village.

"Why don't the villagers fire the catapults?" Takmel asked the giant.

"Perhaps the Mistress' forces are not within range yet," he replied as they both watched the advance.

"Torch the payload," Jonathon commanded.

One by one, the men lowered the flames to the heavy loads waiting in the cradle of the weapons.

Tomas' stomach tightened as he witnessed Joanne's eyes open.

They were black as pitch, with tendrils spreading like spider webs under her skin towards her temples and down to her cheeks.

"By the gods," Simon gasped.

The payloads erupted into balls of flames. Wood, iron and stone engulfed in fire. Jonathon found it hard to believe, even with his own eyes seeing it.

"Loose," he bellowed.

Some men hesitated, surprised by the flaming objects loaded in the catapults.

Several fireballs moved through the sky, arcing high into the air.

"Loose," Jonathon repeated, shouting. "Loose. Loose."

The men snapped back to reality and released the cradles, sending the load into the sky.

"Unfurl," Joanne said in an emotionless, toneless voice.

The fireballs spread open, stretching into ribbons of flames as they fell towards the approaching army.

"Do you see this?" Takmel stared with wide eyes at the spectacle.

"Yes," the giant thundered. "I most certainly do."

The ribbons of fire intensified as they neared the ground, spreading, uniting.

Some men on the ground turned to flee, but it was too late.

Fire swept over the foremost troops before engulfing several rows of men behind them.

Several soldiers continued to flee, set on fire and running blindly across the plain in any direction they could.

Others fell and writhed in agony as the flames relentlessly bit into their flesh.

"Reload," Jonathon called as some of his men stopped to cheer.

Quickly, the soldiers regained composure and reset their weapons.

"Those bitches," Sumaiyya spat as she observed at least five hundred of her soldiers die on the field.

"Keep moving," the commander of her forces yelled. "Advance more hastily as they reload their catapults."

The remaining men started running towards the far end of the open ground.

Jonathon moved his gaze across a large band of men, more than a thousand, running hard towards them.

"Loose," he commanded.

Fireballs stretched into the sky, rising high above the oncoming army.

"Damn," he clenched his teeth. "We overshot our targets."

"Fall," Joanne commanded.

The projectiles exploded, illuminating the sky in bright light.

Fire streamed down onto the advancing men like rain.

Screams of agony and terror echoed across the plain as flames enveloped many of the Mistress' troops.

A loud ecstatic laugh erupted from Jonathon as he witnessed the brilliance of the fire expand over the enemy soldiers. Most of the forces were now lying on the ground, turning to ash.

"Reload," he called.

His men reset the catapults as he kept watch on the field.

Another large number of soldiers still advanced. Their numbers were great; at least seven hundred.

They leapt over the burning bodies of their comrades and continued towards the village at high speed.

The advancing troops were well within the firing range of the catapults. Jonathon needed to move to the next step in the plan.

His smile disappeared as he dropped from his steed and lifted his bow and quiver from the saddle. Smacking the horse on the rump, he sent the beast back to the centre bridge, where it galloped over the crossing and back into the village.

"Archers," he bellowed. "Volley."

A barrage of projectiles zipped through the air, planting deep into the approaching men at the front of the line. The remaining enemy soldiers pushed their injured comrades to the ground, stepping upon them to continue their assault on Woodmyst.

Too close for his men to reload and fire again, Jonathon dropped his bow and quiver in favour of his sword strapped to his back. With his blade brandished high, he started towards the oncoming force.

"Attack," he shouted.

The two armies charged towards each other on the charred fields, shouting and cursing the men before them.

Thirty-Six

The din of battle reached the ruins of the Great Hall.

Swords clashed as men roared upon the fields over the river.

Tomas moved his gaze over the scene as the sun slunk away for the night and the first stars appeared in the sky.

"Tomas," Emily called softly. "They have broken contact."

He turned to the circle of women sitting by the small oak tree. Joanne was looking at him and shaking her head.

Her eyes had returned to normal; there was no sign of the black veins that stretched from them only moments before.

"What is it?" he asked, rushing over to her. "Are you all right?"

"We can't make the fire dance, Tomas," she told him. "The enemy is too close to our people. You can hear them. They fight hand-to-hand. I'm afraid we would burn them all if we moved the flames about as we did before."

"You did well, Joanne," he told her. "You all did. Most of her forces are trampled into the ground and set ablaze. What you've evened the odds out there."

"She still stands," Joanne said, looking towards the mountains to the south.

Tomas followed her gaze.

With such losses on the field, Sumaiyya might consider fleeing so she could rebuild her army only to return another day.

This had to end tonight.

She urged her steed forwards, towards the battle at the far end of the valley. Her hatred for the Seven drew her closer. She needed to destroy the auburn-haired girl.

Driven by revenge, her thoughts consumed with the loss of Yasmeen Svoboda, her lover and prime, she set her beast into a canter.

"What are you doing?" Lavender called after her. "We should retreat. Our forces are expired. Sumaiyya!"

The White Mistress pulled to a complete stop and turned to face the other, stretching out her arm with clawed fingers.

Her eyes turned black, and her scowl was dark.

"Mistress," she barked, tightening her grip. "You address me as Mistress."

Lavender screamed as deep gashes appeared in her flesh around her cheeks. Layer by layer, skin and tissue fell away, exposing her white teeth at the back of her mouth.

Her lips dropped away and tumbled to the dirt as the corners of her mouth ripped wide open, joining the tears over her cheeks into one oversized grimace.

The lavender witch continued to scream in agony as the White Mistress closed her fingers slowly. Teeth and bone made a moist cracking sound. Blood streamed from her right eye as it turned upwards, separating from the nerve stem to float freely in the socket.

"I never liked you," Sumaiyya told her. "Both you and Violet were a constant aggravation. Your incessant giggling and eccentricities didn't belong amongst the Mirikin. Imagine my disappointment when I realised it was only you and Violet remaining at my side. I would have preferred to be here with any other Mistress than you.

"And the one thing that I loathe about you most of all..." The White Mistress brought her fingers closer and closer, balling them tighter. "You both ate people. Both of you were useless and just not right in the head."

She made a fist.

Lavender's head crumpled into a pulpous ball of flesh and bone.

Her body slipped from her horse and slapped to the earth.

Sumaiyya took a deep breath and steered her charger towards the battle in the distance.

Kicking hard, she raced across the plain towards Woodmyst.

"Where is she going?" Takmel quizzed. "What does she think she is doing? She'll get herself killed."

Vonavo watched on in silence.

"Go after her," Takmel ordered.

The giant whipped the reins, urging his horses forward.

"We must go faster," the lad pressed.

"We'll go as fast as we can safely travel, Takmel," the being told him. "My primary task is to protect you, not to place you in danger. If your mother enters the battle, we will not venture any closer."

"But I need to help her!"

"You would help her destroy innocent people, Takmel?"

The boy furrowed his brow as a lone tear streaked down his cheek.

His mother was bent on destroying these people because they simply dared to stand against the tyranny of the Mirikin. By all measures, the coven needed to be destroyed.

And it had been.

Now, only his mother remained, and she continued with her goal.

"She won't stop." Takmel frowned as he watched her in the distance, crossing the plain.

"Will she, Vonavo?"

"No, she will not," the armoured giant replied. "Not until all free men are enslaved or dead."

"Then I must stop her." Takmel's eyes welled with tears. "I must kill my mother."

Loud crashes resounded along the western front as an unseen enemy triggered traps and fell into pits. The sound of shrubbery being disturbed grew louder, and shadowy figures emerged from the depths of the forest.

"Here they come," David called, bringing his sword up to the ready.

Bursting onto the open grass came hundreds of hulking reptilian creatures. They hissed and roared intimidatingly at the men gathered along the edge of the woods, brandishing axes and swords in their large, leathery hands.

"Ugly bastards," Ewan Cunningham sneered. "Aren't they?"

A beast closest to him seemed to understand his words. It raced towards him, raising its axe above its head as it advanced.

David rushed towards it, noticing the old man standing petrified in the corner of his eye.

The bald man swung his blade towards the creature's belly, remembering the conversation in the meeting hall earlier. The reptilian brought his axe down, aiming for David's head.

It was too slow.

David found his mark and slit the beast's belly open, spilling its contents onto the grass.

It fell to its knees, intestines dangling from the wound.

In one swift movement, David spun around and brought the blade of his sword down upon the Agrodien's crown, splitting bone and tissue.

It fell, lifeless, onto the ground.

The large man, fuelled with rage, turned towards the snarling faces of the creatures watching from the tree line.

"Who's next?"

With that, the creatures all raced forwards as one.

Swords clashed against axes and blades as men noisily cursed beasts along the northern boundary of the village. Agrodien and human blood spilled, and the fallen from both sides were increasing in number.

Magistrate Dennison held a firm hand against his ribs as blood trickled over his fingers. One of the Agrodien axes had found its mark.

He remained on his feet, and his sword found the soft place under the attacking warrior's chin where he pushed his blade in so deep that it stuck from the top of the Agrodien's head.

"Are you all right?" Chief Harling called to him.

"No," the magistrate replied. "I think this one might have killed me. The wound is deep."

"Do you want to retreat?" the chief asked. "See if someone can mend you?"

"No," Dennison replied. "We are losing men. I am needed here."

"There's no shame in seeking help," Harling told him as he swung his blade towards an attacker, slicing through a reptilian arm, forcing the enemy warrior to drop his weapon.

The chief lunged and buried his blade deep into the creature's belly before twisting the blade. The beast dropped to its knees.

"I'll remain here until I can't remain anymore," the magistrate told him.

Harling pushed with his boot against the Agrodien's chest, retrieving his sword from the dead reptilian.

"You're a stronger man than me, then." The chief glanced over at him. "I would have gone for a rest for a wound much less severe."

"I doubt that," Dennison replied as he blocked a blow from another enemy warrior.

Keeping his hand against his ribs, he swung his leg out, hooking his foot behind the Agrodien's ankle and pulled his leg back towards him. The creature fell on his back with a heavy thud.

The magistrate turned his sword in his free hand to plunge it into the beast's belly again and again.

At the sound of battle outside, the children in the meeting hall whimpered and cried as their fears overcame them. The women tried their best to comfort the younglings, but their fears overwhelmed them, too. Words of comfort fell upon deaf ears as adult and child gripped each other tightly in hope of survival.

"I want Mama," Alice blubbered as the roar of a distant Agrodien caused them all to tremble and gasp.

"It's all right." Lucy hugged the girl. "We're safe here."

She glanced around for Catherine, looking first to Linet, who was nursing Alan. Lucy moved her eyes around the meeting hall, darting them this way and that, seeing many other women of the village comforting their own younglings.

"Where's your sister?" Lucy stood up. Her gaze moved to the flap of the main entrance to the structure.

It swung in the breeze.

Catherine was gone.

Takmel moved his eyes from his mother and into the village over the river. The cart continued to bump along the road as it moved on into the plain.

But it wasn't the plain, or the battle upon it, that drew his attention.

There was something else that gripped him, pulled him forward.

I can help you, a gentle voice told him. *Come to me.*

"Who are you?" he asked the voice.

"You know my name, Takmel," Vonavo told him.

"Not you, Vonavo," the boy replied. "Another is calling me."

I can help you, it said again. *I will wait for you.*

"Catherine," Lucy screamed as she burst from the meeting hall with Alice in her arms.

Becka was on her heels, grabbing her around the waist and dragging her back inside before she chased the lost girl into the village.

"You can't go out there," the older woman told her. "You do not know where Catherine has gone."

Lucy was distraught. Her face was a mess with tears and snot as she dropped to her knees. She continued to grip Alice tightly in her arms. The little girl grew more and more upset at the sight of the adult woman she trusted falling apart.

"I lost her," Lucy blubbered. "I lost her."

Catherine walked calmly through the village towards the river. Her eyes moved across the battle that was transpiring on the far bank. Her attention, however, remained fixed upon a presence that was further on the plain travelling towards her.

"Come to me." She smiled; her eyes closed as she directed herself towards the centre bridge.

"We should go to help, Tomas," Akasati called. "The Seven have done what they could. We should escort them to the meeting hall and join the battle. We are surrounded."

Tomas didn't want to leave just in case something sparked in the women seated by the young oak tree. He had seen it before. Just when he thought they were done, something would bring them back together and refocus their energy.

But he had to admit, it had been a long time since they fired the last catapult.

"All right," he agreed, turning towards the village. His eyes fell upon a young girl strolling between the houses. "Who is that?"

"Who is who?" Emily asked. "Everyone should be inside."

"There." He pointed with his blade. Suddenly his eyes recognised the individual as she stepped upon the centre bridge. "Catherine."

He ran as fast as he could, but she was too far away to stop. By the time he would reach her, she would be across to the other side.

"Catherine," he called after her. "Catherine."

She couldn't hear him over the din of battle.

"No," Emily cried, racing after her husband, keeping her eyes upon her daughter.

Joanne was next to run after them, followed by the Erilian women.

Catherine found Jonathon's horse upon the bridge. She stopped to stroke its nose before moving towards the battle. The steed turned its head, watching her as she moved closer to the southern bank of the river.

Sumaiyya pulled her charger up to a halt before leaping from its back, landing squarely on the ground with both feet.

The battle was only a few yards from her.

She could smell the sweat and blood as the loud clash of swords rang in her ears. Her thoughts were of the auburn girl. The Black Miss had tested her patience and ultimately took the Sovereign away from her.

The village was so close.

Her goal was so near.

She raised her hand towards the battle, focusing upon the men that blocked her access across the river as she closed her eyes.

Bending her fingers into claws, she pushed towards them.

Suddenly, her men before her fell to the ground, writhing in pain.

She stepped back, surprised.

This was not her doing.

Someone else had entered the battle.

Thirty-Seven

Jonathon stared at the fallen men around him in disbelief. He spun to see his own men still standing, untouched.

Along the line in both directions, the battle continued.

The commander saw the white witch standing before him in the open. At first, he thought she was responsible for this phenomenon.

But why would she take down her own men and leave us standing?

He saw the look of surprise on her face, the same expression that he shared with her.

She looked to him and he to her, staring at each other for what seemed an eternity.

He tightened his grip on his sword.

Turning his shocked look into a scowl, he prepared to attack.

"Out of my way, Commander," a small voice said from behind him.

He turned to see the young, small frame of a little girl standing at the edge of the bridge.

Tomas' daughter.

"You should be inside where it is safe," he told her.

"My place is here," she told him. "Please, step aside."

He did so compliantly.

The din of battle slowly subsided around him as others moved their eyes onto the child by the bridge.

Gradually, all men on both sides lowered their swords.

It's her, Sumaiyya told herself. *But how? She is still a child.*

The White Mistress shook her head.

This must be a trick.

"Step aside," Catherine said to the woman. "I'm not here for you."

"Well," Sumaiyya growled. "I'm here for you."

"I've come for the Maji," the girl told her.

"You wish to harm him?"

"I wish to help him," Catherine informed her, slowly walking towards the woman in white.

"I could help you, too. I know all about you, Sumaiyya Tarkin."

"You know nothing," the witch spat. "Who are you?"

"Catherine," Emily shrieked. "Catherine, come back."

Sumaiyya's eyes moved to the bridge where she saw a man and woman she recognised from many years before. They had aged a little, as had the face of another that she knew beside them. The Black Miss, now older.

Their faces showed fear, concern for the little one before her.

She raced forwards and pulled a dagger from her sleeve. With her free arm, she grabbed the girl around the chest and dragged her back into the field.

"Stay back, man of Woodmyst," she warned, grimacing wickedly. "Or I will slit your daughter's throat."

"No," Tomas cried. "Please. She is just a child."

"Just a child?" The white witch laughed. "Do you see what she has done here? This is no mere child. I could take her and train her, just as I was trained. Do you understand? Just as I was trained. Just as your Black Miss was trained. I'll expose her to men first to strip away her will before I show her kindness, winning her over to me. Making her loyal to me."

"Please, let her go," Emily called, dropping to her knees.

"Kill them all," she barked to her men.

They didn't move. Instead, they dropped their swords to the ground.

"I command you to kill them," she hollered, pressing the blade of her dagger against Catherine's neck.

The soldier's eyes were all fixed on another behind her.

"Mama," the boy called. Vonavo stood diligently behind him, watching over him as he spoke. "It's over. Let her go."

"No," she shouted at him, tears streaking over her cheeks. "They are the ones that killed the Sovereign. They killed my Yasmeen."

"Let the girl go," he yelled. His voice roared like thunder and shook the ground she stood upon.

She dropped her dagger and stumbled backwards, letting Catherine free. To the surprise of everyone watching, the girl ran to Takmel, not to her parents.

He reached out to her and took her hand in his.

"Are you all right?" he asked, looking at her neck where his mother had pressed the blade. With his finger, he lifted her chin to see a tiny surface cut.

"Is there blood?" she asked.

"Nothing more than a scratch," he assured her.

"Men who fought for the Mistresses," Jonathon shouted. "Their time has ended. Fight with free men and be free. Or perish here. What say you?"

"We can't find our commander," one of them shouted. "So we have no more orders to follow. I can't speak for the others, but I wonder if I may join you?"

"Only if you swear your allegiance to Woodmyst," he called.

They remained silent, looking at one another.

"For Woodmyst," he bellowed.

"For Woodmyst," some called back.

He repeated the words, holding his sword high, "For Woodmyst."

"For Woodmyst," the men shouted back more enthusiastically.

"Now aid the men on the western border of the village," Jonathon called to his men. "Kill all Agrodien."

The men ran towards the western bridge as Sumaiyya slunk away, keeping her head low.

"I'm not finished," she hissed.

Stretching her fingers towards the earth, waving her palms towards the fallen bodies of all slain warriors on the field, she moved her eyes over the charred and the butchered alike.

Limbs twitched.

Fingers flexed.

Eyes opened.

Slowly, gradually, the dead began to rise.

"No, you don't," Tomas whispered as he grabbed Jonathon's horse by the reins and leapt onto its back.

"Tomas?" Emily was still sobbing. "What are you doing?"

"I'm going to stop her," he answered, kicking into the steed's flanks and charging forward.

"By the gods," Karlena breathed.

"There are no gods," he called back to her.

He lifted his sword high and directed the steed directly to the white witch.

"Stop, Mama," Tarkin called.

She ignored him, grimacing, chuckling as the fallen soldiers pushed themselves upon their feet. A great number of the burnt bodies attempted to push themselves off the ground, splintering their bones in places so that their limbs broke away, leaving them to drag themselves across the ground towards the village.

Others rose to their feet, body parts dangling from their mass by thin tendrils of flesh. Sinew and bone exposed as gashes opened. Intestines dragging along the ground as they walked towards the bridges.

"Mama." Takmel started forward to intervene, only to feel the heavy hand of Vonavo fall upon his shoulder, keeping him in place.

"Papa," Catherine cried, still holding the boy's hand as she spied her father racing onto the plain on horseback.

Sumaiyya noticed the approaching steed and swept her hand towards the beast.

A dust cloud exploded from the earth in front of the beast, knocking it off its feet so that it toppled over, flinging Tomas into the air.

Joanne and Emily screamed, knowing this wouldn't end well.

He plummeted to the ground hard, skidding across the charred surface and over the remains of men that moved towards Woodmyst.

A sharp pain burned in his back and sternum at the same time as he tumbled over and over.

He came to a stop at Sumaiyya's feet.

His breathing was shallow, and his air came in loud, raspy gasps.

"So, this is how it ends, man of Woodmyst." She smiled.

Tomas locked his eyes upon her as he sat upright.

His legs sat awkwardly in front of him and his energy was being drained with each exhaling breath.

"Vonavo," she called. "Squeeze his head until it bursts."

The giant moved his face towards her.

"No," he replied.

She snapped her head around to glare at the giant.

"I gave you a command," she told him.

"Yes, you did," he said. "But I will not kill another. Not even if you instruct me to do so."

"So," she frowned, stretching her hand towards him. "You would rather die."

Vonavo hollered in pain, dropping to his knees as he clawed at his armour with his monstrous hands.

Takmel turned towards the giant, his eyes wide and his heart pounding rapidly.

"No," he cried. "Mama, no. Stop."

She tightened her grip on the giant, causing him to fall onto his back as he attempted to open his armour at a seam.

"Stop this now, Mama," Takmel called, tears running down his cheeks. He reached his hand out towards her, not wanting to do what he was about to.

But what choice did he have?

"Please Mama," he begged, sobbing. "Please stop."

Her eyes filled with rage as she continued to squeeze Vonavo's life force.

Then there was silence.

Vonavo ceased writhing and sat upright. His face turned towards the white witch.

Takmel lowered his hand as his chin quivered and the corners of his mouth moved down.

Catherine sobbed softly by his side as she kept her eyes on the scene before her.

The dead fell back to sleep as Tomas slumped back to the ground, his hand smeared with Sumaiyya's blood.

She held her hand against her neck, just below her jaw. The hilt of her dagger that she had dropped now stuck from her flesh.

She fell onto her rump as her eyes drifted to the man from Woodmyst. She looked to the wound in his sternum, where the blade of a sword that had pierced through his back still protruded.

The boy ran to his mother's side as the girl ran to her father.

"Papa," she cried, dropping to her knees and wrapping her arms around his neck.

He placed an arm around her and kissed her head.

"Good-looking boy," he huffed to the White Mistress.

They shared a moment, knowing the imminent end for both of them drew near.

"He has his father's looks," she said gruffly.

"What is his name?"

"Takmel," she replied, shedding a tear.

"After your brother," Tomas returned.

She nodded.

Tomas turned his attention to the lad.

"Your father was my friend," he said. "His name was Ivo Hamond. You have a place here with us if you want it."

Sumaiyya slipped to her side as blood drained from her wound and over her clean, white fabric. She took her son's hand and kissed it before directing the lad to go to Tomas.

Her hold, her control, depleted.

Vonavo rose to his feet.

"I am free," he thundered.

Piece by piece, his armour fell to the ground, releasing his form from the prison she had placed him in.

Dark mist seeped from the joins, forming into a mass of black cloud.

Tomas recognised the being as a Gomatha and followed it with his eyes as it drifted away to the east, towards the Lunkhul Forest.

Takmel watched him go momentarily before turning to his mother, sobbing as he crossed the tiny space between the two adults. It seemed like an eternity before he reached Tomas' side.

Sumaiyya rested her head to the ground, watching her boy leave her, suddenly wanting him to become so much more than she had intended.

Tomas, still hugging his daughter, reached up to him with his free hand.

The boy took it and cried as he looked at the dying man.

"Welcome home," Tomas breathed as he remembered the words of his daughter as they sat by the river.

He was going to leave them and never come back.

Looking over to Sumaiyya, he could see that she was no longer breathing. Her eyes were closed as she rested in the deepest slumber of all.

Slowly, he closed his eyes, hearing his name being called in the distance, like an echo through the hills.

"Tomas," Joanne called, racing frantically over the bridge towards him. "Tomas."

Emily was on her heels.

They both darted across the charred ground, tears streaming from their eyes.

Within a moment, they were both falling beside him, weeping profusely, calling his name.

There was no answer.

No reply.

He was gone.

Epilogue

With the Agrodien defeated and their bodies piled and burnt upon the southern fields, the task of building pyres and preparing the dead for their farewell became the primary task for all within Woodmyst.

The help of military men, refugees from Belburn and Oldcastle and the people of the village made the solemn task a swift one.

Takmel had asked for a pyre to be built for his mother. Most had ignored his request, but when the boy tried to pile timber together on his own, several others felt their hearts sink and offered their assistance, including David, Simon and Oliver who had all faced her in some manner upon the snow a decade before.

Tomas' wives begged the council to build both Sumaiyya's and Tomas' pyres near to each other. Their reasoning was that the boy was a part of them through Ivo, and it would only be fair if he was with his family while he mourned.

Lor held Linet tightly as she wept bitterly for losing her brother.

The councilmen and their wives shed tears and sobbed as they considered the children of the fallen man that was much loved by all in Woodmyst. It would come to the responsibility of the entire village to help raise them as their father would have wanted them to be.

Joanne and Lucy held onto each other's hands as they bade farewell to their husband. Catherine and Alice pressed themselves against their mother's legs as they watched the flames engulf their father. Emily fell apart and dropped to her knees, howling as tears streamed down her face.

The Erilian women gathered behind her and placed their hands upon her shoulders, offering what comfort they could.

Catherine reached her hand over to Takmel, who took it into his own. She kept her head rested on Emily's shoulder as she peered into the flames.

"Goodbye, Papa," she whispered as tears fell from her chin onto the earth.

***

The sun was high in the sky and birds were singing as they zipped over the grass, catching insects that fluttered through the growth.

"We'll go to Dweagan and free the women and men that were left behind," Amicia told David as her army mustered near the northern bridge. "I'll send some men back with supplies and farming implements. You'll need to plough that ground again if you want a harvest before the end of the warmer seasons."

"Don't worry," David told her. "I think we can get a good portion of the fields back in condition before your men return. But I appreciate any help you can offer. Will you return to Newholt?"

"It's our home," Jonathon told him. "I think we should, just so the people there can know what has happened."

"Well." Chief Harling smiled from his horse. "You're all welcome in Belburn if you want to join us."

"And here also," David informed them. "All of you."

"Thank you, David." Amicia grinned. "We may take you up on that if we feel Newholt isn't for us any longer."

"Don't hesitate." He took her hand and kissed it. "My lady."

He watched them for a long time as the woman and her army started across the bridge and along the road to the south, followed by the refugees from Belburn, who started their journey back home.

"So," Richard said, moving to his side. "It appears that you have assumed the role of leader."

"I don't desire it, Richard. But I have noticed..." He stopped to swallow the lump forming in his throat. "I had noticed when Tomas was engaged in other duties or distracted by pressing times, others would come to me for guidance."

"Including Tomas," the old man returned.

David nodded as he remembered his friend.

"We have a larger number under our care now," Richard told him. "The people of Oldcastle have no home to return to, so we must allow them to stay with us."

"As I told you and the council this morning," he replied. "Which is why I made my request."

"You have the council's support. We agree we need to expand the village into the ruins and rebuild the wall, with one exception."

"The Great Hall remains untouched so that the oak tree may grow," David said.

"How did you know?" he asked. "We only just met together in your absence."

"Those were my conditions that I put to both Simon and Oliver before you reconvened without me," he answered.

"You knew we were meeting in your absence?"

"Yes," he replied, continuing to watch the travellers on the road.

"How?" Richard asked. "Simon told you."

"No," David shook his head. "Becka did."

"My wife?"

"She knew you were considering me to take Tomas' place," he said. "She thought it was only fair if I had some warning so that I could have time to consider it. Don't be angry at her."

"I'm not," the old man replied. "She was right to tell you."

He turned his gaze to match David's, observing the long procession moving away from the village.

"Why did you request that the Great Hall be left untouched?" Richard asked. "I didn't take you for a sentimental man."

"It holds a history that we should never forget," the bald man replied. "It's where our mothers were taken from us. It's the only place we can go to remember them.

"It's the place where the Seven meet together. There is power there, according to them, and I don't think it's our right to take that away.

"There are children amongst us, and others on yet to be born, who may possess such abilities as those women. So that makes it not just our history, but our future lives there as well.

"It's also where I placed Tomas' ashes," he told the old man. "I went back to the field during the night with Simon and Oliver and collected the ash from his pyre. We placed them around the base of the tree and over the grass inside the ruins of the Great Hall.

"I know they were probably more or less the powder from the timber we used, but we wanted him over this side of the river with us. I told his wives, and they were pleased." David's eyes blurred as tears built on his lashes.

"It was the least we could do," he continued. "After everything he did for us, it was a small token gesture that doesn't speak enough gratitude for what we should show to that man.

"Besides..." He wiped his eyes, "I think Tomas would have wanted it."

The old man frowned as he turned to face the big man beside him.

"He was right to confide in you, David," Richard told him. "Even after he has departed from us, you continue to be a fierce and true friend."

With that, Richard moved away, leaving David to watch the long procession of people leaving Woodmyst. His gaze moved to three tiny figures sitting on the grass by the river a fair distance away, two little girls and one young boy. They waved and smiled at those crossing the bridge to the south.

Something unsettling gripped his stomach as he focused on the boy. He recalled Tomas' words about not hurting the child, but part of him wondered if they had made an error allowing the son of the White Mistress to live.

"Maji," he hissed under his breath.

The boy turned his head, as if responding, and peered directly at the big man.

David tensed his jaw as his unsettling feeling turned into a heightened sense of dread.

About the Author

Robert E Kreig was born in Newcastle, Australia and grew up in its outer suburbs.

He has always had a love for books, particularly well-told stories involving action, adventure and fear.

Some of Robert's favourite authors as a young reader included J. R. R. Tolkien, Stephen King, Orson Scott Card, Ray Bradbury and Frank Herbert. As he grew into adulthood, the list continued to lengthen, adding more influential writers such as George R. R. Martin, Matthew Reilly, Nathan M. Farrugia, Dan Brown, James Patterson, Michael Connelly and Lee Child just to name a few.

Inspired by movies like Star Wars, King Kong, Jaws, Jason and the Argonauts and other great adventure pieces, Robert listened to the voices in his head and entertained the strange visions dancing through his mind to assist him with writing his fantasy series The Woodmyst Chronicles.

Robert has penned ten books for the series which follow the lives of many characters, particularly focussing upon a family who must face many trials before the epic conclusion. Clashing swords, strange creatures, flying dragons and sorcery inhabit the world surrounding Woodmyst.

Robert has also written a standalone book, Long Valley.

Robert currently lives in Canberra, Australia where he hopes to one day become a full-time writer.

Other Books By This Author

THE WOODMYST CHRONICLES

From a faraway land...
...comes a new adventure.
The Woodmyst Chronicles is the story of a small community that faces the hardest of trials in a world filled with darkness, violence and magic.

Books In This Series...
THE WALLS OF WOODMYST
THE SONS OF WOODMYST
THE HEIR OF WOODMYST
THE WARLORDS OF WOODMYST
THE HUNTRESS OF WOODMYST
THE SHADOW OF WOODMYST
THE BRIDES OF WOODMYST
THE GODS OF WOODMYST
THE WEAPONS OF WOODMYST
A FAREWELL TO WOODMYST

LONG VALLEY

In the small community of Long Valley, nestled comfortably beneath snow-capped mountains, people quietly go about their business. Everybody knows everybody and there are no worries to give mind to.

But something has awakened.

A tragic accident near the valley's army base sparks a number of terrifying events, placing the local civilians in mortal danger.

A contagion is subsequently released into Long Valley, infecting pets, livestock, wildlife and people.

It's up to the local law enforcement and a small band of citizens to try to keep the town safe.

In the end, it becomes a struggle for survival as the people of Long Valley are overcome by the urge to feed.

THE CALM VOICE

No one in the remote town of Edwards Hill could have known that she was capable of such carnage.

Least of all her parents, the first to die.

Driven by the gentle words of The Calm Voice, she inflicts a barrage of carnage and death, leaving a trail of blood in her wake.

Her goal is to bring death to all who have hurt her.

All she needs to do is listen to The Calm Voice.

All she needs to do is just focus...

Just focus...

Focus...

The Calm Voice is a dark psychological novel surrounding the actions of one girl on a fateful morning in April, 2017. Kristin Matthews is fed up with her life, her oppressive parents, and her bullying schoolmates. She is compelled by a soothing voice thrumming in her head to seek revenge on those who have wronged her. At the top of her list is a trio of girls who have taunted her to breaking point. After careful planning, she embarks on a deadly rampage through Edwards Hill State High School, bent on destroying all her pain one final time. What follows is a haunting description of the day's events, culminating in an ending no one will expect.

www.whitekeepbooks.com

www.robertekreig.com

www.ingramcontent.com/pod-product-compliance
Lightning Source LLC
Chambersburg PA
CBHW020256120726
47904CB00001B/228